Acknowledgements

Like much in this world, writing a book is a bizarre business. The dichotomy of experiencing life as a creative wellspring and simultaneously hiding from its demands and realities creates a schizophrenic impulse to both devour and disappear. I would like to thank my great friends and family for not disowning me over the past sixteen months, and especially Julia, who has walked this journey with me every step of the way. Her influence is unseen, yet I doubt *Learning to Fly* would be what it is without her love, clever brain and the bountiful joy she brings to my life.

Alison Lowry – I cannot thank you enough for your inspiration, guidance and calming influence. Our Midlands imbizos cemented the building blocks for what was to follow, and your faith and brilliance cajoled me through the difficult months of editing and second guessing. It is unique for a writer to find an editor (and boss) whom he can trust implicitly to share his vision. You are the true mother of this series and what The Guv might call a delinquent visionary. Thanks, also, to the entire crew at Penguin Books who take my mad ramblings, turn them into beautiful books and ensure that they fly off the shelves. I feel like I have an army behind me and the success of Spud is as much yours, as it is mine. Special thanks to Tracey McDonald for thinking big, Janine (Leadfoot) Daniel for breaking the speed limit, and Claire Heckrath for her artistic gems.

Finally I want to thank you, the reader, for taking this journey with me. May these pages bring you joy and laughter and an insight into a world that is both familiar and foreign. After all, that is what you all have gifted me.

SPUD

By John van de Ruit

PENGUIN BOOKS

Learning to Fly

...ublished by the Penguin Group
Penguin Books Ltd, 80 Strand, London WC2R 0RL, England
Penguin Group (USA) Inc., 375 Hudson Street, New York, New York 10014, USA
Penguin Group (Canada), 90 Eglinton Avenue East, Suite 700, Toronto, Ontario, Canada M4P 2Y3
(a division of Pearson Penguin Canada Inc.)
Penguin Ireland, 25 St Stephen's Green, Dublin 2, Ireland
(a division of Penguin Books Ltd)
Penguin Group (Australia), 250 Camberwell Road, Camberwell, Victoria 3124, Australia
(a division of Pearson Australia Group Pty Ltd)
Penguin Books India Pvt Ltd, 11 Community Centre, Panchsheel Park, New Delhi – 110 017, India
Penguin Group (NZ), 67 Apollo Drive, Rosedale, Auckland 0632, New Zealand
(a division of Pearson New Zealand Ltd)
Penguin Books (South Africa) (Pty) Ltd, 24 Sturdee Avenue, Rosebank,
Johannesburg 2196, South Africa

Penguin Books Ltd, Registered Offices: 80 Strand, London WC2R 0RL, England

penguin.com

First published by Penguin Books (South Africa) (Pty) Ltd 2009
This edition published in Great Britain by Penguin Books Ltd 2011
001 – 10 9 8 7 6 5 4 3 2 1

Text copyright © John van de Ruit, 2009
All rights reserved

The moral right of the author has been asserted

Typeset in 10.5/12.5 pt Bookman
Printed in Great Britain by Clays Ltd, St Ives plc

British Library Cataloguing in Publication Data
A CIP catalogue record for this book is available from the British Library

ISBN: 978-0-141-33623-7

www.greenpenguin.co.uk

1992

NEW YEAR'S DAY

TAKING STOCK

PHYSICAL

Freakishly underdeveloped with no real biceps, triceps, pecs, calves, six pack etc ... etc ... The realisation has dawned on me that I'm less than two years away from finishing my school career and yet I still don't look a day over eleven. Despite months of spectacular knackjumping and other verbal pyrotechnics, my voice has hardly dropped below the level of a masculine woman. I had my first shave on New Year's Eve which didn't seem to make any difference, except for the nasty cut on my neck that seeped blood all night and then miraculously stopped on the gong of New Year. This was quite possibly some sort of signal from above that 1992 will offer up greater things than 1991 – or at least be a little less bloody.

EMOTIONAL

After two years of numerous disasters, countless embarrassing situations, and endless turmoil, I find myself in a desperately fragile state of mind. My 'relationships' are a constant cause for stress and I've narrowed the problem down to the simple but unavoidable fact that I'm utterly terrified of women, particularly the ones who like me. My parents are often insane, my friends are mostly delinquents or cretins (or both), and since I have no siblings, I have to unload all my worries on Blacky. This is grossly unfair on an animal that thinks licking his privates in public is generally good form.

There's also glaring evidence of inbreeding in my father's bloodline, which could account for my embarrassingly late physical development. Thanks to my great-great-grandfather repeatedly bonking my great-great-aunt, my goolies are now more famous than I am.

MENTAL

Being surrounded by madness most of the time has left me edgy and disturbed. I think about death at least once a week and frequently have a twitchy left eyebrow, which Mom says is definitely stress related. I do still have my scholarship, although the letter from the school bursar let it be known that the school isn't satisfied with what I have achieved thus far.

SPIRITUAL

I'm fairly sure God exists, although He hasn't exactly come storming through on any of the urgent prayers that I've sent His way. I have a feeling this is because He's either overworked, punishing me for dabbling in the occult with Fatty, or he's reading my mind when I think of Amanda or Julia Roberts. I've also spent many unsuccessful hours trying to work out the meaning of life.

FAMILY

Mom is in a permanently bad mood, which Dad puts down to menopause. Wombat is senile, deranged and suspicious of her own family, and it took my father nearly a week to convince a team of top psychiatrists in the nuthouse that he wasn't insane. Dad called the whole nuthouse debacle at the end of last term a simple misunderstanding, and blamed God and the station wagon for his woes. If you ask me, any person who announces, 'I've had a breakdown!' outside an asylum deserves to have electrodes strapped to his head for a week. I also overheard Mom telling Marge that Dad spent four of the days in the asylum wearing a straightjacket and a nappy! Hardly the sign of a sane man ...

GIRLS

Mermaid

Mermaid and I have decided that we will wait until after school before we have a real relationship. In truth Mermaid decided this on our weekend away at Sodwana Bay with her parents, and because my bottom lip started quivering I immediately agreed. Inside I was screaming No No No! but unfortunately my traitorous lips were stupidly saying 'Okay' over and over. Later on the trampoline I asked her if we could start over again. She gave me a hug and said I was her best friend. My lips then said 'Definitely'. And that was that.

Further bad news is that the Mermaid has suddenly become religious and now reckons she's saving herself for marriage. When I asked her when she would like to get married she answered, 'When I'm twenty-nine.' On the plus side, we did share a passionate goodbye kiss up against her fridge, which was only interrupted when Brutus (Mermaid's boxer) got his head stuck in the rubbish bin and then had a panic attack and pissed himself.

Amanda

Mom didn't let me go away with Amanda and her friends in the holidays because she said there was no adult supervision and that it would encourage my 'drinking problem'. Mom also called Amanda a private school hussy, hell-bent on driving me to suicide. When I broke the bad news to Amanda, she called me a coward and then said, 'Sorry, I forgot you were only fifteen and needed Mommy's permission.'

I haven't spoken to her since.

Christine

Christine invited me to her New Year's Eve party at Salt Rock but I bravely told her I had plans. (Dismal braai with Mom, Dad, Wombat, Uncle Aubrey, Aunt Peggy and Blacky.) She then told me that she wasn't giving up and kissed the phone three times before saying goodbye.

FIVE REMINDERS OF WHY I SHOULD NEVER BE WITH CHRISTINE:

Boggo says she's got the clap.
She's psychotic and slutty (a mixed blessing).
She was Gecko's girlfriend.
She's terrifying.
At least four boys at school think they're going out with her.

Unfortunately, the list of girls in my life remains identical to that of two years ago. This semi-arid love-life situation is becoming serious and requires urgent and immediate attention. The only problem is that I'm still in love with one of them, obsessed with the other, and lately I have had pleasurable dreams about the third.

So here I sit, at my desk in my little room, looking back over the worst holiday in living memory. The Mermaid has sort of dumped me *again* and I'm wondering if life is really just a series of random experiences that deceives you into thinking that you're actually serving some sort of purpose, when actually you are no more important than a mosquito in the greater sewerage works of life?

I now understand why Vincent van Gogh cut his ear off.

Monday 20th January

The atmosphere in the green Renault station wagon was at best gloomy and at worst murderous. Just before leaving home, Mom caught Dad on his stepladder peeping over the fence as our new neighbour was taking her afternoon swim. Mom accused Dad of being perverse and blamed Frank for putting funny ideas into his head. Our new neighbour goes by the name of Amber and because of her being blonde, thin and divorced, Mom has taken an instant dislike to her. Dad pleaded that he was only checking the alignment of the hedge and not being a peeping tom. Mom hasn't spoken to him since, besides barking orders and complaining about finding a tick in the bed.

Further bad news was that the windscreen wipers stopped working soon after driving into a huge electrical storm near Cato Ridge. Dad was livid, and kept lunging out of the window with his jersey to furiously wipe at the windooreen to improve his visibility. He then set off on a long tirade about Renault being infiltrated by commies and said that the French were spending too much time bonking and not enough time at work. Mom snorted loudly to herself but didn't say anything else. I slipped on my Walkman and allowed David Bowie to take me back to school instead.

Ground control to Major Tom
Ground control to Major Tom
Take your protein pills and put your helmet on …

19:15 I dragged my trunk up the final stretch of Pilgrim's Walk towards the grand old red brick buildings accompanied by the loud chorus of frogs and crickets celebrating the rain. I felt twitchy and nauseous and my trunk was heavier than I can ever remember. A thick

6

mist had descended over the school, muffling all the sounds and the hesitant trickle of Pissing Pete standing alone and miserable in the school fountain. Once in the quad I gazed up at the second storey of the house where all the dormitory lights were blazing neon and in each window frame there was a buzz of movement. I looked along towards the third year dormitory at the far end of the building. In the first window I could see a hand repetitively bouncing a ball on a cricket bat, the second window was closed and the third revealed the outline of a very large boy eating something greedily out of an ice cream tub.

Fatty must have seen me approaching because there was a loud bleat, and then the strident voice of Boggo shouting, 'Hey, okes, here comes the resident house lesbian!' There was a chorus of laughter followed by more bleating and a few wolf whistles. I pretended not to hear the mockery and heaved my trunk through the house door. Vern came galloping down like he was running away from a fire and screeched to a halt in front of my trunk at the foot of the stairs. 'Hi, Vern,' I said. Rain Man saluted with a flourish and shouted, 'Spud!' before picking up the handle on the other side of my army trunk. We carried my trunk up the stairs in complete silence and then opened the door to my new home ... and a new member of the Crazy Eight.

And there he sat, perched like a goblin on the end of his trunk, wolfing down a bar of chocolate. It soon dawned on me that everybody was munching a bar of chocolate and staring at me like *I* was the stranger in the dorm. The new boy jumped up and marched towards me holding out his hand. It was pleasing to see that he was a good few inches shorter than me.

I didn't immediately say anything because I was distracted by how pink his face was and realised that the short curly hair on his scalp was glowing like an orb in the neon light. It was so white that it looked like he had been dragged on his head across a halfway line.

'Hello,' he said with a goofy grin. 'You must be Spud Milton.'
    'Hi,' I stammered.
    'I thought so!' he shouted in a high-pitched voice.

The new boy looked thrilled that he knew who I was before I even had a chance to introduce myself.

'My name is Garth Garlic,' he said, pumping my palm with a vigorous handshake. I immediately sensed that this must be a devious Crazy Eight set-up and that I was about to embarrass myself, so I played things cool and said nothing.

'I come from Malawi,' Garlic continued. His eyes then widened into blue circular pools and he asked, 'You ever been to Malawi?'
    I shook my head.
    Garlic looked heartbroken and his big eyes narrowed again. 'You would love it,' he continued. 'Lake Malawi is the most beautiful place in the world and they don't mind if you drink beer there under age.'

Then he said, 'Gee, it's awesome to meet you, Spud Milton. I'm feeling really proud to be a member of the Secret Seven!'

There was a shocked silence around the dorm before Fatty stepped in. With one arm around Garlic's shoulders and eyes that were gleaming with delight, he opened a mouth full of chewed chocolate and said, 'That's the Crazy Eight, buddy – you probably don't want to make that kind of mistake again …' He then gave me a wink and announced, 'His old man's the MD of Nestlé Malawi.' Fatty then swallowed greedily before saying, 'The oke's class.' With that he patted the beaming Garlic on the back and returned to his cubicle where a stack of Nestlé products waited for him slap bang in the centre of his bed.

Boggo was quite obviously sulking. Apparently Rambo had arrived early and immediately welcomed Garlic to the dormitory without discussing the matter with anyone else. Boggo and Fatty were appalled that a stranger could be installed as a fully fledged member of the Crazy Eight without passing a series of worthiness tests that ranged from burping on demand to a graphic description of the females in his family tree. When Boggo complained, Rambo accused Fatty and Boggo of behaving like twelve-year-olds and said the whole Crazy Eight thing was childish and embarrassing.

Unfortunately for Boggo, that was the moment when Fatty discovered that Garlic's dad was the boss of Nestlé Malawi and immediately switched sides before turning viciously on his former comrade and best friend. Boggo clearly wasn't impressed with the way everything had gone, because he spent the rest of the evening scowling into the mirror and exploding his numerous zits into a white tissue.

Rambo is also behaving bizarrely. He hardly said anything the entire evening and is acting like we're all complete strangers.

I watched Rain Man pull out his notebook and sketch a very lifelike picture of Garlic's face. He furiously wrote GARLIC underneath the picture, and then snapped his notebook shut and slid it back under his mattress. He then crouched low on his bed and watched Garlic for the entire evening through the bars of his towel rail.

CRAZY EIGHT HOLIDAY SCORECARD

RAMBO   Thrice bungee jumped off the 216m Bloukrans bridge.

SIMON   Spent a month living in a villa in Monaco. He says scoring girls in the south of France is like shooting fish in a barrel. Simon may have overdone the tanning a bit because he now looks weirdly orange.

FATTY   Videos, Dungeons and Dragons, computer games, eating. Etc.

BOGGO   Has come up with a deadly secret formula for scoring girls. He says it has a proven hundred per cent success rate. He later admitted that he had only tried it on one girl, who hasn't returned his calls since the night he got stuck into her.

SPUD   The worst holiday ever. Sheer boredom, and constant arguments among his family. I told the others about violently kissing Mermaid against the fridge and may have exaggerated things slightly but didn't mention that we'd actually broken up. I also kept Dad's week of madness to myself.

VERN   Went to Swaziland for Christmas and brought a photograph of himself sitting on the loo and two Christmas cards to prove it.

ROGER   Unknown.

GARLIC Lake Malawi.

Garlic has verbal diarrhoea – after crapping on about Lake Malawi for over an hour, Boggo snapped at him and told him if he wanted to be a part of the Crazy Eight then he had to talk far less and preferably not at all. Garlic's face flushed and tears sprang to his eyes. He then said, 'Sorry, guys, I know I talk too much, it's like I have a loose wire between my head and my brain sometimes and I just like say things that I'm thinking, but that I don't really like fully mean. You know what I mean?'

There was a pause and then everybody burst into laughter. Garlic was thrilled and laughed along raucously despite being the butt of the joke. Fatty thumped Garlic on the back and said, 'What a guy!' He then helped himself to another chocolate from Garlic's locker and added it to his pile.

Garlic finished laughing and said, 'Gee, I'm glad I brought those choccies. Dad said they could come in useful if I wanted to buy a few friends ...'

We all laughed again and Garlic once again roared along with us.

It feels weird to be back at school, in a new dormitory, and to have a stranger among us. The good news is that I have my own cubicle this year; the bad news is that I'm sandwiched between Vern and Fatty.

Lay awake listening to Fatty snoring and Vern muttering to himself in his sleep. I waited for the night train to charge by but it never did.

I dreamt that Mad Dog derailed the night train from

Johannesburg with his catapult. I then woke up and couldn't sleep for hours. I lay in bed thinking about how different the dormitory feels.

I miss the Mad Dog.

Tuesday 21st January

6:30   Roll Call

Norman Whiteside read out the names at the first roll call of the year. For this reason, and because he looked overly self-important, I'm backing he's our new head of house. Boggo agreed and said, 'The class of 1992 aren't exactly top of the gene pool.' He then downed his tea and strode off across the quad shaking his head and looking disgusted with life.

Garlic and Barryl were nearly declared missing after spending roll call in the bogs. Apparently, Garlic bailed Barryl up with more talk of Lake Malawi. The shaken Barryl said it was impossible to get away from the prattling maniac, and that Garlic also looked a bit like the *tokoloshe*. Whiteside made a great show of giving the two a severe rebuking and a final warning. He droned on for ages about people taking liberties and disregarding school traditions. His speech attracted quite a crowd because many boys thought he was making an official announcement.

Garlic was greatly upset that he had implicated Barryl and pleaded, 'It wasn't this gentleman's fault. I was talking about Lake Malawi!' A collective groan sounded around the bogs and the crowd began to disperse. Looks like word has already spread about the great peril of Lake Malawi.

To add salt to the wounds, Vern gave both Barryl and Garlic a written warning for Bad Form in the Bogs and Surrounds. Garlic obviously didn't know what was cracking because he said, 'Hey, shot!' and happily stashed the blue chit in the pocket of his crimson dressing gown.

Spike has grown. In fact he looks more and more like his vermin older brother by the day. Unfortunately, he now seems to be at least a head taller than me and to make matters worse he shoulder-charged me as I passed him in the passage near the piss trough. He claimed it was an accident but didn't apologise.

The matrics are all walking around barking orders at people and looking prefectish. Tonight Viking will announce this year's head of house and the 1992 prefects.

16:45 Garlic covered his entire body in Vaseline after his afternoon shower. He then ambled around the dormitory chatting to people about Lake Malawi while stark naked and glistening. Vern thought this was hilarious, squawked with laughter and pointed at Garlic's groin. Garlic then asked Vern if he was retarded. Vern thought this was equally hilarious and cackled away to himself before pointing at Garlic's nuts again and shouting, 'Spud!' Garlic looked a little shocked and backed away to his cubicle where he hurriedly got into his clothes and scurried out the dormitory.

20:00   House Meeting

Viking called the first house gathering a 'Meet and Greet' although it would be more accurately described as a 'Clout and Shout'. Spike farted and tried to pretend it was his chair squeaking on the floor. Tough break for him was that it stank and the entire house meeting had to be adjourned for ten minutes while the Normal Seven were ordered to fan the room with cushions and spray their deodorant. Viking conducted his first thrashing as housemaster and caned Spike with two very meaty strokes. Eventually order was restored and Runt was allowed to continue with his Bible reading.

Viking's introduction was conducted at the general volume of a shout. The poor first years huddled together on the floor at his feet looking genuinely terrified. I remember those days when I kept my eyes glued to the floor, cringing from everything.

'This house,' Viking declared, 'is a complete and utter disgrace!' He then continued with, 'And most of you lot wouldn't cut it in any half-baked platoon!' I felt an elbow in my ribs before Vern's extremely loud whisper of, 'Half-baked Spudoon ...' His crazy sniggering was brought to a halt by Viking who boomed, 'You clearly have something to share with the house, Blackadder?' Vern blushed and shook his head about seven times. He then realised that everyone was watching him so he said, 'Spud!' There was a long pause. Clearly Vern had stumped yet another figure of authority with his rambling nonsense. Viking eventually said, 'Yes well ... um yes indeed ... thank you for sharing that with us, Blackadder,' before cranking up the volume with, 'Now I am going to instil peace and respect in this house even if there must be bloodshed!'

After this heart-warming welcome, Viking announced his 1992 prefects:

HEAD OF HOUSE Norman Whiteside (no nickname). Whose only claim to fame is that his canoe played the title role in last year's

	appalling house play. He was so excited when his name was announced, he embarrassingly punched the air with his fist and shouted, 'Yes, please!'
PREFECTS	Greg Whitton (nickname Eggwhite). His dad is on the board of governors. No discernible sign of personality.
	Meany Dlamini. The school chess champion. (Hopefully he's only called Meany because it rhymes with Dlamini.)
	Leonard Pike!!!!!!!!!!!!!!!!!!!!!!!!!!!!!!!!!!!!

There was uproar in the common room after the prefects were announced. The fact that Pike was coming back for post matric was thoroughly gutting. That he's now a prefect is a catastrophe! Viking must be insane if he thinks that Pike could in any way be a good prefect? Thankfully the swine isn't back at school yet so we didn't have to endure the look on his smug face and his taunting threats.

Viking congratulated the new prefects with shouted congratulations and wild slaps on the back. He then said to them, 'My office – now!' Rambo turned to the rest of the Crazy Eight and said, 'My cubicle – now!'

House Meeting adjourned.

Upstairs Rambo ordered the windows and door shut. Fatty tried to light up incense and candles but Rambo told him to grow up and look sharp. Then Boggo, who had sauntered into the dormitory with his hands casually fondling his pockets said, 'Oh, so now suddenly we're calling Crazy Eight meetings again.'

'All right, we've got a serious problem,' said Rambo, completely ignoring Boggo's taunt.

'This place is insane,' added Simon as he furiously bit his nails.

'Talk about scaling an oke's nuts from out of his jocks,' agreed Fatty solemnly.

Vern shouted, 'Oi!' to let us know that he wasn't happy either.

Rambo waited for complete silence before continuing, 'Right, now listen up. We've got to box clever. We can't have a repeat of last year.' We all nodded back in agreement. 'We can never get bust, never! In fact we can't put a single foot wrong. With Viking and Pike sniffing around like detectives we're gonna have to keep our noses clean – and I mean Omo clean ...' We all nodded solemnly again, apart from Garlic, who chuckled loudly and thought everything was great fun – a clear indication that he's never encountered a human being as dire as Pike before.

'We can't just carry on like we're a law unto ourselves,' continued Rambo, now looking more in control. 'It's a dead end street and it's obvious that something suspicious is going on here.'

I wasn't too sure what Rambo was talking about but if it meant an end to suicidal crazy missions then I'm all for it.

'Oh, and another thing,' said Rambo. 'I'm doing away with democracy. There are members of this group who don't deserve the vote, have no judgement, and are clinically insane. That's the reason the shit hit the fan last year.' Vern stroked Roger forcefully and looked around deviously like he was expecting something to happen. Nothing happened.

16

Rambo cleared his throat and glared at each of us in turn before saying, 'So that is why I am taking over full control of the dormitory.'

There was another long and awkward silence. Boggo looked like he was sucking on a lemon. Fatty eventually summoned up the courage to speak, albeit in his whiny voice. 'So what happens if we don't want to do what you want us to do?' Rambo stared at Fatty for a few seconds before grinning and saying, 'Let's double-cross that bridge if we get to it.' Fatty grinned back like an idiot and said nothing further.

'Right,' said Rambo clapping his hands together. 'Let's go meet the new boys!' His march to the door was stopped by Simon who had clearly had enough of Rambo Stalin's orders. 'Okay, you've told us we are going to stick to the rules and stay out of trouble this year. Then in the same breath you order us to break the rules of the house.' Boggo snorted loudly and shouted, 'Hello – contradiction?' Nobody moved. Rambo stared, but still nobody moved.

It was a classic Crazy Eight stand-off.

'There's no contradiction, Boggo,' said Rambo in an unnervingly calm voice. 'Yes, it's breaking the rules to touch a first year before their two weeks' grace is up. But there's nothing in the rules about a little meet and greet ...'
    Simon shook his head and said, 'If the prefects bust us in that dormitory they won't ask questions.'

Rambo grinned, 'They can't bust us, you piss brain, because they're all in a prefects' meeting in Viking's office. Trust me, it's now or never.'

We reluctantly followed our leader along the passage and watched him throw open the door to the second years' dormitory. Our arrival was met with a horrified silence ...

THE NORMAL SEVEN

The Normal Seven were appalled to see the Crazy Eight. In fact half of them dived onto their beds and desperately tried to hide, while Darryl (the last remaining) made a hilarious attempt at disappearing into his trunk. Rambo ordered them all to sit on their lockers. All obeyed except one: Spike made a big show of lying on his bed and opening up a newspaper. Rambo once again demanded that Spike sit on his locker. Spike ignored him. Rambo strode up to Spike's cubicle and stood over him looking like he was on the verge of violence. I noticed the hands holding the newspaper were becoming a little unsteady.

'My brother's a prefect, in case you haven't heard,' said Spike, trying to appear nonchalant. 'You guys so much as touch me, touch any of us ...' He faded off in a strident voice and waited for Rambo to say something.

Rambo said nothing and instead softly plucked the newspaper out of Spike's hands and began reading it. Spike jerked his hand away in fear of the sudden movement, and there were a few snorts and sniggers from the Crazy Eight.

After about a minute of reading the newspaper Rambo finally spoke. 'Tell me, Spike, why are you reading a newspaper from November last year?' Spike didn't answer and there were a few more sniggers rippling around the dormitory.

'Is it because you're woefully behind the times? Or is it because you get turned on by this picture of Margaret Thatcher?' Rambo flashed us the picture of Margaret

Thatcher dressed in green and looking horsey. The sniggers now turned into loud cackling laughter.

'Or is it because you wanted to try and look cool in front of your mates instead of lying there with your legs open like the dipshit you really are?'

The laughter died away and Rambo turned and made his way towards the first year dormitory. Boggo snapped up the old newspaper, took a brief look at the picture of Margaret Thatcher and then stashed it into the back of his pants before following Rambo.

'Piss off, you wanker.'

It took a few moments for us to realise that the insult had been uttered by Spike, and that his intended target was Rambo. For the second time in minutes Rambo had been challenged on his way out of a dormitory door. This time he stopped and swung around with his jaw clenched and his dark eyes burning.

'I'm sorry, what did you say, Spike?' replied Rambo in his brand new soft and terrifying voice.

Spike stood up and repeated, 'I said, piss off, you wanker!'

Rambo marched up to him and everybody backed away a few paces. He stopped his march centimetres from Spike's face.

'Listen, Spike, what you've just said is insubordination to a senior. You ever speak to me, or any of my boys like that again, I'll go straight to Viking. Am I understood?'

Spike nodded and suddenly looked on the verge of tears. I even found myself feeling a bit sorry for the idiot.

We left again. It was a relief to exit the second years' dormitory because Runt was staring at me and making me feel self-conscious.

THE NEW BOYS

When we arrived in the first years' dormitory they all dropped what they were doing and stood to attention at the foot of their beds like they had been drilled all afternoon by an army sergeant. Unfortunately, Vern strode forward and saluted vigorously at the new boys. Some of them saluted back while the rest stared back at Vern in terrified confusion. Vern held his rigid salute for about thirty seconds while beadily eyeing out the new recruits. When he was satisfied that he had sized them all up, he dropped his right arm, sniffed loudly, and returned to his place in the line.

Garlic looked a little confused by the military developments and asked Fatty, 'Why are these boys saluting us?' Fatty glanced around suspiciously and whispered, 'This dorm is haunted, Garlic. There can be no explanation for the shit that goes down here.' Garlic looked around nervously and asked, 'Voodoo shit or like weird shit?' Fatty closed his eyes dramatically and inhaled through loud nostrils as if sniffing the air for the supernatural. Then he said, 'All kinds of shit.' Garlic's eyes widened like saucers as he nodded slowly to himself and said, 'Same at Lake Malawi.'

Thankfully, Rambo interrupted.

'Good evening, gentlemen. We are the third years and I'm Rambo. We just wanted to welcome you all to the house. And if there's anything, or anyone ... that troubles you, come speak to me first.'

No violence, no bloodshed, nothing. Rambo wouldn't even let Fatty examine anyone's tuck or allow Boggo to interrogate the new boys about their moms and sisters. The first years, I'm happy to report, are all smaller than me and at least three of them are still spuds. In fact I had the weird sensation of feeling my body growing taller while we were standing proudly in front of them.

When new head of house Norman Whiteside came storming into our dormitory to turn the lights out, we were already lying silently in our beds. He looked dreadfully disappointed and didn't even bother to say goodnight before flicking off the lights and slamming the dormitory door.

These are strange days indeed.

Wednesday 22nd January

The rising siren is sheer horror. Mrs Bishop shat on me for falling asleep during Maths dawn patrol and said I was letting my parents, the school and myself down. I felt terrible and did my best to look lively but couldn't stop myself from daydreaming about falling asleep in my own bed at home.

11:30 There was a buzz of excitement in our English classroom as we waited for The Guv to make his entrance. Eventually, there was a lot of shouting and banging outside the door. The Guv came bursting in as if he expected to see an empty classroom and stopped dead in his tracks before looking heavenward and asking, 'And this is the best they could come up with?' He slammed down a large pile of books on his huge oak desk, flung his leather briefcase into the empty fireplace, and collapsed into his chair exhausted. He then cleaned his spectacles with a white handkerchief before replacing them on his head and glaring at us again. 'Good God,' he said, 'it's worse than I thought.'

His eyes fell upon Garlic in the front row. Garlic's face reddened, his eyes swelled and he broke into a great goofy smile. The Guv studied the new man in silence before lighting his pipe. He blew out a huge puff of smoke and continued to examine Garlic like he was an unusual species. Eventually, Garlic could take it no longer and blurted out, 'I'm Garth Garlic, sir. I come from Malawi. You ever been to Malawi, sir?'

The Guv replied in a deep and droning voice, 'Young man, I wouldn't go to Malawi if the rest of the world were ablaze! And I would prefer, Mr Garlic, if you would refer to your hallowed bastion of heathen horror as Nyasaland within the strict confines of my classroom.'

'But, sir,' stammered Garlic, 'Malawi is a beautiful place – and it changed from Nyasaland nearly thirty years ago ...'
   The Guv thumped his fist down on his wooden desk and cried, 'Nyasaland may be thirty, but I'm a hundred and eight and this classroom is my empire!'

The Guv sighed deeply, pulled out his handkerchief, and mopped his brow. He then analysed his handkerchief for some time before saying, 'Who could have predicted that so much mischief could come from such an insignificant little snotrag ...' He looked at us with eyes burning with excitement and intensity. 'Gentlemen,' he announced, 'reach into your bags and unsheath your Othellos.' Once we had taken out our books he peered at us again as if we were about to embark on some mysterious and dangerous journey and said, 'Now, gentlemen, reach into yourselves and unsheath your minds ...'

I returned to the dormitory after lunch to find a massive golf putting competition under way. Simon and Rambo were taking on Fatty and Boggo in an ill-spirited match and, judging by all the sneering and goading, Fatty and Boggo had fallen woefully behind. This wasn't that surprising since Boggo has no hand-eye coordination whatsoever and Fatty was having some trouble squeezing in between the lockers and was often forced to putt left handed with the back of his putter. Garth Garlic was jumping up and down with excitement and chanting the score at regular intervals, which only further enraged Boggo.

Boggo and Fatty eventually called the match off because according to them, 'People were cheating.' They didn't say which people or how they were meant to be cheating. Everyone then left to practise hitting golf shots on the field.

I asked Simon what the sudden golf craze was all about. He glared at me like I was an idiot and said, 'Because the father and son golf day is only six weeks away and this year it's at Victoria Country Club. You'd better start grooving your swing, Spud.'

This is a huge worry. It seems like this golf day is quite a major event – in fact every senior is expected to play and play well. I've never played golf before and neither has Dad, although he did use a three wood to kill a boomslang a few years back. (It turned out the boomslang had already been killed by the gardener, but Dad obviously didn't know this at the time.)

20:30 Narrowly avoided Garlic talking about Lake Malawi again. This time the victims were a couple of frightened first years whom he had unwittingly cornered at the far end of the common room. When I realised what was happening, I pretended to be looking for somebody and immediately raced out of the room, tapping urgently away at my watch. Garlic seemed to be swinging his arms backwards and forwards like he was trout fishing or perhaps whipping a servant. The first years watched him in silence with eyes of fear and uncertainty.

All the first years look identical. They stand out because they are small and foreign in familiar surroundings. I've seen three of them crying already. (Although it could have been the same guy crying three times.) Either way it's a bumpy ride for the newbies. I pity whichever one of those poor sods ends up slaving for Pike. If I were him, I'd slit my throat immediately.

Boggo reckons he's got first dibs on nicknaming the first years. He's already compiled an extensive list of possible names which include: Doggystyle, Gonad and Gastro.

Thank God I'm a senior.

Thursday 23rd January

8am Assembly

The first assembly of the year was delayed until today because The Glock has only just returned from a disastrous skiing holiday to Austria. Apparently, the ski lift on which he and his wife were riding capsized, sending our headmaster and his wife crashing thirty feet into the snow. The Glock escaped with a broken wrist because he landed on top of his wife who cushioned the blow. Unfortunately, the force of the falling Glock broke his wife's back and the poor woman is in traction for three months in a hospital in Vienna.

I must admit The Glock looked a little pathetic standing up at the podium trying to look intimidating with his broken arm and bruised face. I noticed the first years didn't seem to be that scared of him. The Glock didn't threaten us with violent punishment nor ramble on about discipline. He just said a quick prayer, mumbled a meek welcome and walked out.

Outside in the sunlight, Fatty said this was definitely The Glock's bad karma coming back to bite him for the underhanded way he expelled Mad Dog and nearly expelled Rambo last year. Everyone shared a low-key high five and we went our separate ways.

Pike is back. I saw him at lunch. He sat at the prefects' table and seems to have developed an extremely fake ultra-casual walk that he's no doubt been practising in the holidays. The good news is that he's not staying in the house. He's living in one of the post matric residences, although I'm sure that won't stop him from snooping around and tormenting people smaller than himself.

Friday 24th January

Woke up feeling nervous and excited about my chances for the cricket season. Today the school is announcing trial teams from the firsts all the way down to the sixth team (let's hope it doesn't come to that). Obviously, I'm at a disadvantage because I'm only in third year and I'm now competing with matrics and post matrics for places along with all the guys from my year as well. The good news is that the first team spinner from last year (Bongo Wilkens) decided he wasn't going to make Natal Schools after all and has gone to UCT instead. Good man. According to Simon, trials lists are usually an indicator of where you'll end up. I'm praying to make seconds although Simon informs me that I'll only make thirds. Rambo says he'll definitely make seconds and obviously Simon will play firsts. We wait until eleven o'clock. Tick-Tock.

8:00 Dad phoned to wish me luck for the trials announcement. He's convinced I'm about to make my debut for the firsts, possibly as Captain. Unfortunately, he's seriously misguided and semi-insane.

11:00 A jostling crowd had already gathered at the cricket notice board by the time I arrived. I could hear cheering and jeering in equal measure as each boy fought his way to the front of the mob and searched hopefully for his name. I began with the first and second team trial list, which was a grave mistake, because I immediately noticed that my name wasn't there and grew instantly depressed, despite not expecting it to be there in the first place. I pushed my way across to the third and fourth team trial list and then I was overcome by that terrible sinking feeling when I saw my name down at bottom of the page under the column:

EXTRAS

I staggered away from the noisy crowd and returned to the empty dormitory where I lay on my bed for ten minutes to digest the news and stop shaking. My first reaction was that there was some kind of conspiracy against me, led by Sparerib, who is now the second team coach. Is it impossible that somebody could go from U15A to a reserve for the fourth team in one short holiday? Obviously, it is. Worse news is that Rambo was listed in the third team and there's now a possibility that I may well end up playing with Garlic for the fifths!

16:30 When I returned from a private bowling session

in the cricket nets, Meany Dlamini swore at me and said my dad had called seven times in two hours and screwed up his afternoon nap.

'He wants to know what cricket team you're in,' he yelled, before slamming his bedroom door in my face.

I decided to call Dad and put him out of his misery, despite the fact that he's certain to do something extreme when he hears that South Africa's 'next great legspinner' is turning out for the fifths! Thankfully, Dad must have thought that I was joking because when I broke the news, he howled with laughter, called me a cheeky little bugger, and slammed the phone down. Who knows – perhaps sense will prevail at tomorrow's trial match and I'll be promoted to the thirds.

Simon, Rambo and Boggo spent the entire evening offering me coaching hints and sage pieces of cricket wisdom. This despite the fact that Boggo has never played cricket in his life. Vern thought my humiliation was utterly hilarious although I don't know what the cretin was guffawing about because he's the final EXTRA for the sixth team and what's more, there is no seventh team. That officially makes Rain Man the worst cricketer in the school.

21:30 Lights out. Rambo called us to a huddle at his bed and spoke in a very quiet whisper. I can't remember Rambo ever whispering at a Crazy Eight meeting before.

'I've got some news from the inside,' he whispered as we all drew in close.

'Ja, from the inside of your mother,' snarled Boggo in a malicious whisper.

Rambo clonked Boggo on his knee with the rim of his squash racquet and told him to shut up. Boggo collapsed onto the floor pretending to be seriously injured.

He then got up and said his knee ligaments may have snapped. Rambo said Boggo should butch up and continued speaking in his conspiratorial whisper. 'Look, we don't have much time. Word on the inside is that the prefects are after us. I mean *really* after us!'

'It's Pike!' hissed Simon angrily.

'Who's Pike?' asked Garlic with a look of rising dread.

'You'll find out soon enough,' said Rambo.

'So what are we gonna do?' asked Fatty, looking inspired.

'We're gonna be stealthy,' replied Rambo. 'Pike's on duty tonight so he's obviously gonna try something. I want everyone in their beds and total silence. Whatever you do, don't let him goad you.'

The minutes painfully ticked by and I kept thinking about the cricket and Mermaid and felt like a complete failure. By 10:05 there was no sign of Pike. Fatty and Boggo became restless and I could hear whispering and the rustle of Fatty's hand moving about his tuck box. Suddenly there were dark shadows at the foot of the dormitory door which then swung violently open as Pike burst in with Eggwhite trailing behind. Pike burped loudly and shouted, 'Busted, you goat lickers!'

His triumphant shout was met with absolute silence, apart from the faint rustle of a chip packet from underneath Fatty's duvet.

Then Pike said to Eggwhite, 'I bet you the idiots have gone nightswimming! Quick – turn on the lights.' Eggwhite stumbled over the bin while looking for the light switch. Towards the other end of the dormitory there was a stifled snigger. And then harsh light flooded the room.

Pike seemed utterly shocked that we were all sleeping. He woke us up by kicking our lockers and demanded to know what we were all up to. Rambo got out of bed, stepped forward and said, 'We're trying to sleep, Pike.'

'*You're* Pike!' blurted Garlic for whom the penny had just dropped.

'That's a first,' snorted Pike, baiting for an argument. 'It's Friday night – I thought Rambo and his bum chums always did naughty things on Friday night?'

'Not any more,' said Simon, glaring at Pike like he was Satan himself.

'Ohhhhhh,' cooed Pike, 'let me guess. Your mommies and daddies all sat you down and told you to behave yourselves. My, what good little mommy's boys you are.'

Rambo didn't say anything but the whites of his knuckles were showing on the handle of his squash racquet.

'I bet you never thought I'd be a prefect,' said Pike with a self-satisfied look on his face.

'To tell you the truth, Pike,' replied Boggo, 'we never thought you'd pass matric.'

Pike let out a raucous fake laugh and then spat a greeny at Boggo.

Despite Boggo's snapped knee ligaments, he nimbly managed to duck down behind his locker and the missile landed safely on the curtain instead.

Pike snorted dismissively, and with a terrible grin said, 'I'm gonna pick you sorry bastards off, one by one, until there's no one left! And even better, it's legal because I'm a prefect.'

'You're a *prefect*?' cried Garlic in astonishment.

'Who the fuck are you, pink face?' demanded Pike.

'I'm Garlic,' replied Garlic.

'Yeah, well I'm sweet basil so lick my arse,' snarled Pike.

'You're nothing!' shouted Simon, unable to keep himself under control any longer.

Pike sneered and said, 'Well, if I'm nothing then I'm not here and if I'm not here, then that means you miserable fanny farts are talking after lights out. I'll see you all in Viking's office at eight o'clock tomorrow morning.'

Eggwhite tried to persuade Pike that he was being a little unreasonable but Pike shouted, 'Shut up, dick-weed!' and marched out of the dormitory. Eggwhite dithered for a moment before following Pike and gently closing the door behind him.

There was a long silence before Rambo spoke again in his low psychopathic voice. 'I told you to say nothing, but it looks like we're going to have to learn the hard way.'

He didn't say any more and the dormitory fell into a cold silence.

Bring on tomorrow.

Saturday 25th January

BAD DAY BLUES

1) Pike told Viking that he caught us running amok after lights out.

We denied everything and said that Pike had set us up and the whole thing was a conspiracy. Pike then swore on his mother's life that we were 'running amok' last night. Viking believed Pike and thrashed us viciously and with much relish.

2) The third team coach (Norm Wade) doesn't believe in spinners. He told me this as I was measuring my run-up for my bowling trial. After the batsman missed the first

five deliveries of my over he then managed to snick the final ball between the keeper and first slip for a lucky four. Norm Wade gave me back my cap and told me that I was far too expensive and that he had seen enough of my bowling. He then drew a sharp line through my name on his clipboard before calling Stinky to take my place.

3) I was fielding on the boundary when my attention was caught by a green station wagon roaring up Pilgrim's Walk in the direction of the first team field. After about twenty minutes I heard loud hooting and then the station wagon roared back down Pilgrim's Walk and disappeared through the main gates. Ten minutes later, the same vehicle sped back through the gates and raced up Pilgrim's Walk again towards the main field. Despite my cap being pulled down low over my eyes, I couldn't help but notice the station wagon steaming back down Pilgrim's Walk a mere five minutes later. I caught a glimpse of Dad staring grimly ahead and Mom with her head in her hands.

A terrible feeling of doom swept over me and I dropped an easy catch. Norm Wade made another note on his clipboard.

When I returned to the house Runt came running up to me and said, 'Hey, Spud, I heard your dad decked Sparerib.' I stumbled into the common room and was met with loud applause and wolf whistles from a small but lively crowd. Everyone seemed thrilled that my father had attacked our former housemaster.

'Sparerib has been rushed to hospital,' said Boggo and added, 'The dude is FUBAR!' He then took a huge swig of tea and continued doodling on the front page of the house newspaper.

'What's FUBAR?' demanded Garlic, appearing suddenly at the door. Boggo ignored Garlic and added the final touches to his ink sketch of a dog with a penis for a nose.

'What's FUBAR, Spud?' repeated Garlic, his eyes spread wide with curiosity.

'It means Fucked Up Beyond All Recognition ...' said Pike, swaggering into the common room and giving Garlic a healthy shove into the wall. Pike snorted at me and said, 'Nice one, scrotum face. You can't make seconds so you send in dad to beat up the coach! Classy.'

I bit my lip and said nothing.

Pike grinned at me with malicious eyes before announcing, 'See what happens when you let in the white trash ...'

I figured this wasn't the best time to attack a prefect so I walked out instead and slammed the door impressively behind me.

Thankfully, bush telegraph has completely cocked up the story. According to Simon (who was at least there), my father had a heated argument with Sparerib during the morning tea break, and the two men had both pushed each other. Simon said it was Fatty and Boggo who had started the rumours of the punch-up. The good news is that Sparerib wasn't injured and certainly isn't lying FUBAR in hospital. The bad news is that after the argument Dad drove off in a furious rage, hooting his horn, and flashed Sparerib the middle finger through the driver's side window.

He then had to return five minutes later because he had driven off without Mom, who had gone into hiding when Dad blew his top.

17:15 I called home to find out what was going on. My mother said she had been forced to lock Dad in the garage because he was completely out of hand. According to Mom, my father's convinced that Sparerib has it in for me.

17:30 Dad called and apologised for attacking my former housemaster. It was all a bit weird because he sounded like he was reading me a pre-written apology. My suspicions were confirmed when he abruptly stopped and took a long pause, before rebuking Mom for her poor handwriting. Once the badly read apology was finished it immediately sounded like Dad wasn't at all sorry about attacking goblin man. In fact the only thing he said he regretted was that he didn't finish Sparerib off when he had the chance. Dad reckons there's a conspiracy against 'us'. He says it's because the teachers and parents are all snobs and are victimising me because Dad doesn't drive a Mercedes-Benz and look like a ponce. He called Sparerib a squint-eyed little bureaucrat and declared that the entire school was corrupt to the core.

He then said he had to call Sparerib to apologise, told me to hang tough, and rang off.

Thanks, Dad.

Rambo cancelled his dormitory meeting because he said there's a rumour circulating that Pike has bugged the dormitory. We agreed instead to meet him at the old gates at 1pm tomorrow for further updates.

Sometime in the night Roger jumped onto my bed and repeatedly tried to sleep on my face. He eventually gave up and crashed in my armpit instead.

Sunday 26th January

Thank God it's Sunday.

At least I can keep a low profile and not have to talk about the fight. Hopefully, Dad apologised and it's now all blown over.

12:30 The Crazy Eight gathered at the house bench waiting for one o'clock and for Rambo to make his appearance.

12:40 Darryl (the last remaining) approached us, looking more than a little shifty. He eventually produced an envelope from his shirt pocket and handed it over to Boggo. He then galloped back to the safety of the common room. Boggo ripped open the unmarked envelope and we all leaned in to read the contents of the mysterious letter:

Clearly you bird brains have no idea how to look natural! Why not just announce to the entire house that you're up to something? Immediately do as follows:

- *Simon, Boggo and Fatty stay on the bench and talk about chicks.*
- *Spud report to the dormitory with his diary.*
- *Vern and Roger to the bogs for a thorough inspection.*
- *Garlic to the common room to talk about Lake Malawi.*

PS Make sure Vern doesn't do anything retarded!

We tried to disperse in a normal fashion, but it was impossible to stop Vern from behaving abnormally.

The fact that Rambo was watching us from somewhere meant that Vern became instantly preoccupied with discovering his whereabouts. He slunk around the cloisters and even peeked inside the big dustbin outside the library. Eventually, Boggo lost patience with Vern's skulking around like a detective, marched through the house door and trumpeted, 'Fire in the bogs! Fire in the bogs!' Vern galloped into the house like his life depended on it and didn't emerge until 12:59.

THE FINAL MEETING

After about half an hour of hanging around at the old gates, it looked like the big meeting wasn't going to happen after all. It was only then that I spotted a piece of paper stuck right in the middle of the rusty old school gate. It read:

Cross the railway line, pass the dam on the left, and then search for the biggest tree you can find.

PS Tell Fatty to move his fat ass!

The piece of paper was stuck over a faded old gate inscription that read:

Quit ye like men

We started running immediately, with Boggo blaming everybody but himself for the series of blunders that we'd made in the past hour. Then Rain Man fell into the dam after trying to overtake Fatty on a tight bend on the footpath. Vern's shorts were soaked and his left thigh was badly grazed but he didn't seem to care and kept running along with us in a deranged fashion.

Rambo was livid when we turned up so late, but made

no mention of Vern being drenched and bleeding. We sat down in the shade of a towering pine tree and caught our breath. Rambo lit a cigarette but didn't offer anyone else one.

'I think we can all agree we have a problem here,' began Rambo once everyone had settled down. We all nodded in agreement. 'The problem,' he continued, 'is that the problem is more of a problem than you know.'

'You mean it's a conspiracy?' panted Fatty.

'A conspiracy?' gasped Garlic.

'Yeah, Garlic, just like your mother shagging the gardener and you being the last to know,' spat Boggo, fed up with Garlic's constant questions and interruptions.

Rambo said it was obvious that Sparerib had chosen the house prefects for this year and not Viking. This means Pike wasn't chosen by Viking to keep the peace – he was chosen by Sparerib to start a war!

'His final parting shot,' said Rambo.

'Well, you *did* repeatedly bonk his wife,' reasoned Boggo.

'You bonked Sparerib's wife?' boomed Garlic and immediately blushed red.

'Both ways,' added Boggo proudly.

Rambo ignored the interruptions and continued with his theory. 'Pike's living in the post matric residence – why would anybody even want him around the house, except to stir up shit?' Rambo lit up another cigarette and said that Pike is planning on using his brother and the Normal Seven as live bait to lure us into making a mistake. 'The moment one of us loses our cool, we'll get hammered.'

Rambo glared at us with dark eyes as black as the night

and said, 'Viking could be our only hope. From what I know he's neutral … at least for the moment. That's why we can't afford to get bust or tempted or tricked. The more shit we get into, the lower our shares with Viking and the less chance we have of surviving this.'

'It's just like a movie,' said the delighted Garlic, who clearly still hasn't grasped the seriousness of the situation.

'I'm going to create a plan to get rid of Pike,' said Rambo in a solemn voice and then dragged deeply on his cigarette. 'Information will be on a need to know basis,' he continued, with large clouds of smoke pouring out his mouth. 'There will be no more meetings and nobody is to even talk about Pike unless it's to me.' There was a pause. Rambo exhaled again and said, 'This is it, the end of the road for the Crazy Eight.'

There was a silence.

'So we won't know the plan then?' said Boggo eventually, with a grim look and a raised eyebrow.
    'You'll know nothing until it happens,' replied Rambo. 'You may even know nothing *after* it happens.'
    'So you don't trust us?' whined Fatty, looking dreadfully disappointed with the way things were turning out. 'I thought you said it was one for all.'
    'I don't trust anyone any more,' replied Rambo and lit yet another cigarette. 'I'm going it alone.'
    'Jeez, talk about a kick in the nuts,' muttered Boggo, who looked enraged yet heartbroken.

There was another long pause before Fatty spoke in a pathetic voice. 'Can we at least call ourselves the Crazy Eight?'

Rambo shrugged his shoulders and said, 'Suit yourself.' He then stood up and said that he had to spend time alone working on his plan. He strode off before anybody could say anything and disappeared into the pine forest.

While the rest of the former Crazy Eight spent the afternoon complaining about Rambo and his strange behaviour, I lay on the grass, gazed up at the sky and felt immensely relieved that I wouldn't be roped into a suicidal plot to de-prefect Pike or something worse. Life around here is stressful enough without starting a civil war with a psychopath.

Back in the dormitory, Rambo blared U2's Sunday Bloody Sunday from his ghetto blaster.

I won't heed the battle call
It puts my back up
It puts my back up against the wall ...

Monday 27th January

A carefully handwritten note mysteriously appeared on the house notice board just before dinner, inviting third years to join up for Anglican confirmation classes. I'm not so sure if Reverend Bishop's title 'Become God's Sheep!' was the best way to attract people to the church.

Boggo announced at dinner that he and Fatty have already signed up for Reverend Bishop's confirmation classes. He chewed away at a leg of roast chicken and said, 'If you don't get confirmed you may as well kiss your chances of being a prefect goodbye.' Fatty grunted in agreement because his mouth was too full to speak. Eventually he swallowed and said, 'Over ninety per cent of prefects have been confirmed Anglicans. It's a proven fact.' He then speared one of Garlic's roast potatoes with his knife and stuffed it in his mouth.

'You do the maths,' said Boggo and looked around in a smug fashion.

There was a long pause before Simon said, 'Hey, Boggo, aren't you meant to be Jewish or something?'

Boggo swallowed hard before saying, 'Me, Jewish? Nah.'

There was another long pause before Simon spoke again, this time with his mouth curled in a slight sneer, 'Ja, but your name's Greenstein.'

'Your name's *Greenstein*?' bellowed Garlic in surprise.

'Come on, Boggo,' said Rambo. 'What's the story? There's nothing wrong with being Jewish. Hey, it's not like any of us are German!'

'My mom's half German!' confessed Garlic to absolutely no response whatsoever.

'I'm not Jewish,' repeated Boggo in a low voice without looking up from his food. 'My great-great-great-grandfather was, but I'm not.'

'He's not even circumcised,' agreed Fatty as he spread tomato sauce over his roast potatoes.

'So what?' demanded Rambo.

'So,' said Fatty, 'all Jewish okes are circumcised – it's common knowledge.'

'So that means Spud is Jewish then,' said Simon, pointing at me accusingly with a fork.

'Spud's Jewish?' repeated Garlic in an excessively loud voice.

I didn't like the direction in which the conversation was moving so I floored my glass of milk and left the table as casually as possible.

Tuesday 28th January

Raining. All cricket practices have been cancelled for today so still no idea what team I'll be playing for on Saturday.

The father and son golf day is becoming more horrifying by the day. They've already announced what time we're teeing off and who our partners will be. Norman Whiteside said my four-ball included Dad, me, Vern and The Guv.

Vern seemed very thrilled that his 'father' was going to be The Guv. Unfortunately, the cretin doesn't seem to know the first thing about golf and spent the entire afternoon seeing how many golf balls he could cram into his mouth at one time.

I called Dad in a panic about the fact that we may look like complete morons on the Victoria golf course in six weeks' time. My father sounded completely confident about his golfing abilities and said he had more or less mastered the game out on the back lawn yesterday afternoon. He promised to borrow/steal a set of clubs for me, and promised to coach me over the long weekend. My father said he had apologised to Sparerib and all was forgiven and forgotten.

Wednesday 29th January

Still drizzling and gloomy. It's meant to be summer in Africa but everyone is wearing polo neck jerseys, longs and trench coats. Fatty said this was a definite sign that the approaching winter would be the coldest in living memory. He then went on to state that if the temperature ever fell below -10 degrees, your piss would freeze before it even hit the ground. Only Garlic believed him.

Rambo informed us at dinner that he had called a dormitory meeting with Viking just before lights out. He instructed us to say nothing and let him do all the talking. Boggo and Simon were livid that Rambo was going ahead with his plans without consulting the rest of us. Fatty flew into a panic and tore up to the dormitory after prep where he counted every item in his huge tuck box and then carried it off to the second year dormitory where he hid his stash under Thinny's bed. Fatty's terrified that Viking may conduct a dormitory search after the meeting and steal his goodies. He threatened to fart on the head of any second year who so much as peeks inside his tuck box.

21:15 There was a booming shout of 'Right!' from outside the dormitory. The door flew open and Viking strode in looking like he was about to bite somebody to death. He slammed the door shut behind him and pulled himself up onto Garlic's locker where he sat like a badly overgrown schoolboy.

'Right,' he shouted again. 'What is it, Black? Time is money, money is time and neither grows on trees!' Rambo hurriedly stepped forward and told Viking that he was speaking on behalf of the dormitory. Viking's eye's widened and he shouted, 'Is this true, Black?' He then glared at all of us. We all stared back and Viking took our silence to mean that we were in agreement.

Rambo spoke in a steady voice and told our housemaster about how we were being victimised by Pike because of the bad blood that existed from the events of last year. He then informed Viking that we all wanted to play by the rules but Pike was making it incredibly difficult for us. His voice was steady and Viking listened, his head cocked and his large, intense face locked onto Rambo's.

Viking didn't make any comment after Rambo had said his piece. He said he would apply his mind to the problem and then left without even saying goodnight. I heard him shouting at Barryl for brushing his teeth on the stairs before striding off across the quad and disappearing into the drizzly gloom.

Fatty immediately charged off to the second year dormitory to find Thinny and his precious stash of grub. After a complete and thorough inventory it was discovered that three 500g packets of mixed peanuts and raisins were missing feared eaten. None of the Normal Seven would admit to the theft, so Boggo and Garlic held Thinny down while Fatty unleashed a ripper of such force that it blew poor Thinny's hair into a centre parting.

22:06   Fatty found the missing peanuts and raisins in his English file. He said he felt terrible about Thinny and that he would give him a big bar of chocolate first thing in the morning. He said this with such regret that he almost convinced me it was true.

Thursday 30th January

Pike marched into our dormitory after breakfast, mocking us about our meeting with Viking last night. He was all sneers and jeers, but the Crazy Eight remained steadfast and nobody was goaded. Just when it looked like Pike was leaving, he stopped and gazed around the dormitory as if seeing it for the first time. He then announced, 'This dormitory is worse than a whore's handbag.' In truth the dormitory wasn't looking at its best. This wasn't helped by the fact that five minutes before Pike's arrival, Boggo had tied Vern's laundry bag around Garlic's neck. Garlic totally freaked out because he thought he was suffocating to death and trashed everything within a five-metre radius.

Pike said he was reporting the deplorable state of the dorm to Viking and strode out, slamming the door behind him.

'Quick!' hissed Rambo. 'Clean! Clean! Clean!' There was a mad chaotic dash to clean up the dormitory before Viking arrived. Boggo was so desperate that in his panic he hurled the entire rubbish bin out the window.

'Twenty seconds!' hissed Rambo as he forced clothes into an already overflowing drawer. 'The moment we hear someone coming up the stairs, drop what you're doing and look natural.'

There was an excited giggle from Fatty as he juggled a handful of golf balls into his toiletry bag. 'We've got that slimy turd this time,' he chortled. 'When Viking opens that door he's gonna know Pike's a fraud.'

Then there were loud footsteps on the stairs. Rambo shouted, 'Now!' We all lurched into position. It was generally a good attempt at looking normal from the Crazy Eight. Mostly we pretended to be reading or shining shoes except for Vern who had become so panic-stricken in all the excitement that he slithered under his mattress and hid himself from the world.

The door flew open ... and standing in the doorway were Pike and Eggwhite. Pike looked around the dormitory and broke into sarcastic applause. 'Nice one, retards!' he shouted, looking as smug as ever. 'Not only are you siff and untidy, but you're stupid and gullible as well.'

He then sauntered around the dormitory with Eggwhite

following awkwardly behind him. Pike's eyes settled on the huge lump in Vern's mattress. Vern's right foot was sticking out from under the mattress and Roger had strolled out from the underpants drawer to sniff Vern's toes and rub his face against them. Pike turned to his fellow prefect and said, 'Hey, Eggwhite, I'm thinking of trying out for the school high jump team.' He then skipped across to Vern's cubicle, launched himself into the air and landed with a thump on Vern's bulging mattress. There was a terrible gasp from under the mattress and then complete silence apart from Roger scrabbling out the window and down the drain pipe. For a moment it seemed like Rain Man had been squashed to death, but then his exposed foot twitched and a crumpled form in khaki slid out from under the mattress and collapsed onto the floor. Pike stepped back in mock surprise and cried, 'Oh, shit, sorry, Vern. I didn't know you were under there. Sorry, buddy.' He then laughed his cruel laugh and sauntered towards the door. He pulled it open and then stopped, still looking out towards the stairs. In a quiet voice he said, 'Oh, by the way, Rambo, I was only bluffing about telling Viking.' He then turned and smiled at an ill-looking Rambo and sneered, 'Gotcha again.'

Eggwhite checked Vern was all right before he left and clearly didn't look happy with the way things had gone. Poor Vern limped off to class without saying anything and Rambo marched out, carrying a file, his strong jaw locked in an expression of defiance.

16:30 The cricket debacle has gone from bad to worse. The fourth team coach (Mr Cartwright) called me aside halfway through the net practice and said that he thought I was out of my depth at fourth team level. He said I bowled 'donkey drops' and that while I may have got away with it at U15 level, it wouldn't work at fourth team level. The fact that most of the fourth team was made up of last year's U15B side didn't seem to worry the old windbag. I tried to educate Cartwright on the art of using flight and guile to deceive the batsman but the old fossil said I didn't know what I was talking about and sent me off to the fifth team practice.

The fifth team practice was diabolical. The coach, Mr Ashleigh-Meyer, had arrived late and left early. Everybody was running amok trying to hurl cricket balls at each other. I sat on the bank in my cricket whites and didn't join my new team.

So now I'm playing cricket for the fifths. What with Cartwright coaching the fourths, Norm (I don't believe in spinners) Wade in charge of the thirds, and Sparerib coaching the seconds, I may as well quit cricket and take up canoeing, tennis or tug-of-war instead!

21:00   A scribbled note on the house notice board read:

PIKE 2 RAMBO 0

Rambo turned slightly pale when he read the notice. He then ripped it off the wall, and marched up the stairs and into our dormitory, where he stuck the notice above the door with a savage smack. He turned to us and said, 'You telling me this isn't personal?' Everybody nodded and looked serious. Rambo's eyes were on fire but he didn't say anything else and went off to brush his teeth.

Friday 31st January

11:00   It's official. I'm playing for the fifths! On a more positive note, I've been made vice captain. Unfortunately, we don't have a game tomorrow because Blacksmith College only have four teams so this means that the

fifths and the sixths are having a practice match instead.
I still can't quite believe I've gone from the cut and thrust
of U15A cricket to spending my Saturdays bowling to
Vern and Garlic of the cretin eleven!

My father may well have cardiac arrest when he hears
the news.

14:30   Fatty and Boggo both auditioned for the choir.
Boggo says that he's putting down key spiritual building
blocks before he begins his big push for prefect. Fatty
scored a hat-trick after being rejected by the choir for
the third year in a row. Boggo made the tenor section
despite using God Save The Queen as his audition piece.
I plan to mock Boggo relentlessly for the entire year in
payback for first year when he did the same to me.

I didn't audition. One more rejection could drive me right
over the edge.

Saturday 1st February

Cricket practice match against the sixth eleven.

Mr Ashleigh-Meyer arrived thirty minutes late. When
he finally sauntered up to the field he told us to 'Carry
on'. Clearly he hadn't noticed that half the sixth eleven
were having a sword fight with the wickets. Our coach
then retired to a bench under the trees and unfolded
his newspaper. Every ten minutes or so, he would shout
for two people to pad up and for a change of bowlers.
Then he would return to his newspaper crossword and
his smoking. I bowled to a large matric boy called Goat
who had no idea of what was cracking. After getting him
out about five times in six balls, he marched down the
wicket, pointed his bat threateningly at me, and told me
to bowl normally and stop showing off. Goat seemed to

be under the impression that spin bowling was illegal and unsporting. I then bowled 'normally' and took his wicket a further five times before Mr Ashleigh-Meyer shouted 'Next!' from the bench under the tree. I took ten wickets in twenty-four balls and my coach didn't see a single one of them.

Just to rub salt in the wounds I ended up facing Vern's bowling for the twenty-four balls of my 'batting' practice. It was a complete waste of time because Vern only landed two deliveries on the pitch. Other disasters included running into the wickets at the bowler's end and twice bowling the ball backwards.

Am seriously thinking of retiring from cricket. The only problem is that I'm not any good at anything else.

Monday 3rd February

Garlic approached me after lunch with a worried look on his face and hollered, 'Hey, Spud, how's your English oral going?' I told him my oral was called 'The Magic of Theatre'. Garlic roared with laughter and said, 'There's no such thing as magic!' His eyes widened as he announced, 'I'm doing mine on Lake Malawi. Fatty's doing his on the occult, and Boggo says he's doing his oral on my mum.' He then spotted Simon and shouted, 'Hey, Simon, how's your English oral going?' Simon ducked through an archway but Garlic was after him.

21:30   Head of House Norman Whiteside clearly had a big speech planned when he arrived to call lights out. He went on for nearly half an hour about school traditions and taking pride in our behaviour. He obviously realised that he was droning on when Fatty yawned really loudly in the middle of his positive intent bit. After a sour look he said, 'If I hear a single report from the slaves that you've so much as touched them, I'll thrash you so hard that your pictures at home will be crying!' He then declared first year hunting season open and switched off the lights.

Boggo slapped his hands together and said, 'Look sharp, amigos, it's time Brother Boggo christened the first years.' He then sniggered loudly and whispered to Fatty, 'And I'm gonna find out which one of those little twerps has the hot mother who looks like Meg Ryan!'

Boggo's excited announcement was met with a long silence. There wasn't any sign of movement from Rambo's bed. After more of nothing, Boggo pleaded, 'Come on, lads, you heard the man – first year hunting season is open ... It's time for a first year FUBAR!'

At last Rambo spoke. 'Good luck, Boggo. Just change the score above the door to 3-0 before you go.'

Nobody went.

Wednesday 5th February

Christine called. At first I thought she was the Mermaid and I may have sounded a little too excited and loving at the beginning of the conversation. Christine took this as a sign of interest and invited the entire Crazy Eight to a party at her friend's farm next Saturday night. She then asked me to make sure that I brought Vern along because she wanted her friends to meet him.

My Crazy Eight shares are at an all time high thanks to Christine and her party. Even better news is that third years are allowed one weekend leave per term so we won't have to bunk out either. Boggo says he's going to demonstrate his new technique for scoring girls and get

Fatty and Vern well and truly snogged for the first time.

Thursday 6th February

I passed Norm (I don't believe in spinners) Wade in the main quad on the way to Geography. He pretended not to see me and looked up at the sky as if he was greatly interested in the weather.

Friday 7th February

Viking stood up at assembly and announced that there would be a NAPAC production of a play called Wild Coast in the theatre tomorrow night. There was loud hooting and excited murmuring when he added that the show contained scenes of nudity and violence. Viking responded by threatening to personally thrash anybody who doesn't behave in a civilised fashion. Then he dropped the bombshell. Only matrics and post matrics are allowed to attend. Boggo looked up at the roof of the hall and shook his head as if God was playing cruel tricks with his mind.

English Orals!

The Guv was in raucous form during the oral presentations. He interrupted and shouted comments throughout and even made Martin Lesley stop in the middle of his oral and accused him of having the oratorical skills of a dyslexic pygmy. Only after our English teacher had calmed down and carefully reloaded his pipe was Lesley allowed to proceed with his oral on the digestive system of Friesland cows.

When Garlic announced that he was doing his oral on Lake Malawi, The Guv screamed loudly and clutched at his skull like he had a blinding migraine. He then relit his pipe and declared, 'The oral cannot be done!'

Garlic looked crushed. He began pleading with The Guv to hear him out and let him say his oral, but The Guv was having none of it. He slammed his fist into his desk and shouted, 'Either the oral goes or I go!'

Eventually, after much muttering to himself in Shakespearean verse, our English teacher conceded defeat and said, 'Do your damndest, Garlic, and pray, good man, remember, brevity is the soul of wit.'

Garlic launched into his oral with gusto but was brought to a halt after the first line. 'Good God, Garlic!' boomed The Guv. 'Must you insist on shouting? This isn't a fish market in darkest Africa, and you, my lad, are no Winston Churchill!'

'Thank God Almighty,' gasped The Guv as Garlic finally finished his oral to a pathetic ripple of applause. The Guv then asked the class if we had any questions. Rambo surprisingly raised his hand skyward. He cleared his throat and said, 'Sir, I would just like to ask Garlic the name of the predominant rock strata that exist under Lake Malawi itself.'

Garlic's eyes swelled, his face reddened and his mouth opened but no words came out. The Guv glared at Garlic in mock anger and said, 'Clearly, you know very little about your subject. In fact I have my suspicions as to whether you really come from Nyasaland at all. The name Garlic sounds a little queer, too. Have you not considered the possibility, dear boy, that you might not in fact exist?'

Poor Garlic stuttered and pleaded and even offered to run back to the dormitory to fetch photographs to prove his existence. The Guv refused. Then Boggo piped up and said, 'Sir, I think I have a question that will finally establish if Garlic is a true Malawian or a lying impostor.'

Garlic wiped the sweat off his brow with his forearm and looked like a man facing execution.

Boggo cleared his throat and asked, 'What is the national snake of Malawi?'

Garlic shouted, 'Snake?' as if the question made no sense. A murmur turned into a roar of laughter as it became obvious that Garlic didn't know the answer. In desperation he shouted, 'Cobra!'

The Guv rocked back in his chair and raised his hands for silence. He sucked on his pipe and said, 'All right, Greenstein, please enlighten this herbaceous African as to what the national snake of Nyasaland in fact is.'

Boggo stood up and announced, 'The one-eyed trouser snake, sir.'

The Guv thought this was hilarious and took some time to gather himself before saying, 'Garlic, it is clear to me that as a non resident your knowledge of Lake Nyasa is sound and your passion for the topic unquestioned and hitherto unseen.' The Guv motioned Garlic back to his seat and shouted, 'Live long Garlic and never allow anyone to question your existence again.'

The Guv seemed very impressed with my oral on the magic of theatre. He even cheered and applauded after I quoted Orson Welles. After I had finished, he said, 'Milton, your oration has left me itching to tread the boards once more.' The siren rang for the end of the double, and The Guv ended the class with, 'If theatre be the wine of love, drink on!'

15:00 After procrastinating for days about phoning home I finally psyched myself up to tell Dad the bad cricket news. Thankfully, Mom answered the call because Dad had just discovered that his garage door was infested with termites and had rushed out to buy poison. Mom said she would try her best to break the news softly and promised that he wouldn't do anything embarrassing this time.

17:00 I found Garlic sitting on the grass behind the chapel. His eyes were red and it was obvious that he'd been crying. I asked him if he was all right. He nodded but then his eyes filled with tears and he covered his face and turned away from me.

'I hate it here,' said Garlic eventually. 'I'm trying to be friendly like, and everybody hates me. I think I want to go home.'

I explained to Garlic that nobody hated him and that he shouldn't take the mockery personally. I told him about getting my balls polished in first year and how bad things have happened to everyone along the way.

He looked at me with his huge eyes and asked me why I stayed at the school. I heard myself rambling on about school spirit and the extra facilities the school offered. In truth I didn't have a good reason to give him.

I suggested to him that he keep a low profile until he knew how the school worked. I also advised him never to mention Lake Malawi again and to stop shouting random questions at people all the time. He nodded and his eyes filled with tears again.

Then we had an awkward few minutes where nothing was said. I eventually got up to leave but he jumped up too. He said, 'Thanks, Spud. You're my best buddy.' I gave him a friendly thump on the back. Garlic grinned happily and said, 'Hey, what are you doing in the holidays? Why not come to Lake Malawi?'

I ran.

Saturday 8th February

The cricket match against Arlington was a complete waste of time. I took five wickets but it didn't really feel like much of an achievement because the batsmen were committing suicide by charging down the wicket and swinging wildly. The game ended well before lunch but Mr Ashleigh-Meyer said there would be no second innings and immediately dragged the opposition coach off to the staff room for the rest of the afternoon.

18:00 Boggo came charging into the dining hall and said he had just witnessed the actress from Wild Coast getting out of her car and he reckons she's the hottest chick he's ever seen in the flesh. He then said he was too in love to eat mediocre food and tore back to the theatre to offer technical help.

20:30 There was much mocking and jeering as the matrics and Pike set off to watch Wild Coast. Boggo became so desperate that he tried to bribe Meany Dlamini in the main quad and received hard labour for his troubles. Boggo said his quest to be the sound operator was doomed because by the time he got to the theatre there was already a waiting list of twenty sound operators and a fight had broken out over who was manning the follow spot. Boggo says the reason that the third years weren't allowed to attend the play had nothing to do with nudity and age restrictions. He reckons the real reason is that Wild Coast is completely sold out. The local farming community has booked in their droves and a farmer's co-op from Fort Nottingham has reserved over a hundred and twenty seats. Boggo said the whole thing was iniquitous. 'Our folks,' he whined, 'pay shitloads for our education. This play should be for our cultural development, not for a bunch of horny sheep farmers from Fort Nottingham.'

Norman Whiteside, our officious new head of house, had grandly announced that he was forgoing Wild Coast to keep order in the house. Clearly the idiot thought we wouldn't notice him wrapped in a scarf and darting behind the walls in the cloisters. The lure of the naked actress has claimed its second victim.

The school fell silent as the crowds disappeared into the theatre. Rambo, who had from the beginning shown no interest in the play whatsoever, sauntered into the prefects' kitchen and made himself a pot of tea. We sat around on the house bench while Rambo silently drank his tea. Boggo continued his rant about the severe theatrical injustice that had been dealt to us, while we stared out at Pissing Pete and the general gloom of the deserted quad.

Rambo downed his tea with a satisfied smack of the lips and said, 'Right, gather yourselves, gentlemen. It's time for a christening.'

The Normal Seven were awake because we caught Spike tormenting Runt and the last remaining Darryl. Rambo didn't stop in the second year dorm but continued into the first year dorm and closed the door behind us once we were all through. The first years were all asleep or at least faking sleep. Fatty wasted no time in marching to the first cubicle on the left and shaking one of the new boys awake. From under his trench coat he produced the house telephone, which he and Boggo had unplugged and stolen.

Fatty told the new boy that his mom was on the line and handed the first year the receiver. The gullible first year took the receiver in a sleepy daze, placed it on his ear and said, 'Hi, Mom.' Fatty nearly fell over, he was laughing so much. The poor first year didn't know what was going on and looked on the verge of tears.

Boggo then ordered the new boys out of their beds and told them to line up in front of us. The new boys silently obeyed and soon stood shivering pathetically in their pyjamas. Vern strode forward, thumped his left foot into the ground and saluted ferociously. Boggo groaned and Garlic burst into loud laughter. The new boys all saluted back at Vern who, satisfied, took a gigantic step backwards to where he'd been standing before. Fatty closed his eyes and took a deep breath that whistled tunefully through his nostrils. After a few more seconds he said, 'Be seated.' The new boys obeyed immediately.

Boggo pointed at the smallest boy and said, 'Hey, you; dickcheese. Stand up.' The frightened first year scrambled to his feet and stood to attention, looking desperate not to offend. Boggo examined him closely before turning to Fatty and saying, 'I think this is the one. I'd recognise Meg Ryan's nose any day.' Fatty examined the new boy's nose and agreed it was definitely the same as Meg Ryan's. Boggo looked the boy up and down and asked, 'What's your name?' The first year replied with an extremely Spudly, 'Er, sir, my name is Jack.' Boggo nodded solemnly and replied, 'Bad news, Jack. Bishop Boggo is about to knock over the king and ace the queen!' Boggo nodded at Vern who immediately produced a pad of paper and a pen. He then licked his fingers manically and began paging through his notebook searching for a clean page.

'Address?' demanded Boggo. The poor first year coughed up all his mother's details, including her name (Virginia), star sign (Pisces) and favourite food (Lobster Thermidoor). Unfortunately for Boggo, Jack had no idea whatsoever what his mother's bra size was or whether she had any kinky outfits in her closet or not. Boggo ordered Vern to put Jack's mother down for a 32D size bra and a leopard print obsession. Boggo christened Jack with the nickname 'Meg Ryan's Son' and told him it was a possibility that he may soon have to address Boggo as Dad.

There was a triumphant shout from the far end of the dormitory where Fatty had just discovered a gold mine of tuck under a new boy's bed. Immediately the largest of the first years jumped up with a look of panic spreading across his round face. He blurted, 'Sir, that's mine, sir, it's special food, sir, because I have a spastic colon.' While wolfing down a box of wheat cookies, Fatty quizzed the large boy about his spastic colon and took a great interest in each item of tuck and what its health benefits were. The new boy became desperate and begged, 'Please don't eat all my food, sir.' Fatty looked deeply wounded and replied, 'What do you take me for – some kind of animal?' He then poured an entire packet of dried prunes into his mouth and chomped away noisily whilst riffling through the boy's underpants drawer. 'Oh, and don't call me sir,' he mumbled, with prunes tumbling out the sides of his mouth. 'Sir is what you call teachers. I'd rather you called me something like ... Guru.'

'Oh guru my guru!' gushed Rambo as he leant non-chalantly against the door. Even the new boys laughed.

Simon suggested that since the new boy's name is Graham, he should be called 'Fat Graham'. But Fatty was having none of it. He said Graham was well short of obese, and would have to pack on at least thirty kilograms if he wanted to be considered properly fat. We finally all agreed on 'Plump Graham' for a nickname. Plump Graham blushed scarlet and sat down looking humiliated.

'Who's the one with the skew willy?' shouted Garlic immediately. None of the first years raised their hands so Boggo made them all strip from the waist while Garlic and Fatty examined their privates and Vern aimed the torch. The culprit was immediately exposed and the humiliated first year was christened 'Sidewinder' and mocked mercilessly for the next ten minutes.

Boggo christened the fourth boy 'Gastro' without giving an explanation. It then took quite some time to work out whether the final boy was either painfully shy or completely mute. Fatty eventually lost patience with the boy's continuing silence and nicknamed him 'Rowdy'.

Once all the first years had been christened, Rambo stepped forward to speak. I noticed the fear and respect glowing in the new boys' eyes. It seems amazing that without saying a single word Rambo can somehow command focus. It was like some great chief was about to make a dramatic announcement before a historic battle. When he spoke his voice was oddly gentle. 'Boys, I want you to know,' he began, 'that we are on your side. This is just normal initiation. We don't mean you any harm.'

'Ja, right!' chortled Boggo and began shadow humping Meg Ryan's Son's locker. Rambo looked at the first years with a meaningful stare and said, 'Boys, I want to know who's been giving you shit?'

There was a long silence as the new boys refused to meet his eyes.

'Tell me!' demanded Rambo, this time in a more forceful voice. Still nobody spoke. Eventually, Plump Graham raised his hand tentatively and said, 'Sir. Um ... we aren't meant to rat, sir, because we've been told that if you rat, sir ... then you get kind of ... killed, sir.'

'Who told you that?' asked Rambo.

'Sir, we can't say, sir.'

Rambo tried his best to look friendly but ended up looking a little frightening. He said, 'Telling a prefect or Viking is ratting – but sharing this information with me is a display of good school spirit.' His eyes locked onto those of Plump Graham. 'Tell me,' he said once again, his voice growing slightly menacing. 'I want a name.'

Plump Graham looked around nervously but the others seemed to be nodding and egging him on. Plump Graham turned to Rambo and whispered:

'Spike.'

A sly smile spread across Rambo's face as he led us all back to our dormitory.

The Fragile Five

Plump Graham
Sidewinder
Gastro
Rowdy
Meg Ryan's Son

Once back in the dorm, Boggo hurriedly changed into his finest civvies and announced that he was 'bonking out' to find the Wild Coast actress. Rambo warned him that he could be facing expulsion if caught. Boggo stood up proudly and said, 'For her, I'd risk death by firing squad.' He then gave himself yet another blast of deodorant and strode out the dormitory without saying another word.

23:30   Boggo woke us all up to say that sparks were

flying between him and the actress, and that a dramatic shag was looming on the horizon. He said he'd met the gorgeous beauty at the stage door and helped pack her bags and props into the car. According to Boggo, the hot actress then kissed him 'with a tongue that could strangle a boa constrictor' and handed him a red rose before driving off into the night.

I must admit this all seemed a little far-fetched. Boggo is famous for lying about his conquests with women and it's a known fact that the majority of girls find him utterly gross and perverted.

Rambo demanded proof of conquest. Boggo sniggered and pulled a rather crushed red rose out of the back of his pants and handed it over to Rambo. Garlic burst into applause and said, 'I've always wanted to shag an actress!' Boggo told Garlic that he could probably fix him up with one of the actress's hot friends.

Then Rambo began his inquisition:

RAMBO   So you're saying this hot actress walked offstage, picked a rose for you, stuck her tongue down your throat and left?

BOGGO   (After vigorous high five with Fatty) She was gagging for it.

RAMBO   And she kissed you.

BOGGO   Savagely. Kiss and run – brutal stuff.

RAMBO   So tell me, Don Boggo – if this is your rose, why is there a note attached to it that reads:

Katherine

Break a leg my darling
Pieter Scholtz

Obviously Boggo hadn't noticed the note because his mouth fell wide open when he read it. He then tried to convince us that the note had become attached to the rose by accident, but nobody was buying it.

Rambo found Boggo guilty of lying, threw his alarm clock out the window, and accused him of kissing Pieter Scholtz instead.

Boggo said we were all jealous, stole Vern's alarm clock, and stormed off to bed in a huff.

Sunday 9th February

AA MEETING

20:00 I knocked on Lennox's kitchen door and heard a baby begin wailing in a back room. The door flew open and there stood a wild looking Lennox beaming out from behind his bushy beard. He invited me in and I took a seat in his cosy living room. Mrs Lennox poured me some coffee before rushing off to attend to her baby daughter who was trying her best to break the sound barrier.

After twenty minutes of making conversation with Lennox, I began to get the sinking feeling that I may be the only one in the society this year. I noticed Lennox kept glancing at his watch and trying his best not to look alarmed. He even went outside a couple of times in case new members were having difficulty in finding his house. Each time he returned alone, looking more and more hurt and despondent.

20:35   We both heaved a great sigh of relief when there was a loud rapping on the kitchen door. Lennox shot out of his seat, pulled open the kitchen door and led the new recruit into the living room.

It was Rambo.

Rambo grinned at me like he was up to something. He then helped himself to coffee and settled into the rocking chair near the empty fireplace. Lennox confirmed that since there were only two members at the first meeting, I should be appointed president and Rambo the treasurer of the society. Thankfully, he said he would perform the role of AA secretary himself until more boys joined up.

Rambo took a loud slurp of his coffee and said, 'Sir, that's not a democratic decision. Surely there should be a vote on this?' Lennox was rather taken aback at Rambo's confidence and seemed to scald his mouth after gulping his coffee in a moment of panic. I decided against reminding Rambo that he had cancelled democracy forever last week.

'In any case,' said Rambo, 'I have far more leadership qualities than Spud, so it would be common sense to make me president and Spud my treasurer.'

Lennox reasoned that since I had been in the society longer I should be given preference. Rambo scoffed and said, 'But, sir, if seniority was the only criterion for choosing leaders we would still be barbarians charging around raping and pillaging!'

Lennox's face broke into a smile and he said, 'Some would say, Mr Black, that that's exactly where we are right now.'

And thus began a two-hour battle of wits between Lennox and Rambo. I hardly said a word as the pair fought out an epic battle of intellectual ping-pong. Eventually, Lennox looked at his watch with a start and said it was 10:30pm and that we had to end. He then declared that this was the best AA meeting we had ever had and said Rambo was a breath of fresh air to the society. Nothing further was said about who would be the AA president and an elated Lennox led us out with an arm over Rambo's shoulder.

Rambo insisted on walking about twenty metres behind me on the way back to the dorm. It was the most uncomfortable three hundred metres of my life.

Thursday 13th February

Received a long and miserable letter from the Mermaid saying she's 'seeing' somebody else and that she still loves me but wanted me to know the truth.

Boggo sauntered past me as I was re-reading it on my bed and said, 'Never a good sign the day before Valentine's. Never good.'

Fatty followed behind, shaking his head and whistling under his breath.

Spent the rest of the day thinking of Mermaid, her someone else, and death. At least Christine's party on Saturday offers me a shot at redemption.

Friday 14th February

Valentine's Day. 0 letters

Vern has got Spike thrashed by Viking for Bad Form

in the Bogs and Surrounds. This is the first time any punishment has been dished out for the offence and I couldn't think of a more deserving recipient. Unfortunately, this also means that Vern has been given real power in the house, which is the equivalent of giving a chainsaw to a deranged toddler!

Feeling angry with Mermaid. It's like she says one thing to me in the holidays and then the opposite when I get back to school. Clearly she's insane, and I'm altogether better off without her in my life.

Worse than anything, she dumped me in the Valentine's season again! That's twice in a row and totally uncalled for.

Boggo couldn't eat because he's so excited about demonstrating his foolproof pick-up routine tomorrow night. I hope it really is foolproof because I'm getting desperate and my semi-arid love life is quickly turning into the Sahara Desert.

Saturday 15th February

Mr Ashleigh-Meyer called off our match against Highfield because he said the pitch was unplayable. He pointed at the muddy patch two-thirds of the way down the wicket and called it 'a death waiting to happen'. The fact that both teams and the opposition coach were keen to play made no difference and the Highfield team returned to their bus where they spent the entire morning and most of the afternoon.

The Party

18:30 The Crazy Eight lined up at the school gates and handed over our leave permission slips to the security guard. He stamped them without question and handed them all back to us before opening the big gates. Suddenly Rambo was sprinting down the path towards the station. We followed him over the railway lines, through a fence and out onto the road. We eventually found him lighting up a cigarette behind a tree near the entrance to the chicken farm.

'What the stuff was all that about?' gasped Fatty, looking like he was midway through an aneurysm. Rambo took a deep drag on his cigarette and said, 'Let's just call it a life fulfilment exercise ...'

After waiting around for ages in the dark, a rusty Isuzu bakkie roared to a stop in front of us. A cheeky looking guy dressed in a khaki shirt lunged out of the window and shouted, 'You guys the Crazy Eight?' When I got up close to the cab it became apparent that our designated drivers were already as drunk as skunks.

'How come there are only seven of you?' enquired the co-driver before draining a tin of Ohlssons lager and tossing it out the window.

'Fatty chowed the eighth dude,' shouted Rambo as he leapt onto the back of the bakkie. Everyone laughed and soon we were tearing through the night shouting and howling, feeling the chilled air sting our eyes. The hooligans up front swerved from side to side, hooting and laughing hysterically. I held onto Fatty's leg and looked up towards a sky of satellites galloping through space desperately looking for a good time of their own.

CHRISTINE'S PARTY

RATING 7/10

VENUE   Christine's friend's parents' 'cottage' (6 bed-
          rooms, 6 bathrooms, pool, pool room, pool
          table, etc)

HIGHLIGHTS
Good crowd
Amanda wasn't there
Beers were R2 each

LOWLIGHTS
Fatty, Garlic and Vern (twice) threw up
Fatty was caught trying to steal large quantities of food
from the kitchen freezer
Vern's dire spading attempt
Boggo being slapped twice in ten minutes by different
girls
Garlic inviting at least twenty girls to Lake Malawi (not
one of them was interested)
I had a terrible hour or so thinking about the Mermaid
and her new boyfriend and what they might be doing
right then

POINTS OF INTEREST
We're not the only ones who take bets on scoring.
Seems like Christine and her mates have their own tote
running. Any girl brave enough to kiss Fatty receives one
hundred bucks. Any girl psycho enough to kiss Vern will
pocket R400. Nobody claimed the money.
    Only Simon and Rambo (he says) came right last
night. Thankfully, Christine was too busy kissing everyone else to pay me much attention.

Boggo's foolproof scoring theory was a dismal failure.
Aside from Boggo being slapped twice in ten minutes,
Vern made a terrible hash of using Boggo's spading
method and had a mortifying cretin attack in front of
a crowd of about twenty girls. Fatty tried the technique

on a terrified thirteen-year-old girl who looked barely out of primary school. The girl threatened Fatty with a lawsuit and then locked herself in a bathroom until her dad arrived to take her home.

I didn't receive so much as a look or a smile from a single girl.

Monday 17th February

13:30   A handwritten sign on The Guv's gatepost read:

LUNCHEON

Underneath it said:

Strictly no halfwits

I found The Guv in the kitchen wearing a frilly green apron, which he said belonged to his late mother. In his hands he held a savage looking meat cleaver and lying on the counter was a gigantic hunk of black meat.

'Springbok,' he divulged. 'Poor thing – if only it had clung onto life like it clung onto the roof of my freezer.' He then asked, 'How do you like your wildlife, Milton – fried in butter or buggered and boiled?'

Thankfully, we didn't have to eat the springbok that's been doing a Walt Disney in The Guv's freezer since the late seventies. Instead he offered up eggs and bacon and said that occasionally having breakfast for lunch kept his bowels honest and his stools impressive.

The Guv then began to remove the entire contents of his fridge in search of some eggs. I strolled through to his living room to take up my usual position in the armchair at the window. I nearly dropped the books I was carrying when I realised that there was another schoolboy sitting in my chair. 'Rowdy?' I almost shouted. 'What are you doing here?' I was attempting to come across nonchalant but my voice emerged as a strident shout. Rowdy was alarmed by my dramatic entrance and staggered to his feet like he was guilty of a heinous crime.

He didn't say anything other than an extremely soft grunt of 'Sir.' But it was nevertheless pleasing to see that he was looking at me with fear, awe and respect.

'Milton, you must know Simpson,' said The Guv as he entered the living room with two bottles of wine and a corkscrew. I informed The Guv that back at the house he was known as Rowdy, which amused my English teacher hugely. Poor Rowdy blushed and grinned sheepishly but true to form said absolutely nothing. It was more than a little weird talking to The Guv in front of the silent Rowdy. He never said a word and observed the conversation like he was watching a tennis match at Wimbledon. The Guv continued like Rowdy wasn't there except he didn't offer me any wine, which was a disappointment.

The conversation then turned to cricket and The Guv was utterly appalled that I was playing for the fifths. 'Fools!' he shouted while pacing around his living room like a maniac. 'Have these pedestrian people never heard of the refined art of leg break bowling?' The Guv raged on about this being a sign of the times and the end of a golden age in cricket where seductive flight and a rotating ball could melt the miniskirts off buxom women.

I left early. I didn't feel comfortable sharing my innermost thoughts and feelings in front of the silent presence at the window. I marched back to the house in a rage. I was angry with The Guv for inviting somebody else to our lunch. I was angry with Rowdy for sitting there like an idiot and not saying a word. I was angry that another Valentine's Day has come and gone without somebody to share it with.

21:00   Vern lined up the Fragile Five on the top step of the urinal and spent half an hour saluting at them. The Fragile Five never questioned what they were doing, and returned Vern's three hundred odd salutes with serious faces and complete concentration.

Something is up with Vern. After years of watching him closely I've come to realise that it's impossible to know what (or if anything at all) is going on inside his head. But the key is to watch for sudden changes in behaviour. At present his new habits include:

Drawing hundreds of pictures of my laundry bag
Shining his shoes constantly
Putting Roger's tail in his mouth
Shooting an imaginary gun at the roof
Drinking out of his contact lens solution bottle

Wednesday 19th February

Didn't sleep very well. My mind was churning about yesterday's lunch and all the other things that occupy most of the space in my brain. I suppose I can't blame The Guv for helping a new boy who's scared and homesick – after all that was me two years ago. It doesn't feel the same with Rowdy there so perhaps that will be an end to our lunches and our crazy discussions about women, cricket and literature. And perhaps it's also time to accept that Mermaid will always be out of my league and I should probably settle for somebody with smaller boobs and a better personality.

The entire Crazy Eight has enrolled in confirmation classes with Reverend Bishop! Our first lesson is this afternoon – I bet the Rev is dreading it ...

CONFIRMATION CLASS 1

'Be God's Sheep'

God knows what persuaded the school chaplain to select this title for both his first lesson and as a controversial way of attracting new recruits. If it wasn't for the fact that everyone appears to be pushing for prefect, I don't think a single member of the Crazy Eight would have signed up to be religious livestock.

After a long and heartfelt opening prayer, Reverend Bishop opened up his arms in welcome and asked us if we would like to ask him any questions. Vern immediately thrust his hand into the air and asked the Reverend if he could go to the toilet. The chaplain smiled and said, 'Of course, Vern.' Vern grinned at the Reverend but didn't leave his seat. This confused the school chaplain because he stammered quite badly over his next line and fumbled awkwardly with his papers.

'Father?' said Rambo, raising his right hand. The Reverend's face broke into a gentle grin and he said, 'Robert, there's no need to call me Father. Reverend will do fine.'

Rambo looked wistfully out of the window and then back at the chaplain. 'I would rather call you Father, Father because I don't have a father ...' Tears immediately sprang to the chaplain's eyes and he charged over to pat Rambo on the back in sympathy. Boggo snorted derisively from the back of the vestry but didn't mention the fact that Rambo was overheard at breakfast saying that he and his dead father were going to win the father and son golf day.

Overall our first confirmation class wasn't as bad as expected thanks to a fierce debate on the meaning of life and the meaninglessness of school.

Reverend Bishop says that without a deep commitment to and belief in God, no man or woman will ever lead a fulfilling existence. This obviously accounts for why I'm unfulfilled.

Boggo volunteered for every single Bible reading, all of which he carried out with a superior look on his face. His routine was to close his eyes at the end of each reading as if consumed with religious spirit and then whisper, 'Amen.' He would then return to his seat with his Bible pressed closely to his heart. The chaplain was mightily impressed with Boggo's religious passion although Simon lost his cool after Boggo's third performance and blurted out, 'Reverend, I think you should know that Greenstein is Jewish.'

'So is Spud,' said Garlic, pointing at me with a pencil.

Boggo threatened to show everyone his penis, but the chaplain doused the flames by saying, 'Boys, I don't care who or what you are. What I care about is that you are here now. After all, let's be reminded that our Lord and saviour was himself Jewish.'

'Jesus was Jewish?' boomed Garlic in confusion. The chaplain didn't answer Garlic and launched straight into his closing prayer, before raising his arms aloft and saying, 'Now go forth into the world and become God's sheep.'

The Crazy Eight bleated all the way back to the dormitory.

Thursday 20th February

Dad phoned to say our house is infested with termites and that it has to be fumigated immediately. He reckons this is a sure sign that the timber industry has fallen into the hands of incompetent leftists. 'Swines!' he shouted, although it was unclear whether he was referring to the termites or the leftists.

After English, The Guv called me aside and said, 'Milton, I'm sorry I sprang Simpson on you the other day.'

'No problem,' I said.

'The boy became hysterical after class and I'm terrible with tears,' he said as if reliving the moment in his mind.

'It's fine, sir,' I said.

The Guv studied me over the top of his spectacles before saying, 'So as an apology ...' He strode over to his bookshelf. 'I'm giving you this.' He dropped a book into my waiting hands and with one hand on my shoulder said, ' I want you to have it. Read it once a decade until your restlessness dies and you become an old drunken hermit.' He then guided me out of the classroom with his hand on my shoulder. He said, 'It defined my generation, old boy. It awoke my wanderlust and made me ceaselessly unhappy. I wish you greater fortune with it.'

I began reading Jack Kerouac's novel called *On The Road* on the cobbled path back to the house. I think I'm going to like it.

Friday 21st February

Spent all afternoon with Fatty in the archives. Perched up in the northern turret overlooking the quadrangle I felt strangely peaceful and protected from the general madness of the school. I complimented Fatty on the work he's done fixing the place up. He blushed and led me past a shelf labelled POSSIBLE MYSTERIES. The shelf above it was called DEFINITE MYSTERIES and the very top shelf was COMPLETE MYSTERIES.

Other shelf headings included SCANDALS, LIGHTNING STRIKES, MCARTHUR SIGHTINGS, GENERAL GHOST SIGHTINGS, and SEXY BABES. (Fatty admitted that he only made the SEXY BABES shelf to keep Boggo busy while Fatty works on the archives.)

'The teachers never come up here,' said Fatty. 'In fact nobody really ever comes up here except for Boggo and Sidewinder.'

The small gingery face of Sidewinder suddenly appeared from behind a shelf called SUICIDE & UNEXPLAINED DEATH. Fatty pointed at the small boy and said, 'Oh, Spud, you know Sidewinder.' Sidewinder waved nervously and said, 'Afternoon, sir.'

'Afternoon, Sidewinder,' I replied in a formal voice. Fatty explained that the new boy was helping out with general filing and then ordered him off to make us tea and an egg mayonnaise sandwich. Sidewinder seemed desperately eager to please and scampered down the thin turret staircase like his life depended on it. When the first year was gone, Fatty winked at me and whispered, 'He thinks I'm a prefect – how cool is that?'

Turns out that Sidewinder is being bullied by Pike, JR Ewing and Thinny and is more than happy to help Fatty with his archives in return for a place of safety for the afternoons and early evenings. Fatty collapsed into an old armchair with a groan and said, 'Feel free to pull in. It makes a good hideaway when things in the house get a tad intense.' I tried to thank Fatty for the open invite but he interrupted me with: 'You can even write your diary here. I mean ... if you want to. It's nice for me to ... you know ... like, have some company.'

He then pointed out a quotation that he had stuck to the wall with pink chewing gum.

'History does not repeat itself. Historians repeat each other.' *A J Balfour*

'How symbolic is that?' he said proudly like he had written the words himself.

Sunday 23rd February

Bad news for Boggo was that the choir was singing at Evensong. He looked mortified and buried his head in his hymnbook as the choir processed down the aisle. I enjoyed his embarrassment immensely.

I nailed a hole-in-one during a high stakes putting competition just before lights out. Rambo said my putting stroke resembled that of somebody called Dick Faldo. Everyone packed up laughing after that, so now feeling less positive than before.

Monday 24th February

After lunch I retired to the bogs to examine my face. I have a nasty looking pimple on my forehead and a smaller one in the cleft of my chin. There seems to be no good reason for bringing my razor back to school and my hair is dull and brown and a little on the thatchy side. No wonder girls are giving me bat left, right and centre. I wouldn't want to kiss this face either.

To make matters worse, Vern skulked out of the bogs tapping his stopwatch as if I had committed some dreadful sin. Then he fumbled through his pockets and pulled out a pad of yellow slips. He furiously began scribbling and signing, before handing me my first ever yellow slip for Loitering in the Bogs and Surrounds. He then crept back into the toilet stall to wait for his next victim.

Before Spike's thrashing last week for Bad Form in the Bogs and Surrounds, Vern's blue chits were a minor nuisance and mostly quite funny. In these suspicious times who knows what a new yellow chit might dish up? If Vern gets me thrashed for investigating a pimple, that might be the last straw.

Tuesday 25th February

Mom called to say that the house is being fumigated as of tomorrow. This means I'm staying elsewhere for the long weekend. There seemed to be an argument going on about whether Mom and Dad were staying at Marge's or Frank's. I told Mom I would rather stay at school than have to sleep in the same house as the girl who gave me consecutive Valentine's bat and has ruined my fragile self-confidence. Mom obviously knew about Mermaid dumping me again because she didn't ask any probing questions. My mother ended the call rather abruptly because she said she had just spotted Dad leaping off the top of a ladder and disappearing into Amber's garden armed with a 5 metre long pool scoop.

On a more positive note Dad has just bought an M-Net decoder so that he can watch the Cricket World Cup. My mother is naturally terrified that Dad's going to have another attack if things don't go well with our cricket team down under. Mom's also not sure how Dad is going to pay the monthly instalments for the decoder since he hasn't worked in months – she suspects that he's squirrelled away a sizeable nest egg somewhere in the depths of his garage.

Wednesday 26th February

Pleased to announce that South Africa have thrashed Australia in the opening game of the Cricket World Cup. Thanks to M-Net holding all the rights and Australia having nonsensical time zones, the games aren't screened in the common room. I have to rely on word from Simon who mysteriously knows the cricket score no matter what time of day or night.

Dad was ecstatic about thumping the Aussies and phoned again in the afternoon to share the joy. He sounded quite sloshed and sang the first line of Shosholoza before forgetting the rest of the words and then set off on a dirty song about Australian sheep farmers, which he had just learned from Frank.

Thursday 27th February

Pike and Spike mugged Vern in the bogs and roughed him up pretty badly. To add insult to injury, Pike set fire to all of Vern's yellow and blue chits. I'm not sure what the Pikes did to Rain Man but I heard him sobbing quietly into his pillow after lights out. I asked him if he was okay but he didn't reply.

Friday 28th February

REASONS FOR FEARING LONG WEEKEND

1) Our house is now a gigantic circus tent
2) I could be living with my ex-girlfriend
3) I will then have to see her new boyfriend

4) This will make me fall in love with her again
5) Mom and Dad will definitely have a fight
6) I'll be forced to visit my grandmother
7) Tomorrow is Feb 29th meaning this is a leap year
   (Fatty said dark stuff will definitely go down tomorrow)
8) General creeping fear of impending doom

Pike was on the Durban bus. He forced some second years out of the seat behind me and then spent the next two hours tormenting me. I tried to ignore him but it was like sitting in front of a giant blood-sucking mosquito. When we reached the bus stop, I noticed Plump Graham charging across the road to where his tearful mother was waiting. They hugged for so long that Pike eventually shouted, 'Get a room, fat boy!'

Mom met me in the station wagon and showed me some large scrapes on the side door of the car. Apparently Blacky completely freaked out when Dad tried to load him into the car en route to the kennels. My father only made the situation worse when he lost his temper and chased Blacky around the garden with the hosepipe. Blacky then had some sort of emotional dog breakdown, which made Dad emotional because he was feeling guilty about taking Blacky to the kennels in the first place.

'It was a hell of a thing,' said Mom as she stared out at the road from behind a huge pair of dark glasses. I noticed her jaw was clenched which means her mind was ticking and the mood wasn't good. When I asked her where we were staying this weekend, she didn't answer. After some time she said, 'Now, boy, it's all been a little difficult, and I don't want you to freak out because God knows we've all had enough of that this week ...' It's worse than I thought ...

Much worse.

I'm staying at Wombat's!

14:30   Wombat flagged us down on the street outside her block of flats. She then directed us up the driveway and into a parking space like we had never visited her before.

15:00   As soon as Mom left, Wombat turned into Gollum and accused me of coming round to steal her money. My grandmother also announced that my pimples looked revolting, and that I was eating far too many sweets. She then charged off to hide the sugar.

15:05   After hiding the sugar bowl and padlocking the fridge, Wombat became strangely pleasant again and we sat down to a long afternoon of tea and boudoir biscuits. I talked about school and Wombat prattled on about the war.

16:00   Made a gruesome find under my bed. A disgusting plate of fried fish, tinned peas and mashed potato – Wombat said it was my dinner and ushered me into her bedroom to demonstrate an identical plate lying in wait under her double bed. (?)

16:15   The phone rang and Wombat rushed through to my room to say that Graeme Pollock was on the phone. It was just Dad playing nasty tricks on Wombat – he says it's one of life's great pleasures. Once my father had finished his snorting and sniggering, he said he'd organised a braai at Frank's on Saturday night and then a game of golf on Sunday afternoon to save me from the Wicked Wombat of the West.

16:30   My grandmother set off to buy the evening paper, brandishing a very long walking stick. She then made it very clear that when she returned she needed absolute silence because she had to listen to the news, weather, and shipping forecast on the radio. I didn't argue and was just relieved to be alone.

16:50 Wombat returned from her walk with neither her walking stick nor the evening paper. I offered to run back to the shop to buy her paper and find her stick, but Wombat brought up my 'drinking problem' and said I couldn't be trusted with her newspaper money.

16:55 Wombat set off again, this time armed with a yellow umbrella.

17:30 I began to worry that Wombat was either lost or arrested. I thought about calling Mom but decided against it, thinking it would only drive her into a panic.

I really don't think Wombat should be living alone.

17:45 As I stepped into the bath there was a loud knock on the door. I then had to step out of the bath, dry myself, and get back into my school pants and shirt. The knocking became loud banging and general shouting. I eventually opened the door to a bald eighty-five-year-old man brandishing a bread knife. Behind him stood a large crowd of old ladies, including Wombat, who pointed at me with her umbrella and walking stick and cried, 'That's the rapscallion! I heard him using up my bathwater!'

The old man with the knife demanded my name. When I said it was John Milton he immediately looked suspicious. Another old duck glared at me and said, 'They all operate under assumed names these days.' Another old geezer wearing a cream safari suit joined the geriatric lynch mob and suggested the block should hire armed security men to keep the riff-raff out. His name was Mr Jeffreys and everyone agreed with him.

Thankfully, a woman about Mom's age burst through the crowd and screeched, 'Oh, look, it's John Milton.' The crowd began muttering among themselves, unsure what this latest development meant. The woman shook my hand and explained to everyone that I was Wombat's grandson and that she knew Mom. Another old lady said, 'Oh, he's the one at the posh school with the beautiful singing voice.'

Wombat stepped forward as if seeing me for the first time and screeched:

'It's David!'

The old man with the knife kept his weapon raised and seemed to be getting a little hot under the collar. He looked at me savagely and barked, 'Which is it, sonny – David or John Milton?' I told him David was my middle name. Suddenly everyone broke into a cheer and began introducing everyone else to me. I felt like the prodigal son returning from years marauding around the desert on a camel. Turns out, the old guy with the knife is the block supervisor Buster Cracknell whom Wombat accused of yoghurt theft in 1990.

Then an old lady demanded that I sing a hymn. Everyone cheered and excitedly stepped forward to hear me let rip. I tried to explain to the old bat that my voice had broken and that I was no longer a singer but the growing crowd of geriatrics refused to let me go until I had given them a performance.

Jerusalem reverberated around the foyer and my voice sounded pretty impressive. Not quite up to pre ball-drop standards but solid enough to avoid disgrace. Soon the oldies joined in a rousing double chorus followed by applause and more handshakes. There were loud calls for a second hymn but Wombat chased everyone away because she said she was about to miss her beloved six o'clock news.

Once inside the flat, Wombat carefully locked her security gates before turning on me with tears flooding her eyes. 'David,' she gasped, 'I wish somebody had warned me. I'm old now – it's not fair of you and your mother to surprise me like that.' Then the sound of the news pips could be heard from Wombat's radio in her bedroom. Her eyes lit up and she stormed into her room before cranking up her news to a deafening volume.

I'm blaming too many news bulletins for my grand-mother's dementia. It can't be healthy to be confronted with so much bad news on a daily basis.

18:15 After listening to the news, weather, shipping forecast and a dreary tune played on a tuba by a man called Nigel Galleon, Wombat re-emerged in an electric blue ball gown. She poured us both a whiskey and soda without asking if I even wanted one. She reclined in her armchair, took a great gulp of whiskey and began telling me once again how she met Winston Churchill. She went on for ages about the twinkle in his eye and how the prime minister had winked at her and complimented her dress. Wombat looked at me with a cunning smile on her face and said that the only way to win over a girl's heart is to smoke a cigar and never leave home without a stiff collar and tie. She tapped her whiskey coaster with her fingernail and said, 'It's very manly to smoke.'

The night wore on and Wombat's whiskeys made me feel light-headed.

19:56   My grandmother places the radio on a stool in front of us.

19:57   Wombat and I fetch our cold fish in unison and then sit down in front of the radio waiting for eight o'clock.

19:59   Wombat says an emotional grace.

20:00   Nibble a dinner of cold fish, mash and tinned peas while listening to the news.

20:15   After the news, weather and financial indicators Wombat cleared the plates, told me it was bedtime, and began switching off the lamps.

20:30   While Wombat's radio droned on in the background, I settled into my grandfather's bed with *On the Road*. It's set in America in the 1950s. The main character hooks up with a wild bunch of mates and hitches his way across America and back. Kerouac's world suddenly felt a long way from the one I'm living.

I'd take drifting around America like a bum over a life of cold fish and shipping forecasts.

Saturday 29th February

4:30   Awoken by the nasty smell of Wombat frying fish in the kitchen. Buried my head under the pillow but could still smell it.

6:00   Wombat woke me up with a screechy, 'Rise and shine, David!' She placed a cup of tea on my bedside table and ordered me to bathe. The smell of fried fish was still everywhere.

7:15   Leisurely stroll up and down Musgrave Road.

7:55   Return from walk in time for eight o'clock news, weather and shipping report.

8:15   Breakfast. Two grapefruits and another cup of tea. No wonder Wombat is so desperately thin and yellow!

9:00   After breakfast Wombat called for absolute silence while she went over her daily finances.

10:00   Dad picked me up and together we sped off to visit Blacky at the kennels. Dad said that a worried woman from the kennels phoned this morning to say that Blacky has become incredibly stressed and appeared to be eating his front right paw. My father reckons Blacky is neurotic. He shook his head in wonder and said, 'Buggered if I know where he gets it from.'

Poor Blacky looked terrible, curled up at the far end of his cage. His big brown eyes were downcast and he shrank away from the other dogs that barked and yapped incessantly in the cages around him. When Blacky noticed us at the gate of his cage he leapt up and charged towards us. He then started whimpering desperately while licking Dad's face through the mesh wire. The woman in charge was wearing blue rugby shorts and didn't look very impressed when Dad began to get emotional. She said that animals can sense our emotions and that the personality of the dog often takes on that of its owner. Dad sensed that the woman with the rugby shorts was calling him a nutcase so he told her that I was Blacky's owner and that I had a drinking problem. The woman in the blue rugby shorts looked even less impressed and gave us both a stern lecture about taking proper care of dogs.

Eventually, we had to force Blacky back into his cage. The cretinous animal wouldn't walk on its own so Dad had to carry it back into its terrible concrete home. Dad promised Blacky he would be out by Wednesday at the latest but the poor animal didn't understand and curled itself back into a ball and whimpered sadly. Dad tried to cheer Blacky up with some loud whoops and shouts but only succeeded in creating chaos with Blacky's fellow inmates. The woman in the blue rugby shorts stormed back out of her house to see what the commotion was all about but Dad and I were already in the station wagon screeching down the driveway, leaving a huge cloud of red dust behind us.

When I told Dad about what Wombat was feeding me, he shouted, 'As mean as bloody cat shit – even to her own bloody grandson!' He then did a dangerous u-turn in heavy traffic and tore off in the opposite direction.

10:45 Once seated at the Wimpy, my father called the head waiter over and ordered me the biggest fried breakfast on the menu. He ordered himself a Castle Lager.

10:48 Dad drained his beer and called the waiter over again. He ordered another beer and demanded to know why the breakfast was taking so long. The waiter scampered off to the kitchen looking concerned.

By the time my food arrived, Dad was so ravenous that he ate most of my bacon, sausages and fries while telling me a series of stories about Uncle Aubrey's disastrous fishing trip to Coffee Bay. I had to eat faster and faster because Dad kept plunging his fork into my plate and wolfing down whatever he stole at top speed.

17:00 FRANK'S BRAAI

Dad and I arrived to find Mom and Frank's girlfriend Shannon in the kitchen making salads together. The atmosphere was very awkward and they didn't seem to have much to say to each other. Obviously Shannon knew about Mom's poor cooking skills and relegated my mother to washing lettuce.

Hysterical laughter from the braai outside meant that Frank was up to his practical jokes again. I stepped out of the kitchen to witness Frank parading a new cooking apron while my father rolled around on the grass in hysterics.

The apron read:

WARNING!!! SIZZLING BOEREWORS READY TO SPIT!

Underneath the inscription was a phallic arrow pointing towards Frank's crotch.

Frank poured us all champagne and made a toast to Shannon, whom he called his 'Little Squirrel'. Shannon turned twenty on Thursday. Frank placed his arm around her but she didn't seem to be very affectionate and wriggled free of his grasp. He then tried to kiss her but she turned her face to one side before walking back into the kitchen.

What followed was a terrible silence. Dad's eyes were darting dangerously from side to side as he desperately racked his brains for something to say. He finally came out with, 'It's been dry, hey?' My father's eyes then darted from Mom to Frank and then back to Mom again.

'Hell of a thing,' said Dad in conclusion.

The evening went from bad to worse when a flaming

red Mazda 323 zoomed up the driveway and came to a halt on the grass next to the braai. Shannon strode out the kitchen door looking incredibly sexy in tight jeans and high heels. Dad, who was desperately trying to get the party back on track, let rip with a loud wolf whistle. Nobody saw the funny side so Dad darted into the kitchen saying he needed a pee.

Frank and Shannon then had an embarrassing argument right in front of Mom and me. Shannon said she wanted to go out with her friends to celebrate her birthday. Frank refused and then tried to compromise by inviting the crowd in the Mazda to join the braai. A guy with spiky hair in the passenger seat snorted at Frank's invitation and said, 'Nought, dude – this is an old ballie gathering. No offence.' He then banged his hand on the roof and shouted, 'Come on, Shanny, let's hit the road!'

Frank wasn't the same after Shannon left. He didn't even make any more raw jokes. He drank heavily and repeatedly looked at his watch. Every twenty minutes or so, he would slip inside to check if there were any messages on his answering machine.

Sunday 1st March

6:00 Tea
7:00 News, weather, financial indicators
7:15 Walk
7:45 Breakfast
8:00 News, weather, shipping forecast
9:00 Eucharist at St Thomas' Anglican Church

Oh, and how is it that Wombat knows every single word in the Anglican prayer book but can't even remember my name?

11:06 GOLF

I'm really not looking forward to the father and son golf day. If today's performance is anything to go by, the Miltons will be humiliated. I shot 128 and Dad, after boasting on the first tee that he was going to take the course apart, ended up carding a whopping 141 shots. Dad's round included twelve lost balls and an eighteen on a par three where he hit six consecutive shots into the swamp. Frank laughed so much that he had to wait five minutes before teeing off because he said he'd lost all strength in his arms.

The good news is that I now have my very own golf bag and set of clubs. The bad news is that they belonged to an old geezer who died last month. Even creepier news is he had a heart attack on the 8th green of his local golf course. This means he died holding his putter ...

Monday 2nd March

I've never felt so happy to pack my bags and dress in my school uniform before. The long bus trip back to school was an absolute pleasure. I played U2's new beast Achtung Baby twice through as the evening became night and the orange sky changed to navy blue. Sawing guitars shredded my ears as headlights and mad visions flashed by. Spud Milton on the road again ...

You're dangerous because you're honest.
You're dangerous; you don't know what you want.

WEEKEND SCORECARD

SIMON   Went to Mala Mala game lodge where a huge male lion slashed on his dad's car bumper.

VERN   Dug a hole. (?)

BOGGO   Read a box of his mom's old Cosmo magazines
            and says he's (again) cracked the code to
            scoring chicks once and for all. (Yawn)

SPUD   Dodgy Wombat weekend and his first ever
            round of golf.

GARLIC   Went back to Malawi to see his parents and
            thankfully didn't have time to get to the lake.

FATTY   Visited his grandfather in Port Shepstone.
            Fatty says his granddad eats more than he
            does but is as thin as a rake.

RAMBO   Joined a gym and allegedly had sex in the
            toilets with a gym instructor.

Simon and Rambo weren't very impressed with my
golf clubs. Simon said they were so last century, and
that if my golf was as bad as my cricket then I might
as well quit before I embarrass myself. Fatty was most
interested to hear that the previous owner had died
on the golf course. He closely sniffed my putter before
declaring that it reeked of death and was most probably
haunted by the geezer's ghost. Let's just hope he was a
decent putter.

Tomorrow is the Shrove Tuesday pancake race around
the cloisters. Our house team hasn't been announced
yet although Rambo's already begun warming up. He
stole the frying pan from the prefects' kitchen and spent
the entire evening flipping a slice of bread high in the air
and catching it in the pan.

Tuesday 3rd March

HOUSE PANCAKE TEAM

Viking
Meany Dlamini
Rambo
Spike
Sidewinder

We ran in a close second behind King House although we were later disqualified because it was judged that Viking deliberately shoulder charged a first year from Barnes House. Viking was furious about the decision and called it a miscarriage of justice. From where I was standing the collision looked deliberate – particularly the way the first year flew into the wall at right angles to where he was running. The first year knocked a tooth out in his violent collision with the library door and had to be taken to the sanatorium. Viking refused to apologise.

Wednesday 4th March

Because it's Ash Wednesday our confirmation class became a bizarre hour of watching Reverend Bishop chanting in Latin. Vern, who was desperately keen to get involved in the ceremony, began chanting along with the chaplain in complete gibberish. Vern's fake Latin didn't fool anyone, and the chaplain asked him to pray without speaking.

After an eternity of chanting and prayer, Reverend Bishop made a cross of ash on each of our foreheads as a commitment to Christ and a celebration of Lent. Vern then spread the ash all over his face and ended up looking like a coal miner.

12:00   Lennox's History classroom has been stripped, painted and emptied. Apparently the school has decided to turn it into the new computer room. Lennox called it 'a forced removal' and he taught our lesson under a tree as a sign of protest.

Fatty reckons computers are about to take over the world. He also reckons it's already illegal in Japan to vote in elections unless you have your own computer and printer.

Thursday 5th March

The new computers arrived after breakfast. A group of workmen dressed in white lab coats and gloves carried them through the quad to the computer room. Fatty said the reason the delivery company had to wear special suits is because the computers contain dangerous gamma rays that can cause brain tumours if handled incorrectly. Vern wasn't impressed with the arrival of the computers and slunk around the cloisters making notes and drawing pictures in his notebook.

Saturday 7th March

Roger's birthday! Since he is no longer a fully paid up member of the Crazy Eight, Rain Man's cat was spared a trip to the school fountain. Vern bought him a tin of tuna from the trading store at the station, which the stupid animal refused to eat. Fatty once again raided Plump Graham's spastic colon friendly food stash and stole a large packet of cashew nuts and fed Roger three nuts before wolfing down the rest. Roger sniffed the nuts before devouring them like a hungry lion. This means Roger is now a vegetarian or, like me, he's recently gone off fish.

The folks chose the perfect day to watch me playing cricket for the fifths. I took seven wickets for just 23 runs, including a hat-trick. Dad was so excited with my three consecutive wickets that he raced around the boundary with his arms held aloft and screaming for joy. Mom popped open yet another bottle of JC Le Roux and the two of them became incredibly sozzled on the deep cover boundary.

I then scored my first ever half century – although it must be said that I was facing a bowler who looked suspiciously like a girl, and I lost count of how many times I survived dropped catches. By this stage Mom and Dad were well past sozzled and entered the terrifying realm of drunk and disorderly. Then Dad began singing rude songs in a loud voice about Sparerib and Norm (I don't believe in spinners) Wade. It was a relief when I was finally bowled for 57 because at least the madman standing on the pitch roller ceased his loud and slanderous musical tirade against the school staff.

Even Mr Ashleigh-Meyer was impressed with my day's work and told me I was the most talented cricketer he'd ever coached. He then seemed to lose interest in what he was saying, lit up a Chesterfield and sauntered off in the general direction of the staff room.

Sunday 8th March

Simon was beside himself about a brilliant run out by Jonty Rhodes in South Africa's World Cup match against Pakistan this morning. He tried to demonstrate the missile-like dive but ended up grazing his knee and looking like an idiot. The good news is that we won the match and look a good bet for a spot in the semi-finals.

Fatty, Boggo, Garlic, Vern and I set off to the fields with

our golf bags while Simon and Rambo marched off in the opposite direction because they said they didn't want to hang around with hackers.

Boggo elected himself the group's golf pro and gave us a thorough coaching clinic on swinging the club properly. Unfortunately, when it came down to actually hitting the ball, Boggo was worse than everyone except Vern.

Golf has to be the most frustrating game in the world. You can hit the ball perfectly with one shot and then with an identical swing the next shot can be an embarrassing disaster. Fatty hit one ball so far that it sailed over the field and landed on the tennis court, nearly killing Rowdy and Plump Graham who had just begun knocking up for a set of tennis. The rest of Fatty's shots either scuttled along the ground or ducked off viciously to the left. Vern's golf is embarrassingly poor. He seemed to miss the ball more times than he actually hit it. Garlic got the ball up in the air every time but it never travelled further than he could throw it.

After practice we caught up with Simon and Rambo who were hitting balls at the far end of Trafalgar. Simon's golf looks nearly as good as his batting. All his shots ended up in a tight circle and he never seemed to make an error. Rambo hits the ball miles but nearly falls over in the process because he's trying to thrash it so hard.

I must admit that hitting a great golf shot is one of the most splendid feelings I've ever experienced. Unfortunately, I only felt it once.

Monday 9th March

00:30 Fatty stubbed his toe on the corner of my locker on his way back from the bogs. He screamed with pain and said that his toenail was loose. He wailed on in agony and only shut up when Boggo gave him four aspirin and a sleeping tablet, which Boggo later conceded may have been one aspirin and four sleeping tablets. Fatty passed out almost immediately.

Unfortunately, then I couldn't sleep. The realisation struck me that in a mere nineteen months I will leave this place forever and be truly free. The thought was terrifying.

13:00   Fatty's toenail is hanging by a thread. He was in so much pain that Garlic and I had to help him to the san after lunch. Unfortunately, Red Tape was on sanatorium assistant duty and his eyes lit up when he saw Fatty in distress. It's a known fact that Red Tape returned for post matric just so that he could torment more sick and injured boys. Fatty groaned as he realised who was on duty and looked around desperately for the san sister. No doubt he was reliving the moment Red Tape took great pleasure in sending Fatty off to athletics trials last year despite his having a peptic heart murmur.

FATTY   Where's the san sister?

RED TAPE   She crept up your arse! Who cares anyway? Red Tape's in charge around here ...

GARLIC   (*Loudly*) Your name's Red Tape?

RED TAPE   (*To Fatty*) Who in the hell is this freak?

FATTY   He's Garlic. Comes from Malawi, but don't ask him questions or you'll never hear the end of it.

RED TAPE   (*Nodding at me*) I see you brought fag boy

	along with you again. You guys bum chums or what?
FATTY	Look, I'll be honest with you, Red Tape. My toe's pretty bad and I need some medical assistance. I mean we could be talking hospital here ...
RED TAPE	I'm afraid I don't waste my time with stubbed toes.
SPUD	Maybe you could just give me some anti-septic and a bandage and I'll help him.
RED TAPE	I bet you will, fag boy. Bet you'd enjoy it too. Just like you enjoyed having your hair permed last year.
SPUD	It was two years ago actually.
RED TAPE	Whatever. Time flies when you're having fun.
GARLIC	Why are you being so unhelpful, Red Tape? Our friend needs your help and we're not leaving here until you do your job!
RED TAPE	(*After a long sigh*) Well, I suppose I could do something, but I'm kind of busy right now.

We all look down at the pile of Asterix comics lying on the desk in front of him.

FATTY	Please, Red Tape, I swear I'll never ask you for anything ever again. I swear to God.

RED TAPE   (*After a dramatic sigh*) All right, I suppose I could help you, Fatty.

GARLIC   (*With much relief*) Hey, shot a lot, Red Tape, you're a legend!

RED TAPE   (*To Garlic*) No problem, Garlic. Just drop your rods and lie face down on the operating table.

GARLIC   What?

RED TAPE   Well, if this septic toe is as bad as everyone says it is, then we have to see if you and fag boy have been contaminated as well.

Red Tape reaches into the top drawer and brings out a thermometer the size of a church candle.

FATTY   Oh my God, what's that?

RED TAPE   Breakthrough in medical science! Plunge this right up your rectum and we can tell immediately if you're septic ...

GARLIC   (*Backing away towards the door*) Um ... no ... I can't. Sorry, Fatty, I can't. Um ... er ... cheers.

Garlic sprints out the sanatorium door.

RED TAPE   Now look, if you guys aren't going to meet me halfway then the deal's off.

FATTY   But my toe could have gangrene!

RED TAPE   Rules are rules, Fatty. You and fag boy

should have thought all this through before bursting in here and interrupting my lunch hour!

I helped Fatty back to the dorm. When we finally arrived at his bed, I'm not sure which of the two of us was more exhausted.

Fatty then buried his face in his pillow and wept.

Tuesday 10th March

Received another letter from Mermaid who's obviously feeling guilty for giving me Valentine's bat yet again. She rambled on about being worried that she's hurt me and that the only reason she told me about her new boyfriend was that she wanted to be honest and not operate behind my back. (Like last time.)

Not sure if this was something to throw me off course, but she says her new boyfriend is a cricket umpire (?) and a junior minister in her church. She also admitted he's much older than her. That must be a joke, surely – the umpire bit, I mean.

After reading the letter twice for hidden meanings, I scrunched it into a ball and hoofed it out the dormitory window. I then remembered that I hadn't told anyone about getting savage Mermaid bat and tore down the steps before my paper football fell into the wrong hands.

I reached it just in time because Rowdy and Gastro were on the verge of picking it up. I gave them a commanding shout and the two first years bolted away like I was a homicidal maniac.

Wednesday 11th March

Dad phoned to say that they have moved back home at last!

My father reckons the whole house smells like a terrible mixture of fertiliser, Jeyes fluid, and Wombat's cheap perfume. It seems Blacky has recovered well after his stint behind bars.

Friday 13th March

8:30   The Glock called me up in assembly to shake his hand and receive the match ball. I tried to look proud about my hat-trick but as The Guv says, 'Playing for the fifths is like clubbing baby seals in the springtime.'

I kept an eye on Norm (I don't believe in spinners) Wade for the rest of the assembly. Behind his thick horn-rimmed glasses his beady little eyes revealed absolutely nothing.

Roger was behaving weirdly this morning. He kept spraying all over the place and howling mournfully whenever he felt like it. Fatty blamed Roger's behaviour on Friday 13th and said it was a sign that supernatural forces were already at work.

Spent the afternoon with Fatty, Boggo and Sidewinder in the archives. Fatty was desperate for me to join them and even offered me unlimited hot drinks and toast. Poor Sidewinder was up and down the turret stairs all afternoon ferrying drinks and snacks. Boggo tasted his first cup of tea and made Sidewinder take it back down to the annexe because it wasn't sweet enough. When he returned, Boggo complained the tea wasn't milky enough. Sidewinder raced down to the annexe again and returned a few minutes later, carrying a mug and still looking desperate to impress. Boggo took a noisy slurp of tea once again, but then decided it was lukewarm and poured it out the window. The small first year then raced off eagerly to begin the tea-making again. Fatty suggested to Boggo that he lay off Sidewinder since he was going through a tough patch. Boggo reclined on the couch with his legs open and said it was important to keep up standards.

Meanwhile Fatty was rummaging through a drawer of papers labelled SUPERNATURAL REPORTS with a pencil behind his ear and a plate of peanut butter sand- wiches at the ready. He kept calling me over to read out reports of unexplained ghost sightings. Each time he would conclude the point with, 'So come on – you're the boff – explain that then!'

Boggo showed us a picture from a 1981 Scope magazine of a semi-naked nun with pink stars over her nipples. He prodded the nun's pink stars with his fingernail and said, 'God, it's good to be an Anglican!'

Pike spent the entire evening camped outside in the passage in case Fatty tried to make a break for the first year dorm. The swine perched himself in a deck chair and kept making orgasm and ghost noises, and threatening to molest our mothers. Fatty was beside himself that Pike was ruining all his supernatural plans for the evening and kept creeping to the door to peer through the crack to check if the coast was clear. By the time the menace left it was Saturday the 14th and nobody was willing to leave the safety of their beds.

Sunday 15th March

Boggo made us each put up cash for the Crazy Eight Masters Putt-Off. With a grand prize of twenty bucks (Boggo took a sizeable commission as an organiser's fee) there was everything to play for. The rules were simple. There would be one hole only. It would begin in our dormitory, cross the landing at the top of the stairs, pass all the way through the second years' dorm to finish at the far side of the first year dorm. The hole itself was a capsized teacup stationed beneath the old nightswimming window. Boggo made it compulsory for each player to have a caddy to carry our putter and make the whole thing look professional.

PLAYERS AND CADDIES

RAMBO	Plump Graham
FATTY	Sidewinder
BOGGO	Meg Ryan's Son
GARLIC	Gastro
SIMON	Darryl (the last remaining)
VERN	Rowdy
SPUD	Runt

Unfortunately, all the first years had already been booked so I had to bribe Runt into being my caddie. We agreed that in the unlikely chance that I won the grand prize, we would split the winnings 50/50. It was a heavy price to pay but still better than being mocked and disqualified. In the end Rambo narrowly won the competition but only after Simon squandered a good start after becoming badly caught up in Thinny's shoe cupboard. After taking six shots to extricate his ball from inside one of Thinny's Grasshoppers, Simon blew a fuse and threw his putter at Darryl (the last remaining) and blamed his poor caddying for the entire fiasco.

Vern's attempt ended in utter disaster. His first shot screamed down the passage but then hit the edge of the wall and rebounded off down the stairs. The golf ball gathered pace down the stairwell and shot out of the house doors and began bounding across the quad like it was on a Sunday joyride. The ball finally came to rest in a gutter outside the dining hall. Vern's second shot wasn't much better and ended up at the bottom of a drain near the library. Rowdy had to stick his hands through the grate and retrieve the slime-covered ball. After advice from Simon, Vern took a penalty drop and whacked his fourth putt right the way across the quad just as Mongrel appeared through the archway dressed in white and carrying a squash racquet.

Mongrel grabbed Vern by the collar and dragged him off to his office where he presented Rain Man with the choice of being thrashed with a squash racquet or his putter. Vern unwisely chose the squash racquet and now his entire bum is deep purple. To add to his woes he was then disqualified from the competition because we all agreed that it was impossible for a player of Vern's limited skill to putt his ball up two flights of stairs without having a potentially dangerous cretin attack.

With just twelve days to go until the father and son golf day, I seem to be losing the battle, at the very least, not to look like an idiot at Victoria Country Club. I just hope Dad has improved on his dodgy performance at the long weekend. I also hope Frank was joking when he said Dad's swing looked like 'moving cardiac arrest'.

Monday 16th March

Lennox spent the entire lesson talking about the national referendum tomorrow and said it was white South Africa's second chance to cross the Rubicon after PW Botha blew it badly back in '84. Thanks to Wombat's news bulletin fetish I was already well versed on all matters referendum, although I was under the impression that a majority 'yes' vote for change was a dead certainty to win. However, judging by the worried frown on our History teacher's face, it seemed that the 'No' for change voters were growing in rapid numbers due to last minute underhanded racist scare tactics.

Only a moron could want to go back to a government of twelve bald seventy-five-year-olds in safari suits!

Lennox said that if we were really concerned about change in our country then we should call our families and friends and encourage them to vote 'yes' tomorrow.

I rushed off after History to call home and double-check that my parents weren't about to sabotage my future by voting 'no' instead of 'yes'.

PLANNED MILTON FAMILY VOTING

DAD	NO!
MOM	Not sure yet.
WOMBAT	Definitely no.

I tried my best to change my father's mind but he gave me the 'Look at the rest of Africa' speech and said I had obviously been brainwashed by bleeding heart liberals and 'that commy pinko society you got sucked into – ' In the end I resorted to lying and told my father that if the 'no' vote succeeded the South African cricket team would immediately be turfed out of the World Cup! Dad fell silent and said he would double-check this with Frank. Sensing I was having some success, I asked my father to put Mom on the line. I then heard Mom's angry whispering in the background before Dad announced that Mom had gone out and he had no idea when she was getting back.

Called Wombat but she thought I was Dad, and gave me a tongue lashing before slamming down the phone.

If that's the kind of treatment he gets from his mother-in-law I'm not surprised he's always plotting to kill her.

Still, I tried my best in a losing cause.

If the 'no' vote wins by a narrow margin, I think I might punish my father and his dodgy right-wing politics by joining the Communist Party.

23:00 Lay awake thinking about life and the referendum. Not being allowed to vote is a frustrating business – I now understand what drives black people to toyi-toying and smashing shop windows.

Tuesday 17th March

Not only is it referendum day, but it's also Boggo's birthday! Pike, Spike, Meany Dlamini and Rambo held the birthday boy down and shaved his right leg. Boggo screamed hysterically and threatened to kill people, but was easily overpowered and sheared. The contrast between his furry left leg and his clean-shaven right leg caused mass hilarity in the showers soon after 5pm. Boggo says the joke is on us anyway, because the only time he takes off his long trousers, is to shower and shag.

Had a poor night's sleep after a succession of weird nightmares involving Pike attempting to murder me. At one stage in the night Pike marched into the main quad with an angry looking Robert De Niro, who had a large violin case slung over his shoulder. Pike pointed directly at me. De Niro nodded, and then began striding towards the house door with that typically sadistic expression of his. Thankfully, De Niro didn't get the chance to FUBAR me with his violin/concealed weapon, because I leapt out of the window to certain death instead. Thankfully,

I had a soft landing in the main quad, only to discover that I was now half-naked at roll call with Pike reading out the names. After roll call Pike informed me that I wasn't dressed properly and stabbed me in the stomach with his penknife. Everyone laughed and I couldn't get them to stop.

I put these dreams down to concern about the referendum, general fear of Pike, and certain unresolved emotional issues.

18:30   Boggo's spreading about the rumour that there's a major school production this year and he's going to nail a starring role. He nudged Fatty at dinner and said, 'If Milton scored three chicks last time and he was shooting blanks, then I'm gonna nail the entire cast before the end of the first week of rehearsals!' Boggo didn't know what the play was, but reckoned he overheard Viking telling The Guv that it might be a Shakespeare.

Didn't do a stitch of work during prep because my mind was racing with thoughts of Shakespeare and beautiful girls in school uniform.

Wednesday 18th March

SOUTH AFRICA VOTED YES!!!!!

Not only that, my father miraculously also voted yes, but made it very clear that it was a vote for Jonty Rhodes and not for the commies. Further good news was that Mom also voted for change, but only because Marge suggested it might be a good idea. Wombat didn't vote because she went shopping by mistake instead.

I'd like to think that I did my bit. Onward to freedom!

Thursday 19th March

IT'S DEFINITELY A SHAKESPEARE!!

And word is that Viking is directing!

After Mr Ashleigh-Meyer cancelled cricket practice because of his migraine, I snuck off to the bog stream with the collected works of WS. I chose a secluded spot under a thick weeping willow and surveyed the contents page. I figured that if I stared at the list of plays long enough without blinking, then Viking's choice should naturally or supernaturally emerge. It didn't, so I settled for a selection of Hamlet, Macbeth, Twelfth Night and The Merchant of Venice. I then spent the next hour performing Shakespeare in a loud stentorian voice from the cover of a weeping willow beside the bog stream. I must admit my Hamlet was particularly splendid, despite not really knowing the meaning of much of what I was saying. The good news was that I definitely sounded Shakespearian.

Saturday 21st March

As per usual my cricket team received a bloody nose from Kings College. Even more embarrassing was the fact that we played against their sixth eleven. Mr Ashleigh-Meyer's dodgy tactics didn't help matters during the morning session. With our score on 49-4 at the first drinks break and me holding things together at one end with a steady 26 not out, our coach ordered us onto a full-blooded attack. He said I was boring the crowds senseless with my slow batting and that he would retire me unless I immediately belted fours and sixes. I didn't mention the fact that the crowd consisted of the coach's wife, her dog and the team scorer, and started slogging. I managed one more cracking four but was then bowled trying to hit a good ball for six. We were all out for 72 and the game was over by lunchtime.

Simon smashed a brilliant century for the first team. Unfortunately, the game was a draw because Kings College adopted typically defensive tactics and batted for time rather than runs. After his batting heroics a large crowd of admiring first and second years had gathered on Trafalgar to watch Simon hit golf balls into a tight circle with an eight iron.

The rest of us hacked around the athletics field and focused on attempting to get the golf ball airborne. Boggo was clearly jealous of all the attention that Simon was attracting with his eight iron. The idiot sidled up to where Simon was entertaining the crowd and began smashing golf balls in an obvious attempt to steal thunder. After a series of low slicing golf shots and loud laughter, Boggo returned to the hackers with a red face, spat angrily and called Simon an exhibitionist.

Sunday 22nd March

South Africa has been robbed of victory in the World Cup semi-final against England due to rain. Dad called it iniquitous and threatened to hurl his new M-Net decoder in the pool. Simon said it was the biggest rip-off in the history of cricket, and appeared to be on the verge of tears.

20:00   It's official. I am the new President (of African Affairs ...)!!! Surprisingly, Rambo seemed fairly happy with being treasurer after all. Despite the obvious lack of membership I still feel proud to be stepping into the big shoes of Luthuli, particularly in the week when South Africa took a giant leap away from apartheid.

This time Rambo walked with me through the chilled

darkness and back to the dormitory. I was so elated with all the good vibes flowing around me at last, that I even asked him how it was going with his plan to get rid of Pike. Rambo didn't seem to mind and said things were coming together nicely. I told him I was pleased. Then he stopped and stared at me, although I could only see the outline of his face in the dark.

'What's it with you and Pike anyway?' he asked.

'Nothing,' I said in a surprisingly high voice.

'Not some history I should know about?' he questioned.

'No,' I replied.

Rambo didn't talk again after that, so I prattled on about the World Cup all the way back to the house. Anything to avoid another menacing silence.

Wednesday 25th March

After a riotous English class, during which The Guv unsuccessfully attempted to talk Boggo into suicide, I was cornered by an agitated Garth Garlic. He bundled me into a vacant classroom and said he had to ask me a serious question and that he was too afraid to ask anyone else.

He looked around nervously before shouting, 'Please keep this quiet, hey! The last thing I need is for Rambo or Boggo to know.'

'Know what?' demanded the voice of Boggo from the corridor outside.

Garlic jumped in surprise. His face reddened and he blurted, 'Nothing,' in a strangulated voice.

'What do you mean nothing?' enquired Boggo suspiciously, as his face appeared in the doorway. Boggo waited for a response and then in a sharp voice said, 'Come on, Garlic, you finally coming out the closet or what?'

It became obvious that the very small section of brain that Garlic uses for speech had shut down completely. I jumped in and informed Boggo that Garlic was about to tell me about windsurfing on Lake Malawi. Boggo's face recoiled into an expression of horror, and with a cry of 'Holy shit!' the school's worst gossip was gone.

'Spud, I just don't get it,' said Garlic once we were alone. 'Okay, first there was originally the Crazy Eight, but then Lizard died and Mad Dog was expelled for building the tree house.'

'Gecko,' I corrected.

Garlic didn't hear the correction and asked, 'Why then if there was only six and now seven, are we still called the Crazy Eight?'

I opened my mouth to answer but Garlic continued rambling. 'Then the Normal Seven has only six and the Fragile Five really does have five members, which doesn't make sense either.'

I told Garlic that this was an example of irony, and that there being seven human members of the Crazy Eight was an absurdist joke. Clearly the fool had neither heard of irony or absurdism before, because a frown crinkled up his face and he left the classroom far more perturbed than before.

One has to question how Garlic ever made it into the top class for English. Perhaps the rumour of Nestle Malawi funding the new school rugby pavilion deal isn't so far-fetched after all.

17:00   I called Dad to check how his final preparations for the golf day were coming along. My father was in high spirits and kept bursting into loud chanting song about us not being buggered about. Dad reckons he's now playing brilliant golf and boasted that his putting down the passage is so deadly accurate, that he gets bored practising. He asked me what the prizes were, and declared that the Miltons would be presenting those snooty snobs with some serious middle class middle finger on Friday. He then noticed that Blacky was chewing away at the grip of his putter, and handed me over to Mom.

I worry about my father's over-confidence. It's hard to forget him questioning the course record last time he teed off and then scoring a shocking 141. I'm not convinced my father has the right temperament for golf.

Thursday 26th March

Simon has pulled out of the father and son golf day. He said he has to attend a cricket academy tomorrow instead. He then lay on his bed for the entire afternoon with his Walkman blaring and his eyes shut tight as if in a trance.

Spent the afternoon hitting balls with Garlic and Vern, which did wonders for my confidence.

Friday 27th March

FATHER AND SON GOLF DAY

10:00 The day almost began in utter disaster. As the old bus roared into life I realised that I'd left my putter behind in my locker. After some nasty jeering from eighty seniors on the bus I scampered back to the dormitory to find my putter, and discovered Simon lying on his bed in the foetal position. Thankfully, his face was turned away and his Walkman was still blaring so I didn't have to deal with any emotional issues. One thing is for certain: he didn't look like somebody about to leave for a cricket academy ...

Back on the bus, I mentioned to Fatty what I had just witnessed in the dormitory. Suddenly the pimple-ridden face of Boggo appeared above the seat in front of us.

'He's not going to a cricket academy, you dork!' exclaimed Boggo like it was yesterday's news. 'His dad bailed on him last night.' Boggo's large teeth tore away at a piece of string attached to his golf glove. 'Been called to Geneva at the last minute for some business meeting or something. He's feeling humiliated.' He finally yanked the string out and spat it onto the floor of the aisle. 'The guy is completely cut up – he's been practising every day for months.'

Rambo considered this news without demonstrating any emotion whatsoever. Eventually he said, 'So Simon's got daddy love issues ...' He then nodded to himself and said, 'Interesting,' before lapsing into a silence with bright capsules of light burning in his eyes.

Victoria Country Club lies on the slopes of Town Hill surrounded by forest and the great Umgeni River Valley. I must admit that I was a little freaked out when I realised that the entrance to the golf club is uncomfortably close to where our station wagon twice broke down last year. I hope Dad keeps all thoughts of nappies and straightjackets at bay during his round.

My father arrived in striped pants and a checked golf shirt. He did an embarrassing war dance in the parking lot in full view of the club golf captain and the caddy master. He then said he needed the loo and disappeared into the bar.

11:40   Ten minutes until our tee-off time. Still no sign

of Dad and The Guv.

11:42   Help Vern search for his ball after putting it off the practice green into a nearby flowerbed.

11:43   Receive verbal abuse from the irate golf captain, who threatens to report us for violating club rules and vandalising his flowerbed.

11:44   Vern becomes distraught because he can see his ball but cannot reach it without stepping into the now out of bounds flowerbed.

11:46   Vern and I concede defeat and carry our bags towards the first tee while the golf captain strides into the flowerbed and pockets a brand new Titleist golf ball.

11:48   Rambo's dad smashes the ball off the first tee and father and son stride down the fairway in earnest conversation.

11:52   The bar door swings open and my father and my English teacher stumble out into the sunlight.

Showtime!

The Guv looked ridiculous. White shoes, long white socks, white plus fours, electric blue golf shirt and white flat cap. He shouted, 'Stevens!' and his gardener appeared with his golf bag. Stevens was clad in old white cricket clothes that may well have belonged to WG Grace. I'm not sure if Stevens has ever played golf before because he didn't seem to know what was cracking, although he and my English teacher certainly looked hilarious striding along together.

The announcer at the first tee boomed into an old

microphone that was completely inaudible beyond a few paces from where he was standing. I barely made out the announcement: '11:54 on the first tee, Black, Adder, Edly, Milton and Milton.' There was then a worried conversation between the announcer and the golf captain who had just pulled up officiously in his golf buggy. After a long consultation, the stern looking announcer stepped forward and said there was some confusion, as we appeared to have five names down instead of four. He then referred back to his sheet of paper and asked, 'Which one of you is Black?' The Guv looked outraged and shouted, 'Why, surely, man, it's obvious?' The announcer's worried eyes then settled on Stevens dressed in his 19th-century cricket kit. His cheeks reddened while Stevens grinned broadly and handed The Guv his driver.

And at that very moment Vern teed off. It was unfortunate that the golf captain was watching because Vern's wood drove viciously into the ground, digging up a fair portion of the tee box. It looked like a small landmine had exploded beneath his feet and the wild swing only advanced the ball by three paces. There were loud sniggers from Boggo and Fatty who had formed part of a lively crowd around the tee. Vern was startled by the ugly hole he'd made and furiously thumped his foot up and down like he was putting out a fire. He then looked around shiftily to see if anyone had noticed his cretin attack, before skulking up to his ball and quickly picking it up and placing it in his pocket. He then strode back to his golf bag where he loudly counted all his clubs. Clearly, the golf captain and the announcer were flummoxed by Rain Man, having never encountered his bizarre antics before. They were also rather taken aback by the enormous boy who had fallen down the bank convulsing with laughter.

Dad unsheathed his driver with a flourish and strode up to the tee like he meant business. I think I was more nervous for my father than I was for me. I so desperately wanted him to hit a great shot in front of the sniggering Boggo and the other posh dads who had gathered to mock us. My father was nervous and his practice swing looked wild and jerky. I could see his body shivering with nerves and perhaps a few too many beers before the start of play. There was a long pause as he stood motionless above his ball and he seemed to be talking to himself under his breath. Then he smashed it miles down the middle of the fairway. Polite applause rippled around the tee and Dad touched his cap with his left hand like a professional. I was bursting with pride when I teed off. Unfortunately, I lifted my head and the ball squirted along the ground coming to rest just on the fairway. Nobody laughed. Mission successful.

11:54   The Guv smashed the ball into the forest after making a dramatic swing with his driver. As the ball disappeared into the trees he shouted, 'To Zion and beyond, fair adulteress!' The gathered crowd laughed and at last, after all the waiting and practising and fret-ting, the worst was over.

Once Vern, The Guv and Stevens had disappeared into the trees to look for the ball, Dad pulled me aside and warned me not to be distracted by The Guv's shouting and Vern's bizarre behaviour. 'Now watch this shot,' said Dad before topping the ball into a bunker.

Suddenly a ball landed on the green and rolled up next to the hole. The Guv came striding out of the trees and shouted, 'I don't accept cheques, Milton – I will have my pound of flesh!' Dad didn't look amused and slammed his next shot into the wall of the bunker and swore loudly.

My putter is definitely haunted. I missed a putt that was only two feet long. If you aim at the hole, the ball veers off to the left. If you aim slightly right to allow for the leftward veer, it runs dead straight.

My putting didn't improve but we still defeated The Guv and Vern, who became increasingly more bizarre as the day progressed. Even Dad agrees that he isn't at all normal and should be at a special school.

18:00 Showered and changed back into our school uniforms, the sons joined the dads in the lounge for prize giving. The room was warm and buzzing and laughing men with beers were everywhere while Fatty and Boggo sped around selling charity raffle tickets. When Boggo arrived at our table he said he was raffling off the putter Gary Player used to win the 1969 South African Open and that all proceeds were going to a children's charity. Dad bought the story (and six raffle tickets) and told me it would be a great irony if we won Player's putter in this desperate hour of need.

Rambo and his dad were second overall and won a huge hamper of prizes. Dad and I came thirty-fifth out of eighty teams, which wasn't too bad. We won a set of whiskey tumblers and a wood cover that looks like Odie.

It was also interesting to watch Rambo with his dad. He seemed like a completely different person once again. He hung on his father's every word and laughed at all his rude jokes. His eyes never left his dad's face and his mouth was fixed in a glowing smile for the entire evening. (Talk about daddy love issues –)

Dad won the lucky draw! Boggo handed over Gary Player's famous putter and the two had a photograph together for a local newspaper. Dad returned from the stage proudly clutching his putter and looking incredibly chuffed. He sat down and drained his beer. He then declared, 'There must be a God!' My father handed me the putter like he was presenting a royal gift and said, 'There you go, boy – your prayers have been answered.'

It didn't look like the kind of putter Gary Player would use for firewood let alone to win the SA Open. Also the way in which 'Gary' had been scribbled in Tippex on the back of the blade was more than a little suspicious. And then the realisation hit me – I had seen this putter before in numerous dormitory putting contests, and it didn't belong to Gary Player. Boggo gave me a wink and grinned at me from across the lounge. Come to think of it, I'd never heard of the Scottstein Children's Charity before either.

On the bus ride back to school I thought about the holidays. It seems so long since I last slept in my own bed. I even miss Blacky! One more week and then that old familiar scent of freedom ... Just six weeks in and and I'm already counting down.

Monday 30th March

Boggo is now spreading a rumour that Simon has requested a move to another house. Nobody knows what's going on with him. Fatty reckons he's had a full-on emotional breakdown after his dad gave him bat for the golf day. Still we all agree that it's a huge reaction just because his father let him down at the last moment.

Boggo and Fatty made over five hundred bucks in their bogus charity raffle. Boggo didn't even let me keep his putter and said the whole thing was rigged, and that they had decided Dad would win before the day even

113

started. Boggo and Fatty said they would use the money for a huge Crazy Eight party at the end of the year where nobody is allowed to leave until they've vomited and lost their virginity. Rambo then asked Boggo why, if the money was for the Crazy Eight end of year party, had he bought a new mountain bike on Saturday. Boggo said that was his own money and that the charity/party fund was stashed away in a hidden location. I won't be holding my breath for the party.

Grim news. All third years apparently have to meet with both Viking and Eve this term. Worse news is that it's compulsory. Viking is just terrifying – it's like having a massive salivating hairdryer blasting in your face for half an hour. And as for Eve, the supposed counsellor, how am I supposed to look her in the eye when I know she likes it when young men stick their fingers in her bum? Wednesday it's Eve. Viking lies in wait on Thursday afternoon.

Tuesday 31st March

Not for the first time it must be said that Boggo's rumours are true. Simon admitted to Rambo that he had requested a move out of the house. He says he's sick and tired of the constant chaos in the dormitory and wants to get away from Pike. Simon's only desire is to be left alone to play his cricket and pass his exams. He even said he would leave the school if his parents would let him.

Rambo reckons that Simon made up the cricket academy story and definitely had some sort of nervous breakdown over the weekend. Boggo shook his head sadly and said, 'Let's be honest, he wasn't exactly the most exciting character to start with. Now he's got no personality at all.'

18:30 An edgy looking Garlic accosted me after supper and asked if we would still be called the Crazy Eight if Simon left.

'Yes,' I replied, hopefully avoiding another long-winded debate on irony and absurdism. Garlic breathed a huge sigh of relief and turned to walk away. He then swivelled back and said. 'Oh, sorry, Spud, I nearly forgot. Has Rambo told you his plan to get Pike?'

'No,' I replied, surprised by the sudden question.

'Not even at your African meeting thingy?' pushed Garlic.

'He didn't tell me anything,' I replied, and stared him down.

'You absolutely sure?' he asked again.

'Positive,' I said.

Garlic nodded for some seconds while his eyes darted around uncertainly. He then said, 'Cool, Spud, I'll check you at dinner – Fatty says it's mutton curry by the way.' And he sauntered across the quad with his hands clasped behind his back and headed straight towards Boggo who had been slouched unnoticed on the house bench. Boggo furiously waved Garlic away and hissed something at him.

Garlic then shouted back, 'I'm not being obvious!' and disappeared through the house door shaking his head.

Wednesday 1st April

April Fool's Day

As per usual some maniac sounded the rising siren at 4am. The Crazy Eight sniggered in their beds at the pattering feet of gullible first and second years as they stumbled down the stairs towards the showers.

Then another idiot set off the fire alarm during Maths. We weren't even allowed to leave our classrooms so it didn't achieve any purpose other than to make Mrs Bishop even more grumpy than usual. Glad to know that the chaplain's wife would rather see us burn than lose ten minutes of calculus.

The third April Fools joke was my counselling session with Eve.

Eve was at her irritating best during our half hour session. She continually asked me personal questions about my family and private life. She even asked me if I was still a virgin. I nodded innocently and hoped Rambo might be right about Eve having a fetish for fresh meat. Eve tried every trick in the book to get me to spill the beans. At one stage she even leaned forward seductively and revealed a vast amount of her cleavage! But I remained steadfast, and left the counsellor's office feeling heroic, highly aroused and slightly exhausted.

Thursday 2nd April

Received yet another rambling letter from the Mermaid, going on about her new philosophy of life and bragging about how cool things are with her. She said Gavin (the umpire) had introduced her to Jesus and suggested that I should join them at their church if I wanted to be saved. (Saved from what?) She invited me to pop around in the holidays because she's desperate for me to meet her new man. (?) Surely the woman should know that no self-respecting cricket player ever befriends an umpire! I tore the letter into tiny pieces and sprinkled it into the house bin.

I guess I'll mark that box down as Paradise Lost.

17:00 Viking glared at me from behind his desk. His open necked shirt revealed large amounts of sprouting black hair that seemed desperate to escape his chest. The initial evaluation of my grades ran fairly smoothly and Viking didn't shout much other than to offer congratulations and warn me about becoming complacent. He then leant back in his black leather swivel chair and said, 'Milton, the time has come to think about your future. What's the plan once you've left this catshitbox?'

I told Viking that I was planning to study English and Drama. He leaned forward as if I had just revealed the identity of the shooter on the grassy knoll. 'Teacher? Academic? Librarian?' he questioned, with each profession doubling in volume.

'No, sir,' I replied. 'I want to be an actor.'

Viking exploded. Within seconds he was holding me by the shirt and barking a river of spittle into my face from six inches.

'Christ, Milton! Are you insane?' he bellowed. He then came even closer and whispered in a maniacal voice, 'You're going to have to want it, Milton. By God, it's a dog eat dog world out there. It's a life of poverty, are you prepared for that?' I told Viking that I was ready to take the gamble. He thumped me on the back and said that he saluted my courage and audacity. He then glared out of the window as if remembering something nasty from his past before turning back to me and saying, 'Take your chances, Milton, and don't give up hope.'

Viking finally asked me what have been my three greatest disappointments of my school career thus far. After some thought I chose Gecko's death, getting suspended, and last year's house play. Viking nodded sagely and agreed that the house play was indeed a tragedy.

As I was on my way out he asked, 'Mr Pike keeping his distance now, is he?'

I paused, not sure what to say.

'Yes, sir,' I said.

'Good. Good,' said Viking and waved me out of his office.

23:00   I can't contain the excitement in my body. It isn't just the thought of holidays. Tonight I told somebody in authority for the first time that I wanted to be an actor and he hadn't laughed at me, and he hadn't said no. Sure he may have called me insane, but that's expected. I'm a Milton, and I'm going to be a professional actor. And tomorrow I'm going home. Goodnight!

Friday 3rd April

As usual the school was filled with laughter and the sound of metal trunks scraping against cobblestones. Nirvana's Smells like Teen Spirit blared out of the prefects' room and cricket bags, suitcases and folded bed linen were piling up in every corner.

Garlic was so excited about his first proper holiday back in Malawi that he couldn't help himself inviting two-thirds of the dining hall for a week at his cottage on the lake. Fatty stamped out all talk of the lesser of Africa's great lakes by stealing Garlic's entire breakfast, including his glass of milk. Garlic didn't seem to care and continued chewing Vern's ear off about a windsurfer that he said he was receiving for his birthday. Boggo leant in towards Garlic and asked him when exactly his birthday was. Garlic's eyes lit up like flying saucers and he announced, '29th April!' Boggo quickly paged through his diary with a protruding bottom lip. He eventually found the page he was looking for and made a note. He then chuckled to himself and said, 'I see your birthday falls a mere two days into the second term?'

'I know,' cried Garlic, 'but my folks said I could have my windsurfer earlier, so it makes no difference in the end.'

Boggo did his best to stifle his delight, but he needn't have worried because Garlic was already shouting on about his windsurfer again. The poor idiot had no idea that he had just signed his own death warrant – drowning by bogwash.

For the first time ever, Rambo genuinely wished me a good holiday. He shook my hand and said, 'Oh, by the way, the school play is going to be A Midsummer Night's Dream. Thought you might like to know.' With that he turned on his heel and sauntered off towards where his bags lay packed and waiting. Mysterious as always.

It was the perfect autumn morning with deep blue cloudless skies, as I strode towards the bus feeling powerful and in control of my own destiny. I took long confident strides and felt the dry grass yield and crunch under my school shoes. That's more like it.

EASTER HOLIDAYS

13:00 Mom made an embarrassing scene at the bus stop over how much I had grown in the last month. She kept shouting, 'Look at you!' as if I had some control over these things. I quickly bundled her into the station wagon, which thankfully started immediately. Fatty shouted, 'He hasn't grown as much as me, Mrs Milton!' He then laughed raucously and squeezed himself into his mom's car. Fatty's mom drove off without waving and I was left with the image of her scowling miserably into the windscreen while her son chortled with laughter beside her – a picture of sheer happiness.

Dad was waiting for us at the gate when we arrived home. Mom hooted loudly and then raced up the driveway with the old Renault roaring like a Ferrari. Dad closed the gates behind us and galloped after us. He pulled open my door with a cheer but then crashed his head on the station wagon roof in his frantic attempt to help me with my bags. Dad gasped and staggered backwards clutching his head. He then opened his eyes, gritted his teeth and shouted, 'You bitch!' He hoofed the left front tyre with his right foot and then instantly calmed down. He removed his right hand from his forehead and shook my hand with it. An angry red welt was fast developing across his brow and his eyes seemed to be a little crossed. As always when injuring himself, Dad pretended that nothing had happened and staggered into the house with all my bags and suitcases, whistling loudly.

My room felt strangely cool and smelled a little odd. Otherwise everything was exactly where I left it two and a half months ago. A feeling of safety swept over me as I lay on my bed and gazed up at the familiar cracks and lines that make my ceiling unique. Bizarre, how this little room with Wombat's old curtains should be the only thing that I truly feel is mine.

My bedroom door flew open and Dad charged in looking manic and sporting a huge welt on his forehead.

'Your mother tells me you've grown,' he said, as his eyes

darted up and down my legs.

'Leave the poor boy alone!' barked Mom as she squeezed past Dad. 'He's not even out of his uniform yet and you're already bombing him out.' Mom handed Dad two aspirin and the rest of his beer. Dad downed the lot and then continued to stare at me like I'd done something wrong. After a loud burp he seized my Collected Works of William Shakespeare and said, 'Right! That's it – we'll sort this out the old fashioned way.' He then pulled me off my bed and pushed me up against the wall. Shakespeare's life's work landed on my head and Dad furiously pulled a pencil out of his shirt pocket. He scratched an ugly line on the wall, stepped back, and announced that he was at least half a foot taller and that we were all wasting his time. Mom winked at me and said, 'We'll sort this out the old fashioned way.' She forced Dad up against the wall and thumped the book so hard on Dad's head that he yelped. She then scratched a neat line about an inch below mine.

Dad wasn't impressed at all and accused Mom of cheating. When this didn't work he then rattled off a number of excuses, including: my school shoes being thicker than his North Star takkies, my hair being longer than his (which isn't difficult considering Dad's practically bald). He also claimed that he had woken up with a 'kink' in his back and that a good stretch would see him gaining at least an inch and a half on the spine. Mom called Dad a short-arse and hooted with laughter. My father blushed terribly and said he didn't have time to fiddle around with family during office hours and strode off for a little lie down.

Spent the afternoon on the grass with Blacky. I kept trying to begin A Midsummer Night's Dream but understanding Shakespeare is impossible when you have a deranged animal with its heart set on biting your head and barking at your feet.

Saturday 4th April

Dad fired up the skottel braai and fried enough breakfast
to feed an entire platoon. While scoffing down a huge
pile of bacon, Mom casually said that the Mermaid had
called and that I should stop ignoring her. Dad didn't
look up from his breakfast and pretended that he hadn't
heard anything. I nodded but didn't say anything either.
There was a long pause and then Mom said, 'They go to
a wonderful church for young people, you know.'

'Who is they?' I asked.

Mom looked a little alarmed and stuttered, 'Debbie
and her new ... friend. His name's Gavin – very responsible chap.'

Dad grunted with a mouth full of toast and said,
'Helluva responsible bugger.' Nothing further was said,
which was no doubt a great relief to us all.

While tanning at the pool with my Walkman I thought
about the Mermaid and why Mom seems so keen for
me to see her when she clearly has a new and 'responsible' boyfriend. I sense there is some dark womanly
plot afoot. Despite never thinking much of Gecko's
dodgy relationship advice, he did get something right.
The surest way to receive attention from a girl is by
completely ignoring her.

Sunday 5th April

10:00   Mermaid caught me seriously off guard with her
phone call. I was still half asleep when I answered the
ringing phone and wish I had backed my first instinct
not to answer it.

BACK YOUR INSTINCTS, MILTON

122

She invited me to a 'gathering' on Saturday night and said she couldn't wait for me to meet Gavin.

Unfortunately, after planning a clever and biting retort in my head, I blew it completely and said that I couldn't wait to meet Gavin either. She laughed her beautiful laugh, said she loved me, and hung up. Mom's head poked around the corner and said, 'I'm glad, Johnny. She's a dear thing. And I think you're really going to like Gavin – he's very knowledgeable about cricket.'

Spent the day seething about Glorious Gavin. What is the idiot woman up to? Why would anyone want their ex-boyfriend to meet their current boyfriend? And why is it that whenever I get home I feel passionately in love with Mermaid and yet when I'm at school sometimes a whole day will go by without thinking of her once?

Took a long ride on my bike and may or may not have ridden past Mermaid's house several times.

Wednesday 8th April

Ran through a shortlist of possible excuses for cancelling the 'gathering' with Mermaid and her boyfriend.

ILLNESS OPTIONS

Flu (this might require some acting)
Diarrhoea (convincing but embarrassing)
Breathing problems
Burst appendix
Yuppie flu (?)
Stroke
Diphtheria (have to look this one up but it sounds serious)

OTHER OPTIONS

Dead granny
Dying granny
Sick granny
General fatigue and stress
Utter fatigue and stress
Overloaded with work
I have a date (tempting but impossible)
I have a drinking problem
Sudden religious conversion to Buddhism/Judaism/Muslimism

Not a single decent excuse, and thanks to my mother keeping a continual eye on my whereabouts, my cover would be blown if I lied. What I really need is a Ramboesque game plan!

Saturday 11th April

Okay, so it's not exactly Ramboesque, but the key to my plan is attitude. Today I have decided to be in a good mood. Make that a great mood ... I will at no times become desperate and needy with the Mermaid. I will attempt to be friendly to Gavin the umpire, despite the fact that he may well be molesting the love of my life as I write this.

I have also decided to audition for the part of Lysander in A Midsummer Night's Dream. He's a strapping young lover willing to stand up to his elders and follow his heart. Now that I've grown taller than my father and am carrying myself with more authority, I think I'm ready to play a daring young Shakespearian lover with charm and conviction.

Working against me is that while I'm now taller it seems

that only my legs have grown and everything above the waist has remained the same. The fact that I have no muscles in my legs whatsoever means that I look like I'm walking around on very long toothpicks. Also the pimples are becoming a bit of a problem. Mom bought me some Clearasil face wash so hopefully they'll be gone by the time I audition next term.

Still, with the help of some armour leggings, shoulder pads and a dollop of make-up I could certainly look the part.

I'm staying on the front foot. That's final.

THE GATHERING

Mermaid looked gorgeous. No doubt she wore denim and that tight pink top just to unsettle me. Her extremely short denim miniskirt revealed smooth tanned legs that gave me heartburn. The sun broke through a bank of cumulus clouds and her blonde hair sparkled and glimmered in the brilliant yellow light. (Thank you, God, for also getting involved.)

Mom and Dad didn't stick around when we reached Crusaders sports club because they were on their way to a 'bring and braai' at Marge's. This further fuelled the idea that this gathering may all be a grand conspiracy and just like Harrison Ford I'll be the last to know.

Mermaid raced up to the car and I thought I made quite a good show of slamming the door and looking generally cool and debonair. Mom and Dad shot off like they were in a terrible rush. Suddenly Mermaid's arms were around me, and her moist lips on mine. Then there was a loud shout of 'HOWZAT!' from the cricket field. An umpire wearing a large white floppy hat raised his finger solemnly into the air and the batsman left the field shaking his head and casting sullen glances back towards the pitch.

Mermaid shouted, 'Go, Gav!' and the umpire tried his best not to look our way. 'That's him,' said Mermaid delightedly and pointed at the figure in white. Mermaid led me around the boundary to where she had a blanket and a picnic basket neatly laid out. From the edge of the field, Gavin hardly looked much like stiff competition. Tall and gangly with narrow shoulders and a definite old man-ish stoop. I began wondering how it was possible that he snared the Mermaid. Mind you, I snared the Mermaid when I weighed 47kg and spoke like a girl. Perhaps she has a fetish for freaks?

At the end of the over, Gavin lifted his hat and wiped the sweat from his brow with a handkerchief, revealing his badly receding hairline.

'How old is Gavin?' I asked Mermaid, attempting to sound like I was just making polite conversation. Mermaid covered her face and giggled as if she was embarrassed.

'He's twenty-nine,' she said.

There was a pause as I digested this rather disturbing news.

'But I'm going to be seventeen at the end of the year so it's not as bad as it sounds.'

There was another silence and I could feel Mermaid watching me. I kept my eyes fixed on the pitch and chewed away suavely at a grass stalk.

'Why didn't you write back?' she asked.

I shrugged and chewed on.

She then asked me if I was cool with Gavin and her being together. An electric chill ran through my body and a stream of bile travelled steadily from my chest into my throat and no further.

'Definitely,' I lied. 'I want you to be happy.'

Then she touched my arm and her delicate pale hand slid down and found my right hand. Sharp tingles shot through my elbow and out of nowhere a loud heartbeat began thumping away in my armpit. I felt the irresistible desire to lean over and kiss her.

'Howzat!' appealed the bowler in hopeful desperation. Gavin's finger soared into the air. The batsman glared at Gavin for some time before stalking off the field. 'Well done, Gav!' shrieked Mermaid. 'He's got another one!' she said, and clapped heartily as the surprised fielding team exchanged high fives. Gavin looked officious and made a precise note in his small notebook.

Then just as I was completely losing interest in her endless twittering about Gavin, Mermaid absent-mindedly placed her hand on my knee and kept it there for at least thirty seconds. Unfortunately, the hand didn't slide seductively up my thigh as it does in some movies, and returned to her lap instead. I sensed that I might be losing control so I excused myself and headed for the clubhouse toilets. I avoided the toilet in the bar in case somebody shouted at me for being under age and risked the players' change room instead. As I stood on the urinal step and waited for something to happen, I couldn't help overhearing three players vilifying Gavin the umpire in the showers. One of them even accused him of cheating.

A great feeling of warmth spread over me and I found myself grinning like an idiot at the thought that Gavin the Umpire might well be the most hated man in Durban North. He's not too popular in the Midlands either.

Unfortunately, it's difficult not to like Gavin the Umpire.

He's friendly, generous and unthreatening (he still lives at home with his mom). It was also good to see very little physical contact between him and Mermaid, besides a 'bums out' hug after the game that ended early after Gavin's six LBW decisions. On the long drive to the Holy Water Ministry, Mermaid only once placed her hand on his knee and for no more than five seconds. (It felt like a victory at the time.)

Gavin the Umpire is far more responsible than Dad. In fact he seems more responsible than most dads. He looks far older than twenty-nine, too, and drives slower than most seventy-year-olds.

GAVIN THE UMPIRE

- Is studying for a doctorate in theology in Pieter-maritzburg
- Dreams of umpiring in a Test match
- Speaks to Mermaid like she's his daughter
- Looks like the Mermaid's father
- Uses his turning indicators frequently
- Is the youth leader at the Holy Water Ministry
- Believes that too many batsmen use their pads instead of their bat

18:00 The Holy Water Ministry is a large dome-like structure that looks more like a coliseum than a church. Inside, the giant auditorium was abuzz with hundreds of teenagers drinking tea and coffee and chatting excitedly in large groups. Everybody charged up to us when we entered and Gavin the Umpire was besieged by beautiful girls lining up to kiss and hug him. He knew everyone by name and introduced well over a hundred people to me.

A cool hand grasped mine, and our fingers entwined. 'The play's about to start,' said the Mermaid and led me to a bank of vacant chairs towards the back of the auditorium. She didn't let go of my hand when we sat down. Instead she said, 'Johnny, this place has done amazing things for me. Especially Gavin.' There was a loud burst of static from the stage followed by laughter from the gathered crowd who were quickly making their way to their seats. A man with long hair stood up and promised that the play we were about to witness, would be life changing. He then hollered, 'Let's hear it for Heaven's Gates, Hell's Kitchen!' The crowd roared their approval.

Then Mermaid turned to me and said, 'I just want you to know that Gavin and I aren't like ...' And then she abruptly stopped as the lights dimmed and the entire church fell into a respectful silence.

Any thoughts that the production of Heaven's Gates, Hell's Kitchen might be a thrilling theatrical experience were soon snuffed out when Gavin the Umpire appeared in a white wig and beard and announced that he was the Lord Almighty. Obviously most of the audience had fallen for his dodgy performance because they chanted, 'Amen! Jesus be praised!'

All in all it was a worse God performance than Greg Anderson's shocker in Noah's Ark last year.

The less said about the script the better. The play amounted to a series of episodes of teenagers being confronted by the devil (played by a tall woman with a pig snout on her face). In the play, all the stupid teen-agers fall for Pig Face's temptation and end up drinking booze, smoking cigarettes, or lying to their parents. Then the auditorium lights would switch off and there would be the sound of a bus approaching, followed by a screech and a crash. Then the lights would come back up and the teenager would find him/herself at Heaven's Gates. (Quite why everyone was run over by a bus was never explained.) God/Gavin the Umpire would then look through a list and tell the teenager that they weren't allowed in because they hadn't given their lives over to Jesus.

After four of these scenes I got the message, but clearly the playwright felt that he/she/them hadn't driven the point home, because after interval another five sinning teenagers were flattened in the dark by the murderous bus. I began wondering if it was the same bus that killed everyone or whether Satan perhaps conducted his temptations in the fast lane of a busy freeway. Either way the bus driver ended up slaying ten teenagers and wasn't once asked to account before God/Gavin the Umpire.

The play mercifully ended with the final bus victim accepting Jesus into her life just prior to being run over. Gavin the Umpire found her name on the list and led her backstage behind the dark curtain to an eternal life of paradise. There was wild cheering as the Holy Water Ministry head priest jumped onto the stage and called everyone up to accept Jesus into their life and be saved. As one, the throng stampeded forward, and the priest, snazzily dressed in an open necked shirt and flared pants, began laying his hands on people's heads as absolute pandemonium broke out. Kids were screaming nonsensical things and shouting 'Jesus! Jesus! Jesus!'

I slipped out the side door of the church and took refuge in the garden.

21:30   Mermaid gave me a lingering hug and told me not to worry if I was a little overwhelmed with everything because she had been her first time. We then had a definite moment of looking into each other's eyes. It seemed like we were going to kiss but Mermaid broke away and said she had to find Gavin the Umpire and ran off.

Gavin the Umpire attempted to hoodwink me into going to church with them again tomorrow. I told him I already had plans but gave no details. It was a great relief to finally get home. Mermaid jumped out of the car and kissed me goodbye and made me promise not to ignore her again. I solemnly promised, but in the darkness she couldn't see that my fingers were crossed.

Friday 17th April

Good Friday and three days until my sixteenth birthday. Sixteen sounds like a big step up in age. I'm practically a man in most areas.

Sunday 19th April

EASTER SUNDAY

Easter Church service, followed by a lunchtime braai with Wombat. Unfortunately, after a few too many gins and tonic, my grandmother became emotional and told us that she was on the verge of death and announced that this would be our final luncheon together. Mom told Wombat that she was talking nonsense and then promptly burst into tears. Dad raised his beer glass and shouted, 'To new beginnings!' Wombat shouted, 'Cheers!' and floored her entire G&T. Thereafter she became high-pitched and giggly and ate a surprising amount of food for somebody at death's door.

Monday 20th April

SPUD'S 16 BIRTHDAY!

But not sweet ...

BIRTHDAY EVALUATION

PRESENTS

U2's Achtung Baby from Mom (My original got scratched after it mysteriously spent the night in Blacky's kennel.)
Best of Lionel Ritchie from Dad, which he then played on the hi-fi all afternoon.
A 50p British stamp from Wombat
The Wisden Cricket Annual from Mermaid and Gavin the Umpire
A pack of Easter eggs from Blacky

OVERALL RATING (OUT OF TEN)
4

COMMENTS
Just like New Year's Eve, birthdays are totally overrated.

16:00   Returned from a ride and Mom was waiting because Mermaid had called to wish me a happy birthday. She forced me to call her back before even having a shower. Turns out that Mermaid had just left with Gavin the Umpire, so I ended up having a toe-curling ten-minute conversation with Marge instead who wished me happy birthday on behalf of everyone.

Dad tried to get us out to dinner at Mike's Kitchen but I opted for takeaway pizza and a video instead. (Robin Hood: Prince of Thieves. 7/10)

Tuesday 21st April

06:00   Some good news at last! Mad Dog called at the crack of dawn and said he was inviting the Crazy Eight to spend a week on his farm in the July holidays. I said yes without even asking for the folks' permission and noted that I was hopping weirdly from foot to foot like an excited elf.

'Buckle up, Spuddy,' said Mad Dog in an ominous voice, 'because it's going to be the maddest week of your life!'

He then barked loudly down the phone and said he had to call Vern.

'Good luck,' I said.

He roared with laughter and hung up.

I can't wait to see that crazy dog again.

I retired to my room and hatched a plan for extorting permission out of my parents. What with my mother still mentioning last year's escapades I'm going to have to be as stealthy as a cat.

Called Fatty to let him know about the Mad Dog plan. Fatty, who sounded like he was crunching on concrete, said he had already heard about it. 'How wicked is that?' he said before swallowing whatever it was that he was chewing. Then I heard whispering and sniggering in the background. Suddenly a loud voice shouted down the phone, 'Milton, you lesbian!' Fatty hooted with laughter and admitted that Boggo was spending the last week of the holiday with him. The rest of the conversation involved Boggo shouting lame taunts in the background at which Fatty would laugh hysterically and then relay back to me as if expecting me to find them equally amusing.

I finally called it quits when Fatty tried to fart Die Stem into the telephone receiver.

Friday 24th April

9:15 Caught Dad talking to Amber over the fence. When he saw me he hurriedly said goodbye to our neighbour and raced back down the stepladder.

'You won't tell your mother, will you?' he begged with a panicked look on his face. 'She's neurotic about Amber.' He snapped the ladder closed.

'I didn't see anything,' I replied and grinned at my father.

'That's my boy!' roared Dad and punched me on the arm.

'Dad,' I said innocently, 'Mad Dog has invited everyone to his farm for a week in the July holidays.'

Dad was so excited that he not only gave me permission on the spot, but then made me practise my rifle shooting technique, using a cricket bat as a dummy.

Once Dad was satisfied with my performance he announced, 'I'll be damned if my boy enters the wild without a sound knowledge of bush craft.'

He then demonstrated how to tie a reef knot on the hosepipe. I didn't remind my father that I already know all about knots, and didn't point out that my father's reef knot was actually a granny knot.

I'm going to Mad Dog's farm – it's official. Now that's what I call a birthday present.

Monday 27th April

I stole one final look at the photograph Mermaid sent me yesterday via Marge and Mom. It was taken in the garden of the Holy Water Ministry and it revealed a gorgeous blonde girl with wild green eyes laughing into the camera. On her arm is a recently turned sixteen-year-old with two large pink pimples on his forehead. He looks nervous and uncertain and his smile seems a little forced. I flipped the photograph over and written on the back in neat writing was the word:

Faith

HOLIDAY SCORECARD

RAMBO   Travelled to the Seychelles with his dad and stepmom.

FATTY   Videos, video games, Dungeons and Dragons.

GARLIC   Lake Malawi – new windsurfer – enough said.

SIMON   AWOL

VERN   Reckons he ignited a massive cane fire that burned an entire valley and has brought a huge box of matches back to school. Let's hope it was a planned burning and not a case of arson.

SPUD   Narrowly avoided becoming a born-again Christian and may or may not have had a series of erotic dreams about his ex-girl-friend.

BOGGO   Has written a manual on business and leadership called *Scoring with Boggo: From Boardroom to Bedroom*. The idiot reckons he's going to make a fortune out of selling his genius and set the price at twenty bucks. He then produced a large pile of

business cards wrapped in an elastic band
and proudly passed them around.

The card read:

BOGGO GREENSTEIN
BUSINESS MAVERICK AND ORIGINAL CRAZY 8
MEMBER

Printed below were two phone numbers including the
house telephone number (with international dialling
codes), a fax number, and a mailing address. On the back
of the card was a grainy black and white photograph of
Boggo dressed in a tuxedo. Due to the obscure picture,
Boggo looks fairly handsome and there's no evidence
of his widespread acne and his pale skin. There were
loud hoots of laughter all round, but Boggo refused to
back down and said that within a month we would all
be making our own business/shagging cards and buying
multiple copies of his manual.

But just when we thought he was done, Boggo triumphantly produced an electric hair shaver and declared,
'Welcome to the new house hairdresser!' He then licked
his lips repetitively and said, 'If there's one thing a chick
digs more than a business card, it's cold hard cash.' He
then reached into his tartan suitcase and pulled out a
neatly written price list.

HAIR BY BOGGO!

PREFECTS/CRAZY 8	R10
NORMAL SEVEN	R15
FRAGILE FIVE	R20
ARSEHOLES/WANKERS	R25

Rambo said that it's a known fact that all male hair-dressers are homos. He then advised us all to sleep with a cork in our bums for safety. Boggo refused to be cowed by the continuous mockery and said, 'When I'm rolling in cash and surrounded by more hot chicks than Hugh Hefner, don't even think about begging for my soggy seconds.'

After Boggo's revelations and demonstrations, the discussion returned to Simon, whose bed and locker lie empty. Rambo called Simon three times in the holiday and he never once returned his call. Not even Boggo had any gossip to add and said he doubted if Simon was coming back. Fatty was dead certain that Simon was displaying all the classic symptoms of a major nervous breakdown, but then declined to tell us what those symptoms were. Rambo reckons the Crazy Eight is a dying breed and soon there will be nobody left.

Boggo snorted loudly and said, 'Oh, talking about dying breeds, Rambo, how's that big Pike plan coming along?'

Rambo ignored him, but Boggo wasn't letting go. 'Because it's now the second term,' he said, 'and he's still a prefect and still pissing us around big time.'

Still Rambo didn't reply, but Boggo kept goading him. 'So what's the grand masterplan, Rambo? You waiting for Pike to die of old age or what?'

Rambo smiled serenely back at Boggo, who was becoming increasingly irritated with lack of reaction.

Eventually, Rambo shrugged his shoulders and nonchalantly said, 'Pike will be de-prefected before the long weekend.'

Boggo snorted derisively and the conversation soon turned to Mad Dog's farm and once again the mood in the dormitory shifted dramatically. It would seem that the only person who hasn't been invited is Garlic, who sat on his locker looking crestfallen and didn't even ask a single question.

Vern has returned to school a pyromaniac. He sat on his windowsill and lit about sixty matches in succession, watching each one burn to within a few millimetres of his fingers. I fear it won't be long before Rain Man burns the school down with us being cremated in our beds. Thankfully, Meany Dlamini confiscated his matches at lights out and warned him about playing with fire. Vern grinned back at Meany Dlamini and said, 'Meany Dlamini.' The poor prefect clearly didn't know what to make of this and glared at the rest of us through his glasses as if we were somehow responsible for Vern's madness. He then angrily snapped out the lights and closed the door.

Tuesday 28th April

10:00 We have a new Geography teacher by the name of Mr Gordon Bosch, who made us all remove our watches as we entered his Geography classroom. He then locked them away in his desk drawer and led us out of the classroom and into the sunlight.

There has been no explanation for why Mr Erasmus, our former Geography teacher, is no longer teaching us because he hasn't left the school. Boggo said it was because Erasmus was as thick as a plank and couldn't keep up with our class's sheer brilliance. After watching half the class chasing Rooster Illingworth around a bush in an attempt to flick his bum with a ruler, I'm not so sure Boggo's theory holds water.

Bosch led us up the hill past all the staff houses towards

the crest of the hill overlooking the dam. He made us sit down under a tree before saying, 'I'm not going to bother with introductions because you'll get to know me soon enough.' He then took off his spectacles and gave them a clean with the corner of his shirt, which had become un-tucked on the brisk walk up the slope. After he replaced his glasses he said that we were incredibly fortunate to study in a place as rich in biodiversity as this. 'Geography, boys,' he said, 'is about experiencing the reality.' He picked up a small rock and held it up for us to examine. 'Every stone has a story. Nothing just is. Real geographers look for cause and effect.'

For the next hour we followed Bosch around the school estate, examining rocks eroded by wind and analysing examples of exfoliation and oxidation. It suddenly seemed like I have wasted three years learning things that could be easily demonstrated in five minutes. Bosch must be a keen bird watcher because he showed us a hole in the trunk of a thorn tree and told us it was a red-throated wryneck's nest. Sure enough a nervous bird with rusty red patches on its neck squeezed out of the hole and flew off in a panic. Our teacher didn't even mind when Fatty said the wryneck squeezing through the hole reminded him of releasing a prisoner before breakfast. Bosch laughed along but then told Fatty that he would be more comfortable if he used the biological term 'defecate' during his classes. Fatty seemed highly disappointed to leave the nest and move on before he had another chance to see the wryneck squeezing out of the hole again. Bosch also pointed out a jackal buzzard and an olive thrush, which made Boggo snigger and make a rude comment about Eve.

We returned to the classroom to collect our watches. Bosch reckons as Africans, we should be able to tell the time by the angle of the sun.

Rambo argued, 'That's all very well, sir, but what do we say to the millions of watchmakers we put out of work?' Bosch grinned and replied, 'Aha, a socialist?' Rambo said he wasn't a socialist but a realist. Bosch thumped him on the shoulder and said, 'Touché, Black – you're a sharp one.' He then dismissed the class with a cheery wave of his pencil.

11:30 We entered our English classroom to find a pile of books standing well over seven feet high. Frozen like a statue beside the tower of books was our English teacher who seemed to be undertaking some earnest reflection while chewing on the end of his pipe. We all sat down in hushed silence, not sure what exactly The Guv was up to. He ignored our entrance completely and continued with his earnest meditation. Once we were all seated and waiting, he turned to us and said, 'Gentlemen, today we stand at the very brink.' He exhaled an impressive cloud of pipe smoke and then said, 'André Brink, to be exact.' A few sniggers broke out from Boggo and Fatty's desk and The Guv scowled at them like he was about to erupt into a nasty torrent of abuse. Instead he removed the pipe from his teeth and shouted, 'To the man step forth and claim your literature in an orderly fashion.'

Garlic jumped up first and sped to the front of the queue like he was about to receive Christmas presents. He then realised that he was far shorter than the pile of books that now stood before him. He became terribly unsure of himself and tried to back away from the pile for fear of knocking it over. Unfortunately, the class had already formed a tight line behind Garlic and his retreat ended when he bumped up against the stocky figure of Richard Smithers.

'So it's the herbaceous fellow to the fore,' said The Guv

as Garlic looked around desperately. 'Perhaps the garlic now wishes he was a runner bean!' exclaimed The Guv, clearly enjoying Garlic's predicament.

In a swift leap, Garlic landed on The Guv's desk. He then grinned impishly and neatly snapped a book off the top of the pile. He held his set work aloft and announced, 'Sir, we Garlics may be small but we have brains and cunning!' Our English teacher shouted, 'Bravo, old man!' and refilled his pipe while chuckling merrily to himself. Garlic then leapt off the desk and crashed into Smithers who had just stepped forward to reach for his own copy. Garlic bounced back off Smithers and with a high-pitched shout, flattened the entire pile of Brink's *Rumours of Rain*.

After the chaos was over, The Guv stated that the next two months would be a very, very long, dry white season, before winking at me and instructing Rambo to begin reading aloud to the class. Garlic kept his head bowed for the rest of the lesson and buried his face in his book, but he couldn't hide his bright pink ears burning with embarrassment and shame.

17:00   I entered the showers to find Boggo shaving the head of Meany Dlamini. At his feet lay piles of hair of different colours and textures and bulging out of Boggo's back pocket was a thick wad of cash.

'Tenth cut of the afternoon,' announced Boggo proudly.
   'He's making a killing,' said Fatty from the toilet stall where he sat spread-eagled with a block of Gouda cheese, half a loaf of white bread and the morning newspaper at his feet. Meany Dlamini reckons Boggo's doing a brilliant service to the house because the prefects' rate was even cheaper than the barber at the taxi rank in Edendale township. Boggo looked thrilled

that he had undercut the market and told Meany Dlamini that his new haircut was bound to get him laid. The merest hint of a smile spread across Meany's lips and he replied, 'Hey, Boggo, I don't need a fancy haircut to lash chicks.' Boggo was so impressed with Meany Dlamini's sexual exploits that he gave him a twenty-five per cent discount on the spot.

Judging by all the dark muttering from the locked cubicle in the corner, Vern was deeply upset at the sinister new developments occurring in his bogs.

Wednesday 29th April

Garlic's birthday.

15:00 Garlic may just have struck upon the only possible method to avoid a bogwash. The Malawian is the first person in living memory to actually vomit on his attackers *before* reaching the bogs. At present Garlic is hiding somewhere in the hills and still hasn't had his birthday initiation yet. Thankfully, I wasn't part of the lynch mob that was suddenly forced to abandon the bogwash after Garlic erupted at the foot of the stairs.

DRENCHED
Pike
Whiteside
Eggwhite
Rambo
Thinny

SPRAYED
Vern
Spike
Runt
Sidewinder

LUCKY TO ESCAPE (BUT STILL SEVERELY GROSSED
OUT BY THE EXPERIENCE)
Boggo
Fatty
Meany Dlamini
Barryl

Pike was so incensed with Garlic's dramatic escape that
he ordered the Fragile Five out on a full-scale manhunt
(after cleaning up the mess). He said if they didn't
return with Garlic by dinnertime then he was personally
bogwashing the lot of them.

18:00 Garlic was nowhere to be seen at dinner.
Rumours were flying around that he had run away and
that the Crazy Eight was almost defunct with dropouts
on consecutive days. Fatty was the only one undisturbed
by the afternoon's events and helped himself to piles of
uneaten roast chicken and potatoes.

21:25 Pike arrived for a typically gloating lights out.
He called Rambo the captain of a sinking ship and
suggested he should jump before he's pushed. He then
crowed on about mentally cracking Simon and how
Garlic was already halfway back to Malawi. 'That's two
down, five to go!' he said. 'The big question is just who
will be next?' His mean eyes settled on mine and he
grinned, before spitting more venom and switching off
the lights.

Vern sketched a brilliant picture of Garlic's empty bed
lying in moonlit shadow. He then scribbled the name
GARLIC underneath the sketch and stuck the artwork
to his footlocker.

'Things fall apart, the centre cannot hold?'

Thursday 30th April

Garlic was first in line for morning roll call. Looking showered and fresh, he wore a great beaming smile on his face and whistled Yankee Doodle loudly and repetitively. He nudged me in the ribs and said, 'Hey, Spuddy, I think I just beat the system.' Pike didn't look overly thrilled to see Garlic at roll call and read his name out as 'Vomit Face'. Garlic shouted 'Sharks' and resumed his whistling.

13:30 Boggo charged into lunch looking pale and breathless. He carried a large brown box that he thumped down at the foot of the table. 'Oh, my God!' he gasped, and downed a full glass of orange juice, refilled it and said, 'You are never gonna believe it!' He then floored his second glass of orange juice, which ended in a nasty coughing fit. Fatty handed Boggo a glass of water to help with the coughing attack. Boggo downed that viciously, too, cascading water all over himself in the process. Vern thought that Boggo was issuing a challenge and began glugging water out of the jug and succeeded in drenching half the table. Rambo had enough of all this downing madness and ordered Vern out of the dining hall before Norm Wade slapped us with a punishment. Vern grinned sheepishly and left the dining hall with a drenched shirt and staring guiltily at the floor.

Boggo immediately launched into a description of the absolute beauty of Mrs Bosch, wife of our Geography teacher and the new school stationery shop manager. 'If Eve is a six and a half, then Bosch is an eight.' This declared, he began discussing her beautiful long legs at great length. Boggo reckons Mrs Bosch was flirting with him outrageously and that it's only a matter of time until another member of the Crazy Eight romps a teacher's wife.

'Slamdunk!' barked Boggo with a snap of the fingers, coughing loudly again.

'So what's in the box?' asked Rambo, who didn't seem very impressed with Boggo's story. Boggo looked at Rambo like he was an imbecile and said, 'Stationery.'

'Stationery?' repeated Garlic in confusion.

'So how much did you spend?' questioned Rambo without seeming too interested in the reply.

Boggo huffed and puffed and said that he had needed to jack up his supplies what with his business booming and exams around the corner. He also said that there was a tidy special running on dictionaries and thesauruses.

'How much, Greenstein?' demanded Rambo.

Boggo paled slightly and said he'd spent more than eight months' pocket money.

A great roar of laughter echoed around the table but Boggo stared proudly down at his tomato soup and waited for the mockery to subside.

'Business lesson number one,' said Boggo haughtily. 'Spend big to score big!' He then downed his tomato soup, grunted loudly as he lifted up his stationery box, and staggered out of the dining hall.

Friday 1st May

Assembly: The Glock was in his best mood in ages. This is probably due to the return of his wife from Austria after her broken back. Garlic said he saw her walking around the rose garden with a walking stick, although it must be remembered that Garlic has never seen the woman in his life before.

The Guv was absent from class today and Mr Lilly sat in for him. Lilly read out a short note from The Guv saying that he had recently contracted syphilis from a gypsy and that he would be on his death bed until Monday morning by which time we must have read the first ten chapters of *Rumours of Rain*.

He then wrote:

Happy Workers Day
Regards
The Proletariat

Poor Lilly blushed terribly while reading out The Guv's letter, especially the bit about syphilis and the gypsy, and spent the entire lesson unsuccessfully attempting to reload his stapler.

11:00 The rugby trial lists were posted on the notice board. I was thrilled to see my name down as fullback for the fifths. Considering there are eight senior teams and that I'm not particularly good at rugby, this felt like quite an achievement. Rambo is down for the seconds while Vern and Garlic are in the eighth team. Trials begin tomorrow at 10am on Trafalgar.

I returned to the house to find Rambo sunning himself on the bench. He had rolled up the sleeves of his school shirt over his shoulders and appeared to be tanning his triceps. 'What do you think?' he asked me, still admiring the muscles in his arms. I congratulated him for making the second trial team and told him that I was fairly chuffed with making the fifths. Rambo grinned and said, 'Then I take it you haven't read the theatre notice board in the last hour?'

I was already running. Behind me I heard Rambo chuckling and an angry shout of 'Hey!' from Whiteside. But I couldn't be stopped, and sprinted across the quad and down the cloister to where a large crowd of boys had gathered.

A MIDSUMMER NIGHT'S DREAM AUDITIONS!

This will be a joint production with Wrexham College for Girls to be staged from 15-18th September. The Dream is the inaugural production of the new Wrexham Trinity Theatre and participating boys will spend the entire third quarter at Wrexham College, where the teachers of that school shall conduct their studies. Permission for involvement in the production will have to be obtained from your relevant housemasters and will be decided upon such factors as academic achievement and good behaviour.

Lists are posted outside Mr Richardson's office. Please select an audition time and write your name CLEARLY in pencil.

Regret no Matrics or Post Matrics will be considered for the production owing to trials and finals examinations.

Break a leg.

Saturday 2nd May

Viking gave me the hairdryer treatment in the quad outside his office. He accused me of 'fouling up' his audition list. In truth I had crossed my name out three times before finally settling on an audition time. I had initially booked 15:10 on Monday, the first day of the auditions, but then Rambo said I was basically committing suicide because by Friday afternoon Viking will barely remember that I even auditioned in the first place. I then opted for 16:40 on Friday afternoon, but then Boggo said this was a terrible blunder because by Friday, Viking will be so jaded after a week of auditioning that he won't even give me a fair shot – even if I'm brilliant. After much thought I split the difference and settled for Wednesday afternoon, but then Fatty said that he'd heard a rumour that it was Viking's birthday on Tuesday and that it might be one of the rare occasions when he doesn't scream and shout and threaten people. I quickly scratched my name out once again and settled on Tuesday 17:00. Unfortunately, the net result is that I did make a bit of a mess of Viking's audition list.

'If such indecision continues to bedevil your acting career, you're dead in the water, Milton!' boomed Viking at the top of his voice. 'In fact,' he added, 'I have a good mind to bar you from auditioning altogether.' There was a loud guffaw from the house bench where Fatty and Boggo were sitting.

'You have a problem, Greenstein?' barked Viking, his green eyes glaring at Boggo.

'No, sir,' replied Boggo innocently.

'Stand up when you speak to me, godammit!' yelled Viking with clenched fists and teeth.

Boggo moved from a slouch to bolt upright and standing beside me in less than a second. He then tried to sweet talk Viking down from his rage by asking him if it was his birthday on Tuesday. Viking's eyes narrowed, and then he spoke in an unnervingly quiet and vicious voice, 'Do you think a man needs constant reminding that his fiftieth birthday is fast approaching?' Then he bashed the new audition list to his door with a pounding fist and disappeared into his office.

Boggo whistled. 'Jeez, talk about a midlife crisis.' He sniggered and said, 'All right, it's official – anybody auditioning on Tuesday is DOA!'

I took a closer look at the new audition list with many

names already printed.

Tuesday 17:00 J Milton.

Once again:

BACK YOUR INSTINCT, MILTON!

10:00   Rugby trials ...

Since I was knocked unconscious and am now lying horizontal in the sanatorium with a blinding headache and no memory of how I got here, I have stuck the following 'story' into my diary. Initially, Boggo offered to write down today's events directly into my diary but since he is a known diary thief and backstabbing gossip, I refused. I tried to explain to the idiot that I don't have to write down every single episode of every single thing that ever happens to me. That would bore me to tears, perhaps lead to criminal prosecution, and result in my parents and grandmother being institutionalised. Boggo reasoned that as an eyewitness to the 'classic' events of this morning, and in the interests of honesty and integrity, I should allow him to write today's diary entry. We eventually agreed that he would write his entry on a piece of paper and then I would stick it into my diary. Unfortunately, Vern then demanded that I also stick in one of his pictures. I tried to make the point that it was my diary, for my own thoughts and reflections and if they wanted to write in a diary so desperately then they should start their own diaries. Boggo looked at me like I was crazy and said, 'There's no point in starting one now, you've already cornered the market!' Vern nodded in agreement and without the slightest shred of irony informed me that the whole school thought I was absolutely crazy.

I realised that there would be no escape from the vultures, so I agreed, only on the condition that Boggo's 'story' and Vern's 'picture' took up no more than three pages of my diary, and that Vern didn't draw a picture of Roger, my towel rail, or the naked Garlic covered in Vaseline.

Boggo reckoned his piece of writing was going to liven up what must be a pretty boring diary. He then said that I was sure to bore my grandchildren to death one day and that judging by the section he read when he stole my first year diary, my writing was well below average and I needed extra lessons. My head was thumping and I still felt dazed so I told the two of them that I needed some rest. Boggo and Vern sped off immediately to get cracking.

BOGGO'S DIARY ENTRY
(READ AT OWN RISK.)

Spud Milton's Rugby Trial
(A.K.A. SPUD FUBARED BY PIG!!!!!!!)

Due to Spud Milton being such a wuss about others checking
out his diary and stuff, I have decided to write this in
Spud Milton's unique 'head up my own poor arse' diary
style. (What a helmet!!!!) He should have left this diary
up to Boggo 'The cat' Greenstein and you wouldn't have
all these shitty stories about being dominated by semi-
hot chicks and having your balls polished. Ha ha, Funny one
though - you had to be there!!! (What a helmet!)

Anyway if you are reading this in front of a fire and you
happen to be Spud's grandchildren (Gutting!) then I have
two points for you to think about. Firstly, one of your
parents must have been adopted or retarded because
there's no way Milton will ever come right with any chick
unless she's a bit of a Vern. (You know what I mean...
.) The second point is that this is going to be the funniest
story ever, so recharge your drinks, take a piss, or
whatever, because you are going to laugh your lungs out
of your arse! My oath to God, I'm hosing already!!! Even
Rambo says it's the funniest thing he's ever seen - and
Rambo's seen a shitload of funny shit. Anyway - whatever!
The story rocks and Boggo 'the cat' rocks even harder!!

Here goes . . .

10:00 Spud hangs back and tries to look anonymous as Dirty
Harry Hall reads out all the names of all the open teams.

10:05 Spud is unbelievably promoted to the 4ths after
Dicksplash Du Plessis cries off with a pulled hammy -
what a chop!

10:06 Spud looks shit scared before running onto the field for a practice match against the 3rds. He is seen having two slashes behind the bush before kick-off which is lank excessive even by Vern's standards.

10:10 Wacko kicks an angel-raper up-and-under straight at Milton and Pig charges down the field to smoke him one time. Milton drops the ball after having a complete fag attack on the 22m line.

10:11 Milton FUBARED by Pig who runs straight over his head and scores under the poles.

10:15 Spud still lying comatose on the field. (What a loser!)

10:18 Bravely, Boggo and to a lesser extent, Fatty, leap into action and save Spud from a certain death via thrombosis and brain damage. Brave Boggo takes charge of the situation immediately and with helpful Fatty they shoulder the dying Spud and rush him to the san in double quick time. A number of chicks turn and watch us go, thinking to themselves, how much they would like to shag brave Boggo in various disgusting ways. Mrs Bosch even runs after the stretcher for a bit but can't keep up with brave, athletic Boggo and helpful Fatty as they ran like muscular Roman centurions on a rape and pillage mission. If Boggo isn't made head of house or at the very least a prefect after his heroics it will be a complete travesty of justice!

10:25 Spud finally comes round with a girl-like whimper and immediately starts freaking out about his diary being missing. Brave, handsome, athletic Boggo miraculously finds the diary and is then falsely accused of being a thief by groggy Milton in a whiny voice. Blind one — what a moose. How's this — the funniest thing is that Milton (The Meek) is dropped from the 4th team (and the 5th and the 6th and the 7th team) and has to report to the 8th team practice

1

when he gets over being **FUBARED** - talk about a Wall Street crash! This is the second time this year that he has been demoted by several teams in various sports and makes Spud officially the most overrated sportsman in the school - in fact some people refer to him more as a sportswoman!! Ha Ha!!! Anyway it also lends truth to the rumour that Spud is a lesbian.

Anyway, whatever, everyone pissed themselves and it was seriously hysterical. And thanks to Boggo The Brave and Handsome and top class for English, you can never ever say - 'you had to be there!' Because Boggo was.

Sorry I have to go now because Anal Milton said I can only use three pages of his beloved diary. (What's with the diary thing anyway????) Oh and even worse, I have to hand over valuable space for Vern to include a picture of Spud's **FUBARING** by Pig.

Oh and if you're a hot chick (and I mean really hot - not like if your Mom tells you you're hot when you're actually a complete growler) and you are reading this before the end of 1993 then phone 033 362 4001 and ask for Boggo the Love Merchant.

If you read this after December 1993 then write your name, address and bra size on a piece of paper, stuff it in a glass bottle and throw it in the ocean. I'll catch you on the Spring Tide, baby!

I do hereby state that everything I have written is absolute truth - my oath to God. And everything Milton has written about is hugely exaggerated and mostly made up - my oath to God. (Except for all the cool stuff done by the Crazy Eight for which I am mostly responsible.)

Regards
Boggo · The Cat · Greenstein
The Middle of Nowhere...
2/5/92

Okay here follows Vern's picture of the incident...

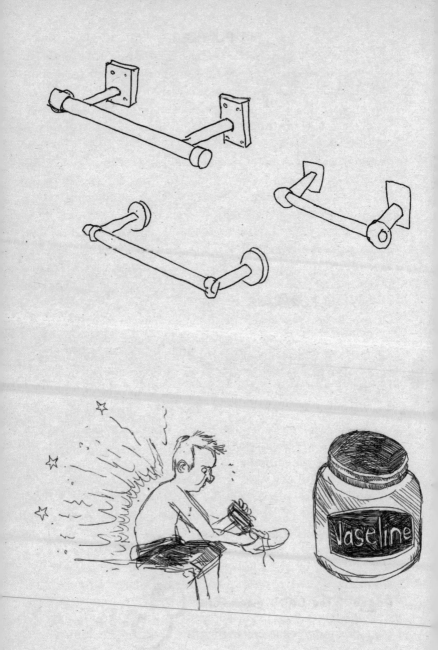

Sunday 3rd May

I've reclaimed my diary. I'm back on my feet and ready to face the world again. Sister Collins says I can leave the san, which is a relief because I was sleeping next to an unhealthy looking first year called Woodrot. (I didn't ask questions.) Sister Collins has also forbidden me from playing rugby this term for fear that another bang on the pip might result in permanent damage. Despite feeling a little dazed and unsteady, I set off determinedly towards the house and ignored the loud sniggers from the common room as I slowly made my way up the stairs.

I didn't care and didn't stop. Instead I packed up the collected works of WS and headed for the hills. Under a tall pine tree on the edge of the forest overlooking the school, I repeated my audition piece well over a hundred times. I returned for roll call (and a few hundred mocking taunts about being stampeded by a Pig) knowing Lysander's monologue better than the names of my family.

BRING IT ON!

Tuesday 5th May

THE AUDITION

16:30   Discovered ten boys standing around the theatre foyer muttering to themselves in Shakespearian verse. I became the eleventh.

16:45   There was an explosion of shouting from inside the theatre after a West second year repeatedly forgot his lines. Viking clearly wasn't impressed with the second year's effort and called him a 'theatrical disgrace'! The boy charged out of the theatre looking devastated. This didn't do much for the morale of the waiting boys. It would seem that Viking's 50th birthday hasn't been a happy one.

16:59   'Next!' commanded Viking from the theatre door. I stepped forward and concentrated on keeping my breathing even and my body relaxed.

'Milton!' roared Viking and led me through the auditorium while ranting on about the dearth of serious acting talent in the school. He then gave me a slap on the back that propelled me up a flight of steps and onto the stage.

One last deep breath and ...

I nailed it! I think.

Wednesday 6th May

Feeling splendid. Yesterday's audition was the best I've ever had because I refused to be nervous and intimidated by Viking's fury and shouting. After the audition he screamed, 'That's more like it!' and told me to keep an eye on the theatre notice board.

I've already checked it twice this morning but thus far there is still only the original auditions notice on which somebody had scribbled *Colin/Colon!!!* in red ink.

I found it difficult to concentrate on schoolwork and Reverend Bishop's confirmation class barely registered a blip on my radar screen. I'm constantly daydreaming about playing a Shakespearian hero and kissing beautiful women dressed in tights in a dark corner backstage.

22:00 Vern has somehow acquired another box of matches and spent the evening lighting one match after another and staring mesmerised at the flame. Nobody could sleep until the cretin had struck up the entire box and finally called it a night. Even Rambo reckons Vern is a serious hazard with his newfound discovery of fire.

Sunday 10th May

WEEKEND DEVELOPMENTS

- Boggo made R250 from hairdressing. His leadership/business/scoring manual has sold seven copies thus far, although it's common knowledge that every member of the Fragile Five bought one after Boggo threatened to hang them out of the window. Boggo denied that this was illegal business practice and called it 'driving a hard bargain'. The two other suckers were Vern and Norman Whiteside, who demanded a refund after reading it. Boggo refused the head of house his refund, but Whiteside threatened Boggo with hard labour until Boggo eventually coughed up the money. He later accused the head of house of being unethical.

- A rumour is doing the rounds that Simon may be coming back to school. Only problem is that not even Boggo knows who started the rumour in the first place.
- Vern set fire to his duvet and then spent the rest of his Saturday night trying to wash the burns out of his linen with Palmolive soap and a pair of dirty underpants.

Monday 11th May

On the way to breakfast I noticed a crowd of boys across the cloister gazing up at the theatre notice board. I raced over and fought my way through the excited crowd – it was the call-backs list of those who had made it through to the second round of auditions. The list was in alphabetical order so it was impossible to know which of the twenty-five names were up for which parts. Seeing my name was more of a relief than a thrill. Seeing Vern's name was a complete shock. Rambo, Fatty and Boggo also made the shortlist, as did Spike, Runt and Meg Ryan's Son. I noticed Geoff Lawson's name above mine along with the irritating Smith, who boasted that he had been offered the role of Oliver in first year before ending up in the chorus line.

Poor Garlic was gutted that he hadn't made the cut. This despite Viking having threatened him with death should he ever audition for anything ever again. He just couldn't understand why Vern had made it through to the second round ahead of him. Garlic, still sporting a puzzled expression and watery eyes, complained, 'Even Meg Ryan's Son got in! He's like barely up to my knee caps!' Fatty placed a friendly arm around Garlic's shoulders and explained that there was no shame in being edged out by Meg Ryan's Son since acting obviously ran in the family and he was also fairly good looking on account of his mom's excellent facial features. Boggo also pointed out the fact that auditioning for the female part of Hermia had probably not been the best idea on Garlic's part.

'How was I meant to know I was playing a girl's part?' protested Garlic as if it was somehow our fault and not his. After sniggering repeatedly like a machine gun, Boggo informed us that he had overheard Viking telling Mrs Bosch that Garlic had repeatedly referred to his character as **Hernia** at the audition. To a chorus of loud cackling laughter Garlic shouted, 'What kind of a name is Hermia anyway? Why can't we do Grease instead?'

Viking has instructed those left in the race to keep our entire Friday afternoon free and warned that the final auditions may run through the evening and into the next morning if he is not satisfied with our progress. Boggo was so excited that he performed a mostly Shakespearian speech from the top of his locker, before pulling down his pants and mooning the dormitory.

Pike bust us talking about the play after lights out and ordered us all to write a five thousand-word essay by Friday as punishment.

The title:

THE GREATNESS OF PIKE!

Not even the vilest primate in history could ruin the mood, and after everything had fallen silent again, Rambo did a Pike impersonation, beginning and ending with slamming the door, that was sheer genius. He had us all rolling in hysterics with Fatty having a near heart attack and Vern crying his eyes out and slamming his fist repeatedly into his locker.

Tuesday 12th May

A notice on the board read:

Old boy G.T. Murray (83-87) has been awarded the Rhodes scholarship to read International Law at Oxford University. In accordance with tradition, tomorrow will be a half-day. Sunday rules apply. Roll call 17:30 strictly enforced.

Right now GT is a school hero!

Wednesday 13th May

It was a fantastic feeling to be packing away my books for the day at 11 o'clock. I wish school were always like this ... As is tradition, a vast game of touch rugby spanning two rugby fields sprang to life without any announcement or notice needed. Standing out on the far right wing to avoid any potential head collisions, the ball was eventually flung across to our side of the field. I positioned myself perfectly to catch it but Garlic jumped in the way and the ball rebounded off his forehead before disappearing back to the other end of the field from where it never returned.

Boggo nearly had a fistfight with Thinny after stealing his bike and driving to Nottingham Road for magazines and supplies. Thinny was seriously steamed up and had to be restrained by JR Ewing and the last remaining Darryl before doing something rash like hitting a senior. Boggo suggested that Thinny should be honoured that he stole his bike, and handed him a business card for good measure. Thinny's face grew very red but he wisely kept his mouth shut. Boggo returned to the dormitory with a bag full of goodies and accused Thinny of having a serious attitude problem. I asked Boggo why, if he has a new bike of his own, does he still use Thinny's. Boggo snapped his fingers in front of my face and said, 'Because mine is a limited edition. By next year it will be worth double the price.' He then tapped his finger against his temple and told me I had no business acumen and suggested I buy his business manual.

23:30   Can't sleep. Worrying about the play. If I don't make it I have no excuses because I've done everything to master Shakespeare. If I can't make The Dream, then what chance do I have of cracking it in the big wide world? Zip.

THERE'S NOTHING TO LOSE!

Thursday 14th May

Spent the afternoon with Fatty in the archives. Thanks to his scoliosis/peptic heart murmur and my concussion, we were able to kick back, drink tea and talk about ghosts instead.

'I've got something mega hectic to show you,' said Fatty as he bustled across the dimly lit room to a freestanding bookshelf called 'Old School'. He pulled down an ancient school magazine and collapsed onto the couch next to me breathing heavily through his mouth.

'This is going to blow your mind, Spuddy,' he said as he furiously flipped through the pages, greedily licking the ends of his fingers at regular intervals. He found the page and thumped the yellowing magazine page down on my lap and said, 'Check it out. Boggo, Sidewinder and I think this guy is the spitting image of you.'

Fatty pointed out a figure in his school uniform in an old black and white rugby photograph. I didn't see any similarity between us, and Fatty looked even more unimpressed when I refused to concede that our chins were identical.

'Anyway,' Fatty continued, 'how's this? Not only do you look identical, but his first name is Milton!'

His name was Milton Montgomery. The photograph was taken in 1913. He was killed in North Africa in 1918.

I pointed out to Fatty that there was a university degree in brackets after Milton Montgomery's name, which clearly made him the teacher seated next to the boy in question. Fatty snatched the photograph back and his face fell as he realised his mistake. Still it didn't stop him saying, 'You've got five years, buddy. You'd better make the most of them,' before disappearing into the storeroom to dig up more nasty coincidences. I then settled into a warm shaft of sunlight at the window to write this.

Friday 15th May

MASS ACTION

In the spirit of the struggle against tyranny and evil, all six surviving and resident members of the Crazy Eight stood in line behind Rambo as we waited outside Viking's office. After a bloodcurdling shout of 'Come!' we filed slowly into our housemaster's office and found him sitting at his desk and poring over the morning newspaper.

'Sir,' said Rambo in a calm voice, 'we have come to hand in our punishment for Pike.'
     'Ah, yes,' said Viking. 'I hear you were having a glorious late night debate on how I might cast my play.' Viking chortled to himself and folded his newspaper into a neat rectangle.

'Sir?' enquired Garlic. He then noticed Rambo's savage glare and hurriedly said, 'Good morning' instead.

'Good morning, Garlic,' replied Viking politely.

Rambo handed over a pile of punishment pages that were utterly blank apart from our names, signature, and the title of course:

THE GREATNESS OF PIKE

Viking wasn't impressed with the piles of blank pages and demanded to know what we were playing at. Rambo spoke for us in his calm, rational voice. 'Sir, we don't deny that we were caught talking after lights out.'

'Good,' said Viking and nodded at us seriously.

'But,' continued Rambo, 'the punishment is undoable because the essay is impossible. In fact after days of thought we have not been able to come up with a single reason for Pike's greatness. The reason – Pike isn't great.'

'Well, make it up, for God's sakes!' Viking instructed us as he thundered his fist into the picture of a little girl holding flowers on the front page of the newspaper. 'Tell the man what he wants to hear and move on!'

Rambo argued that although he was famous for his silver tongue (?) even he couldn't possibly make up so many untruths about one extremely un-great human being.

Viking didn't reply immediately, which meant he was thinking. And if he was thinking then he clearly thought that we at least had a fair point. After a long silence Viking said, 'I have a decision and there will be no arguments. Am I clear?'

We all nodded and waited for our housemaster to deliver his judgement.

'I agree it's a tough assignment,' he said, scratching away at his beard as if he had been overcome with a series of itches. 'Instead of writing a five thousand word essay on Pike, I suggest a five thousand word essay on why I should cast you in The Dream.' We all looked at Rambo for his next move but his eyes never left those of our housemaster.

'Since you were caught talking about Shakespeare, I'll offer you a reprieve. I shall require no more than three thousand words in neat handwriting.'

'Sir!' blurted Garlic. 'How can I write the essay when I didn't even make it through the first round?'

Viking observed Garlic for a moment and then said, 'Garlic, if your essay is persuasive enough, I'll consider suspending your life ban on auditioning.'

We followed Rambo out of our housemaster's office and into the bright sunlight and the buzzing activity of the main quad. Rambo threw his hands into the air and cried out, 'Follow me, brothers. I am the way, the truth and the darkness!' There was a brief pause and then we all followed him into the house.

CALL-BACK AUDITIONS!

Besides a twenty-minute break for dinner, the final twenty-five didn't leave the theatre until just before midnight. Every boy had a shot at just about every male role available and we did everything from solo speeches to improvising scenarios and group work.

All twenty-five boys reckon they've made it – I can see it in their eyes. I can't believe Vern has a hope in hell. He kept everyone laughing with his loony antics, and speaks Shakespearian verse as if it is a foreign language and regularly uses loud Zulu clicks to punctuate his delivery whenever he feels it necessary. Viking gave us absolutely no hint as to who he was favouring and once again instructed us to keep an eye on the notice board. I wish he'd stop saying that, because Fatty is already mocking me about checking the theatre board every five minutes. He reckons if you want something too much you'll never get it. He called it the first universal truth and said it was more reliable than both Murphy's Law and Friday the 13th.

The problem is how do you stop yourself wanting something that you desperately desire? The real universal truth is that there are only nine roles up for grabs so that means more than half of us will be gutted when the cast list finally goes up.

Have decided to limit myself to three trips to the notice board per day (not counting a quick peek on the way back from the tuck shop).

Saturday 16th May

In his obsessive quest to become a prefect, Boggo has signed on as the second team linesman. This, despite the fact that he knows absolutely nothing about rugby and has banned himself from all sport on account of his drastically low iron levels, which afflict him only during the winter and autumn. (Rugby and athletics?) Boggo's iron levels have never been officially examined but he reckons they are hovering just above the danger zone.

14:30 Rambo played a brilliant game against St Giles for the seconds. He scored two tries and made a thundering tackle on the opposition wing directly in front of the delighted school benches. Stupidly, however, the wing pushed Rambo once he had peeled himself off the grass. Rambo grabbed him and dumped him headfirst into the ground. There was a loud roar from the school and then a long argument between the ref, Rambo, our linesman (Boggo), their captain, and the angry winger. The winger had to be restrained by his fellow players because he was pretending to want a piece of Rambo, who by now had his arm on the ref's shoulder. Eventually, the ref penalised us and sent Rambo to the cooler for ten minutes.

The first team won easily, but all the talk was about Rambo and how he had turned the opposition wing into a tent pole. Depending on who you speak to, Rambo is about to be banned from playing rugby, expelled, or promoted to the first team!

The man himself seemed unconcerned about all the fuss and merely noted that his intense gym work over the holidays had seriously paid off. Meanwhile Boggo was outraged with the one-eyed ref who he swore was wearing a St Giles Old Boys' tie after the game.

Sunday 17th May

I got a little carried away with my punishment essay on why I wanted to be in The Dream. I ended up writing 4,168 words and then felt like an idiot.

Mind you, at least that wasn't as dire as Boggo, who said he only wanted to be in the play so that he could act under 'a director of unparalleled genius' who was 'easily the finest theatre director in the school's history'. Boggo then spent the next three thousand words praising Viking and saying what a creative giant he was. He signed off by saying Viking was his favourite teacher ever, and that he felt privileged to know him.

Rambo called Boggo's blatant brownnosing 'sickening' and said, 'It's the worst case I've seen since Spud tried to crawl up The Guv's rear end in first year.'
    'Business lesson number two,' announced Boggo. 'Talk the talk before porking the pork!'

Rambo threw a shoe at him and Boggo ducked out the dormitory.

Garlic ran out of reasons for why he should be cast in the play after a mere two paragraphs. The rest of his essay rambled on about why Vern and Meg Ryan's Son shouldn't have made the second round.

Monday 18th May

8:00 The Glock came out firing on Rambo's side during assembly. He said the whole incident had been blown out of proportion and that the St Giles winger had provoked the scuffle. He then congratulated Rambo on showing restraint (?) and having a fine all round game. He also praised Boggo for his vivid eyewitness portrayal of how the fracas played out. Boggo was thrilled with his mention despite the fact that the The Glock had called him Alan Einstein. Boggo says this is a private joke that he shares with the headmaster and that The Glock is merely doffing a cap to Boggo's superior intellect. I would consider this unlikely because the only time Boggo ever speaks to The Glock is when he gets bust with porn, booze or cigarettes.

Still no sign of the cast list. Boggo tried to get the juice out of Viking after breakfast but our housemaster threw a file at him and then chased him right the way across the quad.

Wednesday 20th May

CONFIRMATION CLASS

There was a sign on the Rectory door instructing us to meet the chaplain in the chapel. Reverend Bishop began the class with a violent sneezing attack and excused himself, before hurrying out of the chapel holding a handkerchief over his nose.

'What a freak,' said Fatty and snapped open a large packet of Cheese Twirls.

Reverend Bishop looked more comfortable when he returned and said that he wanted to dedicate this lesson to silent and earnest prayer. He instructed us to clear our minds of all the things that occupy our daily lives and to speak openly to God. The chaplain believes that too much spiritual time is wasted by not talking openly and honestly with the man upstairs.

'Lay your hopes and fears at his feet and trust that he will guide you.'

We all knelt on cushions in the choir stalls and fell into silence. Apart from Vern that is, who shouted, 'Dear God!' and then began rattling off a long list of his favourite meals. Reverend Bishop ordered Vern to pray in silence, which was a ridiculous order because he should know by now that Vern can't think without speaking and may not think at all.

I found it difficult to drown out the voices in my head. But slowly they grew faint and then faded away completely. Eventually, all I could hear were the rock pigeons cooing in the eves and the distant sound of the old Massey Ferguson cutting the grass on Trafalgar. By now, not even the creaks from the old wooden pews could distract me.

I reached a place where everything felt perfectly still and peaceful. And then I began speaking to Him – or to nobody if He wasn't listening. The voice in my head was stronger than mine and it calmly told God about everything that was worrying me. It didn't even feel embarrassed asking God to pull a few strings and get me into the school play.

The siren rang for dinner. An entire hour had passed with me on my knees and yet I hadn't felt so much as a twinge in my body. I stood up and walked confidently down the aisle and then outside into the stillness of the early evening. I can't say why, but I knew then, in that moment, that I had made the play.

Now that's faith.

Friday 22nd May

Things are hotting up. I have to finish the final 120 pages of *Rumours of Rain* by Monday. Despite The Guv's snootiness about Brink, I think it's an excellent novel, set on the eve of the 1976 Soweto riots. I'm also not surprised to hear that André Brink isn't exactly well loved by the Afrikaans community. I rate Brink a better writer than Charles Dickens, although I wouldn't dare tell The Guv, who has spent the entire term sulking because he was only allowed to teach Othello for six weeks and no Dickens at all.

I also have to research the formations of marshes and ox-bow lakes before next Thursday's Geography field trip to Lidgetton.

Tomorrow is Kings College and the school is cranking up for a major battle. Word on the street is that Kings have their weakest side in years and are ripe for a savaging. It's at times like these that I miss the feeling of throwing on the old rugby jersey and getting psyched up on adrenaline and Tiger Balm.

Saturday 23rd May

Kings College have been absolutely thumped by our first team! The score 26-10!!! Not only that, but Rambo scored a try when he came on as a replacement for Vaughan Michaels who was carried off on a stretcher. It felt odd watching Rambo being hoisted aloft by the school and celebrated as a rugby genius. Think I'm going to seriously rethink the whole gym thing.

There was great comedy to be had at the eighth team match on one of the outer fields earlier in the day. Under the 'coaching' of Mr Lilly and with a dodgy side including both Vern and Garlic, it was no surprise that a crowd of just under a hundred boys had gathered to watch.

Unfortunately, Vern only had a single cretin attack when he attempted to score a try in the corner and dived head first into the corner flag. A nasty red stripe appeared across his pale forehead and he spent the rest of the game furiously rubbing his face and muttering angrily to himself.

Garlic, playing hooker, was even funnier. Every time a scrum collapsed he would stagger up from the bottom of a pile of bodies with large amounts of grass and the odd twig stuck to his hair. He didn't seem to notice and by the second half he was running around with a small compost heap on his head. Late in the game he arose from the bottom of a ruck with a long piece of bandage attached and the crowd went berserk.

It seems that Mr Lilly still hasn't improved in his defensive tactics. His new brainwave is for the entire team to chase the largest opposition player on the field. Unfortunately, the downside of this tactic is that if he passes the ball to anybody else there's nobody left to tackle him.

Final result: Kings 94 – Us 0

Monday 25th May

Boggo returned from the stationery shop with another armload of stationery and looking flushed with success. He reckons he's definitely on the verge of scoring Mrs Bosch. He said she was all over him like a rash and even asked if he had a girlfriend! Not only that, she's promised Boggo thirty-five per cent off his next purchase. He proudly lined up his new Atlas series on his locker and then showed us a pen that used invisible ink that could only be read under UV lighting. Unfortunately, there was no UV lighting to be found in the house.

'Perfect for writing down girls' phone numbers in night-clubs,' said Boggo optimistically as he carefully placed his new pen in his pencil case and zipped it shut.

'Business lesson number three,' he declared. 'When it comes to scoring chicks, think laterally.'

After a loud groan from the rest of us, Fatty showed off an old pair of binoculars that he's borrowed from Mr Bosch so that he can watch the wryneck nest from a safe distance. 'The chicks hatched sometime over the weekend and they're lank protective about people near their nest,' he said, as he polished away at the lenses with the corner of Vern's handkerchief.

Boggo told Fatty that he was also going to use the binoculars for bird watching, but that the only hole he's going to be checking out belongs to Mrs Bosch. He then enacted a graphic scene where he repeatedly smacked her imaginary buttocks and shouted, 'You like that, don't you, Mrs B!'

Wednesday 27th May

Rumours were circulating the dining hall at breakfast that Viking had auditioned the girls at Wrexham College and was considering casting girls in male roles.

'You see!' shouted Garlic with a spoon of yoghurt in his mouth. 'How can chicks play our parts and we can't play theirs?'

'Chicks are welcome to play with my part,' replied Boggo and smacked his lips together. 'Something you amateurs wouldn't know about.' Rambo sniggered at Boggo and called him a desperate virgin. Boggo didn't take kindly to this and retorted, 'Well, Friday is the long weekend.'

'So what?' replied Rambo without showing much interest.

Boggo looked around suspiciously and whispered, 'You know what I'm talking about. You said your big plan would be done by the long weekend.'

'So what's that got to do with you being a virgin?' asked Rambo as he stacked his empty plates together.

'When are we going nightswimming?' asked Garlic suddenly after an awkward silence.

'Nightswimming is for juniors, Garlic,' said Rambo, standing up to leave. 'We aren't fourteen any more.' With that he sauntered off.

On the way back to the house, Viking called me into his office. My entire body became a pulsing heartbeat. Surely this was the moment when he broke the news that I'd been cast as his leading man! But he was only asking me to help him organise the photostatted scripts into the correct order while he continued writing his reports. He didn't even look up until the bell rang for the beginning of prep.

'Carry on, Milton,' he said, and returned to his marking. I finished stacking the neatly stapled scripts in Viking's cupboard and excused myself. I thought about asking but figured it could reveal excessive desperation and ruin my chances.

19:00   The main quad was silent and the cloisters were empty. I began striding towards the house door, but something caught my eye and I slowed down. It must have been a movement but I also thought I heard a dull sound. There was a dark figure sitting on the ledge of the fountain watching me. It was gloomy in the quad but I knew immediately who it was.

'Come here, Milton!' hissed Pike. He stood up and his face caught the light, revealing an expression of anger and suspicion. I turned and ran into the house. He didn't follow. I don't know why but my moment with Pike occupied my thoughts for the rest of the evening. Not even Shakespeare could make me feel happy.

Thursday 28th May

GEOGRAPHY FIELD TRIP

The field trip was fairly interesting, although there is a limit to the excitement you can fire up over an ox-bow lake you've seen many times before. The only real bright spot was when Fatty sank deep into the mud in the middle of the marsh. He completely freaked out because he thought that he was being swallowed by quicksand. It was quite a sight to see Fatty screaming and slowly disappearing into the marsh, holding Mr Bosch's old binoculars in one hand and a packet of peanuts and raisins in the other. What made it even more hilarious was that nobody else sank into the marsh except Fatty. Boggo tried to pull his mate out with one hand but ended up sinking down to his thighs before calling off the rescue attempt and offering to take care of Fatty's funeral arrangements.

We eventually pulled a mortified Fatty out of the marsh with the help of the bus's towing rope and then Mr Bosch made him wash the mud off his clothes in the freezing Lion's River. Poor Fatty looked like a drowned rhino, and was forced to sit on the floor of the bus so that he didn't ruin the seats.

16:55   Return from field trip.

17:00   People are whispering and rumours are flying around that something is going down. According to Runt, Whiteside was called into Viking's office over half an hour ago and hasn't been seen since.

17:20   Whiteside emerges from Viking's office looking pale. He refuses to talk to anyone. Viking storms off in the direction of the headmaster's office looking furious.

17:21   Boggo and Fatty move to the house bench and attempt not to look obvious.

17:30   Find Rambo in the common room and ask him if he knows anything. He shrugs his shoulders and says, 'Beats me.' He continues watching The Bold and The Beautiful.

17:32   Boggo and Fatty are driven off the house bench by an angry Viking, who threatens to thrash them for lingering about near his office.

17:40 Norman Whiteside marches into the common room and switches the television off to a loud chorus of groans. He informs us that an emergency house meeting has been called for 18:00.

17:41-17:59 Whiteside rings a loud hand bell at the foot of the stairs and repeatedly announces the house meeting.

18:00 Viking strides into the common room looking dangerous.

'Right!' Viking roared. The entire house fell into silence. I felt terrified despite not having done anything wrong and poor Vern was almost green with fear.

'Now I'm not going to beat about the bush here,' said the housemaster, 'because by now you are all aware that something is going on in the house.' We all did our best to look surprised.

'This afternoon I conducted a search and discovered cigarettes, alcohol and an illicit magazine in the residence of Leonard Pike. He has been de-prefected, beaten by the headmaster, and suspended for two weeks. He has been banned from entering the house for the remainder of the year, and that decision is final.'

Somebody gasped, and a low rumble of whispering began. I couldn't quite register what Viking was saying.

'I hope this is the final incident of this nature. And let it be noted that nobody, not even prefects, are exempt from the rules of the school and my house.'

It's really happened, although I can't quite believe it yet.

'I have decided against a prefect replacement this year and expect you all to reflect on this over the long weekend,' concluded Viking.

Then he was gone and a great cheering roar erupted

in the common room. Boys were hugging and shaking hands and laughter was everywhere at once. Fatty picked me up and nearly crushed me to death with a wild embrace. I then turned and searched for Rambo but he wasn't among the crowd of cheering boys.

At dinner, a mere ten minutes later, Boggo already knew the whole story. Meany Dlamini smelt smoke on Plump Graham (Pike's unfortunate slave) and ran him in to Viking. Our housemaster then led Plump Graham down to Pike's residence and broke into his room using a sparc key. Plump Graham showed Viking where Pike kept his illegal contraband. Viking hit the roof, called in The Glock, interrogated Spike and the rest is history.

Nobody noticed Rambo until he sat down at the table with a plateful of beef stroganoff. He winked at us and said, 'Happy days, boys.' He then sat down and got stuck into his food.

We ate for a while in complete silence until Boggo couldn't take it any longer and hurled down his knife in frustration.

'Okay, so enough with the undercover agent shit. What did you do to Pike?'

Rambo looked up innocently and said, 'Me? Nothing.'

'Well, either there's something going on that we don't know about, or you're the second Nostradamus,' said Fatty, attempting to stare Rambo down.

'How did you know Pike would be gone by the long weekend?' blurted Garlic, frowning.

'Guess I got lucky,' shrugged Rambo and looked serenely at the ceiling.

'Bloody lucky,' agreed Boggo as he closely examined a strip of beef.

'A toast!' cried Rambo suddenly, raising his glass of milk. 'To luck.'

We raised our glasses.

Before lights out, I noticed Rambo sitting alone on the house bench staring out at the fountain. After some internal debate, my curiosity got the better of me and I decided to join him and strike up a friendly conversation. Unfortunately, as I sat down he stood up. Like an idiot, I immediately stood up too. I felt embarrassed and foolish for trying to treat him like a mate, and no doubt he was about to make me feel like an idiot.

'I'm off to a rugby team talk at Century,' he said. 'You feel like a stroll?' Rambo and I walked along the cloister past Viking's office and then the chapel, before stepping out into the rose garden.

'You're not going to tell us, are you?' I said eventually.
'Nope,' he replied.
'Why not?' I asked.
'Because there's nothing to tell,' said Rambo.
'Well, anyway,' I said, 'well done.'
'Thanks,' he said and smiled at me like we had just shared a secret.
'I'd better get back. Viking's on the prowl.'
'Cool,' he said and began walking away.
Then he stopped and shouted over his shoulder, 'Oh, I've got some good and bad news for you, by the way. Which do you want first?'
'Good news,' I replied.
Rambo raised an eyebrow as if my choice was significant and said, 'We both made the play. Viking told me this morning.'

I was so stunned that I forgot to ask for the bad news. Rambo became a large shadow moving quickly through the roses and onto the cobbled driveway. Then he was gone. I looked up at the stars whirring above my head. The edge of the chapel loomed above me like a ship's sail leading me forward into the unknown. I should never have doubted.

Then I threw my head back, opened my mouth and screamed.

Friday 29th May

LONG WEEKEND!!!

Saturday 30th May

My father is up to something. Firstly he called me out into the garden and then led me deep into the shrubbery. After making sure nobody was observing us, Dad asked me if I would take a drive with him. Since I couldn't think of a single other thing to do instead, I immediately agreed. Dad whispered for me to meet him at the garage in five minutes.

'What's going on?' shouted Mom suddenly from her bedroom window.

'We're just taking a drive,' said Dad in a high-pitched voice from the front lawn.

'Well, don't do anything stupid!' shouted Mom, before slamming the window shut.

Dad and I raced through Durban city in the newly cleaned station wagon. My father kept pointing out dilapidated buildings and saying that they used to be hotels or nightclubs in his youth. He reckons the entire inner city is going to the dogs and soon it's going to look like downtown Nairobi.

Eventually, we found Gale Street and Dad drove very slowly in the left lane for about a kilometre before pulling onto the pavement outside Requiem Funeral Services.

I asked Dad if we were buying a coffin for Wombat. He

laughed loudly and said I had his sense of humour. The light was fading and the Durban sky was dull grey, reflecting our faces in the tinted windows of the funeral parlour. Dad beckoned me to the door and kicked it open like he didn't want to touch the handle. Immediately a loud bell rang and we entered the funeral parlour to find workmen drilling and hammering and generally pulling the place to pieces. Frank was over in the corner, wearing psychedelic welding glasses and furiously sawing at a block of wood.

Dad thumped me on the shoulder and said, 'Boy, I want to officially welcome you to the next big thing to hit the city of Durban.' He then spread his arms wide and said, 'Welcome to Frank's Bar and Grill, Snooker and Darts.'

I didn't know what to say because the place was a mess and a funeral parlour and Dad was waiting for me to speak.

'Wow!' I said, trying my best to look amazed.

Turns out Dad is a junior partner in the business with Frank obviously being the man in charge and the major shareholder. My father reckons that they have also secured a big foreign backer to help bankroll the project. He says the place is going to hum seven nights a week and turn him into a millionaire. There seemed no doubt in his mind that a former funeral parlour on the dodgy end of Gale Street was the way forward to certain richness. Suddenly my father's finger was in my face and he was looking threatening. 'You tell your mother and I'll wring your neck!' he cried, before his face softened and he said, 'Just our little secret.' He cast a glance across to where Frank was hard at work and added, 'You know how she is about old Franky.'

I did my best to look impressed, and raved on about the place on the road home. If I'm truthful, then I predict Frank's Bar and Grill, Snooker and Darts is heading towards disaster.

QUESTIONS & PROBLEMS

1   The name – it isn't very catchy. The acronym F-BAGSAD is even worse.
2   What does Frank know about running a pub?
3   What does Dad know about running a pub's kitchen?
4   It was a funeral parlour. (How do we know there isn't a stray corpse under the floorboards?)
5   The kitchen is being built where the dead bodies were stored.
6   If Dad is keeping this from Mom then he must be financially involved somehow. He's still paying off debt from his now defunct dry-cleaning business. My father says his (illegal) success with Innocent's Moonshine is proof that he has a 'canny knack' for business.
7   Won't Frank and Dad drink all their stock?
8   Turns out, the big international investor is Uncle Aubrey!
9   It's in a dodgy part of town, and across the road from Serpent's Club which has a neon pink ADULTS ONLY sign above its entrance. Next door is an antique pawnshop that appears to be called Best Price Cash Only No 1.
10   Frank's Cressida was broken into last night and his car radio was stolen. His passenger window is now made out of cling-wrap.
11   Frank seems to be building the place himself. This despite being regularly mocked by my father for his various industrial disasters. Dad says Frank is the only man in the world to have made a five-

legged coffee table and reckons it's no coincidence that Frank plugged in his Christmas lights at exactly the same moment that half the province was plunged into a six hour long power failure.

The only positive is that working at F-BAGSAD will at least give my father something to do other than follow the dog around the garden and repeatedly check the alignment of the hedge. I just hope and pray that I'm not around when Dad finally breaks the news to my mother.

I thought about calling Mermaid but couldn't work out what I was actually going to say and even if I really wanted to speak to her in the first place. I'm definitely over women.

Sunday 31st May

Wombat has been moved permanently into a nursing home called Guinea's Rest. It's quite a smart place and Wombat has her own apartment, which she shares with a 24hr nursemaid called Regina. The decision was finally taken when Wombat accused another old lady of theft in the lift and attempted to slam her fingers in the door. Buster Cracknell phoned my mother and suggested that Wombat could no longer live without aid. Wombat's flat goes on the market tomorrow. I hope somebody removes the fish from under the bed before showing it off to potential buyers.

This senility setback doesn't seem to have dampened Wombat's spirits, because she didn't stop prattling from the moment we arrived at Guinea's Rest until we were safely down the stairs and heading to the car. A good eighty per cent of Wombat's drivel was rambling non-sense, although she did mention Churchill twice so she's not completely loony. Mom and I pretended to listen to her gibbering conversations but Dad was overcome with loud sniggering and had to excuse himself when Wombat confused me with her sixty-two-year-old doctor.

Thought about calling Mermaid but decided against it. I mean, what's the point?

Monday 1st June

Phoned Mermaid but hung up after three rings, sensing she wasn't home.

WEEKEND SCORECARD

SPUD   Rather slow moving weekend with family.

FATTY   Drank 9 litres of Coke in 2hrs, eclipsing his old record by well over a litre. Fatty said this was his final Coke drinking record attempt because he had bad gas and his teeth were now permanently furry even after two days of brushing.

RAMBO   Bench pressed 100kg in the gym. This means he could potentially lift both myself and Garlic at the same time.

GARLIC   Stayed with his rich uncle in Johannesburg. Says it wasn't as exciting as Lake Malawi.

SIMON   Still AWOL. With each passing day it seems less likely that he's coming back. There's a rumour that he might have moved to England but nobody knows for sure.

BOGGO   Had to work off his large stationery debt by cleaning out his stepfather's garage. He escaped having to clean out the attic as well when Boggo luckily found a box of his stepdad's dirty magazines in the garage and threatened to tell his mother. Boggo's stepfather took fright and cancelled his punishment. He then handed Boggo a hundred bucks and let him keep the magazines. Boggo wasn't very impressed with the content of his stepfather's porn mags and said, 'It's quite hard to look a guy in the eye when you know he's got a midget fetish.'

VERN   Has returned to school with his right arm bandaged to the elbow after burning himself in the holidays. (Once again, why am I the only one who's worried about Rain Man's pyromania?)

After Whiteside had switched off his light and ceased prowling around, we snuck into the first year dorm to shake Plump Graham's hand and for Fatty to hand over a present on behalf of all of us for ridding the house of Pike.

Plump Graham couldn't believe his eyes when Fatty handed over the huge box of Nestle Malawi chocolates and grinned at the package like it was a beautiful woman. 'Not all of the choccies are spastic colon friendly,' Fatty pointed out and suddenly looked longingly at the box of chocolates himself.

'We're proud of you, Graham,' said Rambo as he shook his hand. Plump Graham became embarrassed, nodding and nackjumping his gratitude. Vern handed Plump Graham a toilet roll as a token of thanks and that became our cue to return to our warm beds where a complicated dream about weightlessness awaited me.

Tuesday 2nd June

CAST LIST FOR A MIDSUMMER NIGHT'S DREAM

The Lovers

Theseus the Duke	Pig
Egeus	Viking
Lysander	Spike
Demetrius	Giles Lazarus

The Fairies

Oberon	Rambo
Puck	Smith

The Comical Mechanicals

Peter Quince	Boggo
Snug a Joiner	Vern????
Bottom a Weaver	The Guv
Snout a Tinker	Fatty
Flute a Bellows mender	**Spud Milton**!
Starveling a Tailor	Geoff Lawson

There's a school outcry over the cast for The Dream.
In what's been labelled a 'hometown decision', Viking is
picking up some flak for casting almost exclusively from
his own house. Vern's inclusion has created the most
surprise, and more than a couple of eyebrows have been
raised at the casting of both Fatty and Boggo.

Although I was hoping to be a lover, I guess I'll have to
settle for being a comical mechanical instead. I may not
have any girls trembling at the knees and begging for
sex, but at the very least I might be funny and attract
the attention of a famous director who needs a smallish

boy with long legs to play a leading role as Julia Roberts' troubled toy boy in a blockbuster movie premiering at next year's Cannes film festival.

Fatty was beside himself with Shakespearian excitement, and Boggo couldn't stop himself pelvic thrusting wherever he went. Fatty's hoping that spending the third term at Wrexham College will mean an opportunity to score his first ever kiss. He says he's not too ashamed to call himself desperate.

Vern seemed rather disturbed by being cast in the play and pulled his duvet over his head. He then pretended to sleep all afternoon, but I could tell by his breathing that he was faking it.

The only disappointment is the casting of Smith in the role of Puck. No doubt he'll march around again like he's in charge and a superior actor to everyone else. Rambo already hates him and has predicted a series of unexplained events to befall him.

If I were Smith I'd take his warnings seriously.

Wednesday 3rd June

'Sin and Forgiveness.'

Reverend Bishop panicked when Garlic and Boggo entered the vestry having a Bible fight. The chaplain's desperate calls for the pair to settle down were completely drowned out by loud cheering and Boggo's nasty goading of Garlic. After chasing each other around the vestry for a while, Boggo eventually Bible-thumped the back of Garlic's head, sending him sprawling into a cupboard door. Garlic leapt to his feet and charged Boggo, nailing him in the ribs with a resounding blow that sent a hollow echo around the vestry. Boggo collapsed into his chair clutching his ribs and complained that the fight was rigged against him on account of Garlic having the far more lethal King James Version Bible. On closer inspection, Boggo was right. His rather thin and harmless looking Holy Bible didn't match up to Garlic's heavy artillery at all.

But the wily Boggo then reached into his bag and withdrew a gigantic *Atlas of the World* that stopped the advancing Garlic dead in his tracks. The chaplain seized on the momentary stand-off and forcefully ushered Garlic to his desk with his own leather bound Anglican Prayer Book.

That's when the chaplain panicked and asked Vern to open the class with a prayer. It was clear that Reverend Bishop regretted it the moment he'd said it, because a shadow of uncertainty crept across his eyes and he repeatedly licked his lips while shifting uneasily from one leg to another.

Vern buried his head in his bag. Then he raised his head, closed his eyes and snorted loudly to clear his throat. What followed was some loud muttering in gibberish Shakespeare.

By now a ripple of sniggers was beginning to drift around the vestry and the chaplain's eyes darted about as if searching for help. Vern then said, 'For what we're about to receive dear lord make us truly grateful.' He then shouted, 'Amen!' and buried his head in his bag once more.

'Does this mean you're serving a late lunch, vicar?' asked Fatty hopefully from directly behind me.

The chaplain eventually regained control of his face and

informed Fatty that he wasn't serving lunch since it was already 16:30. He then asked Fatty not to refer to him as 'vicar' because it was an outmoded Church of England tradition.

'Whatever you say, boss,' said Fatty and popped a Zoo biscuit into his mouth.

Then Vern lit a match and let it burn down to his fingers. After the flame had disappeared, he dropped it, still smoking, into his top shirt pocket and then opened his Bible to a random page before pretending to read.

'Sin,' said the chaplain in a loud voice, 'is the one single thing that's common to all of us. Yes, boys, we are all sinners.'

Garlic looked deeply offended. He raised his hand and called out plaintively, 'But what have I done wrong?' The chaplain smiled warmly and explained to Garlic that he hadn't done anything wrong but he was sure that somewhere in his past he would have sinned against God.

'When?' demanded Garlic with a rapidly reddening face.

A look of panic returned to the chaplain's eyes and a toothless smile spread across his lips. 'We all sin, Garth. We sin because we're human,' he said, and spread his hands gently to indicate all of us.

Then Fatty argued that the chaplain had no right to accuse Garlic of sins if he couldn't come up with proof.

The chaplain grew frustrated with the debate and exclaimed, 'We all sin because we're human, Sidney. Therefore, I can conclude that Garth has committed a sin against God at some stage in his life.'

Fatty wasn't impressed with this explanation and said the chaplain's logic was unsound because there was no proof that Garlic was actually a human in the first place.

Even Garlic roared at that one. The chaplain tried his best to argue back but his strident voice was drowned out by all the cackling laughter. Then Boggo raised his hands for silence and pretended to read out a quote directly from his Holy Bible. 'Let he who is without guilt, cast the first stone!' He then accused the chaplain of casting the first stone at Garlic.

'Is this a personal vendetta between you and Garlic, Father?' asked Rambo innocently while rocking back on his chair.

The chaplain looked terribly guilty and immediately apologised to Garlic for hurting his feelings. Garlic seemed hugely relieved and said, 'Thank God. I thought I was in trouble again.' Garlic then apologised to the chaplain for blaspheming in the vestry. The chaplain accepted his apology and then apologised to the rest of the class in case we were hurt by anything he said during the class.

Rambo smiled gently and said, 'We forgive you, Father.'

The chaplain let us go early without even reaching the part about forgiveness, which is what I thought Christianity is meant to be all about.

I then followed those without sin into the common room to watch the final twenty-five minutes of The Bold and The Beautiful.

Thursday 4th June

The Crazy Eight was assigned to a compulsory tour of the new computer room with Mr Green at 3:30. It was my first look at the new set-up and it was certainly impressive. We all crowded around Mr Green as he showed us how to switch the computer on at the big white box on the floor. The box is actually the computer!

What I thought was the computer turned out to be the monitor. The round thingy you move the cursor with is called a mouse (?).

Vern really struggled coordinating his mouse and eventually had it pressed up against the monitor screen in frustration before Mr Green intervened and banned Rain Man from touching a computer again unless he was watching.

I must admit it was pretty heavy going. It took ages to find the right key to press and I had Boggo sniggering next to me and writing a rude story about Mrs Bosch on his screen.

We finished the tour with a one-minute speed writing competition. I didn't pick up much speed because I could never find the 'U' and 'S' keys on the keyboard and the loud laughter from everyone watching only made me more desperate. After a late charge where I nailed three words in quick succession I managed a grand total of 19 words in my allotted minute.

Fatty was the best with 38 words (including 10 errors) and Rambo was even slower than me and only managed a mere 17 words. Meanwhile Vern clocked up an amazing 394 words. Unfortunately, the only letters he'd used were G and H so he was disqualified.

Before dismissing us, Mr Green said that by the 21st century computers would rule the world. Rambo grinned and said, 'Not if I get there first, sir.' Mr Green laughed.

14:00   An open list for the St Catherine's Senior Social has been posted on the notice board. So far nobody has written their name down for fear of being mocked for looking desperate, although at least thirty boys are hovering around the quad with pencils pretending to be busy examining the various notice boards. Eventually, Rambo broke the deadlock when he wrote Leonard Pike as the first name down. Soon a mad crush of boys descended on the notice board and within seconds a loud scuffling fight had broken out.

I have decided not to put my name down. I have no interest in seeing Amanda kissing somebody in front of me and Christine is just plain scary. With the first Dream rehearsal beginning tomorrow and what with me playing a serious/comic Shakespearian character, I have no time in my life to be pining over girls.

18:00   Boggo said he had written down all our names on the social list because he wanted witnesses when he unveiled his infamous business card plan.

All right, now I'm going! I'll just not think about it until it happens.

Friday 5th June

A MIDSUMMER NIGHT'S DREAM

REHEARSAL 1

The eight boys of the cast waited patiently in the front row of the theatre. Excitement was bouncing off the walls but everybody was playing it cool as if they had strolled in for a drama prac. It was only then that I realised that Crazy Eight members comprised nearly half the cast. What with Pig, Spike (sort of), Lazarus and Geoff Lawson sitting with us, that left Smith alone and separate. Smith seemed to be learning his lines and didn't appear to care that he was already being ostracised due to his poor personality and excessive arrogance.

'Hey, Smith,' said Rambo jovially, 'what you reading there?'

Smith took a while to look up from his book and then glared as if he had been rudely interrupted from something important.

'I'm learning my lines,' he said in a condescending manner. 'I'm playing the lead, so I have more lines than any of you.' He then returned his attention to Shakespeare.

'You little fuck!' hissed Rambo in a loud whisper. Smith's head shot up once again and met Rambo's gaze with a look of mild shock.

'What did you say?' asked Smith, his face reddening.

'I said, are you playing Puck?' lied Rambo. Smith nodded and said it was one of the greatest Shakespearian roles. He then said he was the only one who was up to the job.

The gathered group wasn't very impressed with Smith's arrogance which seems to have grown exponentially since Oliver two years ago.

'Listen, Motherpucker,' said Boggo in a sharp voice, 'I know your mom thinks you're a great actor, but judging by your feeble effort in last year's house plays I'd say you're lucky to have made the cut.'

Smith showed no emotion and said he had more talent in his little finger than we had altogether. He then said that it was common knowledge that Viking was biased and that Lloyd Creswell was passing around a petition protesting against the one-sided casting.

'I mean, look at Blackadder,' said Smith with disdain. 'He's practically a mongoloid!'

Admittedly, Smith had a case.

Thankfully, Viking and The Guv marched down the theatre steps at that moment because Pig had stood up angrily and was advancing on Smith with the intent to damage him.

'Right!' shouted Viking as he leapt up the steps and came to rest in the middle of the stage. He held his hands out and said, 'And so it begins!'

'Bravo!' cried The Guv and burst into applause. We all clapped along and Viking did an elaborate bow. He then leapt off the front of the stage and stood before us.

'Three rules, gentlemen, and three rules only!' he barked.

VIKING'S THREE RULES

Nobody will speak in a poncy voice like Laurence Olivier.
No farting about in the wings.
No dilly-dallying or depravity with the girls.

Viking then acknowledged that there was some controversy regarding his casting selections and said that he was picking up flak from other housemasters.

'But I don't give a flaming rat's arse!' he boomed. 'I have chosen each and every one of you for a specific reason.' He then dropped a bombshell. 'Under no circumstances do I want any of you to act!' There were some puzzled looks from the cast, especially Smith who clearly thought Viking was joking.

'I want you all to be yourselves – particularly the mechanicals.' Viking explained that he had cast the mechanicals because of our 'natural comic rhythm' that, if replicated on stage, may result in audience hilarity.

Smith snorted and shook his head.

'Smith, you have a problem?' enquired Viking with a ferociously raised eyebrow.

'Yes, sir,' replied Smith in a smug tone of voice. 'Fatty and Greenstein are only here to score chicks and have no acting ability whatsoever and Blackadder is basically retarded.'

'I see,' replied Viking as he vigorously scratched his beard. 'And what, may I ask, has Master Smith ever done on a stage at this school?' Smith muttered on about devising the house play and being the most talented actor in the school. His boasting was drowned out by loud laughter and his angular face grew red and angry once again.

'I'll have you know, Smith,' said Viking in a threatening voice, 'that Vern Blackadder's performance as the prompt in Noah's Ark last year was the funniest thing I've ever seen on a schoolboy stage.'

'It was very Andy Kauffmanesque,' agreed The Guv, and burst into more applause that was warmly supported by the rest of us.

Smith didn't argue and the director moved on.

Unfortunately, the mechanicals are going to rehearse at school every Friday while the lovers and fairies (and The Guv) are travelling to the dingy Howick Town Hall to rehearse with the girls because the Wrexham Theatre is still only a pile of workmen's rubble. Boggo and Fatty responded to this news with a loud groan and were severely shat on by the director.

The good news is that we are spending the entire third term at Wrexham College!! There's also going to be an English teacher exchange because The Guv will be teaching at Wrexham, and one of their English teachers will move into his house and teach his classes next term. Bad news for the poor sods left behind is that Mongrel is taking over as housemaster while Viking is away, which could mean we return to a house of devastation and a pile of corpses.

Viking then handed out scripts and explained that he had spent the last week cutting the play down to two hours long. After taking us through his changes page by page it became obvious that Viking had sliced off a good portion of the lovers and fairies scenes and left the mechanicals intact. Smith was appalled to see that half his lines had been chopped. He was still complaining half an hour later when we filed out of the theatre. Once we reached the foyer, Rambo put his arm tenderly around Smith's shoulder and said, 'Remember, Smith, there is no such thing as small parts, only small actors.'

The Guv caught me up just before reaching the main quad. 'Milton,' he shouted, 'are you aware that we have to share a kiss in the fifth act?' I told The Guv that I was aware of it but was trying not to think about it. The Guv agreed it was a dodgy state of affairs but still seemed thrilled to be leaving the school for a term. 'I've never taught young ladies before, Milton. I intend to blow a good deal of hot wind up their skirts!' Then he marched off towards the san, complaining about gout in his drinking arm.

Saturday 6th June

Boggo and Fatty have waged war on Vern!

In fact, the situation has become so bad that both Fatty and Boggo have even signed Lloyd Creswell's petition to have Vern and themselves thrown out of the play.

The drama began after Spike returned from a hockey match and demanded that Boggo give him a cool haircut before this evening's St Joan's Junior Dance. He's the only member of the Normal Seven to be invited and has been heard bragging about losing his virginity tonight. Boggo charged him 25 bucks, which is the standard rate for wankers/arseholes.

After the haircut, Spike was deeply upset with the sight

that met him in the mirror. In truth his whole head was shaved short apart from a long central tuft that had been shaped into a large penis that pointed proudly at the ceiling. Boggo refused to cut it off and said it was a brand new trend and a powerful artistic symbol. (Since yesterday's first rehearsal/meeting Boggo has seldom uttered a sentence without referring to himself as an artist.)

Thinny ran Boggo in to Norman Whiteside, who immediately raced down the stairs in his dressing gown to resolve the crisis. Thinny scampered back into the bogs ahead of Whiteside and pointed at Spike's head. 'You see, sir,' he said desperately, 'he's made Spike look like a dickhead.' Whiteside wasn't impressed with Spike's phallic haircut and demanded an explanation from the hairdresser.

Boggo said the haircut had an artistic symmetry about it and that the style accurately reflected Spike's personality.

Whiteside ordered the offending tuft of hair to be shaved off and gave Boggo a twenty-minute lecture on art being the root of all evils in the world.

A mere twenty minutes later there was another loud commotion in the bogs. This time Fatty was in trouble for instigating a scrumming competition against the Fragile Five after becoming bored with observing haircuts. According to Boggo, Fatty pushed all five of them right the way across the bogs and into the far wall without breaking a sweat. Suddenly Vern leapt out of a locked toilet stall and gave everybody a blue chit for bad Form in the Bogs and Surrounds. Fatty then lost his temper and ate his blue chit. Vern became enraged with Fatty and ran him in to Meany Dlamini, who then thrashed Fatty, Boggo and the Fragile Five with a plank of wood.

Boggo was outraged that he had been thrashed because he wasn't involved in the scrum at all. (Apart from running a small tote on the sidelines.) Fatty accused Meany Dlamini of being a tyrant like Shaka and threatened to drown Vern in the urinal. Further bad news was that Rowdy burst into tears after his thrashing and then blabbed on the phone to his mother.

The bottom line is that Fatty and Boggo now hate Vern and want him killed or at the very least severely maimed. Vern has said nothing since the incident and was last seen watching the news in the common room with Roger the cat and his toiletries.

Sunday 7th June

9:30   Called Dad to wish him Happy Birthday. By the sound of things he and Mom have been hitting the bottle pretty hard this morning. Dad thanked me for the golf shirt (?) and then asked how the rugby was going. I reminded him that I was banned from rugby because of my concussion. Dad grunted and then asked how the play was going. I told him that we hadn't started rehearsing properly yet. He grunted again and then said he had to turn the sausages over and rang off.

11:00   The lovers set off for their first rehearsal at the Howick Town Hall. Boggo was in the middle of firing instructions to Rambo through the back window of the minibus when it abruptly drove off. Boggo chased the vehicle down Pilgrim's Walk and kept shouting orders at Rambo about compiling a list of the hottest girls in the cast and getting names and addresses of all lesbians and potential lesbians.

Thursday 11th June

I think I've finally worked out what happens behind the scenes in this school. The Glock calls all the staff to a meeting on a particular Monday morning. He then threatens to fire them all if they don't crack the whip and get the boys slaving for their exams. The staff return to class frothing at the mouth like rabid dogs, and set us enough work to keep Einstein busy for an entire decade. Not only do they set mountains of work, but they issue threatening speeches about us falling woefully behind the syllabus. Obviously they never blame themselves for these delays, but rather our poor work ethic. Then they conclude their lessons by setting unreasonable tests in four days' time and threatening us with failure/expulsion/beatings and a dismal future.

If I'm going to become a professional actor then surely working on my Shakespeare performance rather than my schoolwork makes more logical sense? Not that logic ever really worked in this place.

Friday 12th June

1st Proper Rehearsal – The Mechanicals

'A Midsummer Night's Dream involves three intersecting worlds,' began Viking, looking like he might have said these exact words many times before. 'The lovers, the fairies and you lot – the rude working class mechanicals who are galvanised to perform a play in the forest for royalty – this is known as the play within the play.' He glugged desperately from a beer mug of water and continued. 'At its heart, The Dream is about love, passion and magic – it's ephemeral.'

Once again Viking demanded that we didn't try and act

but rather 'search for authenticity in every word, thought and movement'. We then read through the mechanical scenes with Viking stopping frequently to bark at somebody for gabbling too fast. He also wasn't very impressed with Vern's gibberish including Zulu clicks.

We didn't rehearse the 'play within the play' scene because Viking says he only wants to block that next term when we begin working on the Wrexham stage. This was a relief because the thought of acting like a woman and having to kiss The Guv in front of everyone was creating some panic.

'Right!' shouted Viking as he moved further upstage, gesturing with his left hand. 'This is where I envisage the forest clearing where the mechanicals meet to rehearse their play in Act I.' He then pulled off his spectacles and glared at us before saying, 'Gentlemen, gather your scripts, it's time to hold a mirror up to nature.'

I picked up my script and in just three short paces I was up the steps and standing on the stage looking out at rows of dark, empty seats stretching away in front of me. Even my scalp was covered in goosebumps.

Saturday 13th June

10:00   Boggo stole Thinny's bike and cycled off to Nottingham Road to buy flowers for the social tonight. He refused to buy for anyone else because he said it was his spading idea and called us a bunch of plagiarists.

12:00   An extremely grumpy Thinny was waiting for Boggo when he returned and a loud argument broke out at the house door. Thinny once again accused Boggo of stealing and Boggo once again threatened to bonk Thinny's mom. 'But you've got your own bike!' wailed

Thinny desperately. 'I actually own three bikes,' corrected Boggo, 'so you should be bloody honoured that I chose yours again.' Thinny shook his head like he was dealing with a moron and then marched off in a sulk.

Armed with his business cards and twelve yellow roses, Boggo reckons he's got more than enough ammo to start up an orgy later.

ST CATHERINE'S SENIOR SOCIAL

I haven't given girls much thought lately because I've had other more worthwhile distractions to daydream about. The hour long bus trip to St Catherine's presented enough time to think about Amanda, become terrified and nauseous, and then issue myself a stern lecture to silence the gutless coward in my head. By the time we reached the school gates, I had righted the ship and was ready for whatever came my way. I then stepped off the bus and my left leg went lame. Limping into their school hall wasn't the ideal first impression, but at least I managed to sneak in behind Fatty so as not to attract direct attention to my sudden and unexplained deformity.

Boggo did a quick circle of the hall and then ordered us outside for a strategy meeting.

Rambo advised Boggo to take it easy and wait until the party really got going before making his move. Boggo refused, and said by later on all the hot chicks would be taken and he'd be left with large girls with body odour. He then produced a rose and a business card and marched back into the hall in pursuit of the hot blonde dancing next to the DJ box.

Boggo returned thirty seconds later and without saying

a word, unzipped Fatty's kitbag, withdrew another rose and galloped back to the hall. He was back a minute later with a feverish look on his face and shouting, 'Come on, Fatty, bring your kitbag, it's like the sardine run in there!' Fatty grabbed the kitbag and charged after Boggo, leaving the rest of us laughing and mocking and mostly talking about our visit to Mad Dog's farm which is now only 20 days away!

I remained on the bench, even after the others had all gone in to dance. I've never once picked up a girl on the dance floor, this despite the fact that everybody else seems to do it all the time. I also didn't want to bump into Amanda and then have to think of something clever and witty to say.

'Spuddy!' came the high-pitched shriek from behind me. It was Christine and soon she was sitting next to me on the bench. She said she was freezing and wrapped her arms around me.

'Why is Dorkhead handing out roses and business cards to everyone?' she asked. I told her it was Boggo's new spading technique and she roared with laughter. 'Okay, if he had given one girl a rose it might have worked ...' She giggled and said that Fatty was too shy to approach anyone directly so he was leaving small piles of business cards on the snacks and drinks tables.

'Should we go somewhere quiet and touch each other?' asked Christine without even changing the tone of her voice. After struggling for breath, I politely declined and said, 'Perhaps later.' Christine told me I was hilarious, stuck her tongue playfully in my ear and ran off.

Back at the dance, it was clear that Boggo's spading plan had backfired spectacularly. Yellow rose petals littered the dance floor and everywhere people were giggling over Boggo's and Fatty's business cards. The two idiots were dancing together towards the far side of the hall and grinning at anyone who looked at them. Poor Fatty was sweating profusely from all the activity and Boggo's dancing style appeared to be a combination of aggressive head butting and a strip show. Unbelievably, Garlic seemed to be coming right with a girl nearly twice his size, while Vern was solo dancing like a robot near the deserted snacks table. I looked around for Amanda but there was no sign of her. I imagine she thinks school dances are beneath her now that she's a Matric.

Then I noticed a girl dressed in school uniform enter the hall. She paused at the doorway for a moment and her eyes scanned the room like a small falcon. She began walking purposefully towards me.

'Are you Spud Milton?' she asked in a shrill voice.

'Yes,' I replied in an even squeakier one.

'You were Oliver?' she asked suspiciously.

'Yes,' I replied in a deep and confident manner.

'You look different,' said the girl.

'I dyed my hair for the part,' I said rather grandly.

The girl didn't look impressed and said, 'My friends used to think you were hot,' and then looked me up and down as if I'd gone to pieces. 'But that was when we were eleven. We've grown out of it now.'

I nodded and didn't know what to say next.

'Anyway,' she said as if she'd suddenly grown decidedly bored with me, 'Ms Lawrence wants to see you in her study.'

'Who?' I asked.

'Amanda Lawrence. She sent me to get you. Please follow me.'

'Right,' I said and stood up.

I followed the girl out of the hall, over a hockey field and across a neat courtyard. A few older girls stood around talking and drinking tea but didn't seem to notice me pass by. My guide then led me up a double staircase and along a narrow passage with a number of closed doors on either side. It all seemed rather surreal, like I was somehow watching myself from the outside.

I was sure I would be suspended if I were discovered in a girls' boarding house at ten o'clock in the evening. In fact, considering I'm already on final warning thanks to last year's Mad House debacle, this may well be enough to see me expelled. The thing was, at that precise moment, I didn't care a damn.

The girl stopped at a door marked HOUSE LEADER. Underneath was the name AMANDA LAWRENCE (6th Form). The girl knocked timidly but there was no answer. Then she knocked louder and a husky voice called out, 'Come in, Samantha.'

Samantha opened the door and entered timidly. 'Spud Milton to see you, Ms Lawrence.'

The husky voice said, 'Thank you.' Samantha nodded and then let me in.

Amanda's 'study' was also a bedroom, a kitchenette and a small library. Her walls were painted white with beautifully framed poetry and song lyrics hanging at odd angles. There was also a painting of a naked girl with red hair standing against the trunk of a large tree.

And there she was – Amanda – lying in bed dressed in cream silk pyjamas with her red locks spread across the pile of white pillows that supported her head. Littering the bed were books, files and notepads filled with writing that now seemed as familiar as my own.

And then her wide mouth cracked and suddenly Julia Roberts was smiling at me. There was nothing to be done, except to fall passionately in love with her immediately.

AMANDA   Hey, stranger, where've you been hiding?

SPUD   I was going to ask you the same question.

AMANDA   I like the new deep voice.

SPUD   Thank you.

AMANDA   Is it real?

SPUD   (*Blushing*)Sort of. It comes and goes. But mostly goes.

AMANDA   (*Laughing*) You're still funny.

SPUD   And you're still ...

AMANDA   ... Beautiful. I know ... Take a look at this ...

Amanda lifts up her pyjama top and flashes a muscular milky white washboard tummy at Spud.

AMANDA   I've been going to gym – religiously.

SPUD   (*More blushing, and sudden unexplained lameness in left leg again*) Wow! (*Pause, awkward silence. He points to the nude picture of Amanda on the wall.*) Nice painting ...

AMANDA	Thank you. My dad is a brilliant artist.
SPUD	Your dad?
AMANDA	Don't be a prude! It's perfectly natural, you know.
SPUD	(*In nodding agreement*) Of course.
AMANDA	How's the Crazy Eight?
SPUD	Simon's left school, maybe for good.
AMANDA	He was the boring guy with blonde hair?
SPUD	That's him. Anyway we now have a new guy. A crazy Malawian called Garlic.
AMANDA	Why is he called Garlic?
SPUD	Because that's his name.
AMANDA	(*Mocking*) Of course. (*Now looking at Spud directly in the eyes*) Why have you come?
SPUD	Because you invited me. Why did you invite me?
AMANDA	To see if you'd come –
SPUD	Well, I did.
AMANDA	I can see that. So ... how's life?

SPUD	Not bad. I got into A Midsummer Night's Dream.
AMANDA	The Wrexham production?
SPUD	I'm spending the third term there.
AMANDA	No doubt you'll fall in love with some stupid simpering girl who thinks you're marvellous ...
SPUD	What do you care anyway?
AMANDA	Okay, I'm jealous, it's irrational. Get over it.

Toe-curling pause.

SPUD	I'd better go. The bus leaves at 11.
AMANDA	Can I at least have a goodnight kiss?

Spud shuffles forward and leans down to kiss Amanda's cheek. Amanda takes Spud's head in her hands and kisses him passionately. They stare into each other's eyes.

AMANDA	How wonderful.
SPUD	Um, maybe we should –
AMANDA	Good to see you again, John Milton.
SPUD	Good to see you, too, Ms Lawrence.

Pause.

AMANDA	Won't you close the door on your way out?
SPUD	Definitely.

Julia Roberts smiles and Spud limps out of the room, along the passage, down the stairs, and out into the freezing night.

Fade to black.

SCORING SCORECARD

RAMBO	Said there was nobody hot enough to get him interested.
GARLIC	Kissed a large girl called Myrtle.
BOGGO	Disastrous night all round. Handed out 100 business cards and twelve roses, and spent the entire night dancing with Fatty.
FATTY	Still hasn't kissed a girl.
VERN	Danced non-stop like a robot for four hours.
SPUD	Kissed his ex-girlfriend in her room and may just have fallen in love again for a few minutes.

Wednesday 17th June

Today forty-six people were massacred in Boipatong township in a clash between the ANC and the IFP. Lennox said he heard a foreign observer on the BBC stating that South Africa was experiencing a full blown civil war.

9 days until exams begin
16 days until Mad Dog's farm!

Friday 19th June

Viking wasn't impressed with the arrival of the annual NAPAC anti-drugs production. Not only were the actors loud and pretentious but their scenery was also far bigger than expected and the afternoon Dream rehearsals had to be moved off the theatre stage and into Viking's classroom instead.

20:00 The NAPAC drugs play was dire. The crowd behaved poorly and the show had to be stopped twice because the audience was talking louder than the actors. Why is it that these anti-drugs plays always talk to you like you're either eight years old or a head case?

CRAZY EIGHT CRITICISMS

SPUD   Weak script and dodgy acting (especially from the guy with the lisp). If that's the standard of professional acting in this country then I'll be a millionaire by twenty-five! 3/10

BOGGO   Lame play, no hot chicks. 0/10

FATTY   Identified a strong yet spiritual component in the play. Unfortunately, the play has also made him want to experiment with mind-altering substances. 7/10

GARLIC   Said the annual production of Grease in Blantyre, Malawi was far better. 4/10

RAMBO	Worst play ever. Reckons that the actors didn't know what they were talking about. According to Rambo nobody freaks out straight after taking a drag of dope. He said the actors should have at least taken the drugs beforehand, so their performances could be more realistic. 0/10
VERN	Made his feelings felt when he set fire to the play programme. 0/10

Saturday 20th June

Mad Dog called and spoke to every single member of the Crazy Eight. He sounded so excited about us all coming up to his farm that he would frequently bark loudly down the line for no apparent reason. He reckons we will have the time of our lives and that he's going to show us what the African bush is really all about. He then said that he still missed the Crazy Eight and asked me to call Simon to the phone. When I told him that Simon had had a nervous breakdown and left school, he wouldn't believe me and demanded to speak to Rambo again.

Rambo reluctantly came back to the phone and did a brilliant Sparerib impersonation, which Mad Dog swallowed hook, line and sinker. Rambo (Sparerib) gave poor Mad Dog a long lecture about his poor behaviour during his time at the school. He even accused Mad Dog of bonking his wife. The rest of us sniggered as Rambo held out the phone so that we could hear Mad Dog's earnest denials and apologies. Rambo then staged a fake tussle in the background and Boggo seized the telephone and began commentating at a loud volume.

BOGGO	Hey, Mad Dog, it's Boggo!
MAD DOG	Thank God, Boggo! Sparerib has just like

	shat all over me for the stuff I did at school ...
BOGGO	Sorry, Mad Dog, I can't talk. Rambo has just attacked Sparerib.
MAD DOG	What?
BOGGO	He smashed him in the face. He's actually drowning him in the urinal as we speak!
MAD DOG	You're joking!
BOGGO	Listen ...

Boggo holds out phone as Crazy Eight scream loudly and make drowning noises.

MAD DOG	Noways! You okes are completely crazy, man! You'll get expelled.
BOGGO	Too late. OOOOHH, that's a great one, Vern!
MAD DOG	Vern?
BOGGO	Hit him with a half-brick.
MAD DOG	Noways!
BOGGO	Spud's just stuck his knee in Sparerib's groin. Ah gee, that's a typically low blow from Milton!
MAD DOG	(*With rising panic*) Hang on, Boggo, this sounds serious. You can't just beat up a teacher – you guys could get gated and the whole holiday will be cancelled.

209

BOGGO   We couldn't stand by while Sparerib shat
          all over you like that – the oke needs to
          learn some respect. All for one and one
          for all!

MAD DOG   (*Sounding a bit desperate*) What's hap-
          pening now?

BOGGO   No, Fatty, put the knife down! He's not
          worth it!

MAD DOG   (*Panicking*) It's fine, Boggo. I don't need
          revenge. I wouldn't have passed matric
          anyway. Tell them to let him go. No hard
          feelings.

BOGGO   Mad Dog, Sparerib says he's ready to
          apologise and he's coming to the phone ...

Sparerib never made it to the phone because Rambo
was floored by hysterical laughter. Boggo ended up telling Mad Dog that we had to take Sparerib to hospital
and hung up.

The phone rang again and Rambo called Runt out of the
common room and ordered him to answer the call.

It was good to see Runt doing fifty press-ups in the
phone room again. Mad Dog still hasn't lost his magic.

18:00 Rambo formally invited Garlic on the holiday
to Mad Dog's farm. The Malawian's eyes widened and
he leapt up and shouted 'Woo hoo!' at the top of his
voice. He then rushed off to call his mom and ask
her to change his flight home for the holidays. I don't
think I can ever remember Garlic being this happy.
Unfortunately, this meant that he couldn't stop jabbering

away uncontrollably and firing unnecessary questions at everyone while we were trying to swot for exams.

Sunday 22nd June

Pike's back from suspension. He seemed to be in high spirits because he chased Meg Ryan's Son along the cloisters with a screwdriver. Whiteside halted Pike's rampage and asked him why he was in the vicinity of the house. Pike gave our head of house the middle finger and disappeared through the archway with a sneering face.

Exams begin tomorrow. Seven days of hell coming up!

Swatting fever is upon us. The school is like a morgue as everybody crams in as much useless information as possible. Tempers are frayed and Garlic has been banned from asking questions because Rambo says it undermines school spirit. Boggo is also grafting extremely hard for a man claiming to have illegal copies of all our exam papers.

Overall, I'm not too worried about anything except Maths, which has to be the most pointless subject ever conjured up by educators.

Wish me luck!!

Tuesday 30th June

Can't write much because my hand is throbbing from seven days of furious scribbling. My right hand has taken on the appearance of a nasty claw, riddled with paper cuts and badly chewed down nails. My handwriting is completely shot and my brain is so heavy with jumbled facts and figures that it has to be rested on a soft pillow at all times. The thought of our Crazy Eight bush experience has seen me through from the beginning. I feel ready to set free my inner monster.

Wednesday 1st July

Mad Dog called and asked to speak to Rambo. Rambo spent nearly an hour on the line to Mad Dog and scribbled down a series of notes on the back of an exam pad.

Apparently Mad Dog was hugely relieved that Sparerib hadn't been smashed to death with a brick. Rambo assured him that he was fine and that everything had been smoothed over. Mad Dog said he's been having sleepless nights about the Crazy Eight being gated for murdering Sparerib.

Great news is that Dad Dog has come up with a surprisingly brilliant idea. In return for working one day on his citrus farm, we don't have to pay a cent for our holiday. All we have to do is sign a temporary worker's slip and Dad Dog will write our holiday off to tax and simultaneously schnaai the tax man! Dad Dog is even sending down a truck to pick us up from the bus stop in Johannesburg.

Fatty and Boggo weren't very impressed with having to labour on their holiday, while Garlic was so excited about the idea of farming that he lost control and asked three questions in quick succession and was promptly hurled in the fountain.

Mad Dog says we are certain to have the best week of our lives and he's hidden two crates of beer and a carton of cigarettes in a secret location for an almighty thrash in the bush.

I'm already packed! The money thing is a huge relief. Dad was meant to have given me cash at the long week-end but said that he'd poured everything into Frank's pub. He promised he would 'wire' money through to me (?) but so far I haven't seen a cent. The thought of borrowing from Rambo or Boggo meant that I would then owe them something.

As my grandmother frequently says, 'There is nothing funny about having no money.'

Thursday 2nd July

06:20   Mom called to remind me about Wombat's birthday and made me write down the number for Guinea's Rest. She then asked if I knew about Dad's pub. She sounded furious and on the verge of interrogating me so I told her that I was late for roll call and hung up.

14:00   FINAL REHEARSAL OF THE TERM: Looks like nobody has learned their lines apart from Vern, who made a great show of throwing his script down on the front of the stage as if he no longer needed it. The fact that the idiot only has six lines in the entire play didn't prevent him from looking incredibly smug and walking around like he was carrying two surfboards under each arm. Viking wasn't impressed with our words not being learned and said if the play were really important to us we would have sacrificed our exams to study up on The Dream instead!

After the rehearsal Viking gave us a sheet of paper detailing all the items we will need next term when we arrive at Wrexham College. He then handed out another page, which was a code of conduct stapled to the Wrexham College school rules.

'Learn these, gentlemen,' shouted Viking, 'because if you so much as step out of line I'll be dealing with you personally!' He then wished us a good holiday and said if we didn't return from the holiday word perfect, he would bury us alive and screaming in his empty swimming pool. 'I have access to the school bulldozer,' he roared with spittle clinging to his beard. Even The Guv looked afraid.

16:50 Called Wombat to wish her Happy Birthday. Unfortunately, she didn't seem to know who I was and told me all about her brain damaged son-in-law and grandson in prison. She rambled on about crime running rampant at Guinea's Rest and accused Regina, her nursemaid, of stealing her unit trusts. I used Mom's system of repeating 'I know, it's shocking!' every thirty seconds or so and it worked like a charm.

22:30 Whiteside took great pleasure in sending Pike back to his house after busting him horsing around in the Normal Seven dorm. Pike apparently swore and spat at Whiteside who in turn threatened to run him in to Viking and get him expelled. Looks like the cage doors are closing in on the school vermin.

Can't sleep. Truly excited about hitting the road and chasing the sun northwards to the great outdoors. Then there is also the whirring fantasy about arriving at Wrexham next term to the welcome of a long snaking line of the most beautiful girls in the country.

Friday 3rd/Saturday 4th July

Assembly: The Glock wished the cast of A Midsummer Night's Dream a successful stay at Wrexham College next term before launching into a ten-minute tirade about obeying their rules and regulations and flying the flag for our school. My feet were tapping and not a minute ticked by without me noticing.

And then we were running and pushing and mocking down the driveway to where a bus waited to take us to Johannesburg.

Unfortunately, that's where the excitement stopped. The 7hr 42 min bus ride to the City of Gold never seemed to end. The further we travelled, so the landscape became increasingly dry, flat and ominous. All I can say is thank God I don't live in the towns of Warden, Villiers or Benoni! Everybody listened to their Walkmans or stared out at the burnt veld and everything was silent apart from the loud roar of the engine and the shrill squeaking that came from my seat every time I tried to get more comfortable. Slowly the great mine dumps appeared like humungous warts growing out of the scarred landscape as we approached the big city.

17:00   We stumbled off the bus at Zoo Lake in the northern suburbs of Jo'burg. Everywhere were pretty moms with beautiful clothes and blonde hair and smart looking men in suits, leaning nonchalantly against the bonnets of their fancy cars.

It wasn't difficult to spot the enormous white truck emblazoned with the emerald green logo:

HOOPER BROS TZANEEN

The driver was a rather stern looking black man called Emmerson who said two boys could ride up front with him and the rest had to travel in the back with the agricultural supplies.

I asked Emmerson how long it would take to reach Mad

Dog's farm. He smiled and said, 'Long way, umfana. Maybe ... eleven hours, maybe twelve hours.' He then lit a cigarette and ordered us to take a pee because he said we wouldn't stop until we reached Naboomspruit.

After fumbling behind his back for some time, Boggo made us draw straws to see which two would ride up front with Emmerson. Unsurprisingly, Boggo drew the longest straw followed by Rambo which means I'm in the back with Vern, Garlic, Fatty, and the agricultural supplies.

Fatty was sulking because Boggo stated that he was too fat to sit up front. To make matters worse, Emmerson had roared with laughter when he laid eyes on Fatty and repeatedly called him Mafuta. We all bought steak and kidney pies because they were the only things left to eat, while Fatty bought just about everything in the shop, including a tin opener, two cans of baked beans and a large jar of Vicks Vapour Rub. He held the baked beans aloft as he came out of the shop and shouted, 'Mafuta gets the last laugh!'

The thought of riding for eleven hours in the windowless back of the truck with Fatty all stoked up on baked beans wasn't a pleasant one. Rambo and Boggo were the only ones who thought this was in any way funny.

Soon Fatty, Garlic, Vern and I were locked up in the back of the white truck like animals being sent to slaughter. There wasn't even anything interesting among the boxes of supplies. Only fertiliser, tools, overalls, and large bottles of liquid that looked suspiciously like acid.

On the plus side, we found a small shuttered window hiding behind a pile of fertiliser bags. Garlic pulled it open and then gasped in the cold night air like a dying fish. Unfortunately, within seconds the back of the truck was freezing cold and Vern angrily snapped the window shut and then put an entire suitcase of clothes on his body. Fatty honourably offered to give us warning if he felt like farting and promised not to eat the baked beans unless it was an absolute emergency.

It seemed to take hours to get through the rush hour traffic around the city and everywhere was the blasting of horns and the whistle of newspaper sellers. In the gloomy light of the back of the truck it was impossible to read without getting carsick. I lay down on a pile of hessian sacks and closed my eyes. All I could feel or hear were shudders and squeaks as the truck took us closer to Tzaneen.

11:00 After dozing off I awoke to find Fatty wolfing down his second can of baked beans using his comb as a spoon.

'Sorry, Spuddy,' he said. 'It was an emergency.'

The rest of the journey was a nightmare. We couldn't even catch a glimpse of the passing world outside. To make matters worse I no longer felt sleepy and Fatty kept shouting 'Bombs away' before letting rip with foul gas that drove me to the verge of suffocating myself in my scarf.

Only Vern looked completely happy with a night in the back of a lorry after spending all day in the back of a bus. He chatted away to himself and kept himself busy drawing sketches of a bag of fertiliser. It's at times like these that being a cretin is a bonus.

Some time in the night we stopped for what seemed like ages. I heard voices outside but couldn't leave the protection of my hessian bags for the frosty night air. I heard the back doors being opened and then the voice of Boggo as the doors were slammed shut again. And then we were moving again. On and on ...

The dust road woke us all up because suddenly we were being flung around, bashed and battered. I looked at my watch.

3:46am

What a night.

The truck finally came to a halt and the back doors were flung open once again. There was the sleepy face of Dad Dog helping us out of the truck. We followed him like zombies into a darkened farmhouse and into a room with bunk beds. Without saying anything we each collapsed onto a bed and I fell into a warm comfortable sleep.

5:45   It was like a nuclear bomb had been released in our warm and cosy bunkroom. Mad Dog began his devastation by turning Vern's entire bed upside down. He then tackled me off my bed, tried to strangle Boggo with an extension cord and leapt on top of Fatty who screamed like a girl. Mad Dog then pulled Garlic out of his bed and barked in his face. Garlic's mouth fell open but no words came out. The room was decimated within seconds but Mad Dog didn't seem to care. We hurriedly threw on our clothes and staggered after him towards the dining room.

Mom Dog isn't at all what I had pictured in my head. With a freckled face and gingery hair tied in a bun she looks younger than most moms. She smiled warmly at us. 'Welcome, boys, sleep well?' she asked.

It was still half an hour from sunrise but the entire farmhouse was awake. Dad Dog had driven off in his bakkie, and servants were cooking in the kitchen while a great roaring fire blazed away in the living room.

'Drink up,' said Mad Dog before I'd even poured milk into my coffee. After my second sip he stood up and said, 'Right, let's go.' We all followed Mad Dog out of the dining room through the living room. Fatty looked longingly at the roaring fire and the soft carpet and said, 'Hey, Mad Dog, china, no offence but we've only had like one hour's sleep ...'

Mad Dog held up his hand and said, 'The rules haven't changed, Fatty. You sleep when you're dead.'

The rules may not have changed but Mad Dog certainly has. He seems to have doubled in size and his leg muscles are gigantic. The dark stubble lining his cheeks makes him look like a fully grown man and even his voice is deeper than I can remember it being. He led us out through the front door and into the yard. The sky was beginning to brighten and everywhere birds were chirping and tractors were firing to life. The frosted ground crunched under our takkies and Boggo was forced to lean against the front door because he said he had brain freeze. Mad Dog, dressed in short pants, a short-sleeved khaki shirt and dark green veldskoens didn't seem to notice that the temperature was below freezing. Suddenly there was some loud growling and barking from the opposite side of the house. Mad Dog looked terrified and cried, 'Oh, shit, boys! Run!'

'Run!' shouted Garlic without moving.

'The hunting dogs are off their chain!' bellowed Mad Dog as he sprinted across the lawn.

'Hunting dogs!' cried Boggo, leaping to attention and forgetting about his brain freeze problems. Then Rambo was running after Mad Dog. Soon the rest of us were running after Rambo. The barking came closer although I didn't dare look round. It was like I was reliving a nightmare. Why is it that whenever Mad Dog's around we continually find ourselves bolting from the Hound of the Baskervilles? Poor Fatty was a sitting duck for the hunting dog and as the Alsatian gained on him he threw himself stomach first onto the frost and pleaded for mercy.

The dog screeched to a halt and then began sniffing the huge lump that lay spread-eagled and terrified on the ground. Then we noticed that Mad Dog was roaring with laughter and clutching at his chest. They weren't vicious hunting dogs – they were Mad Dog's dogs!

Mad Dog only stopped laughing when Rambo picked him up and threw him down on his backside. Then Mad Dog leapt up and dived on Rambo who collapsed to the ground. Thankfully, Boggo broke up the tussle because it was beginning to look like one of those nasty Dad/ Uncle Aubrey play fights.

Boggo's sniggering drew our attention back to Fatty lying dead still on the lawn while being humped by Mad Dog's Alsatian. Fatty didn't know the dog was humping him and clearly thought that if he played dead the dog would eventually move off. We all fell about laughing, especially when Rambo shouted, 'Hey, Fatty, nice girlfriend!'

Mad Dog eventually called the humping dog off Fatty. Turns out the dog is a 'he' and goes by the name of Bakgat. The other two Alsatians are called Slapgat and Drollie.

Poor Fatty copped some more abuse when it appeared that he had been crying while being humped by Bakgat. He cheered up instantly, though, when Mad Dog promised him a fried breakfast to end all fried breakfasts when we returned from our tour of the farm.

Dad Dog owns two bordering farms that are separated by a dust road. The house is situated on the citrus farm and on the other side of the road is the game farm.

'No way!' Garlic was pointing in the direction of the valley. 'Check all those orange trees!' Everywhere you looked was orange and brilliant green.

'Sweetest oranges, minneolas and naartjies in the entire southern hemisphere,' bragged Mad Dog.

We continued down the hill and soon found ourselves among the orange trees. Just when I thought Mad Dog may have grown up, he branded Vern on the back with a gigantic orange. Vern didn't know what had hit him and sped off down the hill in a panic with the three Alsatians in hot pursuit.

Then an arm tugged desperately at my shoulder and pulled me behind a tree. It was Garlic.

'Please officially introduce me to Mad Dog,' he said in a faltering whisper. 'Please, Spud. I don't feel like I can speak to him until we've been properly introduced and too much time has now passed for me to introduce myself without looking like a complete idiot.'

Luckily everyone was distracted with watching Vern eating an orange on a rock like a baboon. I put my arm confidently over Mad Dog's shoulder and said, 'Mad Dog, I want to officially introduce you to Garlic, the new member of the Crazy Eight.'

Garlic was so overcome with meeting Mad Dog that he bowed to him before thrusting out his hand and saying, 'It's an absolute honour to meet you finally, Mad Dog. I've heard so many of your stories. You're a legend.'

A great smile spread across Mad Dog's naughty face, and he pumped Garlic's hand before enveloping him in a bear hug. Garlic was so overwhelmed with Mad Dog's friendliness that he then called him sir by mistake. Mad Dog roared with laughter before saying that Garlic was the perfect replacement for him in the Crazy Eight.

Garlic beamed with pride and said, 'I come from Malawi. You ever been to Lake Malawi?'

There was a collective groan from the Crazy Eight and loud sniggers from Boggo and Fatty, who had stuffed so many oranges in his windbreaker that he looked eight months pregnant.

Mad Dog didn't laugh. Instead he said, 'Of course I've been to Lake Malawi. It's one of the best places in the world!'

'Really?' gasped Garlic.

Mad Dog nodded. 'My mom's cousin has a cottage up by Cape Maclear.'

Garlic's eyes nearly popped out as he uttered a loud gurgle of delight. 'But that's near where our shack is!' he shouted.

And off they went, Mad Dog and Garlic, marching down the hill in earnest conversation about Lake Malawi. Fatty collapsed against a tree with his face covered in strings of orange. 'We're doomed!' he groaned as one hundred per cent pure orange juice dribbled off his chin and onto the zip of his navy blue windbreaker.

We walked back to the house into the rising sun.

8:30   Garlic called it a feast, Fatty declared it a miracle. Trays of eggs and bacon were carried through. Then lids to pots were lifted and suddenly we had mushrooms, tomato bredie, sausages, boerewors, hashbrowns and melba toast. We all gorged ourselves and hardly a noise was heard until the groaning began twenty minutes later. One by one we excused ourselves from the table, thanked everybody we possibly could, and staggered off back to the bunkroom for the sleep to end all sleeps.

19:00   The roaring wood fire in the back garden melted my drowsiness away and soon I was chuckling along at Mom Dog's story about Mad Dog's grossly enlarged head at birth. The Phalaborwa doctor who delivered Mad Dog said it was the biggest head he had ever seen on a baby.

'Pity it had no brains in it,' quipped Dad Dog as he popped open another bottle of red wine. We all hooted with laughter and Mad Dog lunged at Boggo from across the fire with a red-hot poker.

'What the large head did have in it,' said Mom Dog with a cheeky grin, 'was endless curiosity and a strong instinct for the natural world.' We all groaned as Mom Dog put her arm around Mad Dog who became embarrassed and ran away to chop more logs despite the large pile already under the braai drum.

'Brains aren't everything, Mrs Dog,' said Garlic with a serious expression on his face. After more mocking laughter, Mom Dog instructed Garlic to call her Annie or Mom. Garlic blushed deeply in the firelight and seemed almost tearful with emotion.

'There's nothing like the bush, hey?' said Fatty peering around into the darkness. Then he said, 'Surely it's time to throw on the steaks?' Dad Dog topped up his wine and asked Fatty how much he weighed these days. Fatty said he had no idea because just about every bathroom scale only went up to 125kg and the last three he stood on he broke. Dad Dog said he had an industrial scale in his workshop that measured up to 500kg. A great mischievous smile broke across Fatty's face. He glanced at Dad Dog once again and said, 'So how about those steaks, Dad Dog?'

After a long debate it has been agreed that Fatty will be officially weighed tomorrow after breakfast. Fatty said this would give him his best chance of busting through the 200kg barrier.

It was another feast and soon I was overcome with drowsiness once more. I collapsed into bed like I hadn't slept for days and dreamed that Fatty broke the industrial scale in Dad Dog's workshop.

Sunday 5th July

05:30   I was awake even before Mad Dog stormed into the room and let off a large firecracker that exploded somewhere over Boggo's bed and left a burn mark across the wall. This time I was first to the coffee pot and was able to drink half a cup before Mad Dog's excitement got the better of him and he ordered us to set off.

The .22 rifle slung over Mad Dog's shoulder meant only one thing: we were heading for the game farm. As we set off it wasn't clear if the gun was for protection or to kill and maim wildlife. I had a shuddering flashback to my weekend of hiking with Mad Dog last year, when he threw his knife at me and killed everything from a friendly honeyguide to a family cat.

Vern, Garlic and I had to trot to keep up with Mad Dog's stampeding march through the orange trees. Fatty elected to give the morning mission a miss because he said it might make him lose body mass for the big weigh-in. Instead he opted to stay at the farmhouse and ready himself for the big moment with some meditation and packet of tennis biscuits.

At the base of the hill we met up with the dust road and

followed it for about a kilometre. On our right was the citrus farm protected by a low barbed wire fence. To our left was a fence eight feet high and pumping with electricity.

'It's to keep the leopard out,' said Mad Dog as he chewed on a long stem of dry grass.

'Leopard!' repeated Garlic and stopped abruptly in his tracks.

'They can still jump the fence,' said Mad Dog. 'You never really see them unless you go around at night, and even then it's still pretty rare.'

'Is that why you have the gun?' asked Garlic earnestly. Mad Dog laughed and said that unless he shot a leopard right between the eyes, his .22 would be as useful as an umbrella in a hurricane. Mad Dog has only seen a leopard on the farm twice in his life, but reckons he often finds their spoor down in the dry riverbed.

Vern looked around suspiciously as if he thought a leopard may be watching us, while his right hand snapped out a small clump of hair, which he twirled in his fingers.

Mad Dog carefully unlocked the gate and we followed him into the game farm.

'I don't see anything,' said Boggo. 'Where are the animals?'

Rambo kicked his backside and said, 'It's not a zoo, you wop!'

Mad Dog said that if we wanted to track animals we would have to walk silently and look for spoor.

'Found something!' shouted Garlic, causing a huge flock of birds to explode out of the grass nearby. Unfortunately, Garlic's 'spoor' turned out to be the back half of Vern's Adidas takkie.

'Great start,' sniggered Boggo and plucked a blackjack from his sock before holding it up to the light and examining it closely.

There can be no greater feeling than roaming around in the bush at sunrise on a clear winter's morning. Perhaps standing on a stage in front of five hundred people might eclipse it – and it must be said that since I haven't had sex yet, I can't yet confirm how good that might be. Even still, walking around the bushveld on a crisp winter's morning is still pretty splendid and easily in my top three of all time favourite activities.

THE WEIGHING OF FATTY

The gigantic scale had been brought out of the workshop and placed in the driveway. A large crowd made up of Crazy Eight, Mom and Dad Dog and at least twenty farm labourers gathered in anticipation of Fatty's big weigh in. Speculation was rife about how big Fatty might be, with Garlic throwing around the possibility of Fatty reaching a quarter of a ton.

Fatty looked nervous – he's convinced that he's over 150kg and has been overheard boasting to the Fragile Five that he's most probably over 200. It suddenly seemed that he was terrified that his weight might prove a disappointment. Then Dad Dog started goading Fatty and suggested that he might not even make a hundred kilos.

'I've seen bigger sheep than you,' he declared before erupting into leg slapping merriment.

After the chorus of bleating had died down, Fatty took a long and dramatic breath and then stepped up onto the shiny silver scale, which groaned and then creaked under his great girth. The red indicator immediately shot up to 200kg, but then swung abruptly back down to 120kg. Like a seesaw it went back and forth.

'Wait for it!' shouted Mad Dog.

'Wait for it!' echoed Garlic.

And then it came to rest and the gathered crowd applauded.

It's now official. Fatty weighs 137.75kg!

CRAZY EIGHT WEIGHT (IN DESCENDING ORDER)

FATTY	137.75kg (WORLD RECORD FOR A 16YR OLD?)
RAMBO	88kg
MAD DOG	83kg
BOGGO	67kg
VERN	60kg
GARLIC	58kg
SPUD	55kg

Vern then insisted on weighing the different parts of his body.

WEIGHT OF VERN'S BODY PARTS

Right leg	12.5kg
Left leg	7kg
Rear	45kg
Head	0.65kg
Right arm	18kg
Left arm	5.5kg

On this evidence one would have to conclude that Vern isn't exactly what you would call a well-balanced person. In fact that could be conclusive proof at many universities that Vern isn't even human.

Fatty looked a bit disappointed with not cracking the 150kg mark but cheered up when it was discovered that he was nearly 50kg heavier than Rambo.

19:00 'Um ... whereabouts are we?' questioned Garlic from the far end of the dinner table. The Malawian had paused with a massive fork, laden with chicken breast, two carrots and roast potato, just inches from his mouth.

'You see!' observed Boggo, pointing his dessert spoon accusingly at Garlic. 'His mouth wanted to eat, but his brain had a question! He does it all the time!' Boggo nodded his head slowly and said, 'My oath to God, he's a freak of nature.'

Vern thought this was hilarious and began sniggering deviously from his stool beside me. Everyone turned to look at him so he stopped sniggering, said, 'Garlic!' in a loud voice and then stuffed a large roast potato in his mouth.

Mom Dog took pity on Garlic and explained that the farm is situated 40km from Tzaneen and 75km from Phalaborwa. This didn't resolve Garlic's confusion because the only places he knows in South Africa are Johannesburg, Durban airport, and school.

Tuesday 7th July - Working Day

Swam in the water tank, drove a tractor (Mad Dog controlled the gears and I steered), shot rifles, chased baboons, picked about a million oranges and didn't stop laughing at Mad Dog all day. Not bad for a hard day's work on the farm.

After we had knocked off from our day's labour, we each had to sign a form in Dad Dog's office to say that we were temporary workers on his orange farm. It all felt highly official and manly to be working on the farm and signing employee forms. In fact my first full day's work wasn't nearly as bad as I expected. If the acting thing doesn't work out I could always while away my days steering tractors, picking fruit and chasing greedy apes with Slapgat, Bakgat and Drollie.

Wednesday 8th July

9:30 Mad Dog waited until his mom and dad had driven off to Tzaneen for supplies before making his move. He unlocked his father's office and sat in the black swivel seat behind the desk. Then he picked up the telephone and carefully dialled a number.

'Watch this,' he said.

He flicked a switch and the ringing tone sounded through the loudspeaker.

'Who are we phoning?' asked Garlic.

Mad Dog raised a finger to his lips to indicate silence and we waited for something to happen.

'Hello?' said a high-pitched boy's voice that sounded oddly familiar. Mad Dog didn't say hello back. Instead he said:

MAD DOG   Runt, I hope you're feeling strong because I want you to drop for fifty.

RUNT   (*In shock*) Mad Dog! Um ... look, I can't do them now. My mom ...

MAD DOG   I don't care what you're doing to your mom! I want my fifty.

RUNT   (*Whining voice*) But Mad Dog, it's the holidays.

MAD DOG   I don't give a stuff. Now don't make me come back to school and hang you out the window again! Because I will – I've got wheels now.

Pause.

RUNT   Okay, I'll do them.

MAD DOG   And I want good ones all the way down with a horizontal back. None of that arse in the air stuff!

RUNT   Okay. I'm starting now ...

The sound of bangs and movement on the other side of the line. Then followed grunting, puffing, and Runt's breathy voice slowly counting upwards from five. I wasn't initially convinced that Runt wasn't bluffing Mad Dog, but then we heard his elbows clicking repetitively and the mass hilarity started. We were rolling around on the carpet clutching our mouths while Mad Dog shouted menacing encouragement like an army general.

After Runt was done, he sounded on the verge of death and tried to quickly sign off but then Rambo jumped in and shouted:

RAMBO   Sorry, Runt, that was just the warm-up. This is Rambo speaking.

Very long pause.

RUNT   Rambo!

MAD DOG   Rambo!

RAMBO   It's no good having big pecs and biceps if you haven't got the six pack to match so drop for fifty sit-ups.

Pause.

RUNT   How do I know it's really Rambo?

RAMBO   Just the same way I know you spend way

too much of your time staring at Milton!

RUNT   Oh, hi, Rambo! Sorry, I didn't know what was going on.

RAMBO   Story of your life, buddy. Now stop pissing around and let's hear those sit-ups. Feet raised six inches off the ground and no shamming!

RUNT   Okay. Starting now.

And off he went again. Runt struggled quite badly with the final twenty and by the sounds of things may have injured his back. After he had completed his workout, Mad Dog and Rambo shouted congratulations at him and said they were doing this in Runt's best interests. Then Boggo cleared his throat and said:

BOGGO   Runt, you scrawny little piss drop, this is Lord Boggo speaking. But as always you can just call me Viscount Vagina.

Boggo sniggers at his own joke.

Pause.

RUNT   Boggo!

BOGGO   Now look, there's no point in having great chest and stomach muscles if you run like a pregnant woman. So let's see those knees up and running on the spot! Go!

Long pause.

BOGGO   Come on, I wanna to see your commitment,

Runt. Running on the spot. Go!

Boggo beeps his stopwatch and sniggers to the rest of us. There is no sound from Runt's end.

Pause.

BOGGO   Runt?

Pause.

RUNT   (*Quiet voice*) Ja?

BOGGO   Are you running?

Pause.

RUNT   No.

BOGGO   (*Aggressively*) Why the hell not?

Pause.

RUNT   Because I'm not scared of you.

The line went dead.

RAMBO   Some prefect you're gonna make!

Boggo was seething. The more we mocked him, the more enraged he became. In fact I don't think I've ever seen Boggo so angry. He paced around the room kicking the air and said if Runt were present he would shoot him in the balls with Mad Dog's rifle.

'That's quite a small target to shoot at,' said Fatty, but Boggo wasn't in the mood for jokes.

'In fact, I'd bet good money that Vern has more authority than you do,' added Rambo, who was clearly loving Boggo's public humiliation.

'Twenty bucks!' shouted Boggo and thrust out his hand.

'Twenty bucks!' echoed Garlic in alarm.

'Twenty bucks,' agreed Rambo and shook Boggo's hand.

Mad Dog leapt up and began dialling again. The laughter and mockery subsided as an uncertain Vern stepped up to the desk and dramatically cleared his throat.

'Make him run on the spot,' whispered Rambo to Vern and thumped him on the back. Vern nodded and then furiously licked his lips.

The ringing tone at the other end of the line continued but there was no answer.

'He's playing cat and mouse,' said Mad Dog.

'Keep trying. We'll eventually smoke him out,' said Rambo.

Mad Dog tried again and this time a woman answered in an angry voice.

Vern said nothing and his face began to redden.

WOMAN   Hello? Hello? Who is this?

Then Rambo jumped in.

RAMBO   Good morning, madam. This is Oliver Tambo from the ANC. I was wondering if you would like to join our party?

Pause and stifled Crazy Eight chaos.

The woman hung up. Boggo snorted dismissively and accused Runt's mom of being a racialist.

Before the argument could continue Mad Dog shouted, 'Follow me, buggers!' and tore out the office, across the lawn and down towards the orange trees.

While Mad Dog, Vern, Fatty and I dug for worms among the orange trees, Rambo and Boggo settled their argument with a nasty fruit fight. Rambo won, although Boggo managed to thunder a ripe orange into the back of Rambo's head, leaving his hair caked in orange juice. It didn't take long for us to fill two tins with wriggling earthworms before Mad Dog led a charge towards the storeroom to find fishing rods and tackle. He then set off at a steady sprint for the dam with us once again galloping behind, desperately trying to keep up.

17:00   Mad Dog said the reason we didn't catch any fish was because the water was too cold and Vern made too much noise thrashing about in the reeds.

We returned, showered and once again we feasted.

Amazing how nearly a week has gone by in what feels like a matter of hours. Tomorrow we have our big sleep-out in the bush and then on Friday we leave for home. Perhaps I really should be a game ranger if the acting thing doesn't work out?

Thursday 9th July

ONE TO REMEMBER

15:00   Dad Dog dropped us off at the gate of the game farm.

'Watch out for the leopards,' he said. 'It's breeding season.' He then gave us a wicked smile and roared off back towards the farmhouse. We carried piles of blankets and charcoal, a cool box stuffed with food, marshmallows, jerseys, coats, beanies, long socks and a bag of strange things that Mad Dog thought we might need. Mad Dog, as always, was dressed in khaki and carried his rifle.

16:00   At last our host announced that our camping spot had been found. We dropped our heavy loads and collapsed onto the dry grass where we lay for some time basking in the glow of the warm afternoon sun.

'Follow me!' shouted Mad Dog and he galloped off into the bush, barking loudly. Rambo and Garlic lifted the groaning Fatty to his feet as he wailed, 'Is this meant to be a holiday or boot camp?'

16:30   We found ourselves gathered around what looked like an abandoned well. Garlic peered down into the darkness and asked, 'Aren't these wells meant to be lucky?'
   'Not if you fall in headfirst,' snapped Boggo as he stretched his hamstrings on the wall.
   'How deep is it?' blurted Garlic.
   'Nobody knows,' said Mad Dog mysteriously.
   'Could be haunted,' said Fatty, peering suspiciously into the darkness.
   'What's down there?' demanded Garlic again, his eyes wide with curiosity.
   'The bar,' said Mad Dog, as he felt around the inside of the well.
   'What are you doing now?' asked Garlic.
   'Bingo!' shouted Mad Dog and held up the end of a rope that he immediately tied to his left wrist. He then began pulling something extremely heavy out of the well.

Fatty helped Mad Dog haul the package over the lip and down onto the ground.

The bad news was that maggots had eaten away at the box and two six-packs fell out of the package while it was being winched up. The good news was that something had gnawed away at most of the cigarette carton. This was only bad news for Mad Dog, Boggo and Rambo, who say they like smoking.

'Still,' said Mad Dog after Rambo and Boggo's thorough inventory, 'we got 36 beers and 26 cigarettes.'

'That's what I call a party,' said Rambo.

'Follow me,' said Mad Dog and off we ran, leaving Vern peering over the edge of the well and Garlic demanding to know how Mad Dog knew there was booze down there.

17:00 Mad Dog made the bonfire and allowed Vern to set it alight. Vern strode forward with his tongue out and a full box of matches at the ready. I'm not sure if he was already drunk from his first sips of beer or whether he was nervous, but he made a terrible hash of lighting the fire. First the matches kept blowing out in the wind and then he fell over and scratched himself on the wood. Eventually, he was striking about ten matches at a time and throwing the ball of flame at the pile of sticks. Mad Dog came to his rescue and soon we were standing around staring at the flames with the last rays of the sun filtering through the trees and thorn bushes around us.

The night closed in and the half moon blazed away in glossy cream and yellow. The beer went straight to my head and I found myself cackling uncontrollably at Rambo's impression of The Glock falling off a ski lift and onto his wife. I was so merry that I even forgot to say no when Rambo handed out the cigarettes.

'Do you realise,' I said after some silence, 'that the last time we all sat around like this, was the exact minute before the Mad House was busted.'

'That's powerful!' said Fatty.'

And then we began to relive the old times. From the very beginning when we first met each other over two and a half years ago. First it was Vern wetting his bed, then Fatty's moment in the chapel and nightswimming and Vern running away and coming back. Then it was Julian and Bert and Gavin, the weird prefect under the stairs. Finally, it was my friend Gecko who should have been sitting here with me, laughing at how wild and crazy things seemed back then.

Rambo's voice grew softer and he told Mad Dog about Simon's mental breakdown. Mad Dog wasn't convinced about the whole thing and said it didn't sound like the Simon he remembered. He exhaled a cloud of cigarette smoke into the flames and said, 'I played cricket with that guy like every day – he's as hard as nails.' He didn't buy the story about Simon's dad either and said that Simon never really bothered about whether his dad came to his cricket matches or not.

'Maybe,' said Boggo as his finger rose skyward, 'maybe he's got an Oedipist thing going with his old man!'

'You mean Simon's gay?' gasped Garlic in alarm.

'Bullshit!' shouted Mad Dog and leapt to his feet like his mother had just been insulted.

'I'm not saying he's gay,' said Boggo, looking panicked. 'I'm just saying the whole thing is suspicious.'

'What's suspicious?' demanded Mad Dog as he calmly picked up his rifle.

Boggo's eyes darted nervously between the gun and Rambo, who lay relaxed and thoughtful up against the tree trunk. Boggo stammered, 'Hey, don't get me wrong, Mad Dog. Simon's a legend – like the best guy ever. But you had to be there to see it – he was like weird.'

'Ja, well, I wasn't there to see it, was I!' retorted Mad

Dog with sudden ferocity. We all fell silent. It wasn't just that Mad Dog was holding his rifle and looking dangerous, we'd reached a point where we had relived all the old stories worth remembering and now only had new and more interesting ones to tell. Somehow Mad Dog seemed threatened by our new stories and was unwilling to find joy and laughter in any event that he hadn't been a part of. For the first time I can remember the Mad Dog felt like a stranger among us. It was as if he could no longer understand, nor wanted to understand that we were now different somehow. There was no way of telling him that school wasn't the same as before, and the marauding chaos has been replaced with something older and safer.

Eventually, Mad Dog finished cleaning his gun and packed it away, but the more he drank, the more depressed and bad spirited he became. With tears of frustration rolling down his cheeks, he gave us each one final rib-shattering bear hug before passing out next to the fire and snoring like a chainsaw. There was more silence now than speaking, and gradually everyone buried themselves under their blankets and drifted away.

I lay on my back and gazed up at the sky. It didn't take long for those ever charging thoughts and visions to fly into view. I saw Amanda lying in her bed with those beautiful locks of red hair cascading over crisp white pillows. I saw myself running from above and then flying from below. I saw vivid colours and bright yellow lights flashing and then disappearing. And then a feeling of great stillness overcame me and I closed my eyes, but I swear I could still see the stars.

Monday 20th July

HOME AT LAST

Thankfully, Mom's fury about my father secretly pouring his life's savings into Frank's pub seems to be over. Mom reckons she'll reserve judgement until she's seen the place for herself, although she still hasn't ruled out divorce should this business venture go the way of most of the others. The grand opening is scheduled for Saturday the 1st of August. Let's hope the place looks a little less like a funeral parlour or I might become just another sad story youth from a broken home.

Dad is hardly around any more and spends most of his time working at the pub or sawing wood in his garage. He reckons Frank is going all out and has even imported two handmade Swedish pool tables and a state of the art jukebox from Japan.

I'm ashamed to admit that my toes curl when I think of Dad and Frank's pub.

Wednesday 22nd July

My best-ever report card arrived. Apart from the dodgy E for Maths, the rest was enough to drive my father straight to the liquor wholesaler where he bought large amounts of cheap champagne at a discounted rate.

VIKING'S REPORT

Overall, a fine semester for John Milton. In fact, I am happy to report a complete rejuvenation amongst his year group and, as a result, a far happier house environment all round. While this may be largely attributed to new leadership and tighter disciplinary controls, one may point to an improved attitude amongst the third years as a contributing factor.

John has returned mostly fine academic results, Mathematics notwithstanding. Since the boy has indicated a tendency towards a career in the performing arts, this should not be cause for alarm, although it remains a nasty scab on an otherwise unblemished and impressive academic effort.

John is a lively presence around the house and his warm humour and easy charm make him popular amongst his peers. His warmth aside, one senses that he is at heart a loner, far happier scribbling away at his diary than in the company of the greater bustling group. Nevertheless, he has won the respect of the younger boys in the house and continues to take a full part in daily school life.

Despite a nasty concussion at the beginning of the second quarter putting paid to his winter sporting ambitions, he has recently been elected President of the African Affairs society. It is good to see John in his first position of leadership, albeit in a society of just two members. He also auditioned successfully for A Midsummer Night's Dream to be produced, designed, directed, and adapted for the stage by yours truly. John is a young actor growing in skill and stature, who stands on the verge of an important theatrical experience. I wish him luck.

Mr Bosch informs me that he has displayed a keen interest in general wildlife and geology this term. He has also enrolled in optional confirmation classes, which is an indication of a growing maturity and a deeper spiritual connection with God.

I am expecting more from this young man in the days and months to come and trust that he will not disappoint me in his endeavours.

Regards
Mr Richardson BA UED (HONS) Rhodes University

SPUD'S REPORT

Viking has made a confident start to his career as housemaster. Not only has he de-prefected Pike, but he seems to have lowered the general level of violence in the house. Unfortunately, he's had to use extreme violence in the process, which is deeply ironic. On the plus side, he didn't laugh when Spud Milton said he wanted to be an actor, and unlike his predecessor, hasn't tried to ban him from keeping a diary.

Viking is prone to periods of non-stop shouting and frothing at the mouth. He should try to chill out more and be angry less. He recently turned 50 and still isn't married. Nobody is sure why he still lives alone but three reasons are regularly bandied about:

A) All women are terrified of him.
B) He's not straight.
C) He has an unnatural relationship with his cat.

I look forward to seeing how Viking behaves in a girls' school environment and if he has a nervous break-down during the rehearsal process.

Regards
Spud Milton (3rd year senior)

Thursday 23rd July

16:00 Amber phoned and asked me to call Dad. I found my father sawing away at a large block of wood in the garage. When I informed him that our neighbour was on the line, he leapt up and charged past me like Amber might have been calling long distance from Helsinki.

'Don't have a heart attack,' hissed Mom, as she placed a fresh bowl of water inside Blacky's kennel. My father pretended not to hear and didn't stop running until he was inside the house. Minutes later, he stepped casually out of the house, whistling to himself and doing a very bad impression of somebody acting cool.

'Thinking of spraying the roses,' Dad said in a weird voice to nobody in particular. Mom said nothing and returned to the house. Dad then looked at me and said, 'Might as well spray Amber's roses if I'm spraying mine ...' I nodded back at Dad, and for some time we nodded together. 'It makes sense,' he said.

16:15 Caught Mom on top of the stepladder peering into Amber's garden. When I enquired about what she was doing she hurried back down and hauled me into the kitchen.

'Your father is having an affair,' she said, before conceding that she didn't have a shred of proof yet. She then accused Dad of having a permanent midlife crisis and called Amber a dolled-up man-eating bimbo. My mother's voice faded to a whisper as she offered to double my pocket money if I spied on my own father.

I refused.

Later I went riding and re-imagined arriving at Wrexham, and suddenly felt nervous and excited, but more nervous.

Saturday 25th July

Mermaid called to congratulate me on my exam results. She then invited me out to dinner with her and Gavin at his parents' house. 'I'm dying for you to meet his mom and dad,' she said, as if I may find that experience hugely exhilarating. I quickly told her I was going out with friends and she sounded surprised. We agreed that we would see each other next Friday for the official pub opening and she blew me a friendly kiss over the phone.

Why does she keep inviting me to hang out with her boyfriend? What does he really think? Surely Gavin should be jealous of me? If he isn't jealous, then why not? (It should be remembered that Gavin is, after all, an evangelical cricket umpire so truly anything is possible.)

This also means I won't escape the Mermaid this holiday. Let's hope she's suddenly developed a beer gut or a bad case of acne. Most of all, I hope her breasts have shrunk, so that I don't have to feel them rubbing up against my chest when I hug her. I deeply regret promising her that we would be best friends for life. What was I thinking? (Major schoolboy error.)

Dad has banned everyone from seeing the pub until it's finished – he maintains it already looks fantastic. One week until the official opening, and I'm beginning to worry about my father's sanity and marriage should this go the way of all his other business ventures.

Sunday 26th July

5:15   I thought we were going fishing. Firstly, it was still dark. Dad definitely had that manic look in his eye, and the manner in which he shook me awake and spilled coffee all over my bedside table led me to believe that the man was in an excitable mood.

'Low tide at 5:56!' Dad informed me at top volume as the station wagon roared to life. It was still dark and chilly outside and I desperately attempted to return to my dream about the naked woman with the long creamy neck that I was chasing down on horseback. It was such a good dream that my nuts were aching like I'd really been horse riding all night. Not exactly sure how that happens but at 5:45 in the morning I didn't really care.

It was only when we reached Umdloti beach that I realised my father hadn't packed any fishing rods. Dad leapt out of the car, creaked open the boot and pulled out a large pair of gumboots. He then struggled to squeeze them onto his feet and grew red in the face and instantly bad tempered. After a poor attempt at stepping into a wetsuit, he gave up and placed an old pair of goggles and a snorkel on top of his head. He then pulled his yellow rose pruning gloves over his hands and ordered me to lock the car and follow him.

'Um ... Dad, what exactly are you doing?' I asked, watching him struggle through the soft sand in his gumboots.
   'We're catching seafood,' he said. 'I'll be buggered if I have to pay an arm and a leg for mussels and crayfish.'
   'Don't you need a licence for catching stuff like that?' I asked.
   'That's why we're doing it at sunrise on a Sunday morning,' replied Dad as he stuffed a Checkers packet

into his swimming costume. He then charged forward and crashed headfirst into the sea. After the briefest of thumbs ups, he sank below the surface and became a dark crocodilian shape lurking under the water with a luminous orange periscope attached to its head.

My job description was holding Dad's towel, holding the car keys, and on a more general level, holding the fort. A few fishermen stood with their big rods at the far end of the beach where the waves crashed into the rocks. Otherwise the place was completely deserted.

I followed the huge orange sun as it lit up the sea with shimmering prisms of silver light. The sun made me feel drowsy again and as I basked in its warmth, I felt my eyelids grow heavy and my mind become hypnotised by the rhythmical sound of waves crashing onto seashells.

When I woke again it was bright and sweltering and the beach was littered with people. Small kids were playing nearby with a beach ball and it must have been their screams that woke me from my exhilarating dream of running for South Africa at the Barcelona Olympics. Thankfully, I hadn't reached the actual running part, because I sense from that point onwards it may well have turned into a horrible nightmare.

Interesting discovery. Somebody had drawn a giant heart around me while I was sleeping. It certainly hadn't been there when I first sat down. The heart was beautifully drawn and the indentation in the sand where I'd been sleeping lay perfectly where a heart's heart would be.

I scanned the beach. Could a shy but beautiful girl be sending me a message of love? Could it be the pretty girls in bikinis tanning near the lifeguard perch? I stood up and stripped off my jersey and shirt and then sat down again. I scanned the beach again to see if anybody was watching me now. Only the elderly couple in tanning chairs shifted their heads momentarily before turning their attention back to their newspapers.

After summoning up some courage I strolled up to the group of girls and spread my towel no more than five paces behind them. This was a brilliant plan because they were all facing forward towards the sea and I could keep an eye on them while pretending to gaze at the ocean myself.

One of the girls turned around and stared directly at me, although her expression was at best neutral and at worst 'Get lost!' I kept my head down and soon they returned to gossiping about a girl called Janine who had fallen pregnant but didn't know who the father was. I noticed the brunette with sunglasses throwing me the odd glance. I tried to smile at her but my mouth wouldn't open.

Then the brunette with sunglasses asked her friend to rub suntan lotion on her back. The friend was happy to oblige and in my opinion seemed to cross the line of friendship with her excessive rubbing and near groping. I wondered if the brunette might in fact be doing all this intentionally. Perhaps this was her next move? If it was, then I had to make *my* next move … Now that I was sitting just a few paces behind them, there was very little I could do besides starting a conversation.

I waited for the girl to stop talking to her friend and then I blurted out, 'Sorry, what's the time?'
    'Excuse me?' said the girl.
    'Sorry,' I said again, 'I just wanted to know if you had the time on you?'
    'Just after ten-thirty,' she replied.

'Thanks,' I said and grinned like a hyena.

'Pleasure,' she said and smiled back.

I wish the chat could have gone on but there wasn't much to say after she had given me the time. If I was closer I could have said something smooth like, 'That's a beautiful watch. Is it waterproof?'

I began thinking that perhaps this is how so many strangers end up having sex. It has always seemed so impossible, but suddenly I can imagine how it could happen. Even possibly to me – on a beach, with a topless brunette.

I was planning my next move when I caught sight of him. It was like a figure from a nightmare. With gumboots squelching loudly, goggles on his head and a ghastly protruding lump in his costume, which had to be his hidden packet of seafood. He staggered nearer. It was too late to run. There was nowhere to hide, besides burying myself in the sand, but it was too late for even that because my father had already seen me. I prayed that he wouldn't say or do something embarrassing but with the girls already pointing and giggling at the strange frogman marching up the beach, I knew all chances of a dignified outcome were gone.

Twenty paces, nineteen, eighteen … Dad approached in slow motion. My toes curled inwards, as did my fingers. If he kept up his current line my father would practically walk straight over the girls to reach me. What a blunder. There's enough humiliation in my life as it is, there's really no need to commit suicide.

Like a very slow and deadly missile he approached. I could see the whites of his eyes, which I've learned over time is never a good sign. The girls were all watching my approaching father, suppressing their sniggers and trying not to appear obvious. But they were.

Dad was so close now that I could hear the heavy thump and squelch of gumboot on sand. I didn't know where to look or what to do. He was only a few feet from the girls now.

And then he shouted, 'I've got crabs!'

And pointed triumphantly at the great deformed lump in his costume.

I didn't look up again. My face was burning with shame as I heard the loud laughter and shrill giggling from the gossiping girls in their bikinis. One of the girls said, 'That is ... so gross!' And they all laughed again. I turned and hurriedly followed my father up the beach, relieved that the girls could no longer see my face and hopefully never would again.

DAD'S HAUL OF SEAFOOD (illegally poached)

14 crabs
2 fishing hooks with nylon attached
1 octopus, which Dad intends passing off as Norwegian calamari

Dad bemoaned the lack of crayfish and mussels on the rocks and declared that the entire South African coastline has been raped by human greed. He blamed illegal poachers, radical leftists, and the Indians.

On the drive home my father admitted for the first time that all is not well with the pub. Dad and Frank have run out of money and can't even afford booze to stock up the bar. He made me promise not to tell Mom about this and offered to double my pocket money if things went well at the pub. He didn't say anything else on the drive home because his mind was already racing elsewhere.

Tuesday 28th July

The pub is in crisis! The Swedish pool tables arrived by boat this morning. The good news is that they apparently look fantastic. The bad news is that they only work on Swedish currency. It seems that the only way to shoot the balls out of the bottom of the machine is to place a Swedish krona in the slot. There's also been a mutiny against the pub's name – Frank's Bar and Grill, Snooker and Darts. Dad says the name won't work because there are no snooker tables, no dartboards, and all the food is deep fried in oil.

Dad and Uncle Aubrey (small foreign investor) are gunning for the name Franky's.

Just as well Dad isn't hanging around the house, because Mom is livid that he's invited Amber to the pub opening on Saturday without asking her first. My mother thundered up and down the passage shouting, 'I won't set foot into that place if *that* woman is there!'

Wombat has also refused to attend the grand opening because she says the pub's in a common area and she's worried about being gang raped.

Thursday 30th July

The tension is building. In just four days I'll be off to Wrexham to ply my trade as a real actor in an epic Shakespearian play. Mom drove me to the La Lucia Mall to shop for the strange and mysterious things on the Wrexham 'To Bring' list.

TO BRING LIST (AS ISSUED BY WREXHAM COLLEGE)

- Sewing kit
- Shoe polish kit
- Warm coat (our Winters get nippy!)
- Candle (white)
- Candle holder (white or cream)
- Facecloth (white)
- Soap
- Soapdish
- Slippers
- Showering sandals
- Sanitary pads (?)
- Sunscreen
- Homework diary
- Teacup/mug (white or cream)
- Laundry bag (white)

Not sure what the obsession with white and cream is. Mom says it's probably about encouraging a feeling of purity and cleanliness. If that's the case I'm not sure why they are allowing Boggo and Fatty in. Mom reckons private girls' schools promote general snootiness, bitchiness, slutty behaviour and Prog leaning tendencies. Should be an interesting term ...

I did a complete afternoon run through of my lines with my mother. I'm officially word perfect – and feeling extremely confident about that first rehearsal with the entire cast. Mom said the high-pitched girl's voice, which I use to play the character of Thisby in the play within the play sequence, is hilarious and she ended up nearly weeping with laughter. I know she's my mom and all, but she hasn't laughed since Christmas last year so this must be taken as a positive sign.

Dad has finally won the battle and the pub will now

be called FRANKY'S. The deal was sealed after the dartboards failed to arrive by 3pm.

Saturday 1st August

The official opening of FRANKY'S. (The first ever pub owned by a South African Milton!)

19:00 For once I was glad Marge was in the car because Mom was clearly nervous. She kept saying, 'I hope he doesn't make a complete bloody fool out of himself.' Marge tried to persuade Mom to be more supportive, but Mom just shook her head and chewed away at her lips.

19:20 Driving along Umbilo Road and Mom was clearly expecting the worst. She stared out grimly at the dilapidated buildings and kept shaking her head in dismay.

19:25 I noticed a large number of cars lining the street near the pub and a crowd of people chatting away happily at the entrance. In my extremely limited experience of pubs and clubs, this is always a good sign. We parked on the pavement and quickly made our way towards the pink neon sign that read:

FRANKY'S

Underneath was a smaller neon sign in blue that read:

ICE COLD BEER!

To the right of the door was a printed sign that read:

NO MINORS. ENTER AT OWN RISK!

We entered a cosy pub coloured in green and dark wood. A wall of sound greeted our arrival. The pub was packed with so many people that you had to say 'excuse me' every time you wanted to move. There was a massive throng around the bar where Frank and Dad were pouring drinks and joking with the customers.

'But ... but it looks like a real pub,' gasped Mom as she looked around the place in wonder.

'It's wonderful,' said Marge.

'But ... it looks like a real *London* pub!' repeated Mom with her mouth hanging slack in amazement.

Dad sped around the bar to meet us. Mom gave him a big kiss and said, 'It looks like ...' Dad didn't let her finish. Instead he lifted her high into the air and shouted, 'It's a hit!'

'But how?' asked Mom, still looking stunned.

'We were saved by an angel,' said Dad and pointed at Shannon who was busy carrying a tray of burgers out of the kitchen. 'She may have treated poor Franky like a turd, but she's come to the rescue big time on this one!'

By the way Shannon was marching around shouting orders at waiters and bar staff, it would appear that she's in charge of far more than the kitchen. Then there was a loud pop and the champagne began to flow.

Clutching my glass of bubbly, I moved around the pub not recognising a single soul. Bryan Adams' Summer of 69 was playing over the Japanese jukebox and people were dancing where they stood and pouring my father's booze down their gullets.

Either the pool tables were now mysteriously working, or the people of Lower Umbilo carry Swedish currency around, because balls were being sunk and a serious pool competition was under way. It's probably just as well that the dartboards hadn't arrived because somebody would surely have lost an eye in the packed opening night chaos of Franky's bar.

I felt so proud of my dad that I had a lump in my throat. If you hadn't ever been here before you would never know that this place of joy and laughter was previously a cut-price funeral parlour – I bet this is just the kind of place where Shakespeare might have enjoyed a pint.

Good news on the Amber front. She had her arm around a man with silver hair and a smart jacket. I observed her for about twenty minutes from a small nook near the bathrooms. She didn't look in Dad's direction. Not even once. But my spying on Amber was cut short the moment I caught sight of Mermaid at the door. I craned my neck to look for Gavin, but it appeared that he wasn't with her.

I began to observe Mermaid as she made her way through the crowd towards the bar where Mom and Marge were perched on barstools still throwing back champagne. She chatted for a while and then began moving around the pub looking for me. I couldn't delay any longer.

'Johnny!' she shouted when I suddenly appeared in front of her. Unfortunately, she showed no signs of acne and a beer boep. She looked like she always did at night – like a fizzing sparkler ready to explode.

'Let's go to the beer garden.' She had to raise her voice to be heard above the din.

'What beer garden?' I asked. But she was already leading me by the hand towards the door that led to the room where the dead bodies used to lie.

The room was gone. Instead the door led to a messy

backyard where plastic chairs and tables were scattered among workmen's rubble and piles of bricks. It wasn't the most romantic of settings, but at least it was quieter and you could talk without shouting.

'You're a hard man to see these days,' said Mermaid with grin.

I grinned back but didn't answer.

'Gavin sends his regards,' she said and waited for a response.

'Great,' I said and took a big sip of sweet champagne.

'He doesn't feel comfortable in bars. He thinks they're places of sin.'

'Well, that's his opinion,' I said in an icy tone.

Mermaid obviously realised that I wasn't impressed with her comment because she then started rambling on about how nice the pub was and what a great job Dad and Frank had done. I didn't really listen because I felt a rising surge of anger inside me. It had nothing to do with Gavin, and everything to do with her. With every movement of her lips another painful memory returned. I realised in that moment that I couldn't carry on like this. I had to be honest with her for the first time in over two years. I had to tell her how I felt. If I didn't set myself free right now then all I could ever say was that I missed the moment – again. It was time to be a man and stop hiding from the termites that gnaw away at my brain whenever I think of her.

'I don't think we can be friends any more.'

In retrospect my announcement must have come as quite a shock for Mermaid because she was in the middle of telling me about her modern dancing exam.

'I can't do this any more,' I said strongly to drive the point home.

'What?' she said. She looked nonplussed.

'I can't be friends with Gavin and I can't be friends with you,' I said and took a long sip from my empty champagne glass. Mermaid didn't notice the blunder because her eyes had filled with tears.

'But I love you,' she said and turned her face away from me.

It takes a brave and courageous man to hold his nerve when confronted with a beautiful girl in tears. Unfortunately, I am no such man. My anger disappeared and I was struck with the sudden desire to hold her in my arms and kiss her.

'I can't take seeing you with somebody else,' I said in a quivering voice.

'I know,' she whispered. 'I just hoped that if you two could become friends ...' She didn't finish the sentence.

'I can't,' I said.

'I love you,' she said again, more desperately this time. She was crying now and I hardly heard her say, 'I always will.'

'Me too,' I replied and then had to look away.

I felt a feather of a kiss on my cheek, and with a swish of wispy blonde hair she was gone.

And she really was.

Monday 3rd August

It's like my first day at school all over again, except this time I don't fear the unknown. If The Guv is right, and life is just a series of unrelated experiences, then this is definitely going to rank as one of the good ones.

Mom and Dad are playful again. Happiness is everywhere, except in my mind when I think of Mermaid. I carefully packed my suitcase and kitbag, and then sat on my bed and ran through my lines one final time. I stood up, closed the windows and drew my old lady curtains. I then left the tranquillity of my room for whatever it is that awaits me.

18:00 It was a bizarre experience standing around the school entrance neither in nor out. I could hear the usual bustling going on in the quad and the sound of trunks scraping on stone. Boggo set off to rile up the Normal Seven while Fatty made a beeline for the first year dormitory where he pilfered a jersey full of Plump Graham's tuck. Rambo sat on the wall looking composed and snooty, while Vern struck matches happily on the lawn. Eventually, my curiosity got the better of me and I sneaked around the chapel entrance and into the flower garden where I had a clear view of the house door. Norman Whiteside was having a conversation with somebody inside while he leaned nonchalantly against the common room wall.

'What do you mean I'm the only one?' shouted a high-pitched insistent voice from inside the house. Our head of house mumbled something back to the hidden shouter, who clearly wasn't impressed with his explanation.

'Where's Simon?' demanded the loud unseen voice from inside the house.

Whiteside shrugged and then rebuked Rowdy, who was passing by, for having his shirt un-tucked. The first year cleaned himself up and then scurried into the house before Whiteside could begin a lecture.

'So I'm sleeping alone,' whined the unseen voice again. Whiteside sipped from his tea mug and didn't reply. Then the loud voiced boy stepped out of the door and with huge saucer-like eyes begged, 'Can't Mad Dog come back, just for a term?'

Whiteside laughed loudly and didn't reply.

But Garlic wasn't giving up. 'How can there be only one member of the Crazy Eight left?' he demanded.

Norman Whiteside said that in his opinion one was

one too many, and pushed past the desolate Garlic before disappearing into the house. Garlic stared out at Pissing Pete like he was contemplating suicide. He then took in a few deep gulps of air and seemed to completely zone out on the tower clock.

'Don't worry, pink face,' snarled a low and miserable voice. 'I'll keep you company.' Pike slid his arm around Garlic's shoulder. Garlic stood stock-still like he was having a life and death stand-off with a poisonous snake.

Then Vern's demented face leered in beside mine. Clearly the idiot thought I was spying on something interesting and craned his neck to see what I was looking at.

'What you looking at?' hissed Vern in a conspiratorial manner.

'Garlic and Pike,' I hissed back and pointed to where Pike was now strangling Garlic in a half nelson. Vern then said, 'Garlic,' and sniggered away to himself like it was the funniest thing ever.

'You two boys!' shouted an ominous voice from just behind us. It was Viking dressed in tight denim jeans and a leather jacket. 'Milton? Blackadder?' he said loudly when he recognised who we were. 'What are you two boys doing in the rose garden at night?'

'Just looking,' replied Vern and then pointed straight at the chapel wall.

Viking's eyes darted around in confusion.

'Just looking for what, Blackadder?' he demanded as he tried to remain on the offensive. Vern became embarrassed and looked directly at his toes. He then said, 'Garlic!' and squinted his eyes up towards Viking without shifting the angle of his head.

'Garlic?' boomed Viking in surprise.

'Yes, sir, Garlic,' said Vern.

There was a long pause before Viking let out a long sigh and said, 'Very well. In the Hiace, on the double!'

The minibus was parked under a street lamp and I could see the silhouettes of Boggo, Fatty and Rambo arguing about who would ride up front with Viking.

Vern sped through the rosebushes and charged off towards the minibus like there might not be any space left. Viking watched him go and then shook his head and murmured, 'Should be an interesting seven weeks, Milton.'

'Yes, sir,' I replied.

We walked towards the waiting minibus. Viking didn't say anything further and seemed to be lost in thought. I didn't know if I should say something to start up a conversation. After running through a list of conversation possibilities I felt like too much time had passed and starting a conversation would be a bit lame. In the end I remained silent and also pretended to be lost in deep and important thoughts.

Surprisingly, Boggo had won the battle for the front seat and he immediately signalled his intentions when he shouted, 'Let's hear it for the world's greatest director!' as Viking pulled open the driver's side door. We all cheered and applauded and Viking looked thrilled. Rambo's knee slammed into the back of Boggo's seat. Luckily he was wearing a seatbelt because thanks to the power of Rambo's knee and the thin Hiace seats, Boggo might well have been propelled through the windscreen.

'Now listen up!' shouted Viking as he swivelled angrily to glare at us. 'I've already caught Blackadder and Milton in the rose bed. They claim to have been looking for garlic for some hitherto unexplained reason.'

Sniggers broke out from various places but Viking's rage quickly silenced them.

'Now look here, I'm not stupid. If you boys want to stuff around picking roses and romancing girls ... I'll have you sent home sooner than you can say ... mark my words ... if one of you sticks a foot out of line ... so help me God ... you little bastards!'

'Yes, sir,' we all murmured and looked elsewhere, desperately trying not to laugh at the director's nonsensical threats.

'Good!' shouted Viking as the engine kicked to life. 'Now, Mrs Owen will be taking care of you during your stay at Wrexham and she will report directly to me!'

We all nodded and said 'Yes, sir' again.

'Who's at the back?'

'Me,' came the smug voice of Smith.

'Who's me?' roared Viking. 'Godammit, boy, can't you see I have a major Shakespearian production to mount spanning two schools and both sexes. You think I even have time to ask the question, WHO IS ME!'

Smith apologised profusely and identified himself twice. Viking ordered him to find his rifle case and open it. Geoff Lawson, sitting next to me, gasped in panic. Nobody wants to see a rifle in the hands of an unhinged theatre director. Thankfully it wasn't his gun but his cane.

'Pass it around,' said Viking with a wicked grin. 'I want everyone to feel its texture.'

We passed the cane around. It smelled of furniture polish. Back in my old Spudly days this tactic may well have terrified me, but a few years in the funny farm has dished up far worse than Viking's stick. I wasn't the only one who wasn't terrified. Rambo had wedged the cane between his legs and was pretending it was his penis. He then kept resting the tip of the cane on Boggo's ear. Boggo couldn't do anything for fear of riling up Viking so he tried to pretend that he didn't feel his ear turning pink then red then purple.

WREXHAM COLLEGE FOR GIRLS (Pietermaritzburg)

The name was written in black letters on a white gate, which swung open after Viking had hooted impatiently and shouted loudly out the window. It was impossible to see much in the darkness but I was immediately struck by how open everything was. We followed a long driveway, passing signs for squash, tennis, swimming, and the gymnasium. Everything was quiet and chilly and not what I was expecting.

I think Viking may have become lost driving around the Wrexham estate, because it took him at least twenty minutes to find our boarding house. I could feel the excitement building in the car as we craned our heads to get a better view of the school buildings. And who knew, perhaps even a girl.

'Where's the bloody sign?' barked Viking as he screeched to a halt outside a white building marked Elizabeth House. We staggered out of the minibus and were met by a woman who looked like a bulldog. She was also looking angry and stood, hands on hips, ready to attack.

'It's half past eight!' the woman declared. Viking was in no mood for taking crap from the matronly bulldog and ignored her completely.

'All right, Black, Fatty, Greenstein, Milton and Black-adder – get out. The rest stay where you are,' said Viking impatiently.

'Good luck, Spud,' whispered Geoff Lawson. 'I'd stay out of her way if I were you ...' He gave me a jab on the shoulder and a thumbs up.

'Thank God we're not sleeping with the crazies,' I heard Smith say to Spike as we stepped out of the van. Spike didn't answer. The first question has been answered. The Crazy Eight have been quarantined from the rest of the cast and quite possibly the rest of humanity.

'Hurry up, Fatso!' said the matron as Fatty struggled with his bags and stolen tuck. Then she pushed Rambo on the back and said, 'It's past bedtime, you know.' Rambo's back stiffened, but he walked on and didn't reply.

We entered Elizabeth House and discovered that it was, unsurprisingly, painted white and cream. The matron led us down a dimly lit corridor and then into a small common room and kitchenette.

'This is your communal space. It is to be kept clean at all times,' she said before glaring at us accusingly and asking, 'I hope you all brought your mugs?' We all nodded.

Two rooms led off the common room and each had three wooden beds and a cupboard.

'My name is Ms Owen, although round here I'm known as Mr Owen,' said the matron without looking too displeased about being known as a mister. 'I'm in charge here and that means very much in charge.' We all nodded like mutes.

'You can decide on sleeping arrangements among yourselves. You have fifteen minutes to prepare for bed and then I'm turning the lights out.' We all stared at her like stunned mullet.

'You may use the girls' bathroom down the corridor on the right, and please stand the seat up when urinating.' She then turned on her heel and marched out.

I knew how the sleeping arrangements were going to pan out even before Boggo called out, 'Hey, Rambo – why don't you pull in with me and Fatty?'

I looked at Vern and he looked at me. I grinned at him and he grinned at me. We weren't grinning about the same thing.

Tuesday 4th August

6:30   It took quite a while for me to figure out where I was when I first woke up. I could hear the unfamiliar sound of girls' voices and hushed whispers. The sunlight was pouring through the open window and directly onto my face so I couldn't open my eyes properly. Gradually, I became aware of somebody moving around in the little common room next door. There was the clink of coffee cups, hushed whispering and the odd sneeze. Thinking it was Boggo making his tea, I leapt out of bed wearing only my sleeping shorts and a T-shirt, and pulled open the inter-leading door only to be met by the surprised faces of two young schoolgirls dressed in white school uniforms. They both seemed to be examining our coffee mugs closely and gaped at me with guilty expressions on their faces. They couldn't have been older than thirteen and looked even younger.

'Hello,' said the one that looked slightly Spanish. 'My name is Brenda, and this is Penny.' Penny was taller than her friend, with blonde hair and railway braces. She had that look about her that suggested that she might be stunningly beautiful in five years' time.

Right now two inquisitive girls were the last thing I needed and I tried to wave them off and go back to bed but they stopped me.

'Mr Owen has put us in charge of keeping things orderly,' announced Penny. She then rolled her eyes at her friend as if I was a complete moron.

Brenda has a dark complexion with brown eyes and hair, and a rather sweet round button nose. She grinned at me impishly and said, 'We already know who you are.'

'Really?' I asked as I switched on the kettle and tried to play things cool.

'Is Rain Man here?' asked Penny and then immediately covered her mouth as if she had just blown an important state secret. 'I mean Vern,' she said and blushed.

'He's in there,' I said and pointed towards our room. The girls peered into the room as if a large python may just explode through the doorway. They couldn't see Vern properly because he was sleeping under a huge pile of pillows with his face pressed into the mattress.

'You're Spud,' said Penny without too much enthusiasm. Then there was a brief pause before she asked, 'Why are you called Spud?'

'Don't ask,' I mumbled, and stirred away at my coffee in a rugged fashion.

'Is it to do with a potato or something?' continued Brenda, clearly not picking up my definite 'back off' vibe.

'No,' I answered.

Then the other bedroom door creaked open and Boggo stumbled out wearing only a pair of white scants. Unfortunately for him, his eyes were still fastened shut with sleep so he didn't see the girls.

The sight of Boggo's morning glory is so commonplace back at school that nobody even teases him about it any more. The girls, however, screamed in terror and charged out of the common room. Boggo shouted in fright and desperately attempted to cover his groin with one hand while hurling himself backwards into his bedroom and slamming the door behind him. Cackling laughter from inside the bedroom.

The girls peeped their heads around the common room entrance and seemed greatly relieved that Boggo and his boner had retreated.

'Where's he gone?' asked Brenda, looking equally revolted and excited.

'Was that real?' asked Penny earnestly.

'Did he have something in his pants?' questioned Brenda.

'Is he Rambo?' asked Penny.

'Why's he got so many pimples on his back?' said Brenda.

I told the girls that it was a ruler in Boggo's underpants and that he was just playing a practical joke. Penny turned pink and said, 'Okay, blind. Whatever ... Just don't tell anybody we fell for it.'

The bedroom door creaked open and Boggo's worried face appeared in the crack. Then my bedroom door creaked open and Vern's inquisitive face appeared in that crack.

'Spud,' hissed Boggo and beckoned me urgently to the door. 'You've got to get rid of those chicks before my bladder bursts. Also Fatty needs the bogs big time. He says it's a number two.'

'You're gonna have to go now,' I explained to the girls as if talking to morons. 'We need to get dressed and stuff ...'

'We'll be back in fifteen minutes to take you to breakfast,' said Brenda looking somewhat relieved.

'Then it's assembly, and then your first lesson which is a school tour with Mr Owen.' Penny had to stand on tiptoes to tighten the taps in the sink.

'Lucky you,' said Brenda.

I must have looked a little startled by all the sudden orders, because Penny smiled sympathetically and said, 'Don't worry, Spud, we'll be here to make sure you don't get lost.' They left, giggling and gossiping, and looking at each other's watches and arguing about who had the correct time.

Suddenly a huge figure wrapped in a white sheet streaked out of Boggo's bedroom, thundered across the common room and hurtled down the passage. Boggo sprinted closely behind, as did Vern who obviously thought that something serious was going down.

6:40   The five of us crammed into the kitchenette and stood around sipping tea and coffee and waiting for the two girls to arrive. Fatty was on his fifth rusk in a mere four minutes and seemed deeply worried about what awaited us at breakfast.

'Chicks' school,' said Fatty with a mouthful of rusk. 'Anything could happen. They might give us like one slice of bread and a quail's egg.'
    Boggo nodded his head in agreement and said, 'Chicks never eat.' We all nodded solemnly and fell silent. I became aware that the two girls had returned and that they had been watching us for some time and listening to our conversation.
    'Hi,' said Penny standing to attention. 'I'm Penny and this is my friend Brenda. We're going to take you to breakfast.'

The two then turned on their heels and led off. The Crazy Eight were a little taken aback by being ordered around by two small girls and Fatty's mouth hung open in amazement as the two little figures in white disappeared out of the room and into the passage. We followed them like sheep, and soon found ourselves outside in the bright sunlight.

Boggo breathed in the air and smacked his hands together. 'This is it, boys,' he said. 'The holy grail of schoolboys everywhere.'

Everything is so different here. This school brings

new meaning to the term 'open plan' with the different houses and subject departments dotted around over the estate. It almost feels like a university, only everybody looks fourteen and is dressed in white. We didn't speak. We just drank it all in. Even the grass was different. Compared to our school, it all felt so modern and new. Brand new. And neat. Very neat. Most of the girls we passed on the way to the dining hall either stared at us like we were aliens or deliberately ignored us.

Penny and Brenda marched ahead on their spindly legs and seemed immensely proud that they were in charge of the five lumbering idiots following behind.

'That's the senior dining hall over there,' said Brenda, pointing at a large building with white doors.

'We're not allowed in,' said Penny dejectedly.

'You need to walk in, take a tray and then turn left to the food serving area,' said Brenda. 'The food services matron will show you where to sit.'

We marched forward towards the door. But then Boggo stopped and said that Rambo should enter first. Rambo hooted with laughter and announced that Boggo had lost his confidence because two twelve-year-olds saw his boner.

'I haven't lost my confidence,' whined Boggo. 'Besides,' he said, 'I was wearing jocks.'

Rambo chuckled and pushed open the door to a huge throng of noise that grew instantly quiet the moment we entered the dining hall. I felt my face heating up and searched desperately for the trays and something to do with my hands. The hush became a chorus of low whispers and then a few sniggers as Fatty was forced to squeeze through the dining hall door because one flap was bolted shut. The sniggers and whispers became loud laughter when Vern grabbed his tray, became disorientated, and walked into the kitchen by mistake. He returned some seconds later, red faced and muttering angrily to himself.

'It's better than school,' said Fatty as he marvelled at the pile of eggs and bacon that had been slapped onto his plate. Once we had all been served up, the food services matron led us through the dining hall to an empty table standing adjacent to the table of the other boys from the cast.

'Hey, Spike!' hissed Boggo across the aisle. 'Where you guys staying?'

Spike looked a little grim and said they were staying with the headmistress, Mrs Mitchell. Boggo and Fatty sniggered and shared a high five at our luck.

Then came the sound of a gavel pounding and everybody stopped eating and stood up. A rather important looking girl with far too many badges on her blazer arose from the top table and said, 'Welcome back, girls ... and boys.' The senior dining hall erupted into giggles. Then she continued: 'Before we sing grace, I'd like to remind the girls that there are builders on the school premises so please stay away from those areas, which include the new Trinity Theatre. Also remember that matrics are preparing for trials so please be considerate and keep the general noise level down ...'

'I'd definitely do her!' whispered Boggo and poked Fatty in the stomach. Fatty grinned back and Boggo said, 'Headgirls always do the kinkiest shit.'

In my opinion there was nothing kinky about this particular head girl. Especially when she sang the grace in a high shrill voice that made both tables of boys snigger and bury their heads in their napkins. The girls in the dining hall didn't laugh – in fact, by the looks of things, standing up and singing an embarrassing grace could be standard form around here.

After breakfast, Fatty led us into the kitchen to congratulate the food services matron on a fantastic breakfast all round. The matron looked a little startled by the five of us suddenly materialising in her kitchen but was thrilled with Fatty's compliments. She told us that if we ever wanted seconds then she would organise them for us.

'You can count on it, ma'am,' said Fatty and led us proudly out of the dining hall to the courtyard where the two imps were impatiently waiting for us.

'We're nearly late,' said Penny. 'The hall is across the hill.' We sped after the two girls, with Fatty bringing up the rear and complaining bitterly about the general layout of the school. 'This school was either designed by a sadist or a palooka,' he gasped, and added that it was incredibly unhealthy to run with four undigested eggs in one's system.

We came across The Guv who was stalking around in a tweed suit and looking disturbed. He admitted to being completely lost and very near suicide.

'I'm already homesick,' said The Guv, 'and the halfwit responsible for this architectural debacle should be dragged naked through the streets and have his testicles guillotined.'

Fatty agreed wholeheartedly and offered to do the guillotining.

'Come on, boys, keep up, we have one minute,' called Penny in a shrill voice. We immediately fell silent and obediently followed the two girls through an archway across yet another hockey field and into the cream hall.

Fatty reckoned there were about 600 girls in the school hall. Pig said it looked more like 800. Either way it was a lot of girls who all seemed to be looking at us like we were the science experiment that backfired. Poor Vern became a little overcome with being watched and stuck his head under his chair and pretended to look for something until the assembly began. Meanwhile Boggo was scanning the rows of girls and was dividing them into groups of possibly shagable and definitely shagable.

'Good morning, girls,' said Mrs Mitchell, the tall headmistress with large round spectacles and a warm smile. 'And good morning, boys of The Midsummer Night's Dream cast who have joined us here at Wrexham for the next six weeks.' The headmistress smiled at Viking and said, 'And a special welcome to Mr Richardson who has kindly agreed to direct the production which will inaugurate our brand new Wrexham Trinity Theatre.'

Viking leapt from his seat on the stage and bowed to the school with a flourish. There was a brief pause and then the headmistress led a weak applause. After Viking had returned to his seat, Mrs Mitchell said, 'And last but not least, Mr Edly has joined us as an English teacher, and of course, he will also be up on the stage later this term when he plays the key role of Bottom.'

The girls thought this was hilarious and screeched with laughter. The poor headmistress looked flustered and embarrassed and had to stop her speech for an urgent sip of water.

After the welcome and a long and encouraging speech from the headmistress, a series of awkward events followed. Firstly, some girl called Melissa stood up and performed a reedy tune on a clarinet. Then a junior girl who had won a poetry prize jumped up and read a poem about her mother. (Couldn't have been a serious prize if that was the poem that won.)

Eventually, the staff left the stage and filed quickly out of the hall. Weirdly, the entire school stayed behind and then were forced to put up with a further twenty minutes of all the prefects standing up with their blazers covered in badges and making their individual speeches about discipline and being polite and good ambassadors for the school. There weren't even any threats of punishment and violence. At Wrexham, the approach is the exact opposite from our school. Here they begin by appealing to each girl's better nature and then dangle carrots for good behaviour in front of them. One almost gets the feeling that speaking too loudly and giggling at random things is probably about as rebellious as Wrexham gets.

After a chapel service involving several hymns and a single prayer, Mr Owen led us around the grounds at breakneck speed. She barked out names and rattled off Wrexham history as she waddled along in front of us, and only paused to hurl abuse and to insult Fatty.

'Come on, Fatso,' she kept shouting, 'we'll shed some of those pounds before the term is out.' Fatty looked terrified and tried to tell Mr Owen about his scoliosis and peptic heart murmur, but she didn't appear to hear him.

Obviously The Guv has never met a woman like Mr Owen because he shrank down behind Rambo and peered suspiciously at everything over the top of his glasses. At one stage Mr Owen became distracted with lambasting some girls for being late for class. The Guv pulled me aside with a worried look on his face.

'Milton,' he said, 'by God, Milton, I'm terrified. Who

is this woman?'

'It's Mr Owen, sir,' I replied.

The Guv's eyes widened and he turned deathly pale. 'Mister?'

'That's what they call her, sir,' I explained.

The Guv was definitely on the verge of having some sort of freak out because he jabbered away at three times his normal pace. He says he's sharing a house with Viking and it's a living hell.

'The man doesn't stop shouting, Milton. My nerves are fraying, dear boy, and I fear I have become dangerously unhinged ...' He tapped his leg three times with his walking stick and whispered, 'That's why I'm wearing tweed.'

'You two!' shouted Mr Owen. 'What's going on there?'

'Nothing at all, sir,' replied The Guv, before striding off in the opposite direction.

I don't think the tour with Mr Owen really helped because I still don't know where anything is. She wouldn't even let us anywhere near the theatre because it's still in the process of being built. Our tour ended back at Elizabeth House with yet another sharp rebuking from the bulldog about us forgetting to make our beds and clean our rooms this morning.

'This isn't your snooty palace in the valley, you know,' she snarled. 'Round here, we all pull our weight!' She then marched to the door before stopping and asking if there were any questions that anybody would like to ask. Fatty raised his hand and Mr Owen's left eyebrow lifted in surprise.

'Well, fat boy, what is it?' she demanded sternly.

'Er ...' said Fatty, 'what time is lunch?'

THE FIRST RUN THROUGH

It would appear that Viking spent the entire day wrestling

with white tape. By five o'clock he had finally marked out the Trinity Theatre stage dimensions on the school hall stage, although all we could see was a series of taped lines stretching across the floor. When Smith asked our director what all the white lines meant, Viking shouted, 'Oh for God's sakes! Bold lines are levels, straight lines are steps, rectangular stripes are the doors and crooked lines are trees! Exits are marked with dotted lines and all setting is denoted by zebra crossings.' He then glared as us with murderous eyes and barked, 'Now I hope that's crystal clear?' There was a brief pause during which it was deeply hoped that somebody would be brave enough to ask Viking to repeat his convoluted taping system. Nobody said anything and some of us may even have nodded lamely back at him.

'Good,' said Viking before giving us ten minutes to, 'avail yourselves with the subtleties of my intricate set design'.

We all charged up the steps and bounded onto the recently polished school hall stage. It was then that I saw the full extent of Viking's set. It was like a great maze of strange markings in white tape. My memory instantly deserted me, and a flush of terror descended as I realised that I couldn't remember a single thing that he'd just said. Thankfully, I wasn't alone because Spike and Boggo were already having an argument about what line meant what. Vern was hurriedly sketching down the stage design with his tongue sticking out.

'My oath to God,' insisted Boggo. 'Bold lines are steps!' I quickly wrote BOLD LINES ARE STEPS! on the back of my script. But then Spike said, 'On my mother's life, Boggo, bold lines are levels!' I reasoned that swearing on your mother's life showed more commitment than swearing to God, so I wrote down BOLD LINES ARE LEV on the back of my script before my pen ran out of ink.

I'm learning that life frequently does this to me. First it offers you an impossible challenge, which you can't refuse. Then it breaks your spirit by messing about with your ballpoint pen. These may seem like isolated events that can be explained away as coincidences, but I fear not. It's happened far too often to me to be a coincidence. It's this kind of thing that convinces me that I'm not going to make forty and my death will most probably be humiliating and painful – a death that people will still laugh about in three hundred years' time. One day I'm going to sift through every single entry of all my diaries and mark down how many times a stroke of 'bad luck' has followed the issuing of a severe test in my life ...

But then I saw Rambo languishing backstage on the enormous Duke's throne with his feet up on a wooden stool. There clearly wasn't a worry in his mind as he calmly watched the panic unfolding before him.

'Hey, Rambo,' I called in a high echoing voice. 'Do you know what all the different lines mean?'

Rambo chuckled and said he didn't have the first clue.

'Then why aren't you trying to work it out?' I questioned.

Rambo smiled and said, 'Because I have a simple plan.'

'What's that?' I said.

'Stay away from all the lines and never enter first. If you go second then the first person gets Vikinged!'

The logic worked for me. I pulled up a small stool next to Rambo's throne and together we watched the arguments breaking out in front of us.

Vern stupidly left his carefully sketched stage plan behind when he scurried off to the toilet. It didn't take long for Boggo to swoop on it and then begin defacing it

273

with his red and black HB pencil. Somehow he managed to join all the lines up and come up with an incredibly realistic picture of a woman's boob.

'Right!' shouted Viking as he strode through the back of the hall with a large mug of coffee. 'Now I hope you are well acquainted with the stage because I won't tolerate unprofessional behaviour!' We all nodded and looked away. He then ordered us to spend the next fifteen minutes going over our lines and preparing ourselves for what lies ahead.

18:30 Viking isn't in a healthy mood. He's outraged about the theatre not being ready on time. He says he signed a contract that guaranteed him use of the new theatre from the beginning of term and is determined to sue somebody. He's already had furious rows with the headmistress, the builders, and most of the staff. He even made a last gasp effort to move the entire production back to school, which was unsuccessful. The school hall isn't exactly the Sydney Opera House, but we're stuck with it.

19:00 The girls arrived in a group closely followed by the figure of The Guv, wearing a long dark coat and hat and creeping along like he was hiding from somebody. It was obvious that the sexes were checking each other out as the girls filed closely past us. Bringing up the rear were two short little girls who appeared very smug and self-important as they marched past. Boggo slid low in his seat and hid his face in horror as he realised that Penny and Brenda were part of the cast.

'Welcome,' snarled Viking. 'Now, due to gross inefficiency on the part of the school builders we are being forced to rehearse in this neolithic hovel.' Viking's face grew angry and he growled, 'They say we shall have at least three weeks in the theatre, but I'm preparing myself for the worst. This ...' he roared, as he bounded up onto the stage with his arms spread wide, 'is your new home, like it or not.'

He then repeated his briefing on what each taped line meant but said it so fast that by the end of it I couldn't remember a single thing again.

I snuck a quick look along the front row at the faces of the girls, which seemed to be mostly fixed in absolute terror as they watched the director ranting and raving. I then locked eyes with the gorgeous brunette second from the end. She looks like a movie star. Her name is Victoria Perez Hamilton and according to Boggo and Rambo, she's the most beautiful girl in the cast and the school. I hate to say it, but she puts Mermaid and Amanda into some perspective. For just a moment I thought she was really looking at me, but it turned out she was looking at Rambo who was chewing the end of his pencil and looking bored.

Once again the rude mechanicals have been separated from the rest of the cast. The Guv, myself, Fatty, Boggo, Vern and Geoff Lawson were sent to the school library to rehearse our scenes while Viking remained in the hall with the lovers and the fairies. The library is about a kilometre from the school hall but we could still hear the never ending irate shouting and abuse.

The good news is that The Guv has been ordered to assume responsibility for the mechanicals group until we move into the theatre. Viking said this was because he needed to spend time on the nuts and bolts rather than the bells and whistles, although Boggo reckons Viking is deliberately keeping us from the girls because we're the studs of the cast and will distract them from their acting.

The Guv flirted outrageously with the librarian who was waiting to knock off and hand over the library keys. He declared her the most magnificent librarian he had ever laid eyes on. The poor woman blushed terribly and said she was married, before bursting into shrill giggling.

'Lucky man!' declared The Guv as he swung his walking stick under his left arm. Then he announced, 'I myself have married thrice. Bloody business. Bloody business.' The librarian didn't quite know what to make of The Guv. Clearly she had never met anybody so eccentric before. She kept giggling at whatever he said and nervously held onto her wedding ring, which she swivelled round and round on her finger.

The librarian handed the keys over to The Guv. He bowed with a flourish and thanked her for such an enchanting conversation. She giggled again and left in a hurry.

'Did you see that?' hissed Boggo. 'Did you see how he operates – brilliant!'

'Nice spading, sir,' said Boggo jovially after The Guv had finally worked out how to lock the library door.

'Spading?' said The Guv with a look of horror on his face. 'Spading is for agricultural yahoos and other such plodders.' He sniffed dismissively before declaring, 'Greenstein, when I romance a woman, I do so with the full might of a thousand master poets behind me!'

'Nice one, sir,' said Geoff Lawson.

We all looked around at the large characterless library. Like everything in this place, the different shelves of books are well spaced apart and neatly divided into subjects. The cream carpets and white walls gleamed in the bright neon lighting and the hum of the lights made it feel like a science laboratory. The Guv led us to the reading section where we removed the chairs to create an acting space. The Guv then pulled out some candles and lit them before ordering Fatty to turn out the lights.

'Friends,' began The Guv, 'we mechanicals have been harshly set aside as bells and whistles in this Shakespearian charade. Let those lovers and fairies mock us – for we shall have the last laugh and perhaps the only laugh!' He looked around, grinned at us mischievously and declared, 'We have been left to our own devices in this so-called library.' He gazed at the surrounding shelves with an appalled expression. 'I propose that under the cover of darkness we devise a work of such brilliance and hilarity that we steal the show from under the director's nose.'

'Yes!' hissed Fatty with clenched fists. 'We are just as important as the other scenes.'

'And funnier,' said Geoff Lawson looking inspired.

'Let's beat them up!' shouted Vern unable to contain his excitement.

'Beat who up?' Boggo was bewildered.

'The fairies!' said Vern and thumped his fist into his palm.

Vern was obviously confused. Nevertheless The Guv quickly righted the ship when he praised Vern for his anger and advised him to channel it into his portrayal of Lion.

'Right,' said The Guv finally. 'Let us break it all apart and begin again at the beginning.' He pulled out an ink marker, strode towards the white board and wrote down:

THE RULES OF COMEDIC ACTING

1 If you think you're funny, then you're not

2 Keep it real and authentic
3 Use the language, don't fight it
4 Never upstage Bottom (The Guv)
5 If you can hear the crickets chirping outside then immediately scratch your balls and make a funny face

Unfortunately just then there was a loud knock on the door. After taking about five minutes to select the correct key, The Guv flung it open to reveal the impish figures of Brenda and Penny. They both looked a little startled at The Guv's leering face and took a hesitant step backwards.

'Mr Viking sent us to find somebody,' blurted Brenda.

'Dear God!' said The Guv as he recoiled in horror. 'He's taking us one by one!' He then asked whom it was that the executioner had summoned.

'Somebody called Gav,' said Penny.

'Gav?' enquired The Guv. 'There's no Gav here.'

'Well, actually,' said Penny regaining her confidence, 'he said we must get *The* Gav, but that didn't make any sense at all.'

'Dear God, it's me!' gasped The Guv as he staggered back into the library clutching his chest. 'I have been summoned.' He then looked at us and shouted, 'I must follow these grim reaperesses at once!' He looked like he had been dealt a fatal blow and ordered us to run through the lines without him.

'Sir,' said Penny rather loudly, 'Megan O'Reilly says Mr Viking has rabies. Is this true?'

'My good woman,' said The Guv as he pulled on his long coat, 'it's very unlikely Satan would contract rabies.'

'Satan,' gasped Brenda.

'Indeed,' replied The Guv. 'Now if you two young fillies could guide me to a large white room of relief I would be much obliged. I have no intention of perishing on a full bladder.'

The Guv thumped the door closed with the end of his walking stick and was gone.

We didn't end up rehearsing because Boggo found a pile of Wrexham school magazines and spent the next two hours perving over girls in old school hockey photographs and making us judge who was the hottest Wrexham hockey player in history.

The winner – Caroline Roux (1981).

Wednesday 5th August

6:00   Once again I was woken by shrill giggling and sniggering in the common room. Then I heard my door creak slightly before a dark brown eye appeared in the crack.

'Do you want some tea, Spud?' said Brenda.

I said thanks but my voice came out as a croak. She giggled and disappeared. I turned over and nearly fell asleep again but was then awoken by a sharper voice from the crack in the door. 'Does Vern want tea?' This time the eye in the crack was blue.

'He doesn't drink tea in the morning, he only has hot water,' I replied. There was a pause before Penny shouted, 'Does Vern want some hot water then?'

'Yes,' I croaked again.

'Hey, keep it down!' came Boggo's anguished cry from next door followed by loud banging on the wall.

'Sorry!' hollered Penny in a shrill voice.

There was more groaning from the other room and then the sound of clinking coffee cups from the kitchen. Then I heard somebody getting out of bed and the door opened. 'Hey, girls,' said Rambo, 'watch out – Boggo's got a ruler in his pants again!'

There was a loud squeal from the kitchen and the girls tore out of the common room in fright.

'All clear!' Rambo called out, and the enormous figure shrouded in its white sheet followed by Boggo with three towels wrapped around his waist, tore out of the room for the bogs. Rambo grinned to himself and sauntered casually after them.

The girls returned eventually and made us our tea/coffee/hot water. Fatty emerged from his room looking surprisingly fresh and clean. Penny passed him his coffee and then pulled a bundle of choc chip cookies out of her bag. The bundle had been carefully tied with a pink ribbon with a small heart stuck to the end. 'Um ... Fatty ...' Penny began to blush. Pink at first and then scarlet. 'I made these in Home Ec yesterday. I thought you might want them.' Fatty's eyes glazed over as he stared at the cookies. He then looked up at Penny with a look of such love that I nearly became emotional.

'Thanks,' said Fatty as he gently took the cookies from her.

'Hope you don't think they're gross,' said Penny, twisting uncomfortably on her feet.

'They look delicious,' said Fatty, feverishly working away at the knot of the pink bow. He pulled open the bundle and then carefully slid a biscuit into his mouth. After three chews he closed his eyes and groaned with joy.

'You're an actor. How do I know I can believe you?' said Penny, acting coy and flirty. Fatty didn't answer. Instead he shoved two cookies into his mouth at once and collapsed into a chair to focus on his munching.

'He really does like them,' Penny said in amazement and beamed at Brenda who gave her an excited thumbs up. Fatty didn't utter a word until he had eaten every cookie in the bundle. Then he rose up from his armchair and informed Penny that they were the finest choc chip cookies in the world. Penny blushed again and twisted some more on her feet. Then Fatty began blushing as the rest of us dissolved into loud mockery and cruel jibes that sent the girls racing out the room again and shouting for us to follow.

Fatty marched ahead at a breakneck pace. Not sure if he was still hungry or whether he was trying to catch up to the blonde cookie maker skipping along in front of him.

SUBJECTS/ TEACHER COMMENTS/RATING

MATHS (Mr Owen)
Thanks to the unfortunate teacher, Maths promises to be nothing other than sheer misery. Why is it that Maths never clashes with anything? (1/10)

ENGLISH (The Guv)
Despite his strange behaviour since arriving at Wrexham, it's good to have a familiar teacher to see every day. It's also great to see the shock on the girls' faces whenever our English teacher bursts into loud Shakespearian insults and swearing. (9/10)

AFRIKAANS (Mev van Niekerk)
Fairly lively teacher but prone to jabbering on in Afrikaans and losing the class in the process. Boggo rated her as not bad looking and assured us that Afrikaans women are brilliant and vigorous lovers. (6/10)

HISTORY (Mrs Lynne)
Unfortunately, not a very inspirational History teacher, and not strong on the pretty stakes either. Seems to think that good teaching is writing out something on the board and then repeating it in a droning voice before beginning the next sentence. It must be said she does have extremely neat handwriting. (6/10)

GEOGRAPHY (The Spider)
A nasty piece of work, who has already taken an exceedingly dim view of boys attending her class. Kicked Boggo out of the classroom for drawing an obscene picture on the inside cover of Fatty's atlas. (4/10)

SPEECH AND DRAMA (Ms Lindsay)
A pretty brunette teacher straight out of university. Lively, energetic and sexy when doing her stretching exercises. Rambo says he's definitely thinking of seducing her. (8/10)

Friday 7th August

15:30 'It's bullshit,' whined Boggo as he prodded the teabag floating in his mug. 'They said this place was meant to be like Sodom and Gomorrah, with orgies kicking off left, right, and centre.' He flung his teabag into the bin and called Wrexham a disgrace.

Fatty grunted in agreement and slowly ate his way through another bundle of Penny's choc chip cookies.

'I mean ...' continued Boggo, after furiously stirring his tea and making it slosh over the sides of the mug, 'besides classes and rehearsals and meals, we never even get to talk to a chick!'

'Shocking,' agreed Fatty and fed himself another cookie.

'And it's not like we can socialise and spade during classes and rehearsals either,' responded Boggo.

'Mr Owen will get you every time,' said Fatty with a mouth full of biscuit and a sympathetic nod.

'Exactly,' snapped Boggo. 'This place is like a prison. And the only girls we ever talk to are Penny and Brenda who were like still wearing nappies last year.'

Fatty didn't answer and instead pretended to be consumed with dunking his cookie.

'What do you think, Spud?' asked Boggo suddenly.

'Dog show,' I replied and shook my head gravely. This seemed to satisfy Boggo and he nodded back at me respectfully.

'You see – Spud knows his shit. This is classic apartheid divide and conquer tactics!' He then took a giant swig of tea and said, 'My oath to God.' He took another sip and said, 'It's sexist.' Boggo switched the kettle on again and said, 'I mean, don't get me wrong, having unlimited tea is pretty cool, and Penny and Brenda are fairly efficient.'

Fatty nodded again in agreement. 'The hottest slaves I've ever seen.'

Boggo paused in opening a new milk carton, and then spun around accusingly at Fatty. 'What do you mean they're hot?'

Fatty blushed and quickly tried to counter. 'No, no, no, I didn't say they were hot … But I like meant they were hotter than, say, other slaves … like Plump Graham and Rowdy and …'

'You shouldn't be looking at the Fragile Five in that way, buddy. It's not normal,' said Boggo and clicked his tongue as if deeply disappointed.

Poor Fatty tried to justify himself but with every word he said, he buried himself deeper in the manure.

'So what you're basically saying,' said Boggo in conclusion, 'is that Penny is hotter than Meg Ryan's Son, who is hotter than Rowdy, who is hotter than Plump Graham?'

'Does Meg Ryan's son go to your school?' asked Brenda in amazement.

Fatty lurched out of his chair, a look of horror on his face.

'Don't you knock?' enquired Boggo and looked distastefully at Brenda. 'You can't just sneak in. We could be planning something.'

'What are you planning?' asked Brenda.

'We're planning something big,' said Boggo seriously.

283

'Really?' said Brenda with wide eyes.

'But it's going to take a few sacks of cookies for me to open up.'

Brenda giggled and then stared fiercely into my face. 'You've got a phone call, Spud,' she said. 'It sounds like a girl who's really upset!'

'A girl?' I replied in some shock.

'Well, it sounded like a girl,' said Brenda. 'But it might have been a boy with a high voice.'

'Hang on, hang on,' said Boggo sipping frantically away at his third cup of tea in twenty minutes. 'Did this girl ask to speak to Spud, or Spud, Vern or Fatty?'

Brenda stared guiltily back at Boggo and then nodded her head.

'Then, Brenda,' said Boggo in a scornful tone, 'that girl you spoke to on the phone wasn't a girl but a garlic.'

With that Boggo shouted, 'Follow me, gentlemen, it's time for the daily Garlic wind-up.' He slammed down his tea mug and ran from the room on his long, pale, furry legs.

'Hey, Brenda,' said Fatty in a low voice once Boggo was gone. 'Where's Penny?'

Brenda looked him directly in the eyes and said, 'Her duties have been moved to another house. She can't come back any more.'

'What?' gasped Fatty, his face falling.

'JOKES!' shouted Brenda. 'She's at hockey practice, you dork! She's coming to get you for supper and she told me to tell you that she's bringing a surprise.'

Brenda turned and marched out with a triumphant look on her face. Fatty heaved a great shuddery sigh of relief and then a naughty smile spread across his face. He looked at me and seemed to be on the verge of saying something. Instead he slapped me on the back and said, 'Come on, Spuddy, let's go wind up Garlic.'

Sunday 9th August

After a weekend of non-stop rehearsing with The Guv in the library I feel ready to perform in front of an audience, even if that audience is only the rest of the cast. The mechanicals' scenes, thanks to The Guv's direction, are becoming sharp and pacy. With The Guv's Bottom leading the way with a brilliant comic performance, we just follow and everything seems to fall into place. The only negatives are that Vern is still prone to slipping back into gibberish Zulu and loud clicks. I can't see what his Lion looks like because in the play the Lion is chasing me and I have to run around as Thisby screaming like a girl. Judging by the laughter, we're doing okay. The Guv has calmed down to his usual self and the only time he behaves in an odd manner is when Mr Owen is around. There is, however, one serious problem – Boggo seems incapable of remembering his lines. He plays the part of Peter Quince who is the leader of the mechanicals and has been entrusted with directing the play within the play for the wedding of the Duke and Duchess and the Athenian lovers.

I'm not sure if it's stage fright, or his general unhappiness with Wrexham, but he hasn't got it right once in rehearsal and yet when we practise in the common room, he never gets a word wrong. Boggo denies he's got stage fright and has blamed his various blunders on:

Shakespeare
Vern distracting him with sudden movements
Hayfever from the dust on the library books
Being temporarily blinded by the neon lights
The library floor is uneven
My high-pitched Thisby voice making him laugh and putting him off
Fatty's silent farting that only Boggo could smell
The noise outside the library

The lack of a director
Rehearsing in the library
A pigeon roosting in the eaves

Tuesday 11th August

I've been wondering why girls are always opening letters and packages at breakfast. This morning I solved the mystery. At Wrexham your daily post is delivered directly to your table setting ... and there it was: my first post – also the first out of all the boys.

The square cardboard box was covered in shiny red paper, and had already created a stir around our section of the dining hall. I couldn't help but notice traces of butter on the inside fold of the wrapping paper where Boggo had tried to molest my package with his knife. The surrounding tables of girls were also watching me with great interest as I sat down casually with my French toast and freshly squeezed orange juice.

'What are you waiting for – open it,' demanded Boggo in a desperate voice.

'It must be from a chick!' said Fatty as he licked globs of peanut butter off the ends of his fingers. Rambo snorted and pretended that he wasn't in the slightest bit interested in my mystery package.

'Open up,' shouted Boggo. 'And don't even think about opening it in private because we've got keys to your room.'

I must admit I was enjoying all the attention. I also know that with attention comes the threat of disaster and humiliation. I slowly opened the package and lifted off the lid of the box. Inside was a framed picture of Amanda in the nude. It was identical to the one hanging on her wall, except half the size.

Boggo ripped the frame away from me and then uttered a loud yell when he realised that it was Amanda in the nude. Then there was a mad tug-of-war for control of the frame, with me clutching onto one corner for dear life.

'You boys!' shouted Mr Owen, looking livid, hands placed firmly on hips. We all froze in horror with our hands still all holding onto the frame.

'Give that here!' she ordered and held out her hand. Boggo reluctantly placed the framed picture of the naked Amanda into the porky hands of Mr Owen. I felt my skin tingling and prepared myself for the worst.

'Mmm,' said Mr Owen as she appraised the image of my ex-girlfriend in the nude. She then looked at Rambo and said, 'And who belongs to this?' Her gaze returned to the frame and I feebly raised my hand to a chorus of sniggers and giggling.

'You've done rather well for yourself, young man,' said Mr Owen with a surprised expression on her face. 'Such a scrawny, nondescript little chap.' She then handed the naked Amanda back to me and ordered me to keep it in my bag and out of sight. I obeyed and Mr Owen rumbled off, shaking her head and looking astonished that the girl in the picture should be interested in a boy like me.

'It's lame anyway,' said Boggo. 'You can't even see her gazoombies.'

I left the dining hall with the naked Amanda pressed to my chest.

Wednesday 12th August

6:10 'I heard a girl sent you a naked picture yesterday,' said Penny in a loud demanding voice. I was in no mood to be talking to the imps at this hour of the morning, especially about my complicated private life, so I ignored her and made a beeline for the kettle.

'Boggo said in the picture your girlfriend was doing

funny things with a horse,' said Brenda with a nervous expression.

'Never believe a word Boggo says,' I replied. I tapped the kettle a few times, hoping it would boil faster than usual.

'Why did your girlfriend send you a nude photograph of herself?' persisted Penny, clearly not sensing the hostile vibe I was giving off.

'She's not my girlfriend and it's a painting, not a photograph!' I snapped, starting to lose my cool.

'Who did the painting?' asked Brenda.

I was beginning to feel like an idiotic cow who had become stranded in a pond and was very quickly being eaten alive by two vicious piranhas.

'What's your girlfriend's name?' asked Penny as she began preparing Lord Fatty's morning tea.

'You two are worse than Garlic!' I shouted exasperatedly, as the two piranha girls fussed and bossed and questioned about me

'Is Garlic your girlfriend?' asked Brenda.

'More like his boyfriend,' said Boggo as he strode across the common room with a footstool covering his groin.

The girls giggled and Brenda's attention immediately centred on Boggo. 'Would you like some tea, Boggo?' she cried.

'Make me two cups,' said Boggo, carefully guiding the legs of the stool through the common room door.

'Is Fatty awake?' trilled Penny, but Boggo was gone and didn't answer.

'He's hilarious!' said Brenda, still looking at the common room door as if Boggo might suddenly reappear. I took the gap, grabbed my teacup and charged back to my room only to find Vern biting his toenails and laying out the splinters across his pillow.

15:00   Still mulling over Amanda and what she's up to ... Tried to call her, but the young whippersnapper who answered the phone said she was studying for trials and then berated me for calling during 'Quiet Time'.

Friday 14th August

At times I have to agree with Boggo that this is a thoroughly odd school. Perhaps this is the way all girls' schools operate? This may also explain the weirdness of women in general.

Sunday 16th August

THE LIBRARY

13:30 Energy was pumping off the library walls. The mechanicals were finally ready to join the rest of the cast and strut their stuff before the girls. The Guv gave us a rousing team talk beside the theology shelf, and warned us about getting carried away in front of the girls, and being intimidated by Viking's constant ranting and raving.

We then executed a word-perfect run through of all our scenes before The Guv shouted, 'To the school hall at once! We will meet; and there we may rehearse most obscenely and courageously. Take pains; be perfect: adieu.'

He thumped his walking stick into the floor, swung round on his toes, and strode purposefully out the library.

THE SCHOOL HALL

14:30 Nobody witnessed our arrival because Viking was in the middle of a long and abusive lecture on theatrical etiquette. He then informed the assembled group of frightened actors and actresses that they weren't up to scratch and threatened to rehearse all night if things didn't improve.

Despite the disappointment of not working with the rest of the cast and rehearsing in the library, it suddenly seemed a relief to have missed two weeks of Viking's furious temper. From today we will no longer have that luxury.

'Aah!' shouted Viking when he finally noticed the six of us. 'The rude mechanicals have arrived, and I would very much like to see your opening scene immediately.'

Viking ordered the rest of the class to sit around the front edge of the stage and the mechanicals lurched into action. I was engulfed with nausea and my head misted up with the fear of failure. Worse news was that the gorgeous Victoria Perez Hamilton had seated herself no more than five paces from the spot where I spend most of the scene listening to Peter Quince and Bottom arguing.

The whispers faded and Viking called out, 'Right! Act I Scene 2. Begin!'

Boggo, looking as pale as a ghost, staggered forward onto the stage with the rest of us shuffling along behind. And then ... nothing. Boggo didn't say his opening line. There was a long silence as Boggo stared out at the auditorium with unblinking eyes like he was staring at a rapidly approaching tidal wave.

'Well?' came a booming voice from somewhere near the back of the hall.

Boggo was frozen with terror. His eyes seemed to roll back into his eyelids and a soft moan escaped his lips like he might be on the verge of singing.

'What's going on, Greenstein?' demanded the voice at the back of the hall.

'Nothing, sir,' said Boggo, suddenly finding his normal voice. 'I was waiting for your instruction to begin.'

'But I just told you to begin!' The voice was moving rapidly forward.

'I didn't hear you, sir. The acoustics in this place are dreadful.'

Viking leapt up the stairs, taking them in fours. He charged up to Boggo and grabbed him roughly by his jersey. 'Greenstein!' he screamed. 'Do you think I have the kind of time to waste on people waiting for instructions that I have already loudly and clearly given?'

'No, sir,' stammered Boggo, turning deathly white again.

'Right!' roared Viking, releasing his grip on Boggo's school jersey. 'Act I Scene 2, from the top. And make it snappy!'

We marched off the stage prior to making our second entrance. Boggo pulled me aside and whispered desperately, 'What's my first line?'

'What?' I replied, not sure that I had heard him properly.

'My first line!' he repeated in a strident whisper. 'Spud, please help me, it's gone!'

'Act I, Scene 2. BEGIN!' thundered Viking from the back of the auditorium. Fatty gave Boggo a firm shove onto the stage. I could see his legs were shaking badly and he shuffled forward like his knees were about to buckle on him at any moment.

'Is all our company here ...' I whispered, hoping my voice would reach Boggo and no further.

'Is all our company here?' said Boggo in a confident voice.

The Guv leapt forward as Bottom and said, 'You were best to call them generally, man by man according to the scrip!'

The girls laughed at The Guv's Cockney accent and instantly it felt like we were back on track. Unfortunately, there was then another long and awkward silence with Boggo once again staring out terrified and white faced.

'What now, Greenstein?' came the director's voice. 'Line!'

'I know my line, sir,' said Boggo once again in his confident voice. 'It's just that I'm meant to have a scroll to read out the names.'

'Yes ... yes, I know, Greenstein,' said the re-approaching Viking. 'Just mime it or use a piece of paper, for God's sakes!'

'But I'm a method actor, sir,' replied Boggo. 'Like Dustin Hoffman.'

Viking snapped. He charged back onto the stage and grabbed Boggo by the jersey again. He then shouted on about *his* method being the only method to be used around here. Once he was done with his shouting and abuse he boomed, 'Act I Scene 2! From the top and so help me God if we have to stop again –'

We did have to stop again.

Viking blew his top ten seconds later when Boggo forgot to enter through the assigned tape markings and ended up leading the mechanicals through two walls and the Duke's courtyard. This time Viking really cracked. With a swift and dramatic movement he slammed Boggo's head into the prompt's desk. There was a horrified gasp from the girls and Brenda immediately started blubbing. Boggo collapsed onto the floor in dramatic fashion and wailed that his skull was broken in three places. He then blamed all further line fluffs on concussion and was eventually allowed to carry his script by a guilty looking Viking. Thereafter, the scene flowed perfectly, but after all the violence and shouting, the comedy was gone and nobody laughed, apart from when Vern grew bored and started feeling around in his pockets. He was probably looking for his pencil, but the sneaky manner in which he was shifting his hands, made it look like he was up to something unsavoury.

Tried to strike up a conversation with the girls playing Helena and Hermia. It didn't work out so well. After a few minutes of chatting they ended up talking to each other about a science project and then moved off, completely forgetting that I was even there. Guess I'll have to scratch their names off the hit list. The problem is, besides them and VPH there aren't exactly too many other choices.

If this is what professional theatre is really all about, then I'm not so sure I want it to be my career.

Wednesday 19th August

16:00 'Your mom's on the phone,' said Penny in an officious tone. The afternoon sun pouring through the window had defeated both Vern and I. What began as an earnest homework session evolved into an afternoon sleepathon.

'Sounds like she was crying,' said Penny as she led me out of the building and across the courtyard. 'What do you think she's crying about?'

'Dunno,' I replied sleepily.

'Sorry, I wasn't meant to ask that,' said Penny without appearing too apologetic.

Wombat's dead or the pub's gone under. That's what I was thinking. But mostly I thought it was Wombat. I took a deep breath, prepared myself for the worst, and then picked up the waiting receiver. I closed the door of the phone box with my foot but Penny didn't take the hint and waited outside, obviously planning on listening in to some interesting gossip. I opened the door again and asked Penny for some privacy. She said, 'Whatever.' And skulked off looking highly offended.

'Hello,' I said in a voice that wasn't mine.

'Spud!' shouted a high-pitched and rather alarmed voice.

'Yes,' I replied.

'It's me!' said the voice. 'Why did it take you so long to get to the phone?'

I breathed out a great sigh of relief. The good news is that it wasn't Mom and nobody had died or gone bankrupt. The bad news was that I was now stuck with Garlic on the other end of the line.

GARLIC   Hey, Spud, have you scored any chicks yet? Boggo says you guys are having full-on orgies every night.

SPUD   I'm bored with orgies.

GARLIC   Bored with orgies! Hey, tell me, is Vern still acting all moggy?

SPUD   Yesterday he was wearing only one sock at rehearsals.

GARLIC   (*Roaring with laughter*) Noways! What a retard! What else?

SPUD   Um ... that's about it.

GARLIC   What do you mean that's it? What about Rambo?

SPUD   What about Rambo?

GARLIC   What's he planning?

SPUD   Nothing.

GARLIC   Nothing!

Pause.

GARLIC   What else?

SPUD   That's all.

GARLIC   That's all?

SPUD   Yip.

I returned to the common room where Brenda and Penny were watching Rambo doing a physical workout in only a small pair of running shorts.

Sunday 23rd August

Weekends at Wrexham aren't exactly the most exciting days on the school calendar. Aside from meals and rehearsals, we're confined to the house and even then, we have Mr Owen snooping around and giving us stern lectures and firing personal insults. We can't even hang out with the other boys in the cast. Technically we can pay them a visit, but that means hanging out at the headmistress's house with Spike and Smith, which isn't worth the effort.

On the female front, nobody has even come close to scoring. There's a rumour that Victoria Perez Hamilton and Rambo have a secret thing going on, but Rambo has denied it and says VPH does nothing for him. This must surely be a lie. In fact, the only girls I ever really get to speak to are the piranha girls in the morning and afternoons, and Mr Owen, who has taken to sneaking up and ambushing us with a nasty reprimand for whatever rule or regulation it is that we have broken. Further bad news is that Viking is so distressed with the state of the Dream that he's not even allowing the cast to go home for the long weekend. That means no break for five more weeks, by which time living 24/7 in a tiny room with Vern may well have driven me bonkers.

On a more positive note ...

It seems that I can't think of much that is positive in my situation except for the fact that it can't really get much more boring and monotonous.

15:30   Decided to kickstart my internal energy battery with a call home. Nobody answered. I then tried Amanda, but the girl who answered said 'Ms Lawrence' had gone home to study for the weekend. I chickened out of calling her at home because I didn't know what to say if her dad answered. 'Hi Mr Lawrence, thanks a million for creating that great painting of your naked daughter in a seductive pose!'

Not sure if painting your daughter in the nude would classify as more obscene than Vern repeatedly drawing the naked Garlic covered in Vaseline?

After my complete lack of success in the phone box I wandered around the quadrangle for a few minutes, debating whether I should sneak off on a highly rebellious afternoon walk around the school. I thought about scaling a drainpipe and then riding the curtain through the window of a girl's room like Indiana Jones.

'You boy!' shouted Mr Owen from the open door of her

office. 'What are you up to?'

'Just going over my lines, ma'am,' I said in an innocent voice.

'Well, get back to your quarters immediately!' ordered
Mr Owen in a menacing tone.

'Yes, ma'am,' I said, and put my head down and
walked very quickly back to my cell.

21:00 Viking is losing the plot. He's already been
hauled in to see the headmistress because one of the
girls' parents phoned in to complain about our director's aggressive behaviour during rehearsals. He has
daily rows with the building contractors, because with
three weeks until curtain up, the theatre isn't anywhere
near ready yet. It's probably a blessing in disguise that
Viking is losing his voice although his hoarse whispering
into a megaphone is none the less thoroughly disturbing.

Wednesday 26th August

The mechanicals were on fire at this evening's rehearsal.
The play within the play scene was a scream (quite liter-
ally) and my high-pitched Thisby voice was cracking the
girls up. The Guv is brilliant as Bottom and the moment
when Titania (VPH) strokes his donkey ears and kisses
him made the entire cast fall about with merriment.
Our scene brought a broad smile to Viking's face and
suddenly it felt like the sun had broken through the
clouds and everybody relaxed and laughed. It's like a
real school play again – like Oliver.

The long feared kiss between The Guv and myself,
through Wall's (Fatty's) crannied hole or chink isn't as
bad as feared. Because of Fatty's size the audience doesn't
really see anything besides our heads leaning in towards
each other.

Boggo hasn't put a foot wrong since last week's violence. I'm not sure if this improvement is due to him getting over his stage fright or because he's stuck his lines to the inside of his scroll, which he always carries about with him, even when not indicated in the script.

Thursday 27th August

16:00 'It's bullshit!' said Boggo. 'We aren't even allowed to leave the house for the entire weekend.'

'It's a prison,' agreed Fatty gloomily. He then looked sadly out the window and mumbled, 'I miss my archives.'

'Me, too,' said Boggo. 'We're not even allowed to go into Maritzburg to buy stuff, or even just take a walk.'

'You'd think we were a bunch of delinquents.' Fatty absent-mindedly turned over another page of Penny's Femina magazine.

'Let's do something,' said Boggo. 'Come on! We're acting like a bunch of wussies! Where's that good old Crazy Eight spirit?'

'What we gonna do?' asked Fatty as he sized up a full page photograph of Jane Fonda.

'I dunno,' admitted Boggo. 'We could go marauding around, like we did in the old days.'

'Marauding?' repeated Fatty without sounding too keen.

'What you say, Spud?' asked Boggo suddenly turning his attention to me at the sink.

'Let's go marauding,' I said.

'Cool,' Boggo replied. 'That's two in.' He then looked back into my room where Vern was listening to my Walkman and tapping his foot against the wall. 'If Spud's in, Vern's in,' said Boggo, grinning triumphantly. 'That makes three votes, so it doesn't matter what you and Rambo say because we've got a majority anyway!'

'I thought Rambo cancelled democracy forever in January?' said Fatty, flipping over another page.

'You can't cancel democracy,' cried Boggo in exasperation.

'The government did,' I put in innocently.

'Ja, but that's different,' said Boggo as his attention returned to Fatty. 'Come on, Fatty. We all need to let off some steam. It will be legend.'

Fatty shoved half a piece of toast into his mouth and pretended to be caught up in his magazine reading. Boggo's inspiration faded and he said, 'So that's final. We're all in for a Crazy Eight mission tonight?'

Fatty didn't respond and Boggo grew frustrated. He whipped the Femina magazine off Fatty's lap and hurled it out the door and into the passage.

'What's wrong with you?' wailed Fatty and looked helplessly to where his magazine lay.

'Nah, nah, nah, my friend,' replied Boggo. 'The real question is, what's wrong with *you*? You've become this pathetic little lapdog to a frikking nine-year-old.'

'She's thirteen,' sighed Fatty, rolling his eyes like he'd had this conversation many times before. 'And I told you we're just friends.'

'Friends, my arse!' shouted Boggo, seething with anger. 'You're like totally in love with her. I've seen the way you look at her.'

'What?' shouted Fatty with his hands raised. 'What's so bad with hanging out and chatting to her?'

'It's just wrong,' said Boggo and shook his head, appalled with the whole situation.

'Hey,' said Fatty in a high voice, 'I don't complain when you spade girls and stuff.'

'I'm not complaining,' said Boggo looking emotional. 'I just think it's a bit weird that you would rather hang out with an ankle-biter than with your best mate.' Then Boggo's face flushed with embarrassment before becoming angry again. 'Oh, and by the way,' he said spitefully, 'how are you planning to shag Penny without crushing her to death?'

My toes were curling at the sink. I wanted to run straight into my room and bury myself under the bed. Boggo obviously hadn't seen Brenda and Penny standing at the door waiting for us to invite them in. Brenda recoiled in horror when she heard Boggo's final sentence and poor Penny's face turned tomato red. Fatty lurched out of his seat when he realised that the girls had arrived. By this stage, Boggo was in a steady retreat towards his room while Fatty gathered himself before storming out of the common room in a huff, snatching up his Femina magazine as he went.

There followed a long and extremely awkward pause. Once again I was trapped at the sink waiting for the water to boil. I considered abandoning my afternoon tea and making a break for it, but then I reasoned that I should be the only person who shouldn't feel embarrassed in this situation.

An enraged Fatty came storming back into the common room.
    'Bitch!' he shouted.
    'What happened?' asked Boggo, who had been driven out of the bedroom by Rambo.
    'Mr Owen said I wasn't allowed outside and she confiscated my Femina magazine!' He then remembered that he was meant to be angry with Boggo and marched across the common room and threw open the door to their bedroom.
    'Get out!' shouted Rambo from inside. Fatty slammed the door shut and returned to his seat where the argument had begun. By now the piranha girls had moved to the sink and were looking around nervously like they thought a fight might break out.
    'It helps if you switch it on,' said Penny, leaning across me and flicking down the wall switch for the kettle. Now it was my turn to blush. Boggo squawked

with laughter and said, 'What a mullet!' Brenda and Penny both giggled in high voices.

'Well, who switched it off at the wall?' I said, suddenly feeling a bit angry myself.

'All wall switches have to be off at all times, except for when in use ... obviously,' said Brenda in a singsong tone. 'It's in the school health and safety guidelines.' The piranhas looked at me like I was most irresponsible and then set about decanting sugar.

'Fatty, do you want tea?' asked Penny sweetly.

'Thanks,' said Fatty in a morbidly sulky voice. Penny shooed me away and ordered me to take a seat. Clearly both girls think I'm thoroughly incompetent at everything I do. Soon they're going to be giving me directions to improve my acting. That will be the point when I drown one of them in a bucket ...

'Hey, Penny!' shouted Boggo. 'Why do you always offer Fatty tea first?' Penny stopped her efficient sugar decanting routine and blushed again, utterly stumped by Boggo's question.

'Because he's the biggest,' said Brenda, boldly coming to her friend's rescue.

Boggo snorted derisively. 'Well, then you should serve Spud last,' he said, 'because he's the smallest.' He looked around at all of us like we were scum and announced, 'If anyone needs me I'll be having an extremely long dump.' Then he exited to the bogs, slamming the common room door behind him.

The slam obviously attracted Vern's attention, because he lunged his head round the door to see what was going on. When he saw the girls, he whipped his head back into the room and slammed the door shut.

Like sharks we circle the same pond, day after day, waiting for something to happen.

Friday 28th August

LONG WEEKEND (Even longer for others ...)

Saturday 29th August

Boggo bust Rambo snogging VPH behind the theatre after rehearsals. He said it was steamy stuff and Rambo appeared to have his hand up her skirt. Apparently Smith is livid with Rambo because he claims VPH was hot for him and that he was about to make his move. Spike also seems to have come right with Hermia because Geoff Lawson saw them holding hands backstage before the final scene started.

Sensing that love was in the air I tried my luck with Tammy Middlebrook who plays one of the fairies. Unfortunately, Vern followed me in, and pretended to be part of our conversation. He didn't ever say anything, but rocked on his heels thoughtfully with his hands plunged deep into his pockets. Tammy kept watching him with a look of some consternation. Eventually, she said that she had to get back to the boarding house. I took a chance and said, 'I'll walk you back.'

'No, thanks,' she said and after one final stolen glance at Vern she strode off.

I felt embarrassed and angry and shouted at Vern for following me around and buggering up my spading attempts. I then felt terribly guilty because Vern slunk away sadly and stood by himself up against the wall. I looked around to see if there were any other kissable girls going spare, but they all seemed to be taken or gone.

'Come on, Vern,' I said. 'I'll race you back to the house.'

Vern's face lit up with mad excitement. I bolted and Darth Vader galloped after me. I was well ahead of the sprinting Rain Man when I heard a loud shout of: 'HEY, STOP RUNNING, BOY!'

I screeched to a halt, only for Vern to scorch past me sniggering with delight. He then put his hand over his mouth and shouted, 'HEY, STOP RUNNING, BOY.' He cackled loudly again and kept sprinting along as fast as his stocky legs could take him.

It's one thing being fooled by an old primary school trick, it's quite another thing to be outwitted by a cretin! I sped after Vern with all the power my long muscle-less legs could muster.

I am pleased to report that Vern had his comeuppance for his underhanded tactics. His brown Grasshopper shoes slipped in the dewy grass and he catapulted forward in a blur of whirling arms and legs. He then skidded along the grass and crashed into a large pot plant. The spectacular wipe-out instantly drew the bulldog out of her office and Vern was given detention on the spot.

Mr Owen then overheard me sniggering at Vern and gave me detention as well.

Lucky she didn't hear what I muttered about her under my breath when back in the safety of our little room. It would have been enough to make a bulldog blush.

Sunday 30th August

It's raining.

The mechanicals (barring The Guv) have been given the entire day off because Viking needs more time to rehearse the fairies and lovers.

AM Boggo forced us into a game of high stakes poker, and ran us all badly into debt. He even tried to encourage me to use the painting of the naked Amanda as my betting ante once my pocket money was gone. I informed him that the painting was worth well over ten thousand bucks and was well beyond his price range.

Boggo snorted loudly and said, 'But you can't even see her knockers!'

'So what?' said Fatty.

'So it means its value is lowered,' reasoned Boggo as he snapped a joker between his fingers.

'So you're saying,' argued Fatty, 'that the Mona Lisa would be worth more if she was topless.'

'Definitely,' said Boggo and produced an ace of hearts out of nowhere.

Tuesday 1st September

'First day of spring!' announced Penny as she triumphantly ripped open the common room curtains. Grumbling and groaning, we all staggered out of bed to welcome in the new season.

'And,' said Brenda, 'two weeks until curtain up!' Both girls then squealed with delight and rushed off to the dining hall to find us fresh milk.

Rambo said nothing other than, 'I need a cigarette.'

The show is currently running at over three hours in length, which is an hour too long. Viking says this is because we aren't picking up our cues fast enough and are taking too long to make our exits and entrances. I reckon the problem is that Shakespeare had verbal diarrhoea and wrote too many lines for the lovers and fairies.

Wednesday 2nd September

22:30 'Get dressed. We're going out,' was all he said.

'Where to?' questioned Boggo as he pulled a tight pair of jeans over his long johns.

Rambo didn't answer. He just strolled out the door and ambled down the passage with the rest of us lunging for clothes and following after him.

Outside it was damp and cold and our breath turned into great clouds of steam. There was no sign of Mr Owen, or anyone else. We followed Rambo as he disappeared around the house and walked briskly through some open ground before disappearing into a small clubhouse on the main hockey field. Inside Rambo lit up a cigarette and offered it around. Only Boggo took him up on it and the rest of us watched them smoke in silence while keeping an eye out for trouble.

'So what's the plan?' whispered Fatty after Rambo had stamped out his cigarette butt and thrown it outside into a flowerbed.

Once again Rambo ambled off without an explanation and the rest of us followed.

'This is more like it,' hissed Boggo. 'A good old Crazy Eight mission.'

'Jeez, it's freezing!' gasped Fatty.

'Yip – a good old Crazy Eight mission,' repeated Boggo and trotted ahead to walk with Rambo.

We could hear the giggling before we reached the maintenance shed at the building site. The girls must also have heard us approaching because they quickly fell silent and there was a flash of movement at the window. Then the door of the shed creaked open and a girl whispered, 'Rambo?'

'Yebo,' Rambo said and led us through the door into

the dark shed. It was impossible to know who was who in the darkness but it felt like there were at least three girls in the shed already.

'What took you so long?' whispered a girl in a husky voice.

'We had to put on our make-up,' retorted Rambo and the girls giggled.

'Do you want some pipe?' asked the husky voice again.

'Oh, baby,' said Rambo taking the pipe.

Rambo's face was illuminated as he sucked on the pipe. The girl with the husky voice was revealed to have spiky hair and a freckled face. I didn't see the others. Rambo sucked hard on the pipe and the girl kept lighting up the one end. After a short cough Rambo passed the pipe on to Boggo and the girl lit it again.

'Oh, my God,' said Boggo after exhaling. 'What is that?'

'It's all good,' said the girl with the husky voice.

Then it was my turn – the smoke smashed into the back of my throat but I kept inhaling. Heat rose to my face and I instantly felt like I was floating above the ground.

Once everybody had taken a turn, we sat on the hard ground. One of the girls was sitting to my left and our knees were joined together. I had no idea what she looked like or even what her name was but it felt tremendously exciting, sexy and rebellious.

Unfortunately, just as we were settling in for a long night in the shed with three mysterious girls and a pipe, there was a loud clank from outside.

This spooked everyone and the girls quickly hid the pipe and snuck out the shed door.

'Next Wednesday, same time,' whispered one of the girls and I felt a light touch on my arm.

Then we sprinted off in the direction of the hockey field but nobody followed us. Cold and deserted.

'Oh, my God,' giggled Boggo. 'How close were we to

an orgy?'

Rambo hooted with laughter. 'Wait till you see those three in daylight – it ain't pretty.'

'Typical,' sulked Boggo. 'The hot chicks are prudes and all the growlers are goers!'

We made it back safely and I collapsed into bed with a spinning head and a tingle on my arm where the girl had touched me gently in the darkness.

Friday 4th September

Woke up with a blinding headache and rather sketchy memories of last night. Boggo said we had smoked crack cocaine but Rambo, who refuses to tell us what was in the pipe, laughed and said Boggo had a lot to learn about life.

'Still, it's our first Crazy Eight mission of the year,' said Fatty happily and crashed a rolled up newspaper on another fly's head.

11:30 'Nay! Tis a dark day,' announced The Guv as he stalked around our English class. 'The King has been dethroned.' His eyes fell upon mine. 'Tis the final nail in the masculine coffin.' He then shook his head gravely and slowly moved back to his desk.

'You, woman!' shouted The Guv brandishing his stick at a terrified Nora Turner in the front row. 'Who in the hell do you think you are?' Nora's mouth was open but no words were coming out. The Guv then let out a great depressed sigh.

'Herewith your creative essays,' he said, thumping down a pile of pages. 'History has been made by the un-likely Nora Turner. Let the truth ring from the chimney tops: Milton has been beaten at last.' The Guv stared at me grimly before muttering, 'By quite some distance, I might add.'

The girls applauded the fumbling figure at the front desk, who knocked over her pencil case when trying to acknowledge the crowd behind her. Rambo, Fatty and Boggo were beside themselves with joy and erupted into a chorus of war cries.

After class Mr Owen stopped me in the corridor. 'Milton,' she said, 'you and the simpleton, see me after dinner in my office.' She then waddled out looking smug.

'Sex slave!' hissed Boggo before sniggering and making a lewd gesture.

I spent the afternoon rereading my essay. The Guv's right – it's uninspired. I put it down to sharing a confined white cell with Rain Man. It isn't easy being creative when you have a deluded cretin talking to himself continuously in your ear.

Fatty stopped me in the corridor after dinner. 'Hey, Spud,' he said, 'sorry about losing your essay record.' I told Fatty I didn't really care and that my essay was a disaster anyway. He nodded sympathetically and whispered, 'Listen, I was wondering if we could have a chat about er ... stuff?'

'What stuff?' I asked.

'Girl stuff,' he said. 'Well, actually ... um ... Penny stuff.'

'Sure,' I said.

'Thanks, Spuddy, you're a good man.' Fatty looked like an old man with the weight of the world on his shoulders.

Vern refused to follow me to Mr Owen's office. The cretin seemed to think that I was trying to lure him into some sort of sinister trap and ran away from me when I tried to catch him. Our detention punishment is to straighten the high jump mats during sports day next Wednesday.

Hardly the most brutal punishment I've ever faced – in fact I'm quite looking forward to it.

On the way back to the house after rehearsal, I asked Rambo how he had organised the smoking shed escapade. He shrugged and said, 'I didn't.'

In the old days he would always brag about his plans and successes. Nowadays he pretends to know nothing when he clearly knows everything. He even walks mysteriously, like he could be holding back world changing information.

Sunday 6th September

Had yet another dream about the smoking shed. Suddenly had a thought: what if Wrexham, like Rambo, isn't revealing the full truth? Perhaps all these well-mannered ladies in white are also carrying dark secrets?

Monday 7th September

19:00   The anticipated move into the new theatre didn't materialise. The builders wouldn't let us in because there were live wires on the stage and somebody was certain to be electrocuted.

'I have understudies!' roared the director and threw his arms in the air like the universe was against him.

'Very poor form,' agreed The Guv as we made the long walk back up the hill towards the school hall. 'Dastardly place this, Milton!' He looked aggrieved. 'I've discovered that I'm not very fond of women.'

'I know what you mean, sir,' I told him.

The Guv glanced at me out the corner of his eye and said, 'If only I'd discovered that before buying three hideously expensive wedding rings.'

'Yes, sir,' I said and we walked together the rest of the

way in a contented silence.

Tuesday 8th September

19:00 The new theatre is dark and foreboding, but full of creative energy and reeking of varnish and wood shavings. There still aren't any chairs in the auditorium but everything else is perfect, ready and waiting. Boggo was pleased to report a number of dark nooks and crannies backstage that he said were perfect places to get down and dirty with VPH. The great crimson velvet curtain that drapes the stage can swing in just about any direction by remote control from the lighting box. Up on the roof, row upon row of specialist lights wait impatiently like cannons on a navy ship to blast their beams in our faces. The stage is made of light coloured wood and feels slippery underfoot. Viking says there will eventually be 300 seats in the auditorium, although it seems smaller than that. Perhaps they're just very thin seats?

'This is your one week call, ladies and gentlemen,' boomed Viking, once we were all seated on the front lip of the stage. 'We've been landed in this terrible predicament by sheer inefficiency and incompetence, but there's nothing to be done besides clench one's anus and plunder on!'

Viking prowled around the auditorium searching for his words with his hands clenched at his sides like he was holding two large grapefruit. 'Now I've been around long enough to know that the first run through in the theatre is always an abomination,' he said, 'but this is the initiation for this theatre and we shouldn't forget that tonight we aren't just actors – we're pioneers!' He glared balefully at the cast. 'Right!' he shouted, snapping up his clipboard. 'From the top with gusto! And if we overrun, I'll make you little bastards do it all again!' Viking then settled himself down in a large armchair in the middle of the empty auditorium. Beside him on a stool were his cigarettes, a glass of wine, a notepad, and four pens.

'Houselights!' he shouted, and then the angry Viking slowly disappeared into the darkness.

'And ... curtain up!'

22:30 The Dream's running time is down to 2h 35mins. Viking said it was still too slow and blamed it all on Smith's insufferable egomania. 'I could have driven a bus through those pauses!' he shouted as Smith shrank away into the wings and disappeared behind the curtains.

'Tomorrow I want it down to 120 minutes maximum!' hollered Viking to nobody in particular. 'Or we'll do it again and again and again!'

0:14 Vern was making weird breathing noises in his sleep. I thought he might be on the verge of dying so I stayed awake just to keep an eye on him. Suddenly Vern gasped desperately and his whole body shuddered like he was having a fit. I sat up in bed ready to sound the alarm. But then I heard Rain Man letting out a long and satisfied sigh, followed by a firm sniff. That's when the grim realisation dawned that I'd just spent the last ten minutes listening to Rain Man yank his chain! I plunged my head under the blankets and waited for the sheer horror to pass. It did eventually, but by then I was wide awake and my brain was racing along like a roller coaster on different intersecting tracks that looped high into the night sky and threatened to launch me into space before plunging me back down to earth again.

Wednesday 9th September

6:00 'Here's your tea, Spud!' said Brenda in an unnecessarily loud voice. I hoped that once she'd plonked down Vern's hot water on the bedside table, she might have disappeared. Alas, she sat on my bed and continued jabbering on about all the homework she'd completed yesterday.

'Um ... Does Fatty like Penny?' she then said out of the blue.

'Don't know,' I mumbled, still caught up in my dream.

'Oh,' she replied. 'By the way, there's a rumour going around that Boggo's together with Victoria Perez Hamilton.'

'That's because Boggo started the rumour,' I replied, and in that instant I felt myself come back from the edge of dreamland into cold hard reality in white.

SPORTS DAY

Now that's the kind of punishment that makes you want to sin again! Watching pretty girls in tight shorts and vests arching their backs and leaping over the high jump bar is a rather splendid way to spend one's afternoon. Vern and I had a great routine going. I would help the girl off the mat once she had landed and Vern would scurry around pushing the mats back together for the next jumper.

The highlight of the afternoon was watching VPH soaring over the bar and through the air towards me. Further good news was that when I helped her off the mat she smiled broadly and said, 'Thanks, Spud.' I was completely overwhelmed that she even knew my name and forgot to reply, and by the time I could regain control of my on-board computer, she was already back at her mark.

On her second attempt I was ready with a charming compliment but she knocked the bar off, and this time she launched herself off the mats and stormed back to her mark. I hung back, sensing it wasn't a good time for spading and patiently bided my time for her third and final attempt.

She landed on the mats with a tender thump. The horizontal bar bounced a little but remained fixed in position.

'Perfect jump, Victoria,' I said.

'Not quite perfect,' she replied.

And that was that.

PM Found it very difficult to concentrate on my homework. My mind was whirling with the thought of VPH, illicit midnight activities in the maintenance shed and the mystery of women.

Fatty still hasn't returned for his chat about Penny. In fact he seems to be avoiding me. Perhaps he's changed his mind, or no longer trusts me for some unknown reason.

21:00 I asked Rambo if we were skulking out to the smoking shed but he said two weeks in a row was suicide. He looked at me dismissively and asked, 'What – you addicted or something?'

I laughed and made a quick exit but couldn't help feeling disappointed. It wasn't the pipe, or the danger, or even the girls; more like feeling alive and the exhilaration of being touched by a stranger in the darkness.

Friday 11th September

6:05 'My oath to God I didn't write it!' protested Boggo, waving a white envelope in the air.

Fatty saw me emerging from my room and shouted, 'Hey, Spud. Boggo got fan mail!'

Fatty snatched the envelope from Boggo and handed it to me. 'Check it out. It was slid under the common room door sometime in the night.'

Inside the envelope was a card with Winnie the Pooh's grinning face on the cover. Inside the card read:

Dear Boggo (Alan)

Roses are red,
Violets are blue,
Sugar is sweet,
And I like you ...

It definitely wasn't Boggo's handwriting, and if he had sent the card to himself it would have been pornographic.

'It's somebody from the cast,' announced Boggo with absolute conviction.

'It could be anyone,' reasoned Fatty.

'I reckon its VPH,' said Boggo rather confidently. 'I've been sensing an animalistic attraction between us since the first rehearsal.'

'Between you and VPH?' said Fatty in disbelief.

'Trust me,' said Boggo. 'She's sordid.'

Rambo sat back in his chair and smiled smugly, like he was way ahead of the rest of us. Penny fussed about in the kitchen and Brenda was making a lame attempt at cleaning the windows with a small dishcloth.

'Okay, let's say it *is* VPH,' said Boggo, continuing on his express train of thought. 'How do I let her know that I know it's her?'

'It's not VPH, Boggo,' said Rambo casually sipping his tea.

'How do you know?' asked Fatty.

'Three reasons really,' said Rambo suavely. 'Firstly, VPH is madly in love with me. Secondly, she told me that she finds you repulsive. And thirdly, the misguided idiot who sent you that note is in this very room as we speak.'

Fatty's head whipped around to where Penny stood helpless in the kitchen. A look of horror spread across his face like his life was on the verge of falling apart. But Penny was looking desperately across to where Brenda was no longer cleaning the windows and stood frozen with fear. She seemed petrified as she slowly stepped down off the stool on which she had been standing. Then she turned and fled.

I know poor Brenda must have been mortified, but I couldn't help laughing like a maniac. Penny just stood there and watched the rest of us howling at the bewildered Boggo and she eventually said, 'Okay. That's like … really embarrassing.' Then with her head held high she flounced out of the room.

'That's so great!' said Rambo in a mocking voice. 'Now you two can go out on a double date.' The grin instantly fell from Fatty's face and Rambo cruised off to the bogs with a towel draped carefully over his left bicep.

Sunday 13th September

At last we have brought the play down to a far more respectable 125 minutes' running time. Unfortunately, Viking said we were now gabbling our lines and reckoned he couldn't hear at least three quarters of the play. The good news is that the Dream seems to be coming together at the death. It's nowhere near perfect, but it's nowhere near embarrassing either. Everyone tells me my female voice for Thisby is hilarious, but since we haven't yet played to an audience and Viking has banned the cast from laughing at themselves, it's impossible to know if they're being honest or just being friendly. I left the theatre feeling fairly confident, with a spring in my step.

22:45 'Spud!' hissed Fatty from under a small tree in the garden to my left. 'Over here!'

'What's up?' I said.

He shushed me to silence and led me through some bushes, making more noise than a marauding elephant, and out into a clearing of grass, where he collapsed onto a bench like he had just run a four-minute mile. He said we had to talk.

'I'm helluva confused, Spuddy,' he began, shaking his head and heaving for breath in the darkness.

'What is it?' I asked after a long pause.

'It's complicated,' Fatty said. He then looked around suspiciously and whispered, 'Your oath to God you'll keep this quiet and not tell Boggo?' I nodded solemnly and repeated, 'My oath to God.'

'Spuddy,' he said, speaking quickly, 'I know this might be a bit weird and stuff, and like it might sound like – stupid to you because you've had a few hot ... well, you know ... girls and stuff.'

I told Fatty that I could offer him my best advice, but reminded him that all my relationships have ended in disaster. He nodded and said, 'It's just that there's nobody else I can talk to.' I nodded solemnly and Fatty nodded solemnly back at me. Then there was a long pause before he said, 'I think I'm in love with Penny.'

His honesty took me by surprise and a loud and terrible snigger shot out of my mouth like a machine gun and exploded into the night. I immediately covered my mouth and hoped Fatty wouldn't have noticed.

'You all right?' he asked, a note of alarm in his voice.

'Fine,' I said to the dark shadow sitting beside me. 'Just a hiccup.'

'Hold your breath for a minute and think of a waterfall,' advised Fatty in a loud voice. I pretended to hold my breath and Fatty continued, 'I think about her all the time. She's beautiful. I can't ... I can't ...' Fatty ran out of words to describe his feelings.

'It's like you can't breathe properly when she's around,' I said.

'Exactly!' cried Fatty. 'That's exactly it! You see, I knew you were the right guy to talk to.'

'Anyway,' continued Fatty, 'Boggo and Rambo said I could get expelled and arrested for kissing an under age girl.' He paused and then spoke in a low nervous whisper. 'They said because I'm now sixteen and she's thirteen, that would make me a paedophile.'

'As long as you don't sleep together then you'll be fine,' I advised in a responsible voice.

'Really?' came the astonished reply from the darkness. 'But I don't even want to sleep with her. I mean I do, but I'd just be honoured to hold her hand or go on a date.'

There was a long pause before Fatty asked, 'So you sure it's cool, if I like make a move and maybe try ... you know ...?'

'Look, Fatty,' I said, 'Boggo is just screwing around with your mind because he's jealous, and Rambo's just screwing around with your mind because he's Rambo. You follow your heart and let the rest go to hell. You'll never know if you never try.'

Suddenly I was pulled to my feet by enormous arms that enveloped me in an embrace.

'Thanks, Spuddy,' said Fatty with an enormous sigh of relief. 'You're sheer class.'

I gave him a thump on the shoulder. We then walked the long road back to the house and he never once stopped talking about his girl.

Monday 14th September

FINAL DRESS REHEARSAL!

The realisation has sunk in. Wednesday is opening night and then BANG! BANG! BANG! BANG! And it's all over. Strange how this term seemed to drag out endlessly, and now it's thundering forward so fast that soon this will be over. Then I'll need another Dream to chase.

This was my last chance to see the show from the auditorium. Since I'm only in four scenes, I have spent most of the time watching the lovers and the fairies and secretly thinking how I could have played their parts better.

SELECTED CAST CRITIQUE

PIG (Theseus The Duke)
Confuses shouting for good acting and has a serious perspiration problem. 4/10

VIKING (Egeus)
Very realistic portrayal of the angry father. 8/10

SPIKE (Lysander)
A surprisingly good performance from Spike, who appears extremely confident and natural on stage. It pains me to say it, but he acts all the other lovers right off the stage. It's a relief that I only have to see that smug face at rehearsals. 9/10

LAZARUS (Demetrius)
Although he looks like he should be a good actor, he clearly isn't. Frequently stumbles over his lines and appears to be more terrified of Helena than in love with her. Don't quit your day job! 3/10

RAMBO (Oberon)
A fairly good performance that relies too heavily on Rambo flexing his muscles and permanently trying to act the love god. 7/10

VICTORIA PEREZ HAMILTON (Titania)
It's difficult to remain objective when considering VPH. She's good, but hardly Meryl Streep. Unfortunately, it's almost impossible to remove your eyes from her when she's onstage. 9/10 (Two points added for excessive beauty)

SMITH (Puck)
Completely over-the-top performance. His voice has also become more effeminate by the day. Despite Smith proclaiming that he's the only thing worth watching in the show, he's barely above mediocre. 4/10 (Three points deducted for excessive arrogance)

THE GUV (Bottom)
Brilliant performance, even better than his Fagin. He should be acting in the West End instead of wasting his life away trying to teach boys to appreciate poetry and literature. 10/10

BOGGO (Peter Quince)
Despite having to secretly carry his script around on a scroll, Boggo is genuinely funny onstage when he relaxes. His constant bickering with Bottom can be hilarious when he gets it right. 7/10

GEOFF LAWSON (Starveling)
As likeable a guy as Geoff is, it would be an extreme stretch to call him an actor. He speaks in a weird monotone and his movements appear robotic at times. 3/10

FATTY (Wall)
At 137.75kg, Fatty makes a very realistic wall. He's good

at playing dumb and should hopefully get a few laughs from the audience come tomorrow night. 7.5/10

VERN (Snug/Lion)

Very difficult to distinguish between Vern acting and Vern being his normal moggy self. Have no idea how the audience will react to him. Either they will laugh hysterically or be thoroughly disturbed. Everyone's holding thumbs he doesn't panic tomorrow night in front of a real audience and do something cretinous. 6/10

VIKING (Director)

Viking's hysteria is worsening. I don't remember him ever being this wild and angry during Oliver. It becomes very difficult to act confidently when you're terrified of the hot hairdryer screaming in your face. He also terrifies the girls, many of whom have been rumoured to be on the verge of quitting the play altogether. At fifty years of age it's probably a bit late to teach him that you don't have to shout at people to get your point across. 3/10 (Three points deducted for excessive ranting and raving)

Brenda and Penny didn't warrant a rating as the fairies because all they do is flit around speaking in high-pitched singsong voices, which is exactly what they do all day in the common room anyway.

Wednesday 16th September

Grand Opening of A Midsummer Night's Dream

It's a vicious circle. You can't sleep because you're nervous and excited. The more you can't sleep the more you panic because you aren't sleeping in the first place, and the more you panic the longer you can't sleep which then creates more panic and less sleep.

05:00   Vern wasn't in bed. After five minutes of waiting I began to grow concerned that the cretin had made a break for it. It wouldn't go beyond the realm of reason to think that Rain Man could disappear into hiding and derail the mechanicals' scenes and thus the play. Suddenly I was full of rage that Vern could ruin months of hard work and quite possibly an important stepping-stone in my theatrical career. After all, as The Guv always says, 'this world is quite simply divided into those that have played the bard and those that haven't'.

I hurled back the duvet and marched into the common room and was relieved to find Vern standing at the window staring out at the first streaks of the morning while sipping away at a mug of hot water. He didn't seem to notice me and continued to be mesmerised by the view from the window.

I asked him what he was doing and he replied, 'Thinking.'

This isn't a good sign at all.

6:10   Boggo shook his head in disgust. 'Appalling casting,' he said. 'Viking must have been mad to think he could pull it off.'

Fatty and Penny agreed, and said that Vern was certain to have some sort of freak out.
   'My oath to God, he's like the worst upstager in the world,' said Boggo, trying to fish something out of his tea. Fatty nodded seriously and said, 'He can't go like two minutes without scratching his balls or pulling hair out of his head.'
   'Ja,' added Boggo looking terribly wounded, 'and it's always on my best lines.'
   'Vern's retarded,' said Penny rather loudly but without elaborating. We all fell into a deep silence and

considered the possibilities of what might go wrong with Vern tonight.

'I guess we'll just have to wait and see,' said Fatty, hauling himself up from the chair and following Penny out of the common room.

PM Couldn't concentrate on anything other than the play. Grew increasingly terrified as the day wore on and developed a possible intestinal problem.

18:30 Viking delivered a long and inspiring final specch about how his work was now done and how it was all up to us from now on. He told us to enjoy it, and to forget about trying to get it right and instead advised that we should lose ourselves in the moment and express ourselves as actors. Unfortunately, he then said he would be watching us like a hawk and would destroy anyone who dropped the pace.

He concluded with, 'Remember this is a privilege and tonight is a christening. Enjoy, relish, and keep that bloody pace up!'

19:30 Nervous energy was crashing off the walls. Dressed in our workmen's uniforms, the mechanicals paced around the tiny dressing room mumbling our lines to ourselves. Boggo looked genuinely terrified and publicly vowed that he would never do this to himself again. Vern locked himself in the bogs where loud and disturbing muttering was heard. Every five minutes or so a loud voice would blurt out of the tannoy system. 30 minute call, 25 minute call, 20 minute call ...

19:50 Vern still in the bogs and refusing to come out despite Boggo banging on the door and pretending to have the runs. By now my nerves were shot and questions swirled around my disordered mind. Firstly, what happens if the audience is completely freaked out by

Vern and nobody laughs at our scenes at all? Secondly, what happens if Vern gets freaked out by the audience? Then a nasty third question popped into my head. What happens if my Thisby voice is met with the chirping of crickets? And then the fourth and worst question: what if I walk out there and realise that I'm not good enough and never will be?

19:55   'My dear Gentles!' began The Guv as our beginners' call blasted through the tannoy. 'We have come to make the commoners laugh, and so we shall. Fear not the fiery devil of failure, for tonight he shall return unto the Bard what is rightfully his!' There was a snap from the lock of the bathroom door and a hesitant figure with demented eyes staggered out as white as a sheet.

We followed The Guv into the wings where we watched the curtain open and our play begin. The theatre was packed and the audience felt warm and friendly and seemed to be listening carefully to the opening scene. Boggo was shifting from foot to foot and kept opening and closing his scroll to check his lines. My hands shook terribly, as did my knees and just about anything that wasn't completely attached to my body.

'We're on,' whispered The Guv. 'May God help us all.' And he marched out into the bright gleam of the footlights with us trailing along behind.

The school went berserk when the mechanicals filed on. We hadn't said a single word, but the laughter seemed to roll on for minutes. We had to wait and wait and wait for that first line. Not sure if they thought we just looked funny in our costumes, or whether it was The Guv, or even Fatty or Vern that set them off, but either way it felt like the worst was over.

Then Boggo opened up his scroll and promptly turned pale. His eyes darted around the page looking for the correct line. Then he snapped the scroll shut and shouted his first line with a spectacular knackjump. Fatty turned his face away from the stage and his shoulders bobbed up and down. I bit my lip and screamed in my head to stay professional. Then The Guv opened his mouth and the audience roared again. Vern suddenly sneezed loudly and the audience nearly wet themselves, especially after he sauntered off stage and then returned some seconds later with a handkerchief. This obviously happened in the middle of Boggo's first major speech so everything he said was drowned out by the hysteria.

Soon the problem was no longer enough laughter, but rather too much laughter. We struggled on and forced our way through the scene although most of the lines including mine were inaudible. The only thing to be done was to scream out your lines above the din of three hundred junior girls all shrieking with laughter and giggling hysterically. Eventually, the lights faded to blackout. I scurried off into the wings and collided with Spike who was marching on at the same time. I staggered to my feet and limped back to the dressing room where wild hugs and high fives were taking place.

'We're gonna be famous!' trumpeted Boggo. 'How easy was that?'

The second scene was just as chaotic as the first. One got the feeling that the audience were just waiting for the mechanicals to return, because they burst into loud applause and laughter when the lights came up for Act III Scene 1. Vern bowed self-consciously when he heard the laughter and three hundred girls went ballistic again.

During the play within the play scene, a girl in the

front row broke her chair from laughing so hard and was forced to sit in the aisle. Unfortunately, the chair breaking caused further shrieking. It happened as I was galloping around as Thisby with Vern/Lion bounding after me on all fours and growling like a deranged house cat.

The audience raised the roof when the mechanicals came on for the curtain call. They all stood up when The Guv took his final bow.

Standing ovation!

'Now that is Shakespeare!' shouted The Guv raucously in the wings as he gave me a thump on the shoulder. Everyone was manic and throwing their arms around everybody else. I even found VPH wrapped around me for a very sexy second and a half.

Viking burst through the crimson curtains looking wild and savage. His eyes fixed on us like an immense explosion was imminent. Then his face broke into a grin, and a great rasping laugh escaped his lips. Viking was not only smiling, but he was laughing like a madman – it was like seeing two rainbows at once.

Then Viking and The Guv were hugging and dancing on the spot at the same time.
    'It's beautiful!' Viking shouted. He pointed his finger at Vern and roared, 'You, sir, are a revelation!' Vern blushed and looked at his feet. Then he grinned deviously and slunk behind the curtains.
    'Wonderful!' boomed Viking.
    'Your best ever, Victor!' hailed The Guv and thumped Viking on the back.

I strode back to the house before the others. I didn't feel

like flirting and spading girls in the remote hope that one of them will suddenly find me attractive.

Ambling along the path in the clear moonless light, I knew for sure that I could never do anything else and be truly happy again. It's a drug, and I already want my next fix.

Thursday 17th September

Another rip-roaring performance, this time for the senior girls. Tonight I felt more in control and began anticipating the laughs before they happened. The only disaster was when Rambo intentionally switched Boggo's crib scroll with another identical one shortly before curtain up.

Boggo only noticed the problem as we were about to stride onto the stage for our first scene. Without his secret weapon, he fell apart at the seams and had about three blank outs, during which he repeatedly opened up his scroll as if hoping that the lines might magically reappear. The awkward pauses didn't make any difference, because The Guv jumped in and said all of Boggo's lines and his own without it sounding strange. The audience were watching Vern anyway.

Rambo thought his practical joke was the most hilarious thing ever, as did the giggling VPH who stood in the wings massaging his neck from behind. Sometimes it's difficult not to be jealous.

Friday 18th September

6:00 'There's a review in the newspaper!' shouted Brenda through my door like the house was on fire. I heard doors opening and closing and the sound of scampering feet and anxious voices. On the coffee table lay the paper with a picture of Rambo and VPH leaning seductively against a tree.

A Midsummer Night's Dream
(Wrexham School Production)
Director Victor Richardson

Fun Filled School Shakespearian Romp!

The new Wrexham College Trinity Theatre is at last up and running and open for business. The elite girls' college has enlisted the help of boys from Kings College (?) to fill in the masculine gaps where needed. Veteran school theatre director, Victor Richardson, who has coaxed some wonderful performances out of a young and exuberant cast, directs this lively production of A Midsummer Night's Dream. As much as it is a Wrexham production, it is alas stolen from under the girls' noses by some charming and evocative portrayals from many of the boys.

It is, however, Charles Edly (Bottom) who is the greatest scene stealer. His timing is exquisite and with a pitch-perfect accent, he is a constant joy to watch. In fact, his scenes with the rude mechanicals had this reviewer and many others on the opening night writhing in hysteria. One wonders why he's never turned his hand to performing at a higher level?

If there were a criticism it would lie with the lovers' scenes, which often seemed to sag despite the best efforts of Renton Pike, who looks a good bet for the future. The stunning Victoria Perez Hamilton (Titania) probably just shades Robert

327

Black's Oberon by a whisker although Black makes for a forceful presence on stage with his brooding dark looks and villainous face.

Many on opening night felt that Richard Smith's performance as Puck was a little strident and laboured, although this was countered by the wonderful energy and vitality of Leanne Fourie (Cobweb).

And finally those mechanicals ... who make the show a must-see for any lover of Shakespearian slapstick comedy. Often it is difficult to know where the acting ends and the real character begins. This said, however, these lads are a true joy to behold and superbly cast. Perhaps it is the powerful influence of Edly, but the mechanicals demonstrated a lust for their work unseen in many so young. Of the rude mechanicals, the standout was Vern Blackadder who may well be South Africa's answer to Charlie Chaplin. His performance of Snug/Lion was continually fluid and ever present in the moment. His choice of turning Snug into a deranged misfit, gave great depth and balance to the group dynamic. Others to catch the eye were John Milton, whose high falsetto voiced Thisby proved a constant delight to the young ladies in the audience; and Alan Greenstein.

A final mention goes to Peta Cramb for superb and authentic costumes used in the production. Whilst the set may have been suggestive rather than realistic, Cramb's insightful use of colour more than made up for this deficit. A highlight was the incredibly realistic fat suit worn by Sidney Smitherson-Scott (Wall). Hats off to Smitherson-Scott for carrying around such a huge bulk in such *a convincing fashion.*

There is something refreshing about this production and it is certainly worth a visit if only for the hilarious mechanicals' scenes.

Performances tonight and tomorrow at 20:00. Saturday's performance will be preceded by the official dedication of the Wrexham Trinity Theatre and a brief cocktail party during which no alcohol will be served. For bookings and further details, call Wrexham College direct. (Regret cash only)

James Camp
Natal Witness Reviewer

My first review! And it's a good one. Rambo said that the theatre critic was clearly incompetent because not only had he called us Kings College but he also had no appreciation for subtle Shakespearian performances. I must admit, calling us Kings College is a bit of a blunder, but one should never expect too much from the *Natal Witness*.

Today I carried myself around the school like I was a higher life form. It's certainly worth trying, if only to better understand Rambo. Unfortunately, nobody outside of the cast made any mention of the brilliant theatre review, although just about every younger girl I passed swivelled her head as I walked by. This is obviously how Jack Nicholson feels 24/7.

22:30   The folks watched the show tonight. Mom said it was delightful but Dad was less impressed and seemed to have been awake only when VPH was onstage. They both said I was brilliant but that I shouldn't get carried away with 'the acting thing'.

Another high quality show from the working actor. It's all ending too fast.

Saturday 19th September

Final Performance

In typical Wrexham killjoy form, there will be no cast party after tonight's performance. Thankfully, Geoff has come to the rescue and The Guv and Viking have negotiated the use of the Wrexham minibuses to ferry the cast up for a day-long celebration at Lawson's farm on Sunday.

18:00 'What am I gonna do, Spuddy?' asked Fatty looking terribly upset. Once again he had dragged me into the garden behind the theatre. It was on the same bench as our previous meeting, although this time Fatty was too agitated to sit.

'I still haven't kissed Penny and like tonight's the final night,' he said with twitchy eyes. 'I've been trying to kiss her all week but it hasn't been working out.'

I asked Fatty what technique he had been adopting.

'The one from the movies,' he said. 'You know ... like when you get in really close to her face and then both your heads like slide slowly together until you kiss.'

'Maybe it's your breath,' I suggested.

'Nought,' replied Fatty. 'I've been chewing Beechies non stop for a week.'

We fell into a thoughtful silence. Then Fatty said, 'Brenda keeps asking me when I'm going to make my move, and I'm getting nervous and stuff.'

I nodded with an understanding expression but Fatty set off again. 'I was planning to do it at the after-party, but now that's cancelled and it's like blind to do it in the daytime tomorrow when everyone's around.'

'Okay, this is what you do,' I said and I outlined an impressive battle plan for Fatty. He listened intently and repeated everything I said. Once I was finished he asked, 'What happens if she says no?'

'She won't,' I said. 'I promise.'

'Thanks, Spud. Wish me luck,' he said, taking a deep breath.

'Break a leg,' I said, and returned to the theatre, to find the female cast in uproar because Rambo had just dumped Victoria Perez Hamilton in her dressing room.

What an idiot.

22:45 The final night wasn't anything like Oliver. I suppose nothing ever will be. Just like nothing will probably be as momentous and intimidating as my first year at boarding school. The show went by like lightning. One minute I was wishing everyone well for the performance, and the next I was bowing my head to the roaring crowd for the final time. The great red curtain swooped across the stage and it was over.

The mostly adult audience loved it as much as the girls did, and the headmistress soon arrived backstage and said it was the best school play she had ever seen. We all packed up our props and hung up our costumes. Then, under the withering gaze of Mr Owen, we headed sadly back to the house.

23:00 So that's that. Hundreds and hundreds of hours spent on perfecting a mere two. It hardly seems fair that we will never do this again. All that's left is a collection of moments and memories, some of which I have captured, and others that have slipped through the net and will no doubt be forgotten. That thought still kills me.

A great depression has descended as I lie in bed writing

this. It's like a flame has been doused and the colour and light is gone. I thought about home and the holidays, and I didn't feel excited. I thought about going back to school for the final term, and I felt anxious. I then pondered being completely free and roaming around the countryside like Jack Kerouac. Even that felt empty and uncertain. I pulled the duvet over my chin, closed my eyes and waited for sleep to take me somewhere better.

Sunday 20th September

11:00   Fatty made sure that he was sitting next to me on the bus trip up to Geoff Lawson's farm. Since Boggo and Rambo were seated right behind us, we couldn't speak but were able to communicate using the Wrexham technique of surreptitiously passing little notes back and forth:

FATTY Didn't do it. Chickened out.

SPUD Do it today.

FATTY Nought. Scared.

SPUD It's now or never!

FATTY Worried it's too late. P acting weird.

SPUD Nothing to lose.

FATTY Plan will still work in daylight? Blind.

SPUD Even more romantic ...

FATTY How?

SPUD Walk in the pines behind GL's house.

FATTY You sure?

SPUD   Nothing to lose ...

FATTY I'm gonna do it!

SPUD   Remember your chewing gum.

Fatty tapped his breast pocket and winked at me with feverish eyes. Then he turned away and stared out of the window for the rest of the journey.

Viking and The Guv wasted no time on arrival setting up camp on Lawson's veranda. It became obvious that they were planning on some serious wine drinking and storytelling.

'Come on, gents!' shouted Rambo. 'Touch rugby, boys only.' Fatty cheered loudly and was about to thunder out onto the lawn for the game when I grabbed the back of his shirt and gave it a yank.

'Not such a good idea,' I whispered and motioned to where Penny and Brenda were standing around looking spare.

'Oh right,' said Fatty and fumbled in his pocket for his chewing gum.

He then hollered, 'Guys, I'll catch you up. I just want to check what Joseph's planning for lunch.'

I watched him hesitantly approach Penny and Brenda.

Go, Fatty, I whispered to myself. Don't be scared.

Fatty and Penny walked off behind the house together leaving Brenda alone on the driveway and looking awkward.

'Hey, Brenda!' I called. 'Come watch the game.' She grinned with relief and sprinted after me. She then didn't stop talking until we reached the field.

Rambo chose sides, so I was teamed up with the un-coordinated, the effeminate, and the clinically insane.

FATTY'S DONE IT!

I heard the loud whoop from the forest behind the house. Seconds later the pair of lovebirds galloped out of the woods looking flushed and exhilarated. Penny and Brenda immediately raced off to the dam, while Fatty announced that I had a phone call and dragged me up to the house before bundling me into the spare room to break the news.

'I did it,' said Fatty. 'She was a brilliant kisser ... like it was hectic and amazing and just ...' He stood there panting and looking as happy as a human being possibly could.

Fatty reckons he didn't even get to use my system in the end, because as soon as they were behind the first tree, Penny ordered him to kiss her! Fatty said they kissed three times and one kiss went on for at least five minutes. He threw himself down on the bed, which creaked loudly under his weight. He folded his arms behind his head and crossed his feet before saying, 'Girls, Spuddy, they're just amazing, aren't they?'

14:00 Somebody was feeling me up under the lunch table. Unfortunately, it turned out to be Brenda who enquired immediately after lunch if I would like to take a walk with her into the forest. I put on the sweetest face I could and said, 'No, thanks, but thanks for asking.' Poor Brenda looked humiliated and ran away.

I took a stroll around the dam and joined Rambo where he was sitting under a tall tree listening to his Walkman. At first I thought he was going to ignore me completely but then he sat up and removed his headphones.

'Complete wank,' he said.

I thought he was referring to the cast party but it turned out he was talking about everything, from theatre to Wrexham College and VPH.

'Complete waste of our time,' he said. 'I took more pleasure out of being expelled than my term at Wrexham.'

I nodded and didn't know what to say. Rambo said that he was finished with schoolgirls and that older women make better lovers and are less complicated.

'By the way,' he added casually, 'I never got to tell you the bad news.'

'What bad news?' I asked.

'That night in the rose garden? I had good and bad news for you, but you only wanted to hear the good.'

'What's the bad news?' I asked in a faltering voice.

'Pike's after you,' he said.

'Pike!' I exclaimed sounding alarmingly like Garlic.

'Spike told me that Pike saw you ratting to Viking the night before he was busted and he thinks you were somehow involved in his busting,' said Rambo. He watched me closely for a reaction.

'But I was helping Viking sort out the scripts,' I cried, suddenly wondering if Rambo was trying to mess with my emotions.

There was a pause before Rambo said, 'Just wanted to give you advance warning.'

'What should I do?' I asked.

Rambo shrugged like it wasn't his problem and said, 'Stay in the house – he can't get you there.'

'Thanks,' I said, unsure whether I had anything to thank him for.

'Actually, I'm out of here tonight,' he said in a low voice. 'Death in the family.'

'Jeez, sorry,' I said, suddenly realising why Rambo's been so morose lately. 'Who died?' I asked.

Rambo looked at me with absolute scorn. 'Nobody, you toss!' he said. 'You see, that's your problem, Milton, you just believe too much.' He grinned disturbingly and continued, 'It's a sham. I'm going home tonight. I'm outta here. My dad's already on his way.'

'Wow,' I said stupidly. 'Enjoy your holiday.'

'I will,' said Rambo. 'Next term is going to be massive.'

He replaced his headphones and his head began to bob slowly along to Nirvana's screaming guitars and throbbing bass.

Ten minutes before departure, Boggo took a brief walk with Brenda in the woods. He returned five minutes later in a foul mood and said Brenda was the worst kisser in the world. 'I'd rather snog Vern,' he complained to a chorus of mocking laughter.

It was a bumpy ride back to Wrexham because of the mist and the drunken madman at the wheel who kept shouting slurred Shakespeare and goading us with vile insults.

Wednesday 23rd September

22:00   Boggo, Vern and I snuck out to the pipe shed but found it locked and deserted. After snooping around the girls' residences for a while, Boggo said he could hear distant footsteps approaching so we galloped around in terror for a while, despite knowing that nothing was really out there. After taking refuge for a few minutes in the hockey pavilion we agreed that we were wasting our time and returned to the common room for tea instead. Without Rambo illegal stuff is dismal.

I guess I'll never know what was in that pipe, and which girl had touched my arm in the darkness.

Thursday 24th September

13:45 I heard footsteps approaching inside and the white door was flung open in a dangerous manner revealing The Guv dressed smartly in his tweeds.

'Milton!' he said in alarm, as if I was the last person in the world he was expecting. 'Afraid the roast pork is an unmitigated disaster, old boy.' He led me inside a small house with a narrow corridor running through the centre. The terrible smell of burnt pork was everywhere. 'Didn't have my glasses on when I set the oven,' he said, before shaking his head sadly and muttering, 'Terrible business. Terrible business.' He looked at me sharply. 'You're not Jewish, are you, Milton?'

'No, sir,' I replied.

'Well, we can thank Christ for that.' The Guv collapsed into an old rocking chair, beside which a bottle of red wine and a goblet stood waiting. He took a great swig from his very full goblet and asked, 'How about a boiled potato and a stray pork sausage?' I told him a boiled potato would be splendid. The Guv poured me a half goblet of wine, before topping up his already full one again.

'So, good news, Milton,' he said after a minute, peering at me over the top of his spectacles. 'Rapturous applause all round, and tomorrow we leave this antiseptic feline slum forever!'

'Hallelujah!' I shouted.

We embarked on a long and involved discussion about The Dream and The Guv said this was without doubt my finest hour on the stage. 'It eclipses your Oliver with interest,' he declared. It must be noted that he was already drunk when he declared this, so once again I'm not really sure if he was being honest, or if it was the booze that was talking.

'My most stressful moments since World War One,' slurred The Guv as he refilled his goblet yet again. The afternoon wore on and The Guv became completely sloshed. When he started rambling on about VPH and her Mexican harlot mother I politely excused myself.

Before I left, I asked The Guv why he was wearing tweed a day before the end of term.

'I'm in mourning again,' he said in a theatrical manner. He sniffed and looked sadly up at the roof before saying, 'I mourn because at my age, dear boy, you never know when you've just performed the bard for the last time.'

I left without even having my boiled potato.

'Steer clear of that cantankerous lesbian!' he shouted after me and waved dramatically before hollering, 'Onwards and forwards, Milton, with the luck of the Irish!'

The energy is different now that Rambo's gone. We're now in that final lull before the end. I slipped on David Bowie's Ziggy Stardust and tried to drive the thought of Pike's leering face from the back of my mind.

Tomorrow it's home. I'm ready to move on.

Friday 25th September

'Goodbye to White'

The station wagon was idling in the staff parking lot. Dad leapt out of the car when I approached and gave me a huge hug that lifted me clean off my feet. He then shouted, 'Ja, you little bugger!' and punched me on the shoulder. He was wearing a tight red FRANKY'S T-shirt that accentuated his rapidly growing stomach, and very short shorts which looked ridiculous. But today I didn't care. I didn't even feel embarrassed. All I felt was a surge of love and good karma with the world around me. As Dire Straits' Walk of Life blared out of the tinny station wagon sound system, I stuck my head out the window and let the rushing wind scorch my face clean of everything that has stuck to it.

MILTON UPDATE

Franky's is still rocking! Dad claims to be rolling in cash, but in severe debt at the same time. He didn't explain how that could be possible but said he was simultaneously on the verge of mortgaging the house and buying a new car.

Mom and Dad seem to be getting on famously all of a sudden. Dad says the reason is that my mother has finally got over her midlife crisis and 'women's problems'. Mom puts the happy marriage down to Dad spending ninety-nine per cent of his time at the pub.

Blacky was also in surprisingly tranquil form, which Mom also puts down to Dad not being around. Innocence seemed to agree and said, 'Ja, ja, it's better the boss goes to work.' She then twirled her finger around the top of her head like she was indicating my father was loopy.

Through various discussions about Marge, I've surmised that Mermaid and the evangelical cricket umpire are still together.

A question:

If Fatty got severe stick for falling in love with a girl three years younger than himself, then surely the cricket umpire should receive some serious abuse for dating a girl who was still only a toddler when he'd already left high school? This is hardly the kind of perversion one expects from junior ministers of the cloth and people entrusted with making important LBW decisions.

Dad's roses are in full bloom. I have a spectacular view from my window and the smell is fantastic, if a little on the feminine side. I collapsed on my bed and felt properly home. I closed my eyes and zoned out on the sound of buzzing black and yellow rose beetles devouring a white bloom below my window.

Then I drifted off and awoke with a smile on my face.

Sunday 4th October

12:00 Wombat looked resplendent in a long golden gown with great billowing sleeves that looked like something out of a fairytale pantomime. She screamed with delight when she saw me and shouted, 'David!' I gave my grandmother a peck on the cheek and complimented her on her wonderful dress. Wombat said it was nothing fancy and strode off to hook her favourite deck chair in the shade before somebody swiped it. Once seated I caught her staring at my legs.

'Look at those feet!' Wombat said suddenly, pointing a bony finger. 'They're huge!'

'He's only a size seven and a half, Mom,' said my mother.

'You know what they say,' shrieked Wombat. 'Big feet, big clonker!' Everyone roared with laughter, while I rushed off to pour another round of gin and tonics.

By the time I returned with the drinks, Wombat and Mom were already sharing horror stories of people they knew of who had recently been murdered, mugged, attacked, assaulted, robbed, raped or burgled. Dad joined the conversation and kept announcing, 'You wait! We're still living in the good times.'

I stayed out of the depressing conversation about South Africa slipping over the edge into chaos and joined Dad at the braai. My father was poking away at some smoky coals with a long pair of tongs. After a brief complaint about the diminishing quality of local charcoal, he asked me about the play and then wanted to know if I had a new girlfriend. Dad looked around to see that Mom wasn't eavesdropping and whispered, 'Good job you got shot of the Mermaid. She's a flaky – just like her mother.' He then shot a nervous glance at Mom and Wombat and hissed, 'You didn't hear it from me.' Dad pulled me close and said I should enjoy being single while it lasted. Then there was a long pause after which Dad admitted that he would give his left testicle to be single again.

'But don't get me wrong. I love your mom,' he said, looking doubtfully into his beer glass. Unfortunately, then my father's eyes began darting around like he was incredibly nervous or agitated and I felt myself instinctively begin to retreat. I've learned to read the signs with my father – and this was a classic example of a red light flashing.

'Johnny,' he began in a strange voice. 'Um ... I think it's about time we had a little chat about um ... some men's issues.'

I must have looked a little panicked because he quickly said, 'Not now of course, but ... sometime.'

I nodded and watched my toes curl up like withered flowers in the green grass.

There was a long and uncomfortable silence during which Dad attended to the fire and sipped desperately at his beer. Eventually he said, 'Yip.' And then, 'Good times.' I nodded again at what good times they were and kept watching my toes. Then Dad announced, 'Hot, hey?' and looked up at the sky like a stranded man in the desert.

'Very hot,' I agreed.

'Need rain,' said Dad.

'Definitely,' I replied.

'Johnny,' called Mom suddenly, 'Gran wants to know what career you're thinking of when you're finished school?'

I felt three pair of eyes immediately zone in on me. I cleared my throat and in a confident voice replied, 'I'm going to be an actor.'

Dad obviously thought I was joking because he roared with laughter before shouting, 'Hey! Watch this!' and hurled himself backwards into the pool.

Wombat turned to Mom with a horrified expression on her face and asked, 'What on earth does he want to drive a tractor for?'

'An actor, Mom!' said my mother loudly. 'In the theatre.' Just to make sure the old bat had registered.

'Oh, an actor!' replied Wombat in her shrill voice. 'You see, I thought he said tractor. He needs to improve his diction, doesn't he?' There were some hushed whispers and then I heard Wombat saying, 'But there's no money in it.' Mom shrugged her shoulders and whispered to Wombat that it was just a phase that I was going through and that I'd eventually grow out of it.

Wednesday 7th October

Dad brought up my 'relationships' over breakfast again. He said if I needed any advice on anything pertaining to girls or sex, he was the right man to talk to. Then he said that he wanted to have a good, man-to-man chat where we could both put all our cards on the table and be open and honest. I nearly swallowed my tongue and thereafter resolved to avoid my father at all costs for the rest of the holiday.

Friday 9th October

Spent the evening at Franky's with Mom. Dad was busy serving drinks behind the bar and making small talk with the men seated on barstools. It wasn't anywhere near as packed as the opening night, but there were enough drinkers and pool players to make the place feel like it was still buzzing. After Frank had come across to say hello, Mom told me in a confidential whisper that Shannon is seeing somebody else and that there was great tension in the air between her and Frank. Shannon didn't greet us and looked to be extremely busy in the kitchen.

'That girl made a cuckold out of poor Franky,' said Mom. 'Just like that snooty redhead did to you.'

I ended up nodding because I didn't know what to say or how to explain that things are a little more complicated than she always makes them sound.

'You're not still seeing her, are you?' asked Mom in an accusing tone of voice.

'No,' I replied and then wondered if I was lying or not.

'Because she'll drive you over the edge that one,' said Mom. 'A real little madam she was.' With a look of distaste, she added, 'Wrap you around her little finger.'

Mom held out her empty wine glass and Dad charged around from behind the bar to refill it. He then gave her a huge smile and darted back.

'Debbie's doing well,' said Mom suddenly.

'Oh good,' I replied.

'Saw her last Thursday at the Hypermarket,' she continued, as if she was imparting some vitally important information. 'She looked radiant.' She watched me for a reaction. I didn't reply and gave nothing away, and after a pause Mom took a swig of wine and said, 'Lovely girl that. You should have done better by her, Johnny.'

As always, I kept silent. Inside I was screaming with indignation, but what was the point, and where would I begin.

I pretended to fall asleep in the car on the way back from the pub. I couldn't bear any more talk about how I supposedly blew it with the Mermaid.

Here I am, my first holiday at home in months and already I'm avoiding both my parents and counting down the days to get back to school. Now that's saying something, considering what awaits me is a vile psychopath hell-bent on savage revenge for a crime I didn't commit.

Sunday 11th October

15:00 Decided to pack my Swiss army knife in case Pike attempts to slaughter me in the night. Unfortunately, it usually takes me about ten minutes to pull the blade out of the knife itself, which isn't exactly ideal when confronted with pure evil in the darkness. I suppose at the very least I could poke him in the eye with the corkscrew.

Monday 12th October

6:30 Woke up sweating and terrified. I staggered out of bed and fumbled around in my cricket bag until I found my Swiss army knife. I then hurled it back into my drawer and slammed it shut before collapsing onto my bed, panting with exertion.

I dreamed in the night that Pike slit my throat with my own Swiss army knife, and then ruthlessly sucked all the blood out of my neck, until I lay utterly deflated on the dormitory floor.

'The Final Act'

19:30 'It's Spud!' shouted the mad Malawian from his perch on the windowsill of our dormitory. I had cautiously entered the quad after carefully scoping out the scene for Pike. Garlic's shouting wasn't the sort of under-the-radar arrival I was shooting for.

'It's Spud!' shouted Garlic again in absolute delight. He then turned to whoever was in the dormitory with him and shouted, 'It's Spud!'

There was a traffic jam at the house door because Plump Graham and Rowdy had succeeded in wedging Meany Dlamini's trunk between the two doorframes, and Norman Whiteside was in the middle of a long lecture about common sense around the house. Spike and JR Ewing had also gathered but only because they were sensing trouble. Standing in front of me was Meg Ryan's Son, who stood patiently listening to Whiteside's sermon in a blazer that almost reached down to his knees.

'Coming through!' I raised my voice, and stepped forward with great intent. The group of bodies parted for me like the Red Sea and I strode, bags in hand, straight over the top of Meany Dlamini's trunk, into the house and up the stairs.

Everyone watched me go in shocked silence, and I marched up the stairs feeling like something monumental had just changed inside me.

I threw open the dormitory door and was met by the grinning pink face of Garlic.

'Spud!' He shot out his right hand to be shaken. 'Boggo said you'd died!' he said with huge relief after making sure it was really me.

'I was talking about his acting career, you toss,' came the irritated voice of Boggo.

'Hey, Spud, look who's back!' said Garlic, and stepped aside while pointing at a tanned figure with blonde hair sitting confidently on his locker oiling his cricket bat.

'Simon!' I shouted, sounding disturbingly like Garlic.

'Hey, Spud man,' said Simon grinning like he was genuinely happy to see me.

Simon seems different to how I remember him. I'm not sure if it's an act, but he seems more relaxed and laid back now. In fact it looks like he's spent the last six months suntanning on Clifton beach. I didn't know what to say to him. What do you say to somebody who's just recovered from a nervous breakdown?

'Wow!' was all I could come up with in the end.

'I'll show you wow,' said Boggo in a loud voice as he flashed us a poster of a lady whose boobs were twice the size of her head.

Thankfully that was when Fatty bustled through the dormitory door.

'Simon!' Fatty's face lit up.

'Fatty!' exclaimed Garlic. The Malawian was delirious with excitement.

'Bullshit!' said Rambo in disbelief as he entered the dorm after Fatty.

'Rambo!' screamed Garlic.

'How you, buddy?' grinned Simon and jumped off his locker and ran up to Rambo. Rambo dropped his bags and started laughing. The two of them hugged while the rest of us stared.

'Oh, get a room, you two,' came a grumpy voice from Boggo's cubicle.

'Get a life, Boggo,' said Rambo and sauntered off to his own.

Then there was an almighty crash from the general direction of the staircase. We all charged out to find Vern sprawled on his back at the bottom of the stairs, covered in a great number of bags and suitcases. Obviously the weight of his bags had sent Rain Man crashing backwards all the way down to the bottom of the stairs. Garlic rushed down to help the stricken Vern, and nearly wiped himself out in the process. Eventually the cretin staggered to his feet and Garlic helped him slowly ascend the stairs.

Not sure if it was the fall or perhaps the brightness of his tan, but Vern seemed extremely disturbed by Simon's return and refused either to speak or look at him directly. He slunk low on his bed and spied around the side of his locker in a mysterious fashion.

HOLIDAY SCORECARD

RAMBO   Said his holiday was 'intense'.

VERN   Seems to have replaced his fetish for striking matches with a fetish for calculators. He now has three of them – four if you count the one on his watch. (?)

FATTY   Spent the entire holiday with Penny and says they are already talking marriage. He's also lost weight although it's impossible to say how much.

GARLIC   Lake Malawi.

BOGGO   Worked off his outstanding stationery debt at his step-dad's betting tote.

SPUD   Narrowly avoided the terrifying 'birds and

the bees' speech from his father, and suspects his mother could be just as irrational as his ex-girlfriend.

SIMON

After Whiteside switched off the lights, Simon gathered us all in his cubicle before swearing us to total secrecy. Once we had all sworn on our mother's lives, Simon informed us that he hadn't had a nervous breakdown after all. He reckons he spent the last six months playing Sunday league cricket in England for a club called Rotherham. He described his strange behaviour as a ruse to throw everyone off the scent. He reckoned the invitation from the cricket club had come through last year and that Sparerib had denied him permission to miss two terms of school. According to Simon, he and his Dad decided against asking Viking, in case he also refused, so they cooked up the mental breakdown plot using the golf day as an excuse.

'Why do you think I made such a show out of practising for the golf day?' said Simon, with a cheeky grin on his face. 'I was so realistic that I should have been acting at Wrexham instead,' he added, chuckling at his own cleverness.

Simon's excited admission was met with complete silence. Simon desperately rambled on, trying to convince the disbelieving faces that surrounded him, but not even him swearing on his mother's life could sway anyone other than Garlic.

Eventually he grew frustrated. He turned to Rambo and asked, 'You believe me hey, Rambo?'

Rambo grinned mischievously and said, 'Definitely.' Simon took this as winning the argument and immediately demanded a complete retelling of everything he had missed starting from the golf day. Rambo began the story but we all chipped in as we described the demise of Pike (which Simon hugely enjoyed), Mad Dog's farm, and our slightly odd term at Wrexham.

Then it was Garlic's turn:

GARLIC'S 3RD TERM OF HELL!

- Mongrel ruled the house like a bloodthirsty tyrant.
- Garlic was thrashed twice for talking after lights out despite being alone in the dormitory on both occasions.
- Garlic attempted a single-handed nightswimming mission but was captured by the guards near the cricket oval, wearing nothing but his underpants. Since he was over a kilometre from the dam and heading in the wrong direction, he was beaten six for bunking out instead.
- Pike threatened to roger him on a daily basis.
- The entire Normal Seven was thrashed repeatedly.
- Norman Whiteside spent half the term living in the san because he was terrified of his daily meetings with Mongrel.
- The entire house was gated for the long weekend due to general lack of discipline.
- Gastro left the school a mere four days into Mongrel's reign of terror. (Fragile Five is now Fragile Four.)
- The entire house (including Pike) was forced to run the cross-country course every Monday morning at 5:00am, followed by swimming laps in the freezing dam.
- All laughter and fun was outlawed.
- Mongrel snapped a grand total of five canes during his orgy of violence and mayhem.

The longer Garlic went on about his miserable third term under Mongrel, the more Wrexham seemed like a holiday. On a more positive note, however, for the first time since I've attended the school, nobody was expelled during Silly Season.

I perched on my windowsill and gazed out at the empty quad. The last time I heard Pissing Pete's trickle was on the 2nd of July – Wombat's birthday. Suddenly it's now the middle of October and life feels like it's furiously galloping towards something. Aside from my own bed at home, I don't think there is any place I would rather be right now than right here on my perch above my little world.

Tuesday 13th October

06:00 I awoke half expecting Penny and Brenda to charge in with tea and loud announcements. Only Vern was awake, and he lay in bed with Roger thumping away at one of his new calculators like he was on the verge of a major mathematical breakthrough.

06:14 I heard the footsteps of a boy running across the quad.

FIVE ... FOUR ... THREE ... TWO ...

And then the rising siren. Like a programmed machine, I stepped out of bed, grabbed my soapbox and towel and joined the migration of sleepy boys stumbling down the stairs to the showers.

9:00 Mr Bosch was delighted to see Fatty, Boggo and me and gave us a friendly welcome back to the land of the living, before beginning his class on population density. The other boys stared at us like we were crusading womanisers, who had just returned from a highly successful rape and pillage mission. (Obviously Garlic has been spreading wild stories about our supposed orgies.)

After History, Lennox called Rambo and me over and informed us that he had dissolved the African Affairs Society while we were away.

'I'm sorry, boys,' he said with a mournful expression, 'but there didn't seem much point in keeping it alive.' The good news is that Lennox will begin a new society next year and asked us both to sign up for it. Unfortunately, this means that we have to join another society for the rest of this year, which Rambo quite rightly termed 'a ball ache'.

Eve was wearing a see-through blouse during our Drama practical. Underneath it her sexy black bra seemed to be struggling to keep her assets in check, especially when she bent over to demonstrate the perfect spinal stretching technique. Boggo was beside himself with horniness and passed me a note that read:

Imagine 3some Eve + VPH!

Eve's sexy attire also seemed to have Rambo acting in an erratic manner and he wasn't his usual cocky self.

Overheard Spike telling other boys in the common room that he had kissed VPH and felt her up. In his dreams perhaps?

Wednesday 14th October

Reverend Bishop was deeply alarmed that aside from Garlic, we had all missed an entire term of his confirmation guidance. 'We're terribly behind, boys,' he said shaking his head sadly.

He became even more concerned when we informed him that we had been worshipping in a Methodist school chapel for the last eight weeks. Obviously the chaplain has very little respect for Methodists and only stopped just short of calling them outright heathens. We then spent the rest of the class discussing different denominations of Christianity and other religions.

RELIGIONS/CHURCHES DEEMED SOUND BY THE CHAPLAIN

All Anglican churches
Some Catholic churches

RELIGIONS/CHURCHES DEEMED SUSPICIOUS BY THE CHAPLAIN

Most Catholic churches
Presbyterianism
Hinduism
NG Kerk
Judaism (this despite Jesus being Jewish)

RELIGIONS/CHURCHES TO BE VIGOROUSLY AVOIDED

Evangelicals
Baptists
Islam
Jehovah's Witnesses

RELIGIONS/CHURCHES TO BE DESTROYED

Satanist
Buddist
Methodist

To end the class, Reverend Bishop read a 'cleansing' prayer to rid us of any possible Methodist indoctrination and contamination.

After lunch, Boggo pulled me and Fatty aside, and declared that Simon was lying about playing cricket overseas. 'We all saw him,' he whispered. 'Simon had a full on nervous breakdown.' Then he motioned us to follow him up the stairs to the archives room.

Seated on our comfortable chairs and secure from the rest of the school, Boggo nodded proudly like he had just cracked the case wide open and said, 'He wants to be cricket captain and a prefect, so he's putting out the word that he isn't a flaky.'

'He does seem a bit different,' conceded Fatty with a concerned look on his face.

'He's much more relaxed,' I noted.

'That's because he's had shock treatment, you helmet,' cried Boggo. 'My oath to God.'

'How do you know?' asked Fatty warming to the conspiracy.

'Hunch,' replied Boggo.

'No proof?' Fatty looked disappointed.

Boggo shook his head and fell silent. Then he said, 'You know, if Simon gets away with this, one of you two won't make prefect.'

Boggo's logic has it that the battle for head of house is down to a race between himself and Rambo.

'Garlic's old man could buy him a spot, and never count Vern out because in this place anything's possible,' he said, and then looked at us like we should do something about it.

We had to abruptly stop the Simon discussion because the freckled face of Sidewinder appeared mischievously in the doorway. Sidewinder was so excited to see Fatty that he raced up to him and stopped just short of leaping into his arms. He then felt embarrassed and blushed terribly before looking down at the floor.

'Check it out, Sidewinder,' said Fatty fumbling in his blazer pocket for his wallet. After much tugging and negotiating, he eventually wrestled the wallet free, along with a significant amount of the lining of his blazer. He then flicked it open and proudly displayed a photograph of Penny. 'How hot is she?' he said.

'Very hot,' said Sidewinder looking at the photograph and nodding slowly as if highly impressed.

Boggo made loud gagging noises and said he was about to throw up his lunch. Since Fatty was now in full cry about Penny, I followed the muttering Boggo down the stairs and back across the quad to the house.

17:00 Viking called in the Crazy Eight for a meeting in the common room. He closed the door and windows because he said it was a secret meeting, and then proceeded to speak so loudly that the entire school may well have heard. Firstly, he announced that we would need to cover many of the duties for the prefects while they were studying for their finals this term and that we had to set the example in the house once they had left. He told us that he was doing away with Sparerib's old policy of announcing the prefects next year, because he said whomever was chosen would need to prepare mentally during the holidays.

'It's a vital job,' he boomed, 'and I won't be handing out the privilege willy-nilly!'

You could have heard a pin drop in the common room. I looked around at the others who were all watching Viking intently, lapping up every single word he said.

Our housemaster concluded the meeting by declaring that we were all still very much in the running for prefect, and said we should prepare for a great test of our leadership abilities soon. He warned that he would be watching us closely over the coming term before coming to his decision.

We left the common room in silence and then went our separate ways.

It's obvious everybody wants to be a prefect, if only for the privileges of having a slave to make your bed and take your laundry, and hanging out in the prefects' room with free tea and toast. It also means that some of us won't be prefects and will have to deal with being second-class citizens next year.

Thursday 15th October

Rambo threatened to kill Vern if he kept up with his unnecessary thrashing on the calculator before the rising siren. It's still unclear why Vern is suddenly so attached to his calculators, but I'd take the irritating tapping over the striking up of matches.

11:00   I think I'm beginning to understand the way in which the universe works: desire something and you're doomed. Ignore it completely and you get more than you ever dreamed off. The same rule applies to cricket, girls, exam results, and just about everything else in life. Not only that, if you expect nothing, then you can never really feel depressed when you lose out. After all, you never really wanted it in the first place ... I'm going to call it the Universal Law of Desire.

From now on, I'll forget all about girls and sex. In fact girls and sex are the last thing on my mind. Not for me.

Never. No, thanks!

Without having bowled a ball since March and not having given the noble sport of cricket a moment's thought in six months, I have been promoted, not one, but two cricket teams. Howzat?

I checked out the team sheets three times during the tea break just to confirm that my eyes weren't deceiving me. But there it was, typed in at number 6 on the list for the Third Eleven versus Woodridge on Saturday.

J Milton

14:00   Called Dad to tell him the good news. Got Mom instead. She said Dad was down at the pub wrapping up the lunchtime session and gave me the number for Franky's.

Finally got through to my father, who sounded completely sozzled. When he heard the news about my double promotion, he roared with delight and rang the gong for a free round of drinks. There was a huge cheer from the bar patrons and I heard my dad shouting, 'To my son! The next great Springbok legspinner!' There was another roar of men's voices and then the line went dead.

14:30   Norm (I don't believe in spinners) Wade was hardly friendly to me at the thirds' net practice. All he said was, 'Welcome, Milton. You're in the team to bat so don't expect many overs.'

I don't care. Even just batting and fielding for the thirds is an honour.

I was very nervous about bowling in the nets. It felt like my shoulder exploded when I released my first delivery.

Everything was out of whack and disconnected and I felt slightly dizzy and faint. Of course it didn't help that Norm (I don't believe in spinners) Wade was standing right behind me with dark sunglasses and a grim expression on his face.

It took me a few balls to get back into the old rhythm, but pretty soon I began to find my length and it became apparent that most of the third team batsmen had no clue how to face spinners. This shouldn't come as a surprise since their coach has had spinners ruthlessly banished from the team.

Even Rambo and Martin Leslie, who have faced my bowling many times before, seemed to be confounded by my spin and bounce. The coach didn't mention that I got just about his entire team out over the course of the afternoon, although surprisingly he was extremely friendly to me when I was batting and offered me numerous pointers for improvement. After I had finished my batting stint he said, 'Well done, Milton. You will bat at 6 on Saturday.'

I'm in! Rambo didn't say a word to me for the entire practice and seems a bit miffed that he'll have to lower himself to play in the same team as me.

I strode back to the house with my cricket bag slung over my shoulder. The grass was lush and green underfoot, with the gentle afternoon sunshine on my back. Listening to the pleasant cooing of the Cape turtle doves in the trees above me, I suddenly realised how much I have missed the exhilaration of competitive cricket.

Friday 16th October

Boggo charged into breakfast looking like he had some important news to share.

'There's a new slave,' he said, before he had even given himself a chance to sit down. 'His name is Christopher Walton – how fag is that?' He chortled to himself as he drenched his fried eggs in a puddle of tomato sauce.

'Then it's a christening tonight,' said Rambo, smiling and looking eager. There was much murmuring and chewing but nobody actually replied in the affirmative.

'Cool,' said Rambo, and took a large munch of his toast.

We all ate in silence for a while, and then Boggo finally said, 'It won't look good getting bust in the first year dorm.'

Rambo stared at him and Boggo mumbled on hesitantly. 'I mean, after the meeting when Viking said we have to be more responsible and stuff ...'

Rambo finished swallowing his mouthful of toast and then in a teasing voice said, 'I think someone's pushing for prefect.'

'Bullshit!' replied Boggo to the sound of loud and derisive sniggers.

Then Rambo's smile faded and his voice was suddenly laced with menace. 'Don't worry, you won't be a prefect anyway, Boggo.'

Boggo snorted. 'I know I'm not going to be a prefect, I'm gonna be head of house!'

Rambo burst into loud laughter.

'You wanna bet?' challenged Boggo immediately.

'Yes, I do want to bet,' replied Rambo.

'Cool,' said Boggo in a strident voice. 'Tonight then.' With that he crashed his knife and fork together on his plate and left the hall without so much as touching his eggs.

22:00   BOGGO'S BETTING PTY LTD

HEAD OF HOUSE ODDS

BOGGO	2-1
RAMBO	3-1
SIMON	5-1? (50-1)
FATTY	20-1
SPUD	25-1
GARLIC	100-1
VERN	1000-1

'What does the question mark next to Simon's name mean?' asked Garlic as he studied the list on Boggo's three-legged chalkboard with a frown.

'That question mark means what it is,' said Boggo. 'It depends on whether he's lying about his nervous breakdown or not.'

'What breakdown!' roared Simon, really losing his temper for the first time since his return.

'All I'm saying,' said Boggo with raised hands, 'all I'm saying is all that lying on your bed and crying and weird behaviour and shit, didn't look like faking to me.'

'Anyway,' said Simon, 'what difference does it make? The staff all think I had a nervous breakdown anyway, and they are the ones who choose the heads of houses.'

'Ja, but *do* they?' questioned Boggo.

'I have to see Eve twice a week, just to assure her that I'm not suicidal,' Simon said bitterly.

There was a silence and Boggo nodded slowly as if digesting this news.

'True,' said Boggo at last. He then changed Simon's odds to 50-1.

'I only wanted you guys to know the truth because you're my mates,' said Simon into the hushed and uncomfortable silence.

Whiteside's door was open the entire evening, although it was impossible to see if he was inside or not. Rambo eventually postponed the Fragile Five christening until tomorrow.

23:15 All this talk of prefects is unsettling. Everyone seems so urgent and desperate about it. It makes me feel like I should be out there doing something to improve my chances, but I can't help escaping the feeling that pushing for prefect is somehow a little bit shameful and pathetic.

Saturday 17th October

Thirds Debut

I managed 22 runs with the bat, which was a solid enough start to my new career as batsman and part-time spinner. I didn't think I was going to get a chance to bowl, but when the Woodridge batsmen smashed all our seam bowlers around the park, I eventually received a terse nod from Norm (I don't believe in spinners) Wade, and the order to bowl from the other end.

The coach refused to comment on my three wickets for just eleven runs, but he did say, 'Well batted, Milton,' when I passed him in the passage outside the change room after the tea break.

Despite the result being a draw, I'm most happy with my debut in serious cricket. I also scored double the runs of Rambo and took three times the wickets, so it was no surprise that he refused to talk to me for the entire evening and the rest of the weekend.

22:30 Christopher Walton is a perfect Fragile Five replacement for Gastro. Not only is he timid and painfully thin, but he's also cursed with a nasty stutter and an Adam's apple the size of an Easter egg. His stuttering and stammering seemed to become worse when confronted by Rambo's aggressive and intimidating questions. Thanks to his unfortunate speech problems, he was unanimously christened STUTTERHEIM, which Simon assured us was a small town in the Eastern Cape. Since nobody else had a better name to offer (Boggo suggested Gastro 2 ...) we settled for Stutterheim, which both Plump Graham and Rowdy thought to be an excellent choice.

Why do parents think they can just send a boy with obvious problems to a school like this? What do they expect – that he's going to thrive? Mind you, nobody ever gave Vern much of a chance at survival, and he's made the school play and is now whispered in some quarters as a potential prefect!

Stutterheim was deeply embarrassed by his name. I wanted to take him aside and say, 'Get out while you still can, buddy, or it's going to be a very long four years!' But I didn't want to start a conversation in case he got stuck on a word and kept stuttering like a lunatic. In the end I settled for a sympathetic smile and a nice warm, 'Welcome.'

Poor Stutterheim will no doubt try his best against all the odds, but he'd better get used to feelings of terror and embarrassment. I wish him well but fear the worst.

Sunday 18th October

Fatty spent two and a half hours on the phone to Penny this morning. Things turned nasty when Boggo reported his former friend to Whiteside for permanently blocking up the house line. Whiteside tore downstairs and tried to force Fatty off the phone but Fatty refused and said he was speaking his last words to his dying granny. Whiteside paled and retreated with apologies to Fatty. He then gave Boggo a stern lecture on respecting people's right to grieve.

After the lecture, Boggo and Garlic returned to the phone room and began banging on the door and shouting nasty taunts at Fatty who was seated on the floor with the phone cord wrapped around his body. When the banging and taunts failed to prise Fatty out of the phone room, Boggo and Garlic resorted to making loud orgasm noises and shouting things in a mock Penny voice like, 'Oh yes, touch me there, Fatty!' or 'My, my, Fatty, what a big shlong you have!'

Fatty came storming out of the phone room in a seething rage and pushed Boggo against the wall. Garlic took one look at Fatty's face and sped off like his life depended on it. Fatty had Boggo pinned up against the wall and looked ready to punch his lights out. Boggo covered his face with his hands and started whimpering. But just when it looked like Boggo was going to receive the knockout punch that he so richly deserves, Fatty's anger abruptly left him and he ended up whining, 'Just grow up, Boggo!' and storming off in a sulk.

'You see!' said the now livid Boggo as he staggered to his feet. 'Chicks! They screw everything up!'

Free Bounds

13:00 'It's outrageous, Spud,' whined Boggo. 'The oke has completely lost his personality. It's like he's not even my friend any more.'

I nodded sympathetically and looked up at the swaying pine trees above us. It's been a while since my last free bounds and I was ideally hoping to spend it alone reading and writing and perhaps thinking, but Garlic spotted me leaving the house and soon he and Boggo were charging after me with a blanket and a lunch pack shouting, 'Wait up! Wait up!'

'Fatty's changed completely since Mad Dog's farm,' said Garlic with large eyes.

'It's Penny,' said Boggo with a look of disgust.

'He used to be so friendly like,' agreed Garlic.

Boggo shook his head for the umpteenth time and said, 'When last did you hear him fart, or see him eat too much, or talk about ghosts?'

'Mad Dog's farm,' replied Garlic immediately.

'He's becoming anorexic,' said Boggo seriously.

I asked Boggo if he was worried about Simon becoming a prefect.

'No chance,' said Boggo. 'You can't have a manic depressive in a leadership position.' Boggo reckons Simon's excuse about playing cricket in England is a lame attempt at saving face.

'He's certainly not prefect material,' he concluded.

When the time finally came to return to school, Boggo shouted, 'Come on, buddy, let's go cause shit with Stutterheim!' He wasn't talking to me. He and Garlic charged off giggling and gossiping without so much as saying goodbye. I stayed out under the pine trees until five minutes before roll call. Any time not spent talking about prefects should be treasured.

Monday 19th October

17:20 A terrific storm blew up out of nowhere and unleashed a torrent of hailstones onto the school. I watched it blow in from my perch on the windowsill. Lightning flashed constantly against the blue-black sky and not a voice could be heard against the pelting stones that smashed onto the tin roof of the dormitory.

Roger tore into the dorm with his eyes wild and his fur standing upright. Vern immediately leapt off his bed, where he was tapping away at his calculator, and ripped back his mattress. Roger leapt into the bowels of Vern's bed and Rain Man carefully folded back the mattress, stashed his calculator in his locker, and then lay flat on his bed to protect his cat from the violence of the storm.

The furious wind drove me off my perch eventually and onto my bed and sounded like it was repeatedly whipping the school buildings.

And then the electricity failed and we were plunged into darkness with the rain pounding down and nothing to be done but sit and wait.

We were each given a candle to do our homework, but it was useless and the idea was abandoned after Thinny and Runt set fire to a carpet in the second year classroom after duelling with lit candles.

Amidst the chaos, Spike and JR Ewing were also thrashed by Viking because he caught them mocking Stutterheim in the first year dormitory.

Lay in bed listening to the roar of the generator and the pelting rain. Pissing Pete's fountain has overflowed into the quad.

Tuesday 20th October

Power still out, although it's no longer raining. Rogers Hallibut, who has recently been promoted to School Maintenance Supervisor, reversed a bakkie into the main quad and began offloading paraffin lamps, which he lined up in neat rows outside the houses. The school is a mess. Flooded and defeated.

I passed Pike in the quad after breakfast. By the time I saw him it was too late to change course so I decided to flash him a smile and be as friendly as possible.

'Hi, Pike,' I said. Those green slitty eyes glared at me with menace and he didn't answer.

08:00 The Glock called an emergency assembly and said the power failure might take some time to fix and asked the matrics to remain patient and focus on their exam preparation. He then gave us a stern warning about 'opportunistic behaviour' after dark and threatened to expel anyone who acted like a hoodlum.

14:30 Took a stroll around the school with Rambo and Simon to inspect the flood damage. Most of the fields are still covered in huge puddles where the hailstones have melted and pooled on the sodden earth. Branches, leaves and debris are everywhere and the ground staff were busy slicing up a tree that had fallen over at the far end of Pilgrim's Walk.

We came across The Guv who was inspecting the overflowing bog stream and seemed to be prodding at something on the riverbank with his walking stick.

'Freeze!' The Guv shouted. 'Move an inch and I'll have your testicles for high tea!'

We froze where we were and The Guv mumbled on about us destroying his evidence. He prodded at the dark shape in the water and exclaimed, 'Bah, humbug!' He stepped back from the water's edge and motioned for us to join him.

'I thought I might have discovered a corpse,' he declared and tapped the mud off his gumboots. He glanced at Rambo and said, 'Never seen a dead body, you know?' We then began to walk back through the mud towards Pilgrim's Walk.

'So, Milton,' said The Guv eventually, 'you've decided to perambulate with Black and Brown, I see?' The Guv roared with laughter and fixed his gaze on Simon before saying, 'Good to see you, Brown. How was the off season?'

Simon grinned back at The Guv and replied, 'Better than expected.'

The Guv stared back at the gushing bog stream and the debris strewn all over the fields and said, 'God's wrath, boys!' And with the slightest tip of his hat, he set off towards his house.

'What a freak,' said Rambo, although it was unclear if he was indicating the storm or The Guv.

It was a relief to reach the house. I hardly uttered a word for the entire walk and was never brought into the conversation. I was like a shadow to them – like I didn't really exist.

'Ass creeper!' hissed Boggo on my arrival back at the house.

'You just want to be seen as one of the heavies now,' agreed Garlic.

Boggo informed me that hanging around with Rambo and Simon wasn't going to improve my prefect chances.

I ignored his taunts and headed for an early shower because I didn't feel like talking to anyone.

The water was freezing cold.

Wednesday 21st October

Still no power! There's a rumour circulating that this situation may last for over a week. I'm not so sure the school won't break out into a riot before then.

All sports/games have been cancelled because of the waterlogged fields. We are expected to spend all day working in dim light despite the entire house, including the prefects, running amok.

Mr Bosch reckons we had over 8 inches of rain on Monday, and that the wind gusted over 80km/h! He called it a freak weather system, the like of which we may never see again in our lifetimes.

I passed Simon coming up the stairs – I'm not sure if it was just the dim light but it looked like he had been crying.

Thursday 22nd October

Getting used to living in the Stone Age. Boggo reckons the real reason we haven't seen a newspaper or eaten anything other than cold meat and salads since the storm, is because the roads have been washed away.

Fatty said he wouldn't be surprised if we were the last living beings left in South Africa and that the rest of the country has been washed away. He reckons the only reason they haven't told us is because they fear a major riot.

'Jeez!' said Garlic in relief. 'Thank God I live in Malawi!'
    'And the phone lines are still down,' whined Fatty like this was far worse than the entire country being destroyed.
    'It would be the perfect time for a psychopath to strike,' said Rambo, chewing thoughtfully on the end of his pen. 'Think about it,' he said. 'No lights, no phones, no contact with the outside world ...' Rambo looked menacingly at Garlic and whispered, 'You could just pop them off one by one ...'

The dormitory fell silent. A feeling of unease spread about the place and mingled with the aroma of paraffin and candle wax.

Saturday 24th October

'We're gonna starve to death!' Fatty gasped in horror as he examined what had been dished up on his lunch plate. (A slice of tomato, a spoon of potato salad, and a rock-hard bun.)

'Well, you're meant to be the house catering rep,' came the tetchy reply from Rambo as he moved the potato salad around his plate with his fork.

'What am I supposed to do – turn five loaves into five thousand?' protested Fatty as he studied his dry bun.

'Well, at least you could find out what day we're going to run out of food and have to start eating each other,' said Rambo, his voice rising in anger.

'Okay,' said Fatty dousing his tomato slice with white pepper. 'Let's say we did have to eat somebody ... who would be first?'

'Garlic!' came the loud chorus of replies.

Garlic didn't see the funny side of being unanimously elected the first roast after the food runs out.

'Dibs on his liver!' shouted Rambo and prodded Garlic's midriff with a fork.

'Why me?' wailed Garlic, desperately protecting his organs with his arms.

'Because you have skin like a pig,' Rambo told him.

'I bet you Garlic tastes like bacon,' said Boggo.

Then we all roared with laughter because of how stupid that sounded. We left the dining hall in high spirits, apart from Bacon Garlic who hung back nervously like he didn't quite trust us any more.

Sunday 25th October

The electricity came on for a brief ten seconds, then it took the rest of the day off.

Fatty drew the line at porridge for dinner, and stormed into the kitchens to give the caterer a piece of his mind. He returned five minutes later looking ashen and horrified. He collapsed back down onto his bench and said, 'We're going down. It's like Ethiopia in there!'

Fatty said the entire situation was diabolical. All the roads to the school have been washed away, as have half the roads in the Midlands. The kitchens have completely run out of food and they only have porridge left for another day.

'The caterer is on the brink of quitting,' said Fatty. 'He's flipping out big time.'

'Well, we may have to eat Garlic after all,' said Rambo.

Then Boggo set off on a long rant about how the school should refund us our money for this. He accused The Glock of being asleep at the wheel and having no plan B in place in case of emergency.

16:00   Good news at last ... The phone lines have been restored. Unfortunately there was an instant queue of twenty boys outside the phone room including Fatty so I didn't bother.

Monday 26th October

Porridge and darkness.

JR Ewing was thrashed 6 by Viking after he was caught hanging Stutterheim out of the window by his feet.

17:00   Phoned home. It didn't sound like my mother believed me about the storm and the electricity cuts. She said they had also had some rain before changing the subject.

Tuesday 27th October

It has begun. Despite the darkness and lack of food, the teachers have kicked off their dire warnings of examination failure and its consequences. We are now at least two weeks behind the other schools. How the teachers all know this when the phones have been cut off is a complete mystery.

Oh no. I'm afraid I'm far too streetwise to fall for these cheap scare tactics. They may have driven Garlic into near hysteria, but taunts of failure don't wash with Spud Milton. I still don't buy the fact that anyone out there in the big wide world will ever ask me for my third year results. It's just the kind of propaganda the National Party has been getting away with for years.

14:00   Three trucks laden with food and supplies pulled up at the kitchen entrance. Fatty was there to welcome the trucks and examine exactly what food had arrived.

18:00   Lamb stew and rice for dinner! It was one of the most delicious meals I've ever tasted. I pity vegetarians everywhere.

Wednesday 28th October

Still no electricity!

Confirmation Class

Reverend Bishop said the storm was definitely an act of

God and we should be humbled by his awe and power.

'Why would God want to screw up the school, Father?' asked Rambo.

The chaplain blustered and rambled on like all priests do when you ask them why terrible things happen.

'Do you think God suspected there might be sodomy being carried out here like Sodom and Gomorrah?' asked Rambo innocently.

The chaplain blushed and told Rambo that that was unlikely because the storm had affected numerous other areas in the province.

Boggo nodded his head at the front desk and said that God was probably trying to destroy the inbred community of Fort Nottingham but missed. The chaplain conceded that this was possible.

'God works in mysterious ways, boys,' he said, looking uncertainly out the window.

'You telling me,' said Rambo.

And then the lights came on.

The vestry was suddenly awash with bright neon light. Nobody said anything. We just stared up at the light, waiting for it to disappear again. But it didn't.

'Let there be light!' shouted Boggo leaping to his feet.

Reverend Bishop genuinely thought it was a miracle and leapt up and down with excitement shouting 'Hallelujah!' He then said a long prayer in a trembling voice about how God had given us the sign of the light.

After the prayer, he exclaimed, 'God is beckoning you, boys! This is your moment.'

Thankfully, the siren rang for the first time in over a week, because Fatty had become greatly excited by the 'miracle' that we had just witnessed and had both his hands raised with an urgent question.

It was like a whole new world out there. The buzz in the quad is back. Mother Nature's siege has been broken.

Friday 30th October

Fatty and I returned to the dormitory after a languid visit to the tuck shop to find Vern prancing around the room wearing only a pair of my underpants. He didn't seem to think this was dodgy behaviour, despite his infamous underpants thievery and controversial nest making in first year.

17:00   Notice Board Alert

All third years to report to the Great Hall at 20:00 tonight

Boggo's convinced that somebody, somewhere is deeply in the dwang and currently packing his trunk.

'It's probably another one of Glock's pathetic sieges,' said Rambo.

Just in case it dragged on for hours, Fatty took along extra snacks and I brought the laborious *Tess of the d'Urbervilles* by Thomas Hardy. How The Guv maintains it's an example of a fine novel is beyond me ...

Not for the first time, a relaxing long weekend at home has been snatched from our grasp. Instead, seventy-five third years are converging on the Umgeni Valley Gorge for a leadership camp. The third years from each house will reside in a different section of the reserve under the watchful eye of two leadership instructors. These two instructors will observe us for three days and then fill out a report, which will be sent to Viking who will then use this as his basis for selecting his head of house and prefects.

The Glock issued a long and emotional speech on house prefects being the most important entity in the school after him. The seven housemasters all nodded along to this in what Boggo later called 'a nauseating display of arse-licking'.

The leadership camp announcement was a terrible shock for Fatty who cried, 'If rope climbing and stupid obstacle courses are what's going to decide the prefects, then they might as well just give all the positions to the rugby players and leave us alone!'

He didn't mention it, but the real reason Fatty was so upset was because it's now impossible for him to see Penny until December.

Boggo was strangely inspired by the leadership camp idea. After returning from the hall he immediately kicked Plump Graham off a phone call to his mother and dialled up his secret weapon in Tzaneen for wilderness survival tips.

Saturday 31st October

I made another stylish 23 runs for the thirds in our emphatic victory over Lincoln. I bowled one over and took a wicket before Norm (I don't believe in spinners) Wade instructed our captain Jason Wilson to remove me from the bowling attack and bring on the fast bowlers.

Norm (I don't believe in spinners) Wade told me after the innings that he was using my spin bowling as a partnership breaker, and that it was the job of the fast bowlers to take all the wickets.

It still gives me great pleasure to watch his face drop after I've taken a wicket. It's my small rebellion, on behalf of the cause of maligned spinners everywhere.

My father had a complete nightmare today. He drove all the way up to school only to discover that our cricket match was taking place back in Durban. He then roared back down to the coast and was caught in two speed traps, one of which he bribed himself out of. When the station wagon finally arrived at the Lincoln field, we had just shaken hands with the opposition and were packing up our bags to leave. My father was furious and blamed me for the disastrous wild goose chase that cost him over five hundred bucks in petrol, tolls, fines and bribes. 'I thought you were making a fortune at the pub?' I replied after Dad had finished with his bad tempered rage. He seemed a little stymied by my question and eventually said, 'When you're rolling in cash, that's when you realise time is money.'

He then said he was off to the pub and left without shaking my hand.

Norm Wade, despite not believing in spinners, is about the only cricket master who doesn't drink in the opposition staff room after the match. He was first onto the bus and read two cricket magazines cover to cover on the long ride home.

I listened to U2's Achtung Baby, and because I had no other reading material I analysed the words for each song in the album sleeve. For some reason the album makes me highly emotional. The words are sexual and dark. In fact they aren't songs, they're dark poems of love gone wrong. For the first time in ages my thoughts turned to girls, and to two in particular that may well haunt me for the rest of my life.

How far are you gonna go?

Until you lose your way back home
You've been tryin to throw your arms around the world
...

Sunday 1st November (The Dying Season)

Fatty wished me heartfelt luck for the month of November.

'It's the dying season, Spuddy,' he said with a grim look on his face.

I nodded, and informed him that I already had it marked down in the diary.

'Then you'd better also mark down Friday 13th next week, because that's going to be massive.'

Fatty watched me noting down Friday 13th in my dairy and then said, 'Howzat, Spuddy – Friday the 13th and the dying season in one month.' He shook his head in amazement and said, 'Now that's a perfect storm.'

Monday 2nd November

Boggo, Garlic and Vern have begun an intensive training regime for this weekend's leadership camp. I asked if I could join them, but Boggo refused, saying they were working on tactics and secret plans. I watched the three of them marching off towards the gym like they were on important business.

Did ten press-ups in my cubicle when nobody was around. Discovered that I'm badly unfit and have no strength in my arms whatsoever.

Tuesday 3rd November

Even The Guv has jumped on the bandwagon! He gave us a long lecture on how far we were behind in our yearly revision. He blamed us for being incompetent and predicted wholesale failure in our coming exams.

After class I took The Guv to task about his fear-mongering. He told me he was being bribed by The Glock to ratchet up the heat in his classes.

'He's offered me a night with his wife if I successfully terrorise my students,' he confided, before adding, 'I'll do my best to dominate on both fronts.'

I laughed loudly at his joke. At least, I hope it was a joke.

Wednesday 4th November

Confirmation class focused on the taking of the sacrament. Reverend Bishop used red grape juice as the blood of Christ and small ginger biscuits to represent the body of Christ for our trial run. He then demonstrated how we should kneel at the altar and cup our hands and shouldn't ever lunge or gulp at the holy chalice.

We took turns kneeling in front of the chaplain and then sipped from the chalice in his hands. Unfortunately, we couldn't rehearse the body of Christ section because the chaplain's biscuits were stolen during the second prayer. In the end we had to mime it, which didn't quite feel right.

Fatty denied stealing the stand-in body of Christ, despite there being obvious traces of ginger biscuit on his chin.

Friday 6th November

11:00 The first years charged for the exits, eager to grab their bags and flee for their lives. Second years were next, walking at a good pace, but still chatting and laughing with their mates and foes. The third years looked sneaky and distracted, with each boy plotting and scheming about how he was going to tackle the Umgeni Valley, while the matrics, who only have a weekend of slogging ahead, exited the hall slowly, chatting in small groups about what everybody else is spotting or not spotting. The post matrics very seldom lower themselves to attend assembly, since they already consider themselves to be university students and above all other school activities except for sport. Pike wasn't there either, which meant I didn't have to feel insecure or alarmed.

UMGENI VALLEY LEADERSHIP COURSE

11:30   Loud squabbling breaks out on the bus between the different houses' third years. Rambo wins the argument for us outright, after slamming the head of an irritating Century third year called Gibbo into the seat in front of him.

12:20   Bus drops us all off and we are met by a distinguished looking gentleman with silver hair and an immaculate khaki uniform. His lapel is full of badges and he seems to be the man in charge. Long lecture on the history of the Umgeni Valley.

12:55   Crazy Eight pile onto the back of a bakkie driven by an athletic looking blonde female ranger. Boggo perks up considerably and assures us he'll romp the ranger by Sunday morning at the latest.

13:20   We arrive at our little camp, marked by the colour red. Ranger Nicky introduces herself, and then orders us to change into our bush clothes and take a seat around the unlit fire.

13:25   Ranger Nicky isn't impressed with general Crazy Eight attire, especially Rambo's bright red REVOLUTION SUCKS T-shirt.

13:27   Ranger Nicky begins a lecture on teamwork,

mutual friendship and respect for the bush.

13:37   She introduces Ranger Neil, who leaps out of a nearby tent shouting 'Gotcha!' He then skips up to us and says, 'Hello hello hello!'
Nobody greets him.

13:38   Ranger Nicky announces that Ranger Neil has just joined the Umgeni Valley team, after working for three months in the Tsitsikamma forest school camp.

13:39   Rambo asks Ranger Neil why he only lasted three months in the Tsitsikamma. Neil stutters and stammers and eventually says that he prefers Natal to the Cape. Boggo raises an eyebrow and Ranger Nicky soldiers on.

13:50   Crazy Eight are shown to their tent, which consists of two triple bunk beds and a single bed. Rambo immediately seizes the single bed, and Garlic and Boggo grab the lower level. Simon and I choose the middle level and Vern and Fatty are left with the top.

13:51   Garlic and Fatty argue over who should have the lower bunk. Garlic cites fear of heights, Fatty cites fear of the bed collapsing. Neither yields, and both lay claim to the bottom bunk.

13:54   Boggo rubs his naked groin all over the sheets of his bed in case anyone was planning a forced removal.

13:55   Simon informs Boggo that the bed may be infected and he could develop a genital rash.

13:56   Boggo charges out of the tent and into the bush with a bottle of Dettol and a box of tissues.

13:59   Spud Milton ordered by Ranger Neil to return his diary to his tent without giving an adequate reason. Loud sniggers and taunts from Crazy Eight.

14:00-18:30   Rope tying, fire making, flag raising, badge sewing, compass reading, map deciphering, star gazing, sermons on teamwork, tree identification, survival tips, leadership lectures, hygiene lectures, further sermons on teamwork ...

It may have been interesting if we hadn't done and heard it all before during Adventure Club last year. Most of us were bored stiff by hearing Ranger Nicky's tips, and Ranger Neil's irritating sing-song voice and that ever fixed grin only made the time pass slower.

After dinner we split into two teams and had a charades competition. Unfortunately, I had Vern in my team so we lost badly.

After the competition we were asked to choose a partner who we could trust with our lives. Rambo said he trusted none of us and that set Neil off on another Kumbaya love and respect thy neighbour lecture.

I paired off with Fatty. Simon and Rambo paired off, while the combination of Boggo and Garlic meant that Vern was left standing alone and pulling out hair.

Ranger Nicky seemed a little uncertain about how to counter Vern's cretinism and asked him if he was all right. Rain Man turned his back on her and stared into the fire with demented eyes, still plucking away at his head.

'Vern?' said Ranger Neil in a loud voice as he stepped forward like he was just the right man to handle the situation. 'Which group would you like to join?' he asked like he was talking to a man on the verge of leaping off a ten-storey building. Rain Man kept his back to the two rangers and looked around at the three groups of two dotted around the fire. He then pointed at Rambo and Simon.

'I refuse,' Rambo said firmly. Ranger Neil then gave Rambo another sermon on team building and mutual respect. Rambo listened with his arms folded until Ranger Neil had finished and responded, 'If Vern's in my team then I'm going it alone.'

'Me too!' said Simon.

'Vern,' said Ranger Neil in a nervous voice, 'perhaps it's best if you choose another group.'

Vern looked directly at me and then pointed at Boggo and Garlic. The Malawian looked thrilled, Boggo less so.

Before sending us off to bed at the ludicrous time of 19:55, Ranger Nicky reminded us once again that although we will now be working in smaller groups, this isn't meant to be a competition and the manner in which you conduct yourself is more important than the speed with which you complete the tasks. (Good news for Team Fatty/Spud!)

Garlic and Fatty both refused to vacate the bottom bunk and are now officially sleeping in the same bed together.

Saturday 7th November

6:00   Awoke to find Garlic sleeping with his arm around Fatty in the bottom bunk. They both appeared to be smiling. (?)

Rambo and Simon won all three of the morning challenges, which included an obstacle course, a treasure hunt, and a compass and map reading challenge.

Fatty and I came second in two challenges and were disqualified in the obstacle course when Fatty refused to take part and pretended that his scoliosis was playing up. Boggo was livid with Garlic's poor map reading skills and also said Vern was beyond retarded.

14:00 Simon and Ranger Nicky spent over an hour talking on a rock away from the rest of us. Either it was a long-winded spading attempt or Simon's on the verge of another setback.

15:00 Rope jumping.

It was Fatty's worst nightmare. A swinging rope that carries you over the edge of the gorge. Then it's a leap into the air and a crash into the deep river pool twenty feet below.

'Noways, hosays!' shouted Fatty as he backed away from the edge of the gorge. Ranger Nicky was unsympathetic and informed him that there would be no getting out of this one. Fatty shook his head and took a place at the back of the group.

Rambo jumped first and landed safely in the water below. Garlic was next, screaming with delight as he disappeared over the gorge. Boggo followed looking terrified and then it was my turn.

'Go!' shouted Ranger Neil and I jumped out of the tree. Then I was flung over the edge of the gorge. I let go of the rope and sailed through the air like a bird before crashing into the freezing water. Luckily, I quickly moved aside because Vern would have landed on my head otherwise. The Crazy Eight gathered on the riverbank below and waited for Fatty to sail off the gorge. Nothing happened. Boggo and Rambo were already making sarcastic comments about Fatty being a coward and said this could be the end of his prefect chances. Time dragged on and there was still no sign of him.

I eventually decided that as Fatty's partner, I ought to make an appearance and staggered up the bank to the sound of loud slurping noises behind me.

When I arrived at the top, Fatty was crying and pleading with the rangers to let him off because he said he was terrified of heights. Ranger Nicky had no sympathy for Fatty and stood with her fists on her hips and an aggressive look on her face.

The rangers had succeeded in forcing Fatty up into the tree, but now he was refusing to jump and also would not come back down.

I asked the rangers if I could have a chat to Fatty in private. They backed off some distance and seemed to be having an argument about how best to deal with the situation. I raced up the tree to where Fatty was hiding like a nervous gorilla in the foliage.

'I can't do it, Spud,' said Fatty in a quivering voice. 'My oath to God this rope is gonna snap or the tree will snap, or I'll let go at the wrong time and kill myself ...'

I told him to imagine Penny was waiting at the bottom with all the others. If he didn't jump, she would forever think he's a coward and will probably end up going home and snogging Boggo.

I'm not sure if it was my inspiring speech or whether Fatty thought Penny was really waiting for him at the bottom. Either way, he seized the rope, screeched a terrible Tarzan call, and leapt dramatically out of the tree. I watched the vast, screaming figure disappear over the gorge and shouted, 'Let go, Fatty!'

I scampered down the tree and raced up to the edge of the gorge just in time to see Fatty staggering out of the water with his arms raised in triumph. Just for a moment there, I thought it was the dying season and I'd have blood on my hands.

17:00   Our final task was to cook up a chicken potjie-kos. (Ranger Neil insisted on calling it 'Bush Stew.') Each group was handed a small black cast iron pot and a bag of ingredients.

'You have two hours,' said Ranger Nicky as she noted her watch. 'May the best chefs win!'
      Fatty was delighted, and while I set about making a small fire, he sifted through the ingredients and separated the vegetables from the chicken pieces and potatoes. He looked crestfallen. 'Only two pieces of chicken,' he said sadly as he rechecked the bag once again.

Suddenly my partner became a flurry of mad activity. He diced an onion in seconds, although half of it shot off the chopping board and into the sand. Fatty didn't seem to worry about this and piled the fallen onion pieces into the pot without even washing them.

Once the fire was blazing, I joined Fatty to lend assistance, but he told me to back off and concentrate on the fire. He didn't seem very impressed with my cooking credentials and instructed me to leave it all up to him.

I shrugged my shoulders and returned to my little blaze, from where I observed Fatty sampling each raw vegetable and nodding his head solemnly as if he was a famous French chef.

18:00 Growing a little concerned with how many tastings and samplings Fatty was conducting. I tried to warn him about our scarce ingredients, but he said it was vital that the chef takes regular tasters.

'It's a subtle art, Spuddy,' he said rather grandly. 'It all comes down to timing.'

Time ticked on and every few minutes Fatty would plunge his fork back into the cauldron and then scoff something so quickly that he would burn the roof of his mouth. He would then stare out into the darkness and nod slowly as if he was deeply satisfied with the results.

19:00 'It's perfect,' declared Fatty as he carried his pot into the middle of the circle and plonked it down beside the other two. Rambo and Simon were already looking smug while Boggo appeared decidedly twitchy.

Simon and Rambo won again.

I wish they would lose sometimes, just to have that smugness wiped off their faces.

Unfortunately, there was hardly anything left in our potjie by the time it came round to the official tasting. The chicken leg was now just a bone floating in a sauce, and Ranger Neil had to poke around in our pot for ages before finding anything to taste. Turned out the only thing that was left were brinjals – one of the few things the chef refuses to eat.

The only reason we came second was because Boggo thought he had discovered some wild sage growing behind the ablution block and added a huge clump to his pot. Bad news for him, Garlic and Vern was that it wasn't sage but weeds, and their potjiekos was inedible.

Fatty and Garlic remained steadfast and refused to move from the bottom bunk despite Boggo and Rambo's mockery and loud rendition of 'Love is in the air'.

Sunday 8th November

05:30 Awoke for an early morning game walk with our professional tracker Khululani. Despite Khululani showing us numerous spoor and regaling us with stories about leopards that live in the caves, the sum total of the walk was three impala and a zebra, all of which were drinking from the birdbath in the head ranger's garden.

10:00 Ranger Nicky announced that we were now officially working together as one team again. Ranger Neil led us across to the smouldering fireplace and pointed at four empty barrels, eight poles and a mighty length of rope.

Our task is to make a seven-man raft and then sail ourselves down the river for two kilometres where all the rangers will be waiting for us at the finish line. We are competing against all the other houses with the winning team receiving four litres of Coke at the finish line. This may not sound like much of a prize, but after two days of bushwhacking the thought of guzzling ice cold Coke was like heaven.

'Go!' shouted Ranger Neil in a strident voice.
    Immediately an argument broke out between Boggo and Rambo about how to build a raft that could withstand the weight of six boys and a rhinoceros.

10:30 Still arguing and haggling, I try to act as peacemaker but Rambo pushes me away and threatens to hit anybody who breaks his concentration.

10:35 Rambo and Simon build the raft. Garlic pretends to look heavily involved from a safe distance. Boggo and Fatty sulk together under a tree and gossip about Rambo and Simon pushing for prefect. Vern stands so close to me that I can hear the wind whistling in his nose.

11:00 Rambo declares the raft built, and orders Garlic and me to drag it down the slope to the river.

11:08 The raft can't handle Fatty's weight and begins to sink.

11:11 The Woodall third years mock our raft and wave goodbye as they sail merrily down the river.

11:12 Boggo suggests that the raft has been poorly constructed. Rambo throws a rock at him, narrowly missing his head.

11:14 The raft capsizes as Fatty leaps aboard for his second attempt.

11:16 Barnes third years float past, and sneer at our comical efforts.

11:18 Barnes third years disappear around a bend in the river giving us a loud rendition of the wanker chant.

11:20 Rambo attaches Fatty to the raft by means of a rope tied to his foot. We set off, dragging an unhappy Fatty behind us.

11:22 Round the first bend to discover numerous rapids ahead.

11:23 Fatty notices the rapids and begins screaming at

us to untie him.

11:24 Rambo grows irritated with Fatty's persistent screaming and nonchalantly lets out close to 60m of rope. Fatty's desperate hollering merges into the sound of the roaring rapids.

11:25 Vern attempts to untie the rope knot attached to the raft but falls overboard.

11:28 Fatty (still attached to raft) and Vern crash down the rapids screaming in agony.

11:30 Vern manages to stagger out of the river and collapses on the riverbank.

11:55 Our raft comes in stone last, and we are rudely jeered upon crossing the finish line.

11:57 Near dead Fatty crosses the finish line.

After Woodall had finished crowing on about their victory and downing their Coke, we enjoyed a lunchtime braai at the river with the entire third year class of '92. Had a chat to Geoff Lawson who said he's been trying his luck with VPH this term but she's stopped answering his letters. He then asked me if I thought I was going to be a prefect.

'No,' I replied. 'And you?'

'Definitely,' he replied.

Monday 9th November

After breakfast Ranger Neil ordered us to find a quiet space to spend an hour reflecting on what we had learned this weekend.

We all went our separate ways and a great silence descended on the red camp and surrounds. I found a secluded spot in the shade and began reflecting on a weekend of disasters and endless bickering.

About twenty minutes into my meditation, Ranger Neil suddenly appeared and asked me if I was all right. I told him I was reflecting. He then asked me if I had any questions that I would like to ask him. I shook my head and returned to my thoughts. Ranger Neil then crept off to bug the next reflector.

About ten minutes later there was a loud scream to my left. Through the foliage I saw Ranger Neil charging back to his tent in a blind panic.

Boggo claims Ranger Neil interrupted him with his pants down having a slash. Nobody believed him.

16:00   It was truly marvellous to be back at school. It takes a weekend like that to realise how good we have it here. The school buildings looked beautiful as they basked in the afternoon sun. Apart from the odd seeping puddle in the grass, you would never have thought a great storm had ripped through here just a few weeks ago.

I showered for half an hour, but still I reek of the Umgeni River.

There's a rumour circulating that Pike has left school for good, but I'm not letting my guard down.

Tuesday 10th November

Viking hauled the Crazy Eight into the common room and shat all over us for our behaviour this weekend. He said he had received a very poor report from the rangers who rated us the most uncooperative third year group in the school.

'Now I'm not going to single out individuals,' roared Viking, 'but I will be reconsidering the number of prefects I select for next year.'

He then informed us that our leadership duties begin tonight. Rambo and Simon have been selected to take the first and second years for prep. Viking left with a scowl on his face looking like if he had it his way, none of us would be chosen as prefects.

20:30   Rambo had absolutely no trouble with the first years, who kept rigidly silent for two hours. Simon gave Spike and Thinny hard labour for throwing paper jets at each other in the second years' prep classroom.

Boggo reckons Simon is pushing hard for prefect. He said it was disgusting to witness a good man sell his soul to the devil for a mere position of power.

Wednesday 11th November

One week until exams begin. The slogging has begun.

Reverend Bishop announced that we had eighteen days until the confirmation service, and that we had fallen woefully behind.
What's new?

18:00   Gloom and doom at the dinner table. Word's out that Eggwhite is staying for post matric. This means, despite the fact that he's the most ineffectual prefect in recorded history, he will definitely be a prefect again next year.

'Why the hell is he doing post matric?' asked Fatty, looking the most alarmed I've seen him in ages.

'Because he's as thick as pig shit,' replied Boggo. 'He can't get into varsity on his current results, so he's gonna try sneak in the back door.'

'What back door?' questioned Garlic.

'The same back door I use when I visit your old lady,' retorted Boggo, biting the skin around his nails.

'So one of us won't be a prefect because of Eggwhite,' said Fatty.

'And ...' interrupted Boggo, 'we'll have to spend the whole of next year with Eggwhite poking his nose into everything we do.'

Simon shook his head and said that he hated Eggwhite. For a man who claims to not want to be a prefect, he seemed ill at ease. Perhaps it's a result of the nervous breakdown, but Simon seems harsh and extreme and very quick to anger.

'Let's kill him!' whispered Boggo without appearing to be joking.

Rambo spooned some rice into his mouth and said, 'Who knows – perhaps Eggwhite will be our next head of house?'

We ate the rest of our chicken à la king in a troubled silence.

Boggo and Fatty have been ordered to take prep tonight. Clearly Viking thinks they are the next most responsible third years. Even Garlic agreed that my chances of being a prefect now are as good as gone.

I'm expecting nothing. Looking down, thinking up.

Thursday 12th November

16:00   Eggwhite emerged from the bogs and appeared to have been crying. I asked him how his exams were going but he didn't answer and walked sadly out of the house.

Vern and Garlic have been selected to take prep tonight. Either Viking thinks I'm an imbecile, or I received a terrible report from the rangers. Vern managed to keep the first years silent but Garlic lost control of the second year prep classroom, which descended into loud arguments and Garlic threatening to stab Spike in the eye with a compass. Garlic had to be relieved of his duties by Meany Dlamini a mere half an hour into the prep session. He returned to our classroom with eyes bulging with indignation.

'I guess we can scratch Garlic off the list then,' sniggered Boggo.

Poor Garlic sank into his chair and buried his head in his hands.

'Hey, look on the bright side, Garlic,' said Boggo cheerily, 'at least you were asked to take prep.'

I ignored him and ploughed on with my revision.

Friday 13th November

FRIDAY THE 13th!

08:00 Fatty faced a mutiny. Nobody except Vern was willing to call up ghosts in the first year dorm at midnight. He begged and pleaded and tried to convince us that we had a ninety per cent chance of calling up Macarthur. We all remained steadfast and Fatty fell into a morbid sulk.

Lunch: Fatty and Vern have vowed to have their séance without us.

The Guv was on edge today because of Friday 13th. He said it had nothing to do with superstitions, but more about it being his wedding anniversary.

'Which wife?' I asked.

'Haven't the foggiest,' replied The Guv and continued to stare out the window like he was waiting for something nasty to happen.

23:57 Whiteside bust Fatty and Vern before they had even reached the second year dorm. He gave them hard labour on the spot and sent them back to the dormitory in disgrace. Rambo and Boggo thought the whole thing hilarious and Boggo took great glee informing them that they had now blown their chances of being a prefect.

'So that leaves Rambo, myself and Eggwhite still standing,' announced Boggo struggling to hide the joy in his voice, 'with psycho Simon the dark horse.'

Simon didn't reply. Perhaps he was sleeping.

Saturday 14th November

We lost badly in the return fixture against Blacksmith. I made a duck and didn't bowl. Norm (I don't believe in spinners) Wade doesn't like losing and didn't say a word to the team after the game. Worried I might get dropped again.

Sunday 15th November

Rambo led a twenty-second silence before breakfast to mark the day of Gecko's death. It should have been thirty seconds, but halfway through Garlic shouted, 'How long are we keeping silent for?'

Gecko seems a long time ago now. I no longer feel any pain when I think about him, and I don't think about him as much as I did. Perhaps my brain finally twigged that he wasn't coming back after all. Or maybe it's just that life carries on and there's nothing we can do about it.

Monday 16th November

17:30   'Hey, Spud!' called Whiteside from the door of the prefects' room. He beckoned me over and ushered me inside. Whiteside collapsed into a large armchair surrounded by notes and sighed.

'Matric's a bitch,' he grumbled. 'You just wait, third year is nothing in comparison.' He stared at the carpet. 'Just one more week and I'm out of here!'

I asked him what he was doing next year.

'WITS,' was the reply. 'Best university in the world.' We were both silent. 'How's the pushing for prefect going?' he asked suddenly.

'Terrible,' I said. 'Everyone hates everyone else.'

Whiteside laughed and casually informed me that I would be conducting house roll call every morning for the rest of the week.

'And I want you downstairs showered and changed by 6:20 every morning.'

I promised Whiteside I would do my best and made for the door before he began one of his infamous lectures. 'Oh –' he shouted, 'and make sure Thinny and Runt are looking respectable.'

'Definitely,' I said, and left the prefects' room.

'What's going on?' demanded Boggo the moment I stepped out. He and Garlic were glaring at me suspiciously, like I might know something incredibly valuable.

'Nothing,' I replied and tried to push past them, but Boggo grabbed my arm and held me back.

'So what was that chat with Whiteside all about then?' he asked, his face inches from mine.

'He gave me a lecture on house respect,' I lied.

Boggo eyed me shiftily for a moment and then he and Garlic moved off to the house bench to talk about me.

I'm not sure why, but the conversation with Whiteside gave me the creeps. After writing yesterday that I don't think of Gecko much any more, I haven't stopped thinking about him since. Being hauled into the prefects' room by the head of house was a little too much like déjà vu. Especially in the dying season ...

I wonder how Gecko would have been acting if he were still with us. I'd like to think that he would have given pushing for prefect the middle finger, and hauled me up to Hell's View to talk about something more important.

Tuesday 17th November

'Right! Line up!' I shouted at the crowd of boys milling about the house entrance. Rambo stared at me with uncomprehending eyes and Boggo's expression turned from disbelief to gob-smacking horror. I tried to sound as commanding as possible and ignored the whispering that suddenly spread throughout the house.

'Graham!' I shouted. 'Sharks!' came the immediate reply. I let out a great sigh of relief – there would be no embarrassing mutiny or loud mocking. Apart from Rambo, Boggo and Spike, I was accorded the respect of a prefect. My hands were still shaking when I set off for class, but inside the adrenaline was pumping and I walked with long comfortable strides across the quad knowing my that my every movement was being observed.

I saw Pike lurking around outside Viking's office just before lunch. He couldn't see me because I was well hidden behind a pillar. Even still, I crouched low and kept incredibly still.

I lost my appetite and skipped lunch altogether.

20:00 There's a rumour buzzing around the house that I'm the next head of house! Everybody seemed to think that my taking roll call this morning was a sure sign. Boggo says if the rumour turns out to be true, then he's definitely leaving the school. He went on to accuse me of buying Whiteside's backing by means of sexual favours.

I informed Boggo and the others that I didn't give a damn about being a prefect, and all I was concentrating on was tomorrow's exams. He sneered back at me and called me a liar.

Wednesday 18th November

EXAMS BEGIN!

Friday 20th November

Rambo didn't rock up to roll call this morning. No doubt this was a deliberate attempt to challenge my authority. I decided not to rise to his bait and ticked his name off anyway. This probably wouldn't be the time to start a civil war with Rambo anyway.

Garlic must rate as the worst private detective ever. The idiot has been following me closely since Tuesday. He even followed me into my History exam despite not taking History himself.

17:00 I pretended to be walking off towards the fields but then hid around the corner of the crypt before pouncing on the unsuspecting Garlic as he blundered after me. It didn't take long for him to cough up the story, and it was exactly what I was expecting. Boggo has ordered Garlic to tail me, and then report back to him on the hour every hour.

Garlic apologised profusely for spying on me and said he was being blackmailed by Boggo, who had threatened to run him in to Viking.

'What have you done wrong?' I asked the now miserable Garlic.

'I don't know!' he replied. 'That's the whole problem.'

Garlic peered around to check that the coast was clear and then whispered, 'Boggo says he could have me expelled at a moment's notice.'

'Expelled for what?' I asked again.

'Dunno,' replied Garlic. 'But it means that if I don't follow you around then I won't be a prefect.'

When my voice emerged it sounded loud and aggressive. 'What's the big deal with being a prefect?' I asked. Garlic stared at me with absolute astonishment and then burst into laughter like I was the idiot.

'Are you mad?' he shouted. 'Being a prefect is so cool.'

GARLIC'S REASONS FOR WANTING TO BE A PREFECT:

- Nobody can boss you around.
- Tea and snackwiches are made for you whenever you want.
- You can tell people you're a prefect and not be lying.
- You never have to make your bed or pick up your jocks, or take your laundry.
- The prefects' room is like having your own private lounge.
- Everyone respects you.
- You can punish anyone you want to whenever you feel like it.
- You don't feel like a loser.
- You get a prefect's tie, which you can wear at job interviews to impress bosses.
- You're guaranteed to score more chicks.

- People take you seriously.
- You rule the world.

And then it sank in. I do want to be a prefect. I do want all these things. I also want to be taken seriously and be respected by the other boys. I want to sit in front of the fire in the prefects' room and read a good book with only a cup of tea and an egg mayonnaise for company. I want to walk around the house like I own the place. I want it all desperately!

After Garlic completed his long and loud list of reasons, I reassured him that I didn't want to be a prefect and ordered him not to follow me around any more. He promised he wouldn't, and then followed me back to the house, where we both hung around the bottom of the stairs looking authoritative.

Monday 23rd November

10:30 Since everybody else was writing Science exams, and Boggo's sarcastic comments and Garlic's endless questions were beginning to irritate me, I decided to head to the nets for some bowling practice. I felt like I needed some exercise to clear the mind before my final three exams and working on your bowling action is better than taking a jog.

I wasn't sure if I was breaking the school rules, so I kept a low profile and circled around the side of the chapel before trotting quickly across the cricket fields towards the nets.

It all felt a bit odd from the start because nobody was around apart from a few ground staff. After all, it was Monday morning. I sensed I was being followed, but presumed it was Garlic. Every few paces or so I would catch movement out of the corner of my eye and swing round and scan the numerous trees and bushes for the crouching Garlic. But there was nothing.

I cursed myself for being paranoid and ran the rest of the way to the cricket nets.

After loosening up, I bowled a few balls and then walked into the net to retrieve them. I turned around once I had gathered up the three cricket balls, and that's when I saw him.

He was blocking the entrance of the cricket net and walking slowly towards me. His terrible leering face was fixed in an evil grin and we both knew I had no escape. My eyes desperately scanned for holes in the netting wire that encircled me, but it was useless.

This was like something out of my worst nightmare. How could I have been so stupid? My brain gave me three options: run straight at Pike and try and knock him over, attempt to dodge him, or scale the netting, leap over the top, and run like hell. I decided on the third option which in hindsight was yet another drastic decision.

Pike caught my foot as I was on the verge of escape and pulled me crashing down to earth.

'Backstabbing bastard!' he hissed as his knee drove powerfully into my stomach. I heard myself gasping and then a terrible pain enveloped my entire chest. I tried to plead my innocence but no words came out. He pinned me to the ground and his strong hands wrapped around my neck and began cutting off my air supply. I was convinced he was going to suffocate me to death. I could see it so clearly – I was going to be this year's dying season victim!

'Keep still,' hissed Pike, his eyes burning green with

excitement. I prepared myself for the worst, but it was far worse than even that. Suddenly his tongue was in my mouth and he was kissing me. I tried to pull away but his hands held my head down. I heard a terrible agonising moan, which I now realise must have been me.

It was worse than cutting me with a knife, worse than polishing my balls. I wanted to vomit.

'Hey!' came the shout. 'Hey, Spud!' It was Garlic, running towards the nets shouting his lungs out in panic. Pike pulled his face away and stood up wiping his mouth and looking weirdly excited like he did after cutting me in first year.

'That's something to remember me by,' he said, and spat nonchalantly on the ground.

And then with one final satanic glare, he turned and walked away.

'Hey, Spud!' gasped Garlic. 'You okay?'

I nodded and tried to speak but couldn't. I felt so nauseous that I threw up in the cricket net. Garlic watched me and kept asking me if I was all right, but I couldn't answer.

'It looked like he was trying to strangle you or something,' said Garlic.

A wave of relief passed through me. Garlic hadn't seen or he would have said so.

'That's what happened,' I gasped. 'That's exactly what happened.' I spat on the grass, but was still unable to get the taste of him out of me.

'Thanks, Garlic,' I said after pulling myself together.

Garlic grinned and shouted, 'Just as well I was following you!'

We began to walk back to the house in what I hoped would be silence, but Garlic asked, 'Why does Pike hate you so much?'

'I don't know,' I replied.

And I doubt I ever will.

Thursday 26th November

The matrics and post matrics have officially left the school. The leavers' war dance/haka was abysmal and it looked like most boys hadn't bothered to rehearse.

Rambo was called in for a thirty minute meeting with Viking. When he emerged it was with a self-satisfied smirk on his face and he just gave a shrug when Boggo asked him what was going on. With the heads of houses announcement due tomorrow, it doesn't take a brain surgeon to realise that Rambo is going to be our new head of house.

Boggo called it a no brainer, but couldn't hide the disappointment from his face.

I watched Pike leaving from the top of the bell tower. His final act was to shout a mocking taunt at Eggwhite who had come to see him off. I watched the Pikes' red BMW slowly make its way down Pilgrim's Walk and didn't take my eyes off it until it left the gates.

Pike's gone forever, and he's taken my fear with him.

Friday 27th November

07:20   'The Last Breakfast'

08:00   Assembly. The Glock left the head of house announcements for last and it was a surreal experience when it finally did come.

Simon Brown stood up as our new head of house and marched proudly forward to shake The Glock's hand. Surprisingly, Rambo whistled loudly and looked genuinely happy for Simon. Garlic roared in confused delight, but poor Boggo looked utterly shocked and slowly shook his head in disbelief.

Lunch: Simon sat with the staff at the top table. (Already with his new badge emblazoned on his blazer.)

'It was obviously going to be Simon,' announced Boggo, despite having him at 50-1 on his betting board. 'It was a no brainer.' He stuffed his mouth full of sausage.

'Why was it a no brainer?' asked Garlic.

'Because, you turd,' mumbled Boggo with his mouth full, 'he's going to be captain of cricket next year.'

'But I thought you said he didn't have a chance because of the nervous breakdown?' persisted Garlic.

Boggo was seething. He thumped down his glass of milk and, ignoring Garlic, stared daggers at Rambo. 'You're such a prick, Rambo! You freeze us out and hang us out to dry.'

'What have I done?' asked Rambo innocently.

Boggo was raging but couldn't find the words. Eventually he shouted, 'What was yesterday's meeting with Viking all about?'

I expected Rambo to shrug nonchalantly but his eyes darkened and his face grew serious.

'You really want to know about my meeting with Viking?'

'Tell me truth, Rambo,' said Boggo.

'Viking offered me head of house but I turned him down.'

Silence.

'But why?' asked Fatty, incredulous.

'For shit's sakes, Fatty, open your eyes!' snapped Rambo. 'For head of house it's a year of babysitting first years, dealing with Viking and nagging mothers. It's a year of being a petty policeman and catching people talking after lights out. And it's a year of being shunned by your fellow matrics and prefects.'

More silence.

'So why did Simon get it?' asked Boggo grimly.

'Because,' said Rambo, 'I told Viking that he was the only one of us capable of running the house.'

'But he's insane!' cried Boggo, tears welling in his eyes.

'Who isn't?' said Rambo and left the dining hall.

We ate the rest of the meal in silence with everyone casting regular glances up towards the top table where Sparerib and Simon were chatting and laughing together like old buddies.

Like everything this week, it didn't seem real.

'Hey, Spuddy,' whispered Fatty as we were leaving the dining hall, 'do you realise that this morning's breakfast was the last time the full Crazy Eight will ever eat together?'

'No,' I replied.

'Weird, hey?' said Fatty, shaking his head like he couldn't quite comprehend it either.

He then told me to mark it down in my diary before returning to his archives room, where he has been hibernating for the last two weeks.

16:00 Exams are done! Feeling dazed all the time. Concerned I might be on the verge of a weird psychological event. I told Fatty that I felt continually dazed and that my eyes were sore. He said I should report to the san immediately because it sounded to him like a brain tumour.

In the end, I borrowed/stole two Disprin from Garlic's locker and slept until dinner.

20:00 Simon has moved into Whiteside's room and taken over full control of the house! He even shat on

Vern for running up the stairs before prep.

Saturday 28th November

CRICKET VS ST JAMES

10:30   I was standing at my position on the backward square leg boundary enjoying the sights and smells of my final cricket match of the year, when my attention was drawn to a large white Mercedes Benz speeding along Pilgrim's Walk. The Mercedes pulled up to our field and stopped on the far bank. Thinking it was a St James parent, I returned my attention to the cricket and made a brilliant stop on the boundary that set the people now getting out of the Mercedes into loud cheering and shouts of 'Go, Johnny!'

It's been a week of shocks, but this one I could never have dreamed.

My father has bought a brand new Mercedes Benz! He's so proud of it that he refused to move more than a few feet from the car in case it was threatened by a stray cricket ball.

The Mercedes wasn't the only thing that's new. My mother was dressed in a full-length skirt, and the picnic table was littered with fancy things like feta cheese and snoek paté. Dad refused to have more than a single beer at lunch because he said he wasn't the sort to drink and drive.

'Now we look just like all the other parents,' beamed my mother. 'You don't have to be embarrassed by that bloody car any more.'

I asked Dad what had happened to the station wagon.

'I got a bloody good price for her considering the state she was in,' said my father proudly. But then his eyes looked sad as he thought of the old bird. There was a pause and he said, 'Her time was up.' He fell silent. 'And your mother hated it,' he said eventually. 'But at least we keep the memories, hey, Johnny?'

But then my father looked up at his new car and the sadness fell away as pride returned to his face.

'Life,' he said shaking his head with wonder, 'you just never can tell.'

16:30 I watched the Mercedes speeding away and wished it were the station wagon instead. I never got to have one last ride in the roaring green beast before she was taken away.

But then again, it's the dying days of the dying season and the monster must be fed.

Sunday 29th November

19:00 CONFIRMATION SERVICE

Boggo and Vern had to be baptised before we could begin the confirmation service. Rain Man got a terrible fright when Reverend Bishop splashed his forehead with holy water. He lurched back and shouted 'Oi!' as if the chaplain was trying to drown him. There was loud laughter from the chapel gallery so Reverend Bishop quickly baptised him before moving on to Boggo, who looked like a man being dragged forward to the guillotine.

The Bishop of Natal is an impressive looking man. With his silver hair and a neatly cropped beard, he looked both serious and friendly simultaneously. No wonder he was made the Bishop. His voice was gentle and deep but it easily reached up into the gallery and through the doors and beyond.

I knelt down in front of him and closed my eyes. He then said:

'Do ye here, in the presence of God, and of this congregation, renew the solemn promise and vow that was made in your name at your Baptism; ratifying and confirming the same in your own persons, and acknowledging yourselves bound to believe, and to do, all those things which your Godfathers and Godmothers then undertook for you?'

'I do,' I said.

And before I knew it, I was confirmed. The chapel bells rang out and the congregation stood as we left the chapel.

Monday 30th November

I can already hear the unzipping of suitcases and the clanking of metal trunks being dragged through the cloisters. Friday can't come soon enough for everyone.

The confirmation service ended a week of personal storms and it seems like God may finally have called a truce on hailing daily surprises on my head.

I would have to call last night a watershed in my life thus far. Not that I really ever felt the presence of God during the service, but somehow when I left the chapel, it felt like everything that went before, everything that I had done, or not done, was wiped clean. I felt forgiven.

No more regrets, no more looking back, and no more fear.

17:00   Boggo bribed Plump Graham and Rowdy to have a loud discussion about Rambo outside Viking's office. Among other things they had to declare that Boggo was their favourite for prefect, Fatty was a paedophile and that Rambo and I hadn't joined a society this term.

The backstabbing plan failed because Viking charged out of his office and shat all over the first years for disturbing his marking.

21:00 Simon has conducted his first thrashing. Spike and JR Ewing were beaten with a cricket bat after attempting to drown Stutterheim in the urinal. If Simon's beatings are anything like his cover drives, the two delinquents won't be sitting down anytime soon.

Wednesday 2nd December

Fatty has broken yet another school record: 207 minutes on the phone to Penny. When he'd finished his call, his voice was hoarse and he was visibly exhausted from his marathon effort.

'Forty-six hours to go,' was all he could say with a skip and a devilish grin.

18:00   Meg Ryan's Son sang the solo for Once in Royal David's City to a packed congregation.

He has a beautiful voice and with his angelic face and big blue eyes, I can only thank God that he wasn't around two years ago, or there's no way I would have ever played Oliver!

This chapel is what I'll miss most when I'm gone.

Thursday 3rd December

It was after dinner. Rambo, Fatty, Garlic and I were sauntering back to the house talking about anything but prefects. That's when we heard it. It was Garlic who caught it first, but Rambo who stopped sauntering and raised his hands for silence. We turned our faces up towards the first year window from where the sweet music was playing. It was a song of great melancholy, but it was also a sign from God.

'Is he singing the word nightswimming?' asked Rambo.

'It's the new REM,' said Fatty. 'I heard Sidewinder has it.'

'What's REM?' asked Garlic in alarm.

Rambo was already running. Up the stairs, through the second year dorm and then bursting into the slave dorm where the Fragile Five sat huddled in Sidewinder's cubicle mesmerised by what they were hearing.

Rambo made a beeline for Sidewinder's CD player and ejected the CD immediately. He lifted it out of the machine with a delicate hand and said, 'Sidewinder, if you let me have this until breakfast tomorrow I'll make sure nobody lays a finger on you ever again.'

'Deal!' said Sidewinder like he had won the jackpot.

'Hey, sir!' said Plump Graham excitedly. 'There's a song on there called Sidewinder Sleeps Tonight.'

But Rambo was off again, back to our dorm where REM's Nightswimming blasted solidly for two hours.

There was nothing for it but to answer the call from above.

22:30   We stripped down to our jocks, sniggering and mocking. Garlic was leaping up and down endlessly repeating the word 'nightswimming'. We scuttled out of the dormitory and hovered on the landing.

'Should we tell Simon?' asked an excited Boggo.

Rambo shook his head. 'He'll probably try and stop us,' he said.

'That's bullshit,' Fatty said. 'He's Crazy Eight and that means he's coming along!'

Fatty barged into Simon's room and emerged some moments later looking glum.

'He's not coming,' he said, 'but promised he'll turn a blind eye.'

'How gracious of him,' said Rambo coldly.

We paused again at the top of the stairs.

'Which way, gents?' asked Rambo with a cheeky grin. 'The old way or the new way?'

'Let's do it in style,' replied Fatty. 'I may have lost weight but I still don't trust that flippin' window.'

We laughed and followed Rambo down the stairs like we owned the place. The six of us strolled through the deserted house door and out into the quad. It felt wrong and right, like we were going back in time. Except the people around me now felt like men and my large shadow made me look just like them.

'Let's go,' said Rambo and he took off through the archway and into the night.

'Wait up!' hollered Fatty, but we were racing, unable to slow down, our footsteps beating out a discordant rhythm on the lush grass passing beneath us. With a soundtrack in my head and no limits of space and distance I galloped forward relishing each pant, each exhalation of bad energy pouring out of me.

The water was cold but nobody cared. Boggo and Rambo hurled Garlic in and then dived on top of him. Vern stood waist deep thumping the surface of the water with both hands while Fatty repeatedly made gigantic bomb dives that echoed around the hills.

'BUSTED!' came the shout from behind us as Simon leapt off the bank and soared over our heads with his fist raised in triumph.

'Simon!' shouted Garlic in delight.

'Garlic!' shouted Simon in mock alarm.

Then we laughed and dunked and dunked some more.

We swam until after midnight and then they were sprinting again. I couldn't keep up. I had let out everything that was inside me and could do nothing but walk slowly back to the house. I will always remember how tranquil it felt to be walking alone through the school in the middle of the night, and for possibly the first time in my life, I feared nothing.

This is officially the last night that I will ever sleep in a dormitory again.

I stayed out on the ledge until late thinking about the stars and the universe and if God really did create it all. And then for the final time, I stepped down onto my bed and slid my diary under the mattress. I slept like a log.

Friday 4th December

D-DAY

8:00   Viking called it a 'final house meeting' but everybody knew what was about to happen. I took my place between Fatty and Garlic and waited for Viking to stop waffling about discipline and cut to the car chase.

I admit I was suddenly afflicted with a bad case of pins and needles on my face and neck. My hands were trembling so I held them tightly together like I was praying.

'The time has come,' said Viking, 'to announce the prefects for 1993.'
    He looked around the room sternly and seemed to be greatly enjoying dragging out the suspense.
    'These gentlemen will lead the house with distinction,'

he continued, 'and they have all demonstrated the qualities that will make them fine prefects and leaders of men.'

There was utter silence; even the first years seemed to be rapt by the coming announcement.

'Before the new,' boomed Viking, 'we begin with the old. Greg Whitton will be returning for post matric and shall once again continue as a prefect.'

There was a pathetic ripple of applause and it was probably just as well that Eggwhite wasn't there to witness it.

Viking waited until there was complete silence before saying, 'The three new prefects for 1993 are ... Robert Black, John Milton and Sidney Smitherson-Scott. Congratulations.'

I shook Viking's hand and he handed over my tie. The house cheered and whistled. I shook hands with Rambo who appeared as cool as ice, and Fatty, who seemed utterly shocked and bewildered by the announcement.

'Follow me, gents,' said Rambo, after Viking had concluded the meeting. Fatty and I followed him into the prefects' room. Simon was already waiting for us, languishing in an armchair and looking highly pleased with himself.

'Slave!' roared Rambo, as we all collapsed into the comfortable armchairs. Within seconds there was the sound of scampering feet and then a timid knock on the door.

'Come!' ordered Simon in a threatening voice. Rowdy and Stutterheim poked their uncertain faces around the door and Simon spread out his hands like he was about to perform a miracle and said, 'Tea and egg mayonnaise for the prefects, please.'

'Yes, sir,' said Rowdy and the pair hurried off to the kitchen.

Fatty grinned at me and said, 'I think I could really get used to this.'

Then he placed his feet up on the table and laughed like a madman.

10:45   I caught up with The Guv after assembly.

'Ah, Milton,' he said with a great smile. 'You're not the only one who's been promoted, old boy!'

I asked if he had by any chance unseated The Glock. He roared with laughter and beat his walking stick repeatedly into the ground. 'Not yet!' he cried. 'But I am coaching the first cricket team next year!'

I couldn't help the huge grin enveloping my face, especially when he said that unlike certain unmentionable others he was an evangelical believer in the power of the spinner.

'Well done, old boy,' he said ruffling my hair. Then he winked at me and whispered, 'The rest is easy.'

And off he strode, like he always does – never giving a shit.

11:00   'We've come to help carry your trunk, sir,' said Rowdy and the nodding Plump Graham as they suddenly appeared in my cubicle.

It took me a moment to realise that they weren't taking the piss, and then I said, 'Er ... thanks,' all the while feeling a bit surreal and uncomfortable in front of the others. Vern looked deeply hurt that he was no longer needed to carry my trunk and sulked on his bed while stroking Roger in a vigorous fashion.

After shaking hands with Vern, Garlic, Rambo, Fatty and Simon, I sauntered out of the house, past the devastated boy slumped on the house bench who ignored me when I said goodbye, and strode across the quad and through the great archway.

'Congratulations on being a prefect, sir,' said Plump Graham.

'Thanks,' I said.

'We were worried Mr Greenstein was going to be chosen,' said Rowdy.

Poor Boggo, he probably hates me right now, but one day he'll realise that he fell foul of the dreaded Universal Law of Desire.

I stood around for some time waiting for my dad to arrive. Plump Graham and Rowdy seemed perfectly happy to wait with me and chatted to each other about what awaited them in the holidays. I then hung my head and laughed at my own stupidity. All this time I had been waiting for a green Renault station wagon that would never arrive.

And then I saw him, parked directly in front of me, killing himself with laughter, and banging his hand repeatedly on the steering wheel.

My father.

'Do you want us to pack your trunk into your dad's car?' asked Plump Graham.

'No, thank you, boys,' I replied with someone else's voice. 'I think from here on in, I'll manage just fine.'